"For a fast-paced story full of fun, action, mystery, and love, I highly recommend you treat yourself to *Trouble in Store* by Carol Cox. Her delightful characters and historical accuracy provide a delightful read!"

—Judith Miller, bestselling author of the
HOME TO AMANA series

"Carol Cox has done it again! From their first meeting in the mercantile, Melanie and Caleb jumped off the page and into my heart. Their story made me laugh, cry, and fall in love all over again. *Trouble in Store* is a do-not-miss read!"

—Kathleen Y'Barbo, bestselling author of *Flora's Wish* and the
ROCKY MOUNTAIN HEIRESS series

"A sweet romance with a suspenseful touch of murder mystery makes Carol Cox's *Trouble in Store* a great read!"

—Julianna Deering, author of *Rules of Murder*,
A Drew Farthering Mystery

"One of my favorite writers has produced another winner. Complete with romance and intrigue, this book is bound to keep you turning the pages to the happily ever after."

—Hannah Alexander, author of *Keeping Faith*

"Trouble in store? You'd better believe it. The action in Carol Cox's novel, set in Cedar Ridge, Arizona, in the wild days of the Tombstone gunfights, delivers more punch than a cowpuncher's spurs, while romantic tensions grow between Melanie and Caleb to build up to a satisfying conclusion."

—Eric Wiggin, author of *The Hills of God* and *The Recluse*

"A spunky, determined heroine, a stubborn, clueless hero, and an intriguing mystery that pulls you in and makes your mind swirl, blend together to create a charming historical romance you'll add to your keeper shelf."

—Vickie McDonough, award-winning author
of 26 books and novellas

"Start with the nostalgic allure of the Arizona Territory in 1885, stir in the suspense of a murder mystery, and season it with the thrill of romance. The result is the pièce de résistance *Trouble in Store,* which you won't soon forget."

—Sandra Robbins, Christian romance author

"*Trouble in Store* grabbed me from the very beginning. . . . a page-turner of a tale that encompasses suspense, a murder mystery, romance, and a wonderful journey of faith. The secondary characters are so richly drawn, the twists and turns of the plot so intriguing, that I just couldn't put the book down. I look forward to reading everything else by this author!"

—Roxanne Rustand, author of *When He Came Home*

Books by Carol Cox

Love in Disguise
Trouble in Store

TROUBLE IN STORE

A Novel

CAROL COX

BETHANYHOUSE
a division of Baker Publishing Group
Minneapolis, Minnesota

Published by Bethany House Publishers
11400 Hampshire Avenue South
Bloomington, Minnesota 55438
www.bethanyhouse.com

Bethany House Publishers is a division of
Baker Publishing Group, Grand Rapids, Michigan

Printed in the United States of America

Library of Congress Cataloging-in-Publication Data
Cox, Carol.
    Trouble in store / Carol Cox.
        pages cm
    Summary: "Melanie and Caleb both claim they inherited the mercantile in
Arizona Territory. But when a body shows up on their doorstep, there is deeper
trouble in store"—Provided by publisher.
    ISBN 978-0-7642-0956-7 (pbk.)
    1. Inheritance and succession—Fiction. 2. Arizona—Fiction. I. Title.
PS3553.O9148T76 2013
813'.54—dc23   2013002696

Unless otherwise identified, Scripture quotations are from the King James Version of
the Bible.

Scripture quotations identified NASB are from the NEW AMERICAN STANDARD
BIBLE®, Copyright © 1960, 1962, 1963, 1968, 1971, 1972, 1973, 1975, 1977, 1995 by
The Lockman Foundation. Used by permission.

Cover design by Jennifer Parker
Cover photography by Mike Habermann Photography, LLC

Author represented by Books & Such Literary Agency

13 14 15 16 17 18 19   7 6 5 4 3 2 1

To Wyatt:
Our family's newest native Arizonan

Trust in the Lord with all your heart
And do not lean on your own understanding.
In all your ways acknowledge Him,
And He will make your paths straight.

Proverbs 3:5–6 NASB

1

MARIETTA, OHIO
APRIL 1885

Are the children ready, Miss Ross?"

"Yes, ma'am." Melanie Ross bobbed her head, trying not to wince at her employer's clipped tone. She shot a quick glance at Mrs. Deaver's daughter and son to make sure nothing had happened to mar their appearance since her last inspection.

Five-year-old Olivia stood on Melanie's left, long golden curls framing her cherubic face and cascading over the wide collar of the pink dropped-waist dress so carefully ironed by Melanie the night before. The little girl's eyes glowed with anticipation, and the dimple in her round left cheek deepened when she offered her mother a bright smile.

Mrs. Deaver's features softened enough to give her daughter a fleeting smile in return.

On Melanie's right, Clarence Harrington Deaver Jr. dug the toe of his black patent-leather shoe into the Aubusson carpet, his dark scowl indicating the nine-year-old's distaste for the blue velvet suit, complete with lace collar, designated as his attire for the afternoon.

His mother drew her lips apart in an unconvincing parody of a smile. "You look quite the little gentleman, Clarence. We're all going to have a lovely afternoon, aren't we."

The boy pushed his lower lip out farther, and she bent toward him, her voice carrying a hint of steel. "I want you to be on your best behavior today. You can do that for Mother, can't you?"

When young Clarence's demeanor didn't alter a whit, she changed tactics. "If you're a very good boy, I'll make sure you have a chance to ride your pony after the guests have gone."

The boy's scowl only darkened. "I want to ride Prince now."

Melanie decided to step in before she had an out-and-out mutiny on her hands. She spoke in a crisp tone. "I'm sure we can find plenty to do this afternoon, Clarence. In the meantime, you'll be a good boy and mind your mother, won't you." She held his gaze until she received a grudging nod and heard Mrs. Deaver's sigh of relief.

The moment his mother looked away, Clarence's features took on a thoughtful expression that put Melanie on immediate alert.

Mrs. Deaver regarded her son again and nodded approval. Turning to Melanie, she said, "You may take them down the main stairs now. Our guests will be arriving in just a few minutes, and I want the children to be on hand to greet them. And," she added with a wry smile, "for our guests to see them while they're still spotless, before they've spent the afternoon playing outside."

Melanie paused in the act of herding her young charges

toward the staircase. Surely she hadn't heard correctly. An afternoon outdoors—in those clothes? She could only imagine the effect hours of romping outside would have on Olivia's pink dress . . . let alone Clarence's velvet suit.

Turning back toward her employer, she injected all the tact she could summon into her question. "Are you sure you wouldn't rather have them stay inside so their playing doesn't interfere with your gathering? It's such an important event, after all."

The hint of steel returned, this time in Mrs. Deaver's eyes. "Nonsense. It's a perfect day to hold our get-together outside, and all the children playing on the lawn will make a charming picture, one our guests will remember when it comes time to endorse my husband's candidacy."

"*All* the children?" Melanie focused on the word that concerned her most.

"Didn't I mention that?" Mrs. Deaver trilled a rather forced laugh. "The Martins and Templetons are bringing their children along."

Melanie selected her words with care. "And you want them all to play outside? While your party is going on?"

Mrs. Deaver's tight smile showed no hint of budging. "It would surely be far more difficult trying to keep them all cooped up indoors on a beautiful spring day like this. Don't you agree?"

Melanie clamped her lips together, knowing full well that her opinion wasn't really being solicited. She made a mental head count, trying to keep her consternation from showing on her face. The Templetons had two children, and the Martins three, meaning she would be riding herd on seven youngsters instead of only two.

She fought back a sigh. Clarence was capable of creating enough trouble on his own. Add Johnny Martin to the mix, and no telling what could happen. The two boys had a long history of trying to outdo each other's escapades. The time they'd tried to see who could throw balls of mud higher onto the white plaster walls of the Deaver's home sprang to mind. Melanie flinched and banished the memory as quickly as it came. No doubt about it, she would have her hands full keeping the two of them out of trouble.

She shot another glance at Clarence and caught the look he sent her way, one that promised "I'll do whatever I want to, and you can't stop me" as clearly as if he had spoken the words aloud.

"Yes, ma'am." Shaking off her sense of foreboding, she shepherded the youngsters down the broad staircase and through the ornate entry hall to the front portico, where carriages had already begun to pull up and deliver their passengers.

Melanie stood back as Mrs. Deaver collected the children and walked over to join her husband, who stood on the portico greeting their guests.

A portly man paused to smile at the little group before he clapped Mr. Deaver on the shoulder. "That's a fine-looking family you have there, Deaver. Just the kind of image we want our next congressman to have."

Clarence Deaver Sr. swelled at the words. "Does this mean I have your endorsement, Judge Conners? Your support in the upcoming election would mean a great deal to me."

"That's a strong possibility. I'm hoping we can discuss some of the finer points of your stand on the issues this afternoon." The judge leaned over and pinched Olivia on the cheek, eliciting a spate of giggles from the little girl, then turned to young Clarence and ruffled his hair. "Ah, yes. A chip off the old block."

Melanie saw the way the boy narrowed his eyes and balled his hands into small fists. She stepped forward, ready to avert disaster, but Mrs. Deaver apparently recognized the signs, as well. Draping one arm around her son's shoulders, she turned and beckoned Melanie forward with her free hand.

"Some of the other youngsters are arriving, Miss Ross. Why don't you take the children to meet them." She waited until Melanie drew nearer to add, "And make absolutely certain that none of them go near the stable. I won't have this party ruined by having the children smelling of horses."

Melanie dipped her head and took the children by the hand, tightening her fingers around Clarence's to keep him from running off. She walked with them to the driveway, where Olivia greeted the Templetons' daughters and Johnny Martin's sisters with squeals of delight.

Clarence sauntered toward Johnny with a show of non-chalance intended to deny his mortification at his blue velvet attire. The boys ducked their heads and began talking in low tones, casting an occasional look toward Melanie and her other charges.

Recognizing the need to keep all seven children occupied, Melanie clapped her hands and pasted a bright smile on her face. "Let's all go over in the shade and play a game of tag." She waved her hand toward a grove of stately walnut trees midway between the stable and the Muskingum River. The area was clearly visible from the tables that had been set up on the expansive south lawn, but far enough away that childish voices wouldn't disrupt the important gathering.

The five little girls scampered off, hand in hand, taking

care to skirt the end of the low fieldstone wall that separated the carriage house from the main lawn. Johnny and Clarence immediately clambered onto the wall and walked along the top, holding their arms out wide like tightrope walkers.

Melanie cringed. "Come down from there this minute," she ordered. "If you fall and ruin those clothes, I'll never hear the end of it."

The boys grumbled but complied. Clarence stuck his tongue out at her as they ran off to join the rest of the group.

Melanie followed, wishing with all her heart that the hours would pass quickly. It was going to be a long afternoon.

Will this day ever end? Melanie tucked a stray piece of chestnut hair back into the coil on her neck, wondering if she could possibly look as bedraggled as she felt after an afternoon spent trying to keep all seven children occupied and out of trouble. After playing several rounds of tag, they had chased butterflies and watched ants carry bits of grain to their nests underground. Melanie let them walk near the river's edge under her watchful eye to observe a mother duck teaching her babies how to dive for food. And every fifteen minutes or so, she squelched yet another request from Clarence to let him ride Prince. Herding cats would have been easier.

Up on the driveway, carriages were being summoned in preparation for the guests' departure. Melanie drew a relieved breath, knowing the end was in sight. Johnny and Clarence had been watching an anthill for the past half hour, and the little girls were sitting in a circle—looking like a ring of flowers in their pastel dresses—telling stories.

"Where's Clarence, Miss Ross?" Olivia's voice broke into

Melanie's thoughts. "I want him to tell us one of the stories about King Arthur and his knights."

Melanie turned to point toward the anthill at the base of the tallest walnut tree. "Why, he's right . . ." And the glib response died in her throat. Johnny lay on his stomach, tormenting the worker ants by blocking their way back to the anthill with bits of gravel. But Clarence . . .

Where was he? Melanie knew at least part of the answer. He'd sneaked off again, the little wretch.

Tamping down the urge to stamp her foot, she did another quick head count to reassure herself she only had one truant to deal with. One, two, three, four, five, six . . .

No one but young Clarence among the missing. Melanie pressed her lips together and scanned the area. Where had he gone?

Her annoyance mounted as she pivoted in a slow circle. He'd been easy enough to spot before. What could he be up to now?

Up near the house, attentive servants hovered by the tables while the Deavers circulated among their guests. Melanie's gaze followed the gently sloping lawns, sweeping across the grassy expanse that stretched from the house to the riverbank.

Sudden fear clenched at her stomach. *Not the river.* Visions of Clarence falling in and being swept away to a watery grave filled her mind. Panic lent wings to her feet, and she raced toward the water's edge.

"There he is!" Olivia's shrill voice pierced the afternoon stillness.

Caught up in her dark imaginings, Melanie craned her neck, straining for any sight of a small dark head bobbing above the swirling current.

"No, Miss Ross! Over there!"

Other voices took up the cry, and Melanie whirled around to see all six children jumping up and down, pointing toward a spot on the other side of the grove, beyond her range of vision. She moved past the trees to see a dappled gray pony charging across the lawn, with Clarence clinging to his back like a burr.

The spirited animal's hooves threw up clods of dirt as he galloped across the grass toward the walnut grove. Clarence held fast, his hands twisted in the pony's creamy mane. He lifted his head, and his eyes lit up when he spotted Melanie.

"Yah! Yah! Look at me!"

Melanie's hand flew to her throat. He was going to break his fool little neck. "Clarence Deaver, you stop that pony now!"

The boy's only response was an insolent smirk as the pony turned away from her and headed straight toward the tables where his parents were chatting with their guests, oblivious to the scene being played out on the lawn below them.

"No, come back!" Catching up her skirts, Melanie sprinted after him, knowing she could never catch up with the fleet-footed animal, but hoping she could somehow divert its path and avoid certain disaster.

Even as she ran, she watched events unfold as if living out a bad dream. She recognized the exact moment the adults of the party became aware of what was going on. Their mouths dropped open—first in shock, then in horror—as the pony and its rider bore down on them like a cavalry charge. Shrieks from several women rent the air, joining the cries of the excited children behind her.

The low fieldstone wall lay directly in Clarence's path.

Melanie redoubled her speed and called his name again, knowing as she did so that he couldn't possibly hear her over the pounding of the creature's hoofbeats and the mingled screams.

Melanie continued moving forward, although something seemed to be dragging at her limbs, as if she were trying to run through the waters of the Muskingum. For one moment, she felt sure Clarence was going to guide the pony away at the last second. Instead he kicked the animal's ribs and leaned forward, urging it to jump the low wall. But rather than jumping, the pony shied away and slid to the right.

As in a haze, she watched Clarence part company with the pony and tumble through the air over the wall. The pony skidded to a stop, allowing Melanie to hear the thump when Clarence landed on the turf. His body bounced slightly upon impact; then he lay still.

On the other side of the wall, Mr. Deaver ran toward his son, his wife only steps behind him. A handful of servants brought up the rear.

The Deavers reached the boy a few seconds ahead of Melanie, who had to slow down to climb over the wall. Clarence's mother took one look at her son's still form, let out a shriek, and fainted dead away. Her husband caught her before she hit the ground and scooped her up in his arms.

"Arthur," he barked at one of the footmen, "carry Master Clarence inside, and then send for the doctor. Bertram, go get smelling salts for Mrs. Deaver."

Turning to leave with his wife in arms, he caught sight of Melanie. His anxious features froze into an icy mask. "Miss Ross, see that the other children are dealt with. As soon as you've done that, report to Clarence's room."

2

By the time Melanie calmed her frightened charges, returned them to their equally distraught parents, and gave Olivia into the care of one of the housemaids, the doctor had arrived and been ushered upstairs to Clarence's bedroom.

She ascended the back stairs and made her way along the third-floor hallway, feeling her feet drag more with every step. What would she find when she reached the boy's room? She shuddered, remembering Clarence's landing on the unforgiving ground, the thump, the bounce . . . and the awful stillness that followed.

Dark thoughts tumbled through her mind. Was Clarence still alive? Alive, but crippled? Dread gripped her, and she stumbled. Young Clarence was a mischief-maker—no doubt about it—never happier than when stirring up trouble for the servants, for his sister, and for Melanie herself. But he was still a child, a much-loved son.

And he had been in her charge.

She reached the end of the hallway and paused outside the open door, taking a moment to gather her courage. Low tones filtered from the bedroom into the hall.

"Will he live?" Distress sharpened Mrs. Deaver's voice.

"Of course he'll live, Eleanor." Melanie recognized the doctor's gruff tone. "A sprained shoulder never killed anyone, at least not in my experience. As far as I can tell, a few bumps and bruises are the only other injuries he has. Your son is a very lucky young man."

Mrs. Deaver's grateful sobs echoed the relief in Melanie's heart. Feeling somewhat reassured, she took a deep breath and stepped through the doorway.

Clarence lay on his bed, his face nearly as pale as the starched white sheets. Strips of bandage wrapped around his body, binding his right arm to his side. His mother knelt at the far side of the bed, clutching his free hand and weeping. The doctor stood with his back to Melanie, returning his instruments to his black leather bag.

At the foot of the bed, Clarence Sr. loomed like a bird of prey, his features taut with anger. "How did this happen, son? That's what I want to know."

"Don't be too hard on him, dear," Mrs. Deaver pleaded. "He needs to rest."

Her husband ignored her, never taking his eyes off the boy. "What were you thinking? How could you be so foolish as to get on that pony, especially after your mother gave you strict instructions not to?"

Clarence's lips trembled as he met his father's stony glare, and he spoke in a piteous tone. "Miss Ross told me I could."

Melanie's gasp announced her presence. All three adults in the room swiveled their heads in her direction, awaiting

17

an explanation. Robbed of speech, Melanie could only stand rooted to the spot, shaking her head.

On the opposite side of the bed, Mrs. Deaver caught her breath in a loud sob. "After we placed such confidence in you? How could you?"

Trying to shake off the sense of unreality, Melanie tore her gaze from their accusing faces and looked down at Clarence, who stared up at her with guileless blue eyes.

His shameless duplicity loosened her tongue. "Mr. Deaver, that is not the way it happened. Tell them the truth, Clarence."

With a quick glance to make sure the adults were not looking at him, Clarence met Melanie's gaze straight on and gave her an insolent grin, the same kind she'd seen the time he denied putting spiders down the neck of his sister's dress.

He'd gotten away with that misdeed, but she wasn't going to let it happen again.

Mr. Deaver's harsh tone cut across her musings. "And what exactly is the truth, Miss Ross?"

Melanie felt a rush of heat flood her cheeks. "I was tending the children—all seven of them—as directed, making sure I kept the boys away from the stable. I turned around, and Clarence was gone. The next thing I knew, he was on the pony, heading straight for you and your guests. I tried to stop him, but he kicked Prince in the sides and made him run even faster." She spread her hands. "You saw what happened next."

A little of the starch went out of Mr. Deaver, and he turned his attention back to the bed. "Is this true, son?"

Clarence twisted his face into a grimace and manufactured a plaintive moan, which elicited another sob from his mother.

"Is it true?" Mr. Deaver repeated. "Did you take your pony out without Miss Ross's knowledge?"

Clarence pushed out his lower lip and blinked his eyes until tears appeared along the lower lids. "I know I wasn't supposed to, Father. I just wanted to show you how well I could ride so you'd be proud of me." He whimpered again. "I was doing fine until she came running after me, waving her arms and shouting. That's what made Prince shy like that. That's what made me fall off. It never would have happened if she hadn't scared us both."

Melanie stared openmouthed at the little prevaricator, her mind in a whirl. She cast her thoughts back to the moment she'd spotted Clarence on his pony. In her mind's eye, she could see it all clearly—the way she'd run across the grass at top speed, skirts bunched up in her hands, calling the boy's name and demanding he stop.

A sick feeling washed over her, and her assurance wavered. *Had* she been responsible for the accident?

Mr. Deaver seemed to read the uncertainty on her face, and his lips tightened. "We entrusted our children to your care because we believed we could rely on you. Obviously, that confidence was misplaced. This afternoon's debacle is an example of a deplorable lack of judgment at best . . . and extreme negligence at worst."

"But . . . but . . ." Melanie struggled to find her voice. She stretched out her hand to Mrs. Deaver. They had always been on cordial enough terms. Surely she could count on her as an ally now.

The look she received in return showed Melanie she had miscalculated. This was no longer the face of a woman who wanted someone to mind her children while she flitted from party to party, focused on bolstering her husband's political aspirations. This was the face of a mother tigress whose favorite cub had been injured. Mrs. Deaver gathered Clarence to her bosom and fixed Melanie with an icy stare. "I can never trust you with my children again. Ever. You obviously have no idea what you're doing."

Melanie reeled as though she had received a physical blow.

Mr. Deaver pointed toward the door. "Pack your things, Miss Ross. I want you out of this house today."

Melanie fumbled for the doorframe and gripped it hard. Her vision went gray, but she heard his voice clearly enough through the fog that seemed to have settled into the room. "I'll see to it that you never again find employment as a governess in Marietta—or anywhere in the state of Ohio."

Melanie pushed away from the doorjamb and blinked back the fog. The mist cleared in time to see a triumphant gleam in young Clarence's eyes as she turned to leave.

Thirty minutes later, Melanie set the last of her neatly folded blouses atop the other clothing in her small trunk and fastened the latches. Retrieving her crumpled handkerchief from the dressing table, she dabbed at her eyes, but the sodden linen square did little to wipe the moisture away. She reached into her open carpetbag to pull out a fresh handkerchief and swiped at her face again.

Catching sight of herself in the oval mirror, she took in her red-rimmed eyes and swollen cheeks and shook herself. Tears wouldn't remedy her situation. If they could, the number she had shed since leaving Clarence's bedroom ought to have made a drastic change in her circumstances. But nothing had altered since Mr. Deaver gave the order to leave. Her fate had been sealed.

From the reactions of the other servants she'd encountered on her way back to her room, she suspected one of the maids had been listening outside the door and wasted no time in spreading the word of her dismissal. A sympathetic smile from any of the staff would have been a welcome balm, but their stoic expressions and downcast eyes, averted as if she were some sort of pariah, denied her even that small comfort. Once again, she was reminded of the distinction between a governess and the rest of the household staff—not ranking high enough to be considered part of the family but too high to have any friends among the other servants.

Melanie cast a glance around the small room that had been her home for the past year, wondering if she had forgotten anything in her haste to pack. She had no way of leaving a forwarding address, so if she left anything behind it would be gone forever. Her abrupt sacking left her with no time to make plans, and she hadn't the slightest idea where she would spend that night, let alone what place she would call home in the future.

Mr. Deaver had made his position clear enough: Her days as a governess were over. He prided himself on being a man of influence, and his vow to blacklist her had been no idle threat. He had the clout to do exactly as he promised, and Melanie had no doubt he would follow through on his threat. Any hope of employment in Marietta was closed to her.

But where would she go? She clamped her hands against her mouth and caught her breath in a ragged sob. How she longed to pour her heart out to her beloved grandparents, whose wise counsel had never failed to bring relief during her growing-up years. But if her grandparents were still living, she wouldn't have been in this situation in the first place.

A low moan escaped her lips. With no family or close friends to call upon, her options weren't just limited, they were nonexistent. What was she to do with her life now? Melanie felt another spate of tears coming on and pressed the heels of her hands against her eyes.

The thought of family reminded her of the few treasured keepsakes she had tucked away in the bottom of her carpetbag. Rummaging under her toiletry items and a lawn nightgown, she pulled out the slim box and spread its contents on her dressing table. Her throat constricted when she looked at the meager collection: her mother's cameo brooch, a pair of blue hair ribbons, a packet of envelopes—reminders of a hope-filled girlhood and happier times.

Melanie slipped the top envelope loose from the ribbon holding it in place and smiled despite her misery when she looked at the familiar handwriting. The last letter from her cousin George, written a year ago, just after she had come to work for the Deavers. Her last living relative at the time, George had gone to his reward only eight months after writing the letter, making this final missive doubly precious.

Though knowing she ought to finish packing her carpetbag instead of reminiscing, Melanie slid the thin sheet of paper from the envelope, filled with a longing to relive her last connection with someone who loved her.

Dear Melanie,

It has been far too long since I wrote. I have no excuse for ignoring you, other than things have been busy here in Cedar Ridge. Staying on top of business at the mercantile keeps both Alvin and me hopping like a couple of old bullfrogs.

You sounded a mite lonely in your last letter, Melly-girl. I know life has handed you some hard knocks, but remember that as long as I'm around, there's someone in this world who loves you. What's mine is yours. Anytime you want to shake free of Ohio and come out here to Arizona, there's a job and a place to stay waiting for you. Your pretty face would do a lot to brighten up the store, and we could always use your help.

Next time I see you, I'll have some new ribbons for your hair, unless you're too grown up to use those any longer. If that's the case, you can have your pick of anything the store has to offer. Nothing is too good for my Melly-girl.

Your loving cousin,
George

Melanie pressed the letter to her chest and stifled a sob. The son of her father's oldest brother, George had been closer to her parents' age, more of an uncle than a cousin to her. How she had treasured his infrequent visits while she was growing up, when he would hold her spellbound for hours with tales of his travels and adventures in mining camps around the West. Even after he settled down to run a mercantile with his longtime mining partner, Alvin Nelson, his letters had been a bright spot in her life.

If only he were still alive! Shortly after her grandparents passed away, she had considered going out to live with George.

Instead, she decided to seek employment as a governess—one of the few occupations available to genteel young women of straitened means—thinking that by staying in the area where she grew up, she could maintain a sense of security among familiar surroundings. Melanie looked at her packed trunk and felt her throat swell. So much for security.

She dropped her hands into her lap and looked out the window. "Lord, why did you have to take him away?" If George were alive, she'd head west in a heartbeat.

A wistful sigh escaped her lips. She bent her head again and skimmed the letter once more, smiling at the way her cousin's love for her showed in every line. Her lips curved even more at the mention of the hair ribbons. And the promise of work and a roof over her head—wouldn't that be lovely?

Even though she'd never expected to take George up on his suggestion to join him, just knowing a home was there if she ever needed it had been a comfort on the days when her duties as a governess had become almost unbearable. In her present circumstances, it would be far more than mere comfort—it would be a lifesaver.

Sliding the letter inside the envelope, she pushed it back into the packet with the rest. Its edge caught on another envelope, forcing it out the other end of the stack. Melanie pulled the letter free and smoothed it flat on the desktop, her heart hammering when she recognized the return address.

Dated just after last Christmas, this one had been written by Alvin Nelson, George's partner in the Ross-Nelson Mercantile, telling her of George's passing and effectively severing her last tie to a living relation.

She scanned the first part of the letter quickly, remembering its painful news all too well. Then her eyes fastened on a paragraph farther down the page:

> George was the best pard a man could ever have, and I mean to be as true a friend to him as he was to me. I know how much you meant to him. Every time he showed me that tintype of you as a little tyke, I could hear the pride in his voice when he called you his Melly-girl. I want you to know I've kept everything he left behind, and it's all yours. I'll be sure to keep it safe, should you choose to come out and claim it—and I hope you do. I would be most pleased to make your acquaintance and get to know the young cousin he talked about so much.

> Your obedient servant,
> Alvin Nelson

In her initial grief at learning of her cousin's passing, Alvin's invitation hadn't even registered, but now Melanie's fingers tightened on the paper in her hand as she stared unseeing at the wall before her, phrases from the letter dancing through her mind.

"I've kept everything he left behind. . . . I'll keep it safe, should you choose to come out and claim it."

A seed of hope sent up a fragile tendril. Cousin George might have departed this mortal coil, but perhaps his promise could hold true after all. Alvin Nelson was a man George liked and trusted. A caring soul, from the sound of his missive. After all, he had extended an invitation for her to travel to Arizona to meet him and claim whatever George had left behind.

Melanie's breath quickened. Once they met, mightn't that invitation expand into an offer to stay on and work in the mercantile? George's letter indicated they would be glad for some additional help. Wouldn't that hold doubly true, now that Alvin Nelson was left to run the store on his own?

Her imagination soared, picturing her arrival at the mercantile and Mr. Nelson's warm greeting. She could almost hear him asking her to stay on, offering her a job and a place to live. Everything would work out. It had to. And wouldn't it be lovely? All she had to do was get to Arizona. . . .

The reminder of her circumstances punctured the happy scene she'd been imagining as effectively as a pin pricking a child's balloon. Alvin Nelson might be willing to take her under his wing and give her a home as she hoped, but the fact remained that she would have to travel to Arizona before that could happen. And she couldn't do that without money for train fare.

Tears filled her eyes once more. Her employment ran to room and board, plus a small monthly stipend for personal expenses. She didn't need to check her small purse to know the amount there wouldn't cover the cost of a train ticket. The purchase of a much-needed cloak in January had eaten up most of her savings, and the meager amount she'd managed to put by since then would barely cover a night's lodging, let alone train fare for a cross-country journey.

She clasped her hands, crinkling Alvin Nelson's letter between her fingers. "What am I supposed to do, Lord? I have no place to go, and no one to turn to but you. My grandpa always said you hear the prayers of your people, so please, *please* hear me now."

A sharp rap on the door jarred her from her prayer. Melanie

took a moment to blot her eyes again before she pushed away from the dressing table and opened the door. Jarvis, the butler, loomed in the hallway.

He held out a sealed envelope. "Mr. Deaver sends this message and wishes to know if you are ready to leave."

From Jarvis's careful tone and the stiffness of his features, Melanie suspected he was dreading the worst—fits of tears and desperate pleas for more time. Well, she wouldn't give him the satisfaction. Forcing a dignified nod, she took the envelope and turned away to open it before the butler could take note of the way her hands trembled.

What more could Mr. Deaver have to say to her? He had made it clear enough that she couldn't expect a recommendation from him. Mystified, she tore open the flap and sucked in her breath when she saw a small packet of bank notes wrapped inside a folded paper. The note was brief and to the point:

Consider this your severance pay.

She stared from the written page to the bank notes and back again. Had a prayer ever been answered so quickly? The amount she held in her hand wouldn't set her up to live in a lavish way, but it would pay her way to a new life in a new home . . . and that was all she needed.

Whispering a heartfelt thank-you, she turned back to Jarvis. "You may tell Mr. Deaver I am packed and ready to leave."

She swept up the mementos and tucked them—along with the heaven-sent cash—into her carpetbag and snapped the latch shut. Looping the handle over her arm, she faced Jarvis with a calm smile. "Please see to it that my trunk is taken to the train station."

The butler's eyebrows soared toward his hairline. "You're leaving Marietta? You couldn't possibly have found a new position so quickly."

Melanie's smile broadened as she pressed the carpetbag close to her side. "My days as a governess are over, Jarvis. I'm going to Arizona."

3

CEDAR RIDGE, ARIZONA TERRITORY

Caleb Nelson knelt beside a packing crate and leaned on the pry bar, straining as he levered the last nail out of the top. With a screech of protest, the obstinate nail popped loose and flew through the air like a bottle rocket before coming to rest under the mercantile counter.

Leaning the crate lid against the counter, Caleb bent over and peered underneath the work surface. In the dim light, he could just make out the nail's slender form . . . alongside a scrap of paper. He retrieved the nail, then stretched his arm out again to fish out the piece of paper.

Not another one. Caleb stared at the crude printing on the crumpled scrap in his hands, wishing he knew what lay behind the menacing words.

Get out of Cedar Ridge. We don't want your kind here.

A slightly different wording this time, but similar in tone to the other notes he had come across while cleaning out the Ross-Nelson Mercantile after his uncle's death, and in the months since then. The open hostility had shocked him at first. Uncle Alvin had been a man without a speck of malice, one who tried to live out his beliefs by caring for his neighbor. Caleb couldn't imagine anything his uncle might have done that would warrant such ill will.

Even if he had committed an offense worthy of such venomous messages, why had they continued to appear after he passed away? Caleb frowned as he examined the paper, wondering what lay behind the menacing words . . . and whether the sender would remain content to send anonymous notes, or if the spiteful comments would one day be backed up by equally malicious actions.

"Papa?"

The urgent whisper interrupted his musings. Caleb wadded up the bit of paper and stuffed it into his pocket, taking care to smooth the anxiety from his features before he turned to face his son. "What is it, Levi?"

Chocolate-brown eyes—so like Corinna's—gleamed with excitement. "Over there, Papa. It's the lady that looks like an *S*."

Caleb swiveled his head around to follow the six-year-old's pointing finger. Over the counter, from his crouched position, he could make out Ophelia Pike standing by the shelves near the potbellied stove.

"The lady that looks like an S." Caleb cringed at his son's creative description of the mayor's wife. After the school shut down temporarily following the teacher's elopement with an officer from Fort Verde, Caleb had spent his evenings teaching Levi his letters. He'd felt proud of his accomplishment, knowing Corinna would have approved. Now he wasn't so sure.

"Mr. Nelson, I need your assistance." The woman's sharp

voice rang through the mercantile like a fire bell. "You've placed these cans too high for me to reach."

"I'll be with you in just a moment, Mrs. Pike." Caleb got to his feet and swatted the dust from the knees of his denim trousers. Then he bent again to slide the crate against the counter so as not to trip unwary customers. He picked up a few stray pieces of excelsior that had drifted to the floor and tucked the strands of the packing material back inside the top of the open carton.

Straightening, he dusted his hands together and had taken one step toward Mrs. Pike when he spotted his son eyeing the new shipment with speculation. Caleb pointed at the crate and fixed Levi with a stern gaze. "Don't get into that," he ordered. "And make sure Freddie stays in his box. I don't want him scaring the customers." Levi's pet frog had already brought complaints from several of the local women.

"Yes, Papa." Levi offered him an angelic smile.

Knowing better than to trust that innocent expression for a moment, Caleb shot the boy a warning glance and hurried off to help his customer. It wouldn't take more than a moment to pull a can or two from one of the higher shelves and hand it to her. Then he would get right back to the crate before inquisitiveness overcame Levi and led to a disaster. The six-year-old possessed the curiosity of any number of cats, and the idea of him deciding to help unpack the shipment of crockery dishes didn't bear thinking about.

Caleb crossed the store to where Mrs. Pike stood waiting, facing the rows of shelves in a way that gave him a full view of her profile. Seeing herself as a leader in fashion, she had adopted the newly revived form of the bustle. The one she wore today made her skirt jut out from the back of her waistline like a narrow shelf. With her jutting chin, squared shoulders, and accented derriere, her silhouette did resemble the letter *S*. The moment the thought popped into his mind, Caleb averted his eyes and felt a wave of heat creep up his neck.

He cleared his throat. "What can I help you with, Mrs. Pike?"

"I need you to hand me two cans of stewed tomatoes." She pointed at the uppermost shelf and grumbled as he got them down. "It would be a great help if you didn't insist on setting the items I need up so high. How do you expect anyone to reach them? Assuming, of course, that your intention is to sell your merchandise and not merely put it out on display."

Caleb grimaced and glanced around the store, hoping his other customers hadn't heard the woman's complaint. It was a futile wish. He knew it as soon as he saw the sympathetic glances directed his way. Mrs. Pike's voice carried throughout the store like that of a trained stage actress.

She fixed him with a piercing stare. "My husband wanted me to check with you about the bunting we'll need for the Founders Day celebration. Have you ordered that yet?"

"Not yet," Caleb admitted. "But there's still well over a month until Founders Day. We have plenty of time."

Mrs. Pike sniffed. "Don't put off until tomorrow what can be done today. Procrastination is a sign of weak character."

Caleb swallowed. "Yes, ma'am. Has the mayor thought any more about purchasing fireworks for the event? I could go ahead and add them to the order for the bunting."

Mrs. Pike lifted her chin. "Mayor Pike has not changed his mind. He intends to uphold his promise to the citizens of Cedar Ridge to manage the town funds wisely. Bunting can be used for a number of years. A fireworks display is a momentary diversion—hardly the best use of the town's money. You could learn from his example of sound business practice, young man."

Caleb put on his most conciliatory smile and held the cans out for her inspection. "Shall I ring these up for you, or do you have other shopping to do?"

The tip of Mrs. Pike's pointy nose twitched like a rabbit's. "That isn't the brand I'm accustomed to buying."

But it's the only brand I carry now. Caleb bit back the retort before he spoke it aloud. Uncle Alvin had been most emphatic about treating customers with respect, regardless of their attitude. Keeping his customers' goodwill would be vital to the mercantile's success, especially with competition from the emporium that had opened the previous autumn. He couldn't afford to alienate any patrons . . . including the demanding Mrs. Pike. Instead, he reached back up to replace the cans on the shelf.

"Young man, did I say I didn't want to purchase those? Just set them aside on the counter while I look through—" Mrs. Pike gasped and stared past Caleb's left shoulder with an expression of horror.

Caleb whirled around. A dusty cloud nearly obscured the sight of his son squatting beside the open crate, his skinny arms flailing as he tossed a double handful of excelsior into the air with a whoop.

"It's snowing, Papa!" Levi's voice rang with glee as the fine wood shavings cascaded over his head. "You said we might not get to see snow again once we moved to Arizona, but I'm making it snow now. Watch me!" He scooped up another handful and flung it overhead.

Caleb stared in disbelief as he took in the sight of excelsior drifting down to blanket his son, the floor around him, and the shelves nearby.

Mrs. Pike harrumphed. "Really, Mr. Nelson, you need to keep that boy under control." Her nose quivered, punctuating her statement. "If he was my son, I'd know how to put an end to such behavior."

With a sniff, she turned toward the door. "I can see you have your hands full, with that mess to clean up. I'll be back another day . . . unless I decide to take my business to Mr. O'Shea instead."

"What about the tomatoes?" Caleb held up one of the cans, but Mrs. Pike never broke stride as she exited the store. Through the window, he could see her angling across the street in front of the Cedar Ridge Saddlery, making a beeline for O'Shea's Emporium at the other end of town.

Heaving a sigh, he put the cans back on the top shelf and turned back to the mounds of shavings that littered the floor. Levi had evidently tired of creating his snowstorm and was currently engrossed in lining up his tin soldiers along the shelf under the counter. Caleb pinched the bridge of his nose between his thumb and forefinger, wishing he were a better father, one who knew how to cope with Levi's behavior.

He couldn't deny that there was some truth in what Mrs. Pike had said. He couldn't expect customers to feel comfortable in the mercantile when they never knew what the boy might do next.

But how was he supposed to corral his exuberant son? Spending his days inside the mercantile was no life for an active six-year-old. Levi ought to be burning off that excess energy by playing outdoors under the watchful eye of his mother.

And that was where the problem lay. The only eyes available to watch the boy were Caleb's, and evidently he was doing a mighty poor job of trying to be both mother and father.

"Don't let her get to you."

Startled by the voice at his elbow, Caleb spun around to find Earl Slocum leaning on the counter, a grin creasing his grizzled cheeks. "Excuse me?"

"The Pike woman. I heard what she said."

Caleb grimaced. "You and everyone else in the store."

Slocum's grin widened. "Not to mention anybody outside who was within earshot." He clapped Caleb on the shoulder. "Don't worry. My sister had three boys who were the same way. You're doing a fine job. He'll grow out of this, but right now you just have to roll with the punches. In the meantime, it looks like you have some sweeping to do."

He left the store chuckling, and Caleb crunched across the excelsior to the back room, found a broom, and went to work. The store might not be a suitable place to raise a rambunctious child, but it showed substantial promise from a business standpoint. Cedar Ridge boasted only a couple of hundred residents, but the growing number of miners and ranchers in the outlying areas, plus the soldiers who rode in occasionally from Fort Verde, provided plenty of customers to give him and Levi a comfortable life . . . providing Levi didn't chase them all off first.

Twenty minutes later, he had swept the shavings into a neat pile and wiped the shelves clean of excelsior and dust. The store was free of shoppers for the moment, as good a time as any to finish unpacking his newly acquired merchandise. He bent over and tugged the crate into the open again, removing the excelsior with care to reveal the set of crockery within.

He lifted the first piece out and examined it carefully, pleased to see that it appeared to have survived the journey without breakage. He set the plate on the counter and was bending to retrieve the next when the bell over the door jingled.

He turned to see a comely, chestnut-haired young woman enter the store, carrying a brocade carpetbag. He didn't recall seeing her before, and he would have remembered—he felt sure of that. Caleb brightened—new customers were good for business.

Thankful that he'd finished sweeping up the remains of Levi's "snowstorm," he set the second plate beside the first and smoothed his hair back with both hands, eager to make a good impression.

His new customer stopped a few feet inside the door and stood staring around, taking in the shelves and stacks of merchandise. Maybe she needed help finding something. He'd started to move out from behind the counter when she pivoted suddenly and marched straight toward him.

Caleb put on a welcoming smile. "Good afternoon. May I help you?"

The woman looked at him with clear gray eyes. "I'd like to speak to Mr. Nelson, please."

Caleb blinked. "I'm Mr. Nelson."

A tiny frown puckered the creamy skin between her delicate eyebrows, and she gave her head an impatient shake. "Mr. *Alvin* Nelson?"

Caleb's smile dissolved. "Oh. Alvin was my uncle, but . . . ."

She turned away from him, hoisted her carpetbag, and set it down onto the counter with a thump. Rummaging inside, she pulled some folded papers from its depths and fixed him with a stare that reminded him of a prim schoolmarm. "Would you go fetch your uncle, please? Tell him Melanie Ross is here in response to his letter."

The man behind the counter didn't move. He stood as if frozen, staring at her with his mouth gaping open and a glazed look in his eyes. Melanie began to wonder if he was hard of hearing. Or simpleminded. Or both.

The bell jingled behind her as the door burst open, and a lanky man strode into the mercantile.

"Hey, Caleb, did that carbolic salve I ordered come in yet?"

Caleb—she assumed that was the deaf man's name—whipped his head around at the sound of the other man's voice, looking like someone who'd just been roused from a deep sleep. "Yeah, it's in the back. Rafe brought it in on his wagon two days ago. I figured you'd show up looking for it soon. I'll bring it right out."

Melanie narrowed her eyes as she watched him disappear through the open door behind the counter. His prompt response ruled out intermittent deafness, and his wits seemed to be quick enough when he wished them to be.

She drummed her fingers on the counter. Had she been a bit too abrupt? Violated some unspoken code of the West, perhaps? But all she had done was state her name and request to speak to Alvin Nelson.

She turned around to take a closer look at the store and realized the tall stranger looking for something called carbolic salve now stood beside her.

"Oh my!" Melanie took a quick step backward and clapped her hand to her throat.

He doffed his sweat-stained gray Stetson and held it to his chest. "Afternoon, ma'am. . . . Or is it miss?"

"It's miss. Miss Ross." Melanie drew herself up and spoke in a dignified tone that belied the sudden flutter of her heart. "And you would be . . . ?"

The corners of his eyes crinkled when he smiled. "Will Blake. I own the Diamond B out east of town."

Melanie let her shoulders relax and allowed herself a slight smile. "It's a pleasure to meet you, Mr. Blake. Am I to assume the Diamond B is the name of a ranch?"

His grin broadened. "That's right. I'm runnin' ten thousand head of cattle on some of the prettiest range God ever created."

Caleb Nelson emerged from the back carrying a sturdy crate filled with small square tins. His eyes widened when he saw the two of them in such close proximity. "I'll put that on your tab, Will. Is there anything else you need?"

"Not today." With a courtly nod in Melanie's direction, the rancher placed his hat back on his head, then took the heavy wooden box with no more effort than Melanie would have used to pick up a kitten. "The pleasure was mine, Miss Ross. I look forward to seeing you again . . . that is, if you're going to be around for a while."

The warmth in his tone emboldened Melanie to speak with more confidence than she felt. "Thank you, Mr. Blake. I hope to be here for quite some time."

Caleb Nelson's frown deepened. He opened his mouth as if to speak when the rancher turned to leave, but he was interrupted by the door swinging inward again, this time to admit a short woman of about fifty, nearly as wide as she was tall. Strands of graying hair had escaped her bun, and the loose tendrils danced around her head.

The storekeeper stepped around the counter. "How may I help you, Mrs. Fetterman?"

Melanie cleared her throat. "Mr. Nelson, ignoring me will not make me go away. I need to discuss this matter with your—"

The irritating man brushed past her as if he hadn't heard a word.

The woman smiled. "I'll be fine, Caleb. You go ahead and tend to this young lady. She was here before me, after all. I'll just browse along the shelves while I'm waiting."

Mr. Nelson rounded on Melanie with a harried expression.

"Thank you." Melanie nodded her appreciation for the other woman's courtesy. When her reluctant host seemed inclined to go tend to his customer anyway, Melanie stepped directly into his path, blocking the way so he couldn't continue forward without walking right over her. "As I was saying—"

The bell jangled again. Melanie twisted around to glare at the infernal instrument as a young man and woman entered the store. While her attention was thus diverted, Mr. Nelson managed to elude the blockade she'd created and dodged around her to greet the newcomers. "Mr. and Mrs. Henderson! What can I do for you?"

The couple motioned him over to the side. "We need to order a few things," the man said. He gave a quick glance at Melanie and lowered his voice. "Baby things."

His wife looked down at the floor and blushed.

Caleb clapped the father-to-be on the shoulder. "My congratulations on the happy news. Let me pull out a couple of catalogs. I'd be glad to go over them with you."

Melanie let her breath out in an exasperated huff. At this rate, it would take all afternoon for her to get more than two sentences spoken at once. No telling how long it would be before she'd have another opportunity to send Mr. Nelson for his uncle. And as busy as the store was, why wasn't the uncle there taking care of things?

On the other hand, if this afternoon was any indication of their usual level of business, it shouldn't be hard to persuade Alvin Nelson that her help was needed in the store. With all her heart, she hoped his demeanor in person would reflect the kindly tone of his letter, and that he wouldn't take an unwarranted dislike to her as his nephew seemed to have done. He had to let her stay, he simply *had* to. The thought of being set adrift on her own was unbearable.

She glanced over at the heavyset woman, who was now sorting through an array of small bottles. Perhaps this was a heaven-sent chance to prove her worth.

Stowing her carpetbag behind the counter, she crossed the smooth wooden planks to the far end of the store. "Is there anything I can do to help you?"

Merry blue eyes squinted at Melanie through thick spectacles. "Would you be a dear and read this label for me? My eyes aren't what they used to be, and I can't always read this tiny print." She held up a bottle, indicating the large red letters at the top of the label.

Melanie looked at the bold print and swallowed. *Tiny?*

The gray-haired woman tapped the bottle with her forefinger. "Is this Dr. Bell's anti-pain remedy?"

Melanie looked at the bottle, then back at her myopic customer. "Oh no, ma'am. What you're holding is Dr. LeGear's—" she glanced at the rest of the label and lowered her voice— "flatulence remedy for horses."

Instead of showing the slightest trace of embarrassment,

the woman exploded into gales of laughter. "My, oh my. I could have sworn this is the same thing I gave Mr. Bledsoe when he complained of a toothache." Speaking more to herself than to Melanie, she added, "I wonder if that's why he looked a bit peaked after he took it."

Melanie pressed her lips together. Faulty eyesight could explain a lot about the wispy hair and the smear of what appeared to be flour on the front of the woman's dark gray dress. Melanie only hoped her customer didn't make too many mistakes of that kind, especially when it came to cooking. Her husband must have a cast-iron stomach.

She scanned the shelves and pointed to a shelf holding a number of patent medicines. "Why don't we look over here? I'm sure we can find what you need."

A smile glinted in the other woman's eyes. "That's mighty nice of you, going to all this trouble to help a stranger."

Melanie recognized her opportunity and extended her hand. "I won't be a stranger for long. My name is Melanie Ross. You might have known my cousin George."

"Why, yes I did." Her companion beamed. "George was a fine man, bless his soul." She squinted and peered at Melanie closely. "I should have guessed you were some relation of his. Now that I look for it, the family resemblance is as plain as day."

Melanie devoutly hoped not. Cousin George was a dear man, but he'd been as bald as a coot and had a nose the shape of a potato.

Her customer sniffled. "It was a sad day for us all when he passed away so sudden-like."

"Yes, I miss him more than I can say. We were the only family each other had. That's why I'm in Cedar Ridge. I've come to see his partner about helping out in the mercantile." She glared toward Caleb Nelson, still engrossed in helping the young couple with their order. "If I ever get an opportunity to speak to Mr. Nelson."

At that moment, three more customers entered the store, and the other woman chuckled. "It looks like you may have to wait on that a bit."

"I don't mean him," Melanie began. "I'm talking about his—" Her words were cut off by a ruckus at the door.

"Land sakes!" The older woman planted her hands on her broad hips. "What are those two up to now?"

Melanie turned to see two gangly cowboys wedged in the doorway. They elbowed one another, grunting and struggling, until they finally burst inside the mercantile like a cork popping from a bottle.

The pair looked around the store wild-eyed. Catching sight of Melanie, one of them pointed and hollered, "There she is!" He shoved his companion out of the way and raced toward her.

The other cowboy, not to be outdone, leaped over a crate holding washboards and skirted around a stack of blankets, knocking them askew as he ran past. They both skidded to a stop in front of Melanie at the same instant.

"I got here first," the taller one, a skinny blonde, declared.

"Nosirree." The shorter one glared up at him, his scraggly beard bristling. "I did!"

The blond-haired man appealed to Melanie. "Ma'am, you be the judge. Who won?"

The older woman elbowed Melanie and spoke in an undertone. "I'd say it was a dead heat."

42

Melanie finally found her voice. "What on earth is going on?"

"That's what I'd like to know." Caleb Nelson strode toward them, his face as dark as a thundercloud.

The two men looked at Caleb, then at each other, and then at Melanie. They both started talking at once, their words tumbling over each other.

"My name is Dooley Hatcher."

"Ma'am, I'm Rupert Hatcher."

"I work for the Diamond B."

"I've been with Mr. Blake three years now."

"Mr. Blake told us you were in town, and—"

"I wanted to be the first—"

They glared at each other and spoke in unison.

"Will you marry me?"

4

When Mrs. Pike had stormed out earlier, Caleb didn't think his day could get any worse. But the last thirty minutes had just proved how wrong a man could be. Since the gray-eyed woman walked inside his store, she had managed to completely disrupt his day—first her demand to speak to his deceased uncle, followed by her flirting unconscionably with Will Blake, and then the incident with the half-witted Hatcher brothers.

Just the thought of the mess the two had created in their mad dash made Caleb grit his teeth. Before shooing them out of the store, he'd assessed the damage they'd done and promised to let Will Blake know he could expect to see that amount added to the Diamond B's store tab. That brought them back down to earth in a hurry, although both of them left casting sheep eyes over their shoulders at the trouble-making stranger.

After he finished writing up the order for Mr. Henderson and his expectant wife, the store was quiet again, with the exception of Idalou Fetterman, happily absorbed in looking through his stock of ribbons and notions. It was as good a time as any to deal with Miss Ross—whatever her business— and send her on her way.

He straightened his vest and cleared his throat.

The back door flew open and banged against the wall adjoining the mercantile's small kitchen. Micah Rawlins, owner of the livery across the street, burst inside the mercantile, his eyes wide. "Caleb, you better come quick! There's a fire in the alley."

All thoughts of Miss Ross forgotten, Caleb followed Micah outside at a gallop and saw several townsmen kicking dirt on a small blaze that had engulfed a patch of dry weeds along the edge of the alley. Caleb grabbed several burlap feed sacks from a stack near the back door, tossed them to the other men, and joined them in beating the flames into extinction.

Andrew Bingham, the town's barber, staggered around the corner of the building carrying two wooden buckets filled with water. Two men sprang to help him lift the heavy buckets and douse the last embers.

Chest heaving, Caleb leaned against the wall of the mercantile to catch his breath and surveyed the scorched area, watching to make sure no sparks flickered that would set the fire off again. He shook his head and turned to Micah. "That was too close. If it had spread another five feet, it would have caught the back wall of the mercantile." He looked around the alley and frowned. "Any idea how it started?"

Micah's lips tightened into a grim line, and he nodded toward the opposite end of the alley, where Earl Slocum was holding two small boys by their shirt collars. Caleb's mouth went dry when he realized Levi was one of them.

45

He covered the length of the alley with quick strides and knelt before his son. "What happened?"

Levi glared back, his lower lip thrust out in a manner Caleb suspected was intended to make him look tough.

Caleb took the boy by the shoulders and saw the rebellious light in his eyes flicker. "Tell me what happened, son."

Levi jerked his head toward the other boy, who stared at Caleb with a frightened expression. "I told Percy I could start a fire with my magnifying glass, and he said I was full of beans. So I showed him."

"You showed him." The words came out in a flat monotone. Caleb swiveled around and pointed toward the blackened patch of earth near the mercantile. "Do you realize you could have set the store on fire?"

"Not just the store," added Slocum. "If that building had gone up, it would have spread from there and taken out most of the town."

Caleb got to his feet and held out his hand. "Give me the magnifying glass."

Levi balked for a moment, then reached into his back pocket and handed it over. "When do I get it back?"

"You don't." Seeing his son's stricken expression, Caleb pressed his point home. "Not until you're old enough to use it for the purpose it was intended. Your actions today could have caused grief for a lot of people. You need to spend some time thinking that over this afternoon, and we'll talk about it at home this evening.

"For now . . ." He prodded the boy's shoulder. "You're going to stay in the store for the rest of the day, where I can keep an eye on you."

"But me and Percy—"

"Percy is going home, too." Caleb shot a questioning glance at Earl Slocum, who nodded back.

"I'll be happy to escort him home and let his daddy know what he's been up to." The older man tightened his hold on Percy's collar and led him away.

Caleb marched Levi back inside the store and pointed to the boy's special hiding place under the far end of the counter. "You can play inside your fort until it's time to go home."

Levi opened his mouth as if to argue but seemed to think better of it and ducked under the counter, where he kept an assortment of small toys.

Caleb waited until he was out of sight, then pulled out his handkerchief and mopped his forehead, trying not to let on how much the incident had shaken him. How was he ever going to manage raising a child on his own? Levi's actions could have cost him the store . . . and seen the whole town go up in flames.

Thanks to the quick actions of the local men, disaster had been averted. But what would Levi come up with next?

The mercantile had a good reputation around town, but he was still keenly aware of the need to prove himself. He had gotten along well enough with the locals in the three months he'd been in Cedar Ridge, after Uncle Alvin decided the store was too much for one person to manage alone and requested Caleb's help. Still, he knew he was far from winning everyone over completely—Mrs. Pike being a case in point. And today's near catastrophe hadn't helped. But he was determined to make a go of it. He had to, for Levi as well as for himself.

He tucked his handkerchief back in his pocket and stifled a groan when he saw that Miss Ross hadn't moved from her earlier position. He beckoned her toward him with a curt nod, intending to move behind the counter to establish his position of authority. As he circled around the end, his foot caught on something and he stumbled. Looking down, he saw the woman's floral brocade carpetbag.

"Is it true?" She kept her voice low, but the concern in her tone carried clearly enough.

Caleb jerked his head back up, wishing with all his heart that it was time to close the store and bring an end to this madhouse of a day. "Is what true?"

"People have been coming in and out of the store since you ducked outside, and I couldn't help but overhear them talking. They said the fire was set deliberately. By . . ." She pointed toward the counter, indicating the spot where Levi had disappeared.

As if his private troubles were any of the nosy woman's business! "That matter has been dealt with, and needn't concern you." Caleb drew his lips down as he picked up the carpetbag and thumped it on the counter. "Miss Ross, you seem to be operating under some misapprehension. I'm sorry you've traveled out here for nothing, but the truth of the matter is—"

"—that my late cousin, George Ross, was one of the proprietors of this establishment. He always told me I had a place to live and work here at the mercantile. When your uncle wrote to tell me of George's passing, he invited me to come out and get acquainted. I took that to mean the offer of a job and home still stand, so I decided to take him up on it. And here I am."

Her blithe assumption of a warm welcome—a home, no less!—rocked him on his heels. "I'm afraid that isn't possible. You see—"

Miss Ross planted her hands on her slim hips. "Mr. Nelson, over the past four days, I have traveled by train, stagecoach, and freight wagon." She tilted her chin and glared up at him. "I did not go through all that just to be brushed off like some bothersome insect."

Caleb winced and pinched the bridge of his nose. "You don't understand."

Her voice rose a notch. "What I understand is that this really doesn't concern you. The person I need to speak with is your uncle. Please get him immediately, or at least tell me where I can find him."

Caleb splayed his hands on the counter and leaned forward. "I have every reason to believe that he is in heaven, Miss Ross." He looked directly into her shocked gray eyes and spoke in a level tone. "My uncle passed away last month, leaving me in sole charge. While I am aware that he and your cousin ran the mercantile together, he was the surviving partner and, as such, inherited the store when George Ross died."

The stunned expression on her face gave him the first moment of satisfaction he'd felt since she'd marched into his store. It was a pleasure—no, a relief—to see her at a loss for words. Unfortunately, that state of affairs didn't last long.

She fixed him with a penetrating gaze. "So am I to assume that you are his heir?"

"That's right." Caleb pressed his lips together to hide a smile of triumph. Miss Ross had been a little slow on the uptake, but the truth was beginning to dawn on her at last.

"I see." Her gaze faltered, and she bit her lower lip while her fingers tapped a rapid beat on the counter. Then she drew a shaky breath and turned back to face him. "In that case, it would appear that you are the one I need to deal with."

A sense of foreboding prickled in Caleb's mind. Something in her tone warned him she wasn't ready to pick up her carpetbag and head back to wherever she came from.

Melanie Ross squared her shoulders and lifted her chin. "Everything my cousin told me about your uncle implied he was a man of his word. I would hope that you are as much a man of honor as your uncle was reputed to be."

Caleb opened his mouth, then closed it again, unable to form a coherent sound. Finally he managed to croak out, "And just what do you mean by that?"

She held up the folded papers she'd waved at him earlier. "George Ross was one of the proprietors of this establishment. When he died, he left everything he owned to me. Surely that would include this store—or his share of it, at least."

Her voice seemed to take on confidence with every word she spoke. "I believe the sign outside reads the *Ross-Nelson Mercantile*. Am I correct?"

Caleb nodded.

"Then not only is my name on the sign, but it's on there first."

Caleb wagged his head back and forth like a punch-drunk boxer. Taking the papers from her, he scanned both documents, then read George Ross's letter again. "I have no quarrel with the idea that your cousin left his personal belongings to you. My uncle once pointed out that they're packed away in a trunk upstairs. But there is nothing here that specifies he planned to leave any part of the mercantile to you. As I said earlier, he and my uncle had a partnership. Therefore, when your cousin passed away, the store became my uncle's. And he left the store to me."

Miss Ross stood for a long moment, then dipped her head

in a brief nod. Taking the letters from him, she slipped them back into her carpetbag and snapped it shut.

Caleb sighed, savoring his moment of victory.

She looked up at him and pursed her lips. "I wonder if the local constabulary will see things your way. Would you kindly direct me to the marshal's office?"

A punch to his solar plexus couldn't have taken Caleb's breath away more effectively. He felt sure of his legal standing—fairly sure, anyway—but he was also aware of Marshal Hooper's tendency to follow his own interpretation of justice rather than the letter of the law.

Coupled with that, it was no secret that the town's lawman had a weakness for damsels in distress. He could see it now—Melanie Ross waltzing into the marshal's office, batting those flashing gray eyes at him, giving him a winning smile, and manufacturing a tear or two.

Who knew what might happen then? The marshal might give the whole store to her, and boot him out altogether. It wouldn't help a bit that Levi had already alienated the marshal by kicking him in the shins. Twice.

Caleb swallowed hard. He could see the handwriting on the wall. If she went to the marshal—especially since news of Levi's latest misdeed had surely swept through the town—he might be out on the street before suppertime.

He couldn't let that happen. The store was all he had.

Miss Ross eyed him closely, tapping her foot as if on a telegrapher's key. When he didn't respond right away, she gathered up her carpetbag, spun on her heel, and marched toward the door.

"Wait!" Caleb raced around the counter to intercept her. "Let's discuss this rationally."

A slight tremor tugged at the corners of her lips, and a hopeful light sprang into her eyes.

Caleb steadied his breathing and spoke in a soothing tone. "I think we got off on the wrong foot. You've had a long journey and a trying day. Why don't you take some time to rest and recuperate a bit? Your arrival has come as rather a shock. Give me a chance to think things through, and we can talk about it more in the morning."

Her smile broadened, revealing a tiny dimple in her right cheek he hadn't noticed before. "That's a fine idea. I am sure everything will look brighter to us both after a good night's sleep. Now . . . where am I to stay?"

He shrugged. "That's a good question. Cedar Ridge doesn't have a hotel."

"Oh?" Her smile faded and the dimple disappeared.

He swiped his fingers across his lips to hide his grin. Cedar Ridge might be an up-and-coming place, but it didn't have much to offer in the way of housing for a respectable young lady on her own.

"No, we don't get a lot of people just traveling through. Visitors either have family living here, or they bring their own bedroll and come prepared to rough it on the ground. There hasn't been much call for a hotel."

"I see," she said slowly. Then she brightened. "Cousin George once mentioned that he lived above the store." She glanced toward the back stairway; then a flicker of doubt showed in her eyes. "Or do you live up there?"

"No, my son and I have a house nearby. Uncle Alvin had it built soon after they opened the store." He drew a deep breath. "I suppose you could stay in George's old room, although there isn't much up there in the way of furniture anymore. My son, Levi, goes upstairs to play sometimes, but he's happy to crawl around on the floor with his toys."

Seeing her hope fade, he took heart and pressed on. "We had a couple of big winds last month. They blew an awful lot of dust though the chinks in the walls. That hasn't bothered Levi, but then, he's all boy. He doesn't mind the dust . . . or all those spider webs."

"Spider webs?" Her voice came out in a tiny squeak.

Levi scrambled out from under the counter and faced their visitor with a grin. "Yeah, there are some really big webs up there."

Caleb smothered a smile at his son's unwitting help. "But a good going over with the broom should take care of them. I'm pretty sure we got all the black widows cleared out." He turned to a back shelf and picked up four empty canning jars, which he set before her on the counter.

She eyed them warily. "What are these for?"

Caleb repressed a chuckle. He hadn't been stretching the truth, and he wasn't about to, but he had a feeling the truth would be enough to send her clamoring for a return trip to Fort Verde on Rafe's freight wagon.

He leaned toward her and spoke in an earnest tone. "You fill them with water, then set the bedposts inside them. It'll keep the scorpions from climbing into your bed. I haven't seen one inside for a month or more, but you never know. Better safe than sorry, don't you think?"

Miss Ross swayed slightly. Caleb almost felt sorry for her. Almost.

"Isn't there *any* place to stay in town?"

Caleb had hoped he could avoid that question, but he knew she'd find out if she checked with anyone else. "Well, there's

Mrs. Fetterman. She takes in boarders from time to time. She might have a room open."

Miss Ross's face lit up. "A boardinghouse? Why didn't you say so in the first place?" She hefted her carpetbag again. "Tell me how to find it."

"Why don't you just ask Mrs. Fetterman?" Caleb pointed over her shoulder toward the lone remaining shopper.

Melanie Ross swiveled around in the direction he pointed, and her eyes widened. "Fetterman? I thought her name was Bledsoe."

"No, Hiram Bledsoe is one of her boarders. Mrs. Fetterman is a widow. She keeps a clean house, and I hear she's quite a cook."

As if overhearing her name, Mrs. Fetterman looked up and smiled, waving a bottle of Dr. LeGear's horse remedy in her hand.

Miss Ross looked back up at him and sighed. "Where might I find a broom, Mr. Nelson? I believe I'd rather take my chances with the spiders."

5

The next morning Melanie laid her soiled work dress across the ladder-back chair next to the window and looked around her new room with a sense of accomplishment. By the time she'd cleared the area around her bed and made sure no spiders or scorpions lurked beneath the covers, her energy, already in short supply after her long journey, had run out completely, and she'd fallen asleep without another thought of the creatures that might be lurking.

But she'd risen before daybreak, refreshed and alert, and had determined to make her new lodgings livable before it was time to open the store. After sweeping everything from the ceiling to the floor free of its thick coating of dust—plus one sticky web she recognized as the home of a black-widow spider—she located a bucket and cleaning rags in the storeroom off the back of the mercantile and filled the bucket at the pump in the small kitchen downstairs. A strenuous application of water and elbow grease left the room and its contents gleaming. Not a palace, by any stretch of the imagination, but comfortable enough to call her home.

The brass bedstead and the oak dresser with its matching mirror suited her well enough. She had noticed some bedding on the mercantile shelves the previous day. She could select a comforter and blanket in lively colors to brighten up the room. Perhaps she could find some wallpaper in a feminine pattern to cover the rough-cut lumber on the walls. In time—assuming she was allowed to stay—she could make it into a cozy retreat. But it would do for now, and it was hers . . . for the time being, at least.

She checked the jars of water under the bedposts, thankfully free of vermin, and shuddered. When Caleb Nelson had handed her the jars, the look in his eyes made it plain that he didn't want her there. So she had hoped his talk about spiders and scorpions had been an exaggeration, a ploy to send the eastern tenderfoot running back home. But after coming across those black-widow webs, she had to reassess her opinion. Apparently, one couldn't be too careful in the wilds of Arizona.

And that caution wasn't limited to undesirables of the lower species. Melanie glanced across at the chair she had propped under the doorknob the night before. In all their years of correspondence, Cousin George had always spoken of Alvin Nelson in the highest terms. Though she'd never met Mr. Nelson in person, her trust in George's assessment of his character was such that Melanie hadn't had the slightest qualms about throwing herself on his mercy. Though Caleb Nelson was Alvin's nephew, she didn't know the first thing about him. As she'd told him the previous day, she hoped he was a man of honor like his uncle . . . but she wasn't taking any chances.

After washing in the basin she had carried to the dresser,

she lifted her yellow flowered dress from the peg on the wall where she'd hung it the night before and shook it out hard, just in case. Relieved when no insects of any description tumbled to the floor, she slipped the dress on and checked her hair in the mirror, pleased to see that the smooth coil was still in place. She was almost ready to descend the stairs and embark upon her new life in a thriving mercantile. But first . . .

Making herself comfortable on the edge of her bed, she reached toward the nearby table for her mother's Bible, the first thing she had unpacked the night before. Pulling it onto her lap, she opened the leather cover and thumbed through the well-worn pages, looking for encouragement.

The jolt she felt upon hearing the news of Alvin Nelson's death had rocked her far more than she hoped she'd let on. After receiving his letter inviting her to come to Cedar Ridge to claim George's possessions, she hadn't entertained the slightest doubt that she would receive a warm welcome from him. His nephew, however, proved to be a whole different story. His reaction to her coming had shattered her hopes and let her know in no uncertain terms that she could expect no kindly offers of assistance from him. Her claim to owner-ship of half the store had shocked her nearly as much as it had Caleb Nelson, coming into her mind as an unbidden, but welcome, flash of inspiration she had acted on at once.

Despite her bold assertions, she wasn't nearly as certain of her legal standing in regard to the store as she'd indicated to Caleb, but she wasn't about to let him know that. If she had to make her place there by brazening it out until he got used to the idea, so be it. And he would have to get used to her being there. There was no place else for her to go.

Her fingers turned another page in the Bible, and Melanie

recognized the story of the children of Israel wandering between Egypt and the Promised Land. She read the familiar passages, drawing from them a sense of hope and comfort. The Israelites, too, had been looking for a home and a place to belong. She smiled as she returned the Bible to its resting place. If God could take care of the Israelites in the wilderness, He could surely do the same thing for her in her new surroundings.

Fortified by that encouraging thought, she started for the door, ready to head downstairs. As she approached, she spotted a crumpled scrap of paper near the wall. She picked it up and frowned. How had she missed that in all her cleaning efforts?

She smoothed the paper between her fingers. It had writing on one side. Holding it up to the light, she turned the note so she could read it.

If you know what's good for you, get out of Cedar Ridge.

What on earth? Melanie carried the note over to the window to take a closer look. Whoever wrote it would never win any awards for penmanship. The scrawled lines were more like angry slashes than flowing script.

She stared again at the venomous words, an uneasy tingle of fear creeping up her spine. Had she missed it during her earlier cleaning, or had the note been slipped under her door after she scrubbed the floor? If that was the case, she could think of only one person who wanted to see her leave.

Melanie glanced again at the chair blocking entry to her room and swallowed hard, wondering if her precaution had protected her from more than a hostile warning. As unwelcoming as Caleb had been, he didn't seem like the kind of person who would stoop to writing anonymous notes. But who else could be responsible?

She started to wad the note in her palm, then stopped. If she intended to stay on in Cedar Ridge, she would need to face Caleb every day as they worked together in the store. They couldn't maintain any kind of working relationship if he harbored such bitter animosity. As little as she relished the thought, she would have to speak to him about it. Slipping the note into her pocket, she started down the stairs, bracing herself to meet whatever challenges lay ahead.

The afternoon before, between arguing with Mr. Nelson and talking to Mrs. Fetterman, she hadn't been able to do more than give the interior of the mercantile a cursory glance. So this morning she took her time perusing the layout of the store and its merchandise, feeling a twinge of nostalgia as the familiar sights and smells took her back to her early years. Growing up in the store her grandparents owned had apparently left more of a mark than she'd realized.

The setting, though, couldn't have been more different. She crossed the store to gaze out the front window. Back in Ohio, she would have looked out at a neat row of red-brick buildings, with shoppers bustling to and fro and carriages lined up along the tree-lined street. Here, the air was filled with a haze of dust stirred up by rough wagons on the dirt road.

Melanie moved to the front door and stepped out onto the porch, where a row of board-and-batten structures faced her. She studied the names over the doors, knowing she ought to familiarize herself with the other businesses in town. The livery stable lay directly across the street, next to the black-smith's shop and Cedar Ridge Saddlery. To the left of the livery stood the barbershop, and farther to her left, the town's saloon, the Silver Moon, plied its trade.

She saw nothing in the immediate vicinity that spoke of di-rect competition for the mercantile. *Good*. Her mood bright-ened as she went back inside to continue her survey.

As she moved from one section of merchandise to another, she made mental notes. The first thing they needed to change was to move the patent remedies away from the veterinary supplies—so there would be no repeat of the previous day's incident with Mrs. Fetterman.

She stopped in front of a set of shelves holding an assort-ment of men's shirts, long underwear, and denim work pants. Pairs of heavy boots hung from hooks on the adjacent wall. Melanie pursed her lips as her gaze traveled past the shelves and took in the displays beyond. Work clothes, guns, saddles, and harnesses. Stetson hats, tools, and bags of seed—items aplenty for the men of Cedar Ridge. Practical and utilitarian. But apart from a haphazard selection of fabric, ribbons, and a few ready-made dresses, there was precious little to entice the women of the area to come in and browse. Where were the bonnets, the notions, the array of fripperies that would draw ladies into the store and cause them to linger?

She would speak to Caleb Nelson about ordering some bonnets and lace, and maybe some finer dishes than the heavy crockery sets she saw lined up along a shelf near the counter. That would make a start, at least. And they could set up dis-plays for the finer things in such a way that the women would have to walk past them in order to get back to the canned goods. Her grandparents had done the same thing in their store back in Ohio, and she knew from personal experience how effective that type of placement could be.

The back door swung open, and Caleb and Levi Nelson entered the store. After a quick wide-eyed glance at Melanie, Levi ducked under the counter and disappeared. Caleb hung his jacket on a peg near the door, then aimed a stern look toward the counter. "No snowstorms today. No loud battles between your tin soldiers, and don't bother the customers. Do you understand?"

A muffled voice answered from the space beneath the counter. "Yes, Papa."

Caleb reached for his storekeeper's apron hanging by the door. He drew up short when he spotted Melanie, seeming startled by her appearance, as if he'd been hoping yesterday's altercation had been a bad dream.

Tamping down her irritation, Melanie pasted a bright smile on her face. "Good morning! I've been looking around, and I have some ideas I'd like to discuss with you. I believe they'll make a marked improvement in the store." Without giving him a chance to object, she launched straight into her plans for making the mercantile more appealing to their customers.

Caleb's eyes grew wide, and he pushed his hands against the air. "Hold on a minute. What makes you think you know what the customers want?"

Melanie planted her fists on her hips. "I understand what a woman finds appealing when she enters a store, and this"— she swept her arm in a wide circle—"is not it."

Caleb's eyebrows dipped low, and he took a deep breath. "You may have some good ideas, but you don't know Cedar Ridge and the people here. This isn't Ohio, or any part of the East, and we do things a little differently here."

He pointed to a chair near the back wall. "Why don't you just sit over there and watch the way things go for a day or two?" He shot another look at Melanie. "Or even a week. By then, you'll have a better idea of how the store functions before you go trying to turn everything upside down."

"But I'm only trying to—"

"Have you ever run a store, Miss Ross?"

Melanie narrowed her eyes. "On my own? No. But I helped out in the store my grandparents owned in Ohio. And I know the kinds of things women expect." A happy thought struck her, and her mood brightened. "That can be part of my contribution to this enterprise. It's obvious you need a woman's point of view in running this mercantile."

Caleb took a step toward her. "And it's obvious you don't know the first thing about the seller's side of the business. If I go spending money on things that may not sell, that money comes right out of my pocket."

Melanie stood her ground, refusing to be intimidated. "Right out of . . . that reminds me. I need to ask you about something." She reached into her pocket and pulled out the note. Summoning up her nerve, she looked him squarely in the face. "I know you're none too happy about my being here. I found this note in my room this morning. Did you leave it there?"

Caleb took the paper from her and gave it a quick glance. His lips tightened. "No, I didn't. It has nothing to do with you." He tucked the scrap into his apron pocket.

Melanie waited for a further explanation, but he remained silent. He obviously didn't want to discuss the matter further. Fine, let him have his own way . . . for now. That didn't mean she would dismiss the note—or its ominous implications—but they had plenty of other things to discuss at the moment.

"If you're not going to let me implement these ideas right away, at least tell me what I can do to help."

Caleb sighed and glanced at the walnut mantel clock on the shelf along the wall behind the counter. "We don't have much time, so pay attention."

He led her to a small office next to the storeroom. Melanie took in the spare furnishings: a small table, a rolltop desk, and a pair of file cabinets.

"I keep all the records here," he said. "Orders, shipment receipts, and customer accounts." He swung around and walked back into the mercantile so quickly that Melanie had to scramble out of his way to avoid a collision. She aimed a glare at his back.

Just outside the office door, he stopped at the chair he had indicated to her earlier. Beside it stood a square table with a stack of books on top.

"This is where the catalogs are kept. I can't carry everything, so this is where I help customers look to find items I don't normally stock."

"Like the baby things that young couple was looking for yesterday."

"Exactly." He patted the stack of catalogs. "Come to think of it, this might be the best place for you to begin. Why don't you sit here and go through them all. It will give you a chance to familiarize yourself with what's in them and the way they're organized. That way you'll be better equipped to assist customers when I think you're ready to start helping out."

And in the meantime, it keeps me out of your way. She understood his ploy perfectly. It was the same one she'd used to keep lively children from getting underfoot while making them feel they were doing something useful.

"And over here . . ." Caleb walked to the end of the counter and reached underneath it, pulling out a sheaf of papers. "Here's a list of the inventory, along with the prices for each item. You'll need to know all of those before you can write up orders. And here is where I keep track of any purchases made on credit. Later, those need to be entered in the journal in the office under each customer's account."

Melanie listened, trying to absorb everything he said as he went on talking about which customers could be trusted to pay bills and which ones he didn't extend credit to. "That's important to remember," he emphasized.

She nodded, wondering if she would ever be able to retain it all. Was that the point? She narrowed her eyes and studied him closely. Maybe he was purposely trying to overwhelm her with the flood of information.

"Some customers require special handling," he went on. "Ophelia Pike, for instance. She is the mayor's wife, so make sure she's treated well. I can't afford to lose her business."

"Speaking of our women customers," Melanie interjected, "I wanted to talk to you about rearranging some of the merchandise a bit. For instance, if we—"

The mantel clock bonged the hour. "We'll have to talk about that later," Caleb told her, seeming relieved by the interruption. "It's time to open, and I'm already running behind." He reached inside the storeroom door and retrieved a broom.

Melanie snatched it out of his hand. "At least I can help you by sweeping." She started toward the front door, but Caleb caught her by the elbow.

"You always start with the back stoop first."

Melanie bristled. "You mean it's one more way to keep me out of contact with the customers."

Caleb chuckled, and a smile creased his cheeks in a way she could have found appealing if he weren't so hard to get along with. "Not at all. It's simply a matter of logic. If you start by sweeping out front, everyone who sees you assumes the store is ready to open. By doing the back first, it gives you a chance to take care of that chore before things get so busy you may not have time to do it at all." His smile deepened. "This has nothing to do with you, really. It's something Uncle Alvin taught me when I first came here."

Melanie swept the back stoop as quickly as she could. By the time she put the broom away, Caleb had already tended to the boardwalk out front and was greeting their first customer of the day, a slender man dressed in a checkered shirt, denim pants, and tall-heeled boots.

"Good morning, Slim."

The newcomer nodded but didn't speak. He held his dusty hat in one hand and kept the other behind his back as he peered around the store.

Caleb frowned and raised his voice a bit. "Slim? Can I help you?"

The cowboy spotted Melanie just then, and his face lit up. He pulled his hand from behind his back, and she saw he held a nosegay of spring wild flowers. "Mornin', ma'am. These are for you."

"Now, just a minute," Caleb sputtered.

"I'm Slim Applegate of the Diamond B. Some of the boys were talking about you last night, and I—"

"Out," Caleb ordered.

The smile faded from Slim's face, and he looked at Caleb

65

with an expression that reminded Melanie of a sorrowful hound dog. "I'm not doin' any harm. I just wanted to talk to—"

Caleb pointed at the door. "If you don't intend to buy anything, you need to get yourself and your flowers out of my store pronto. And tell the rest of the Diamond B crew that goes for them, too."

"Can't I at least leave the flowers?"

Caleb took them from Slim's outstretched hand and shoved them toward Melanie. "All right, you've left your flowers. Now go."

Slim backed toward the door, holding his hat over his heart. "Just remember, ma'am. The name's Applegate."

Caleb shut the door behind him with a decisive click and turned toward Melanie.

She glanced down at the flowers in her hand, then back up at Caleb, catching his glare full on. "Don't blame me for that. I have no idea why this is happening. These men don't know me from Adam—or should I say, Eve—so why on earth would they want to come courting?"

Caleb started to speak, then shook his head. He picked up a keg holding an assortment of brooms and carried it out to the boardwalk, leaving Melanie alone with her bouquet.

She found a jar in the kitchen and filled it with water, then placed the flowers in her improvised vase and carried them out to the square table.

Caleb returned, accompanied by a square-shouldered man wearing a charcoal gray suit and bowler hat. The newcomer's eyes lit on Melanie for a fleeting moment, then his gaze slid past her as if she held no more interest for him than the roll of brown wrapping paper above the counter.

Caleb brushed his hands off and turned to the other man. "What can I get for you today, Doc?"

"I need a new supply of Dr. Copp's White Mountain Bitters. And some pipe tobacco."

Caleb nodded. "That shipment with the bitters came in yesterday. If you'll give me a minute, I'll go unpack the crate."

Melanie studied their customer while Caleb hurried to the back room. His sturdy build was matched by a square face, but the bags under his blue eyes, the sagging cheeks, and drooping brown mustache added years to his appearance and made him look more like a tired night watchman than a medical man. She stepped out of his way when he walked past her to peruse the back shelves, and her nose crinkled at the sickly smell of stale alcohol that trailed along in his wake.

She moved to a spot near the front window and waited until he paid for his purchases and left the store before approaching Caleb. "That man is a doctor?"

He nodded. "From what I've heard, despite his appearance, he's a fine physician . . . or he used to be, before his drinking started to take a toll on him."

Melanie walked back to the table that held the catalogs, praying she wouldn't need the doctor's services anytime soon. Seating herself on the wooden chair, she pulled the top catalog from the stack and opened it. After examining a few pages, her gaze drifted past the counter and out across the store. In her mind's eye, she could see a bright, appealing space, filled with merchandise arranged to draw the interest of everyone who entered. And she could create such a space, she knew it.

If she were ever given the chance.

She watched Caleb straightening a stack of blankets and swallowed back her disappointment. Determination and tenacity were traits she admired, but refusing to even listen to her suggestions was carrying it too far. He talked about the worry of losing money invested unwisely, but her ideas would only improve the business. Why couldn't he see that?

A slow smile curved her lips. That was what he needed to do—*see* the changes instead of arguing about them. She would reorganize the store on her own and present the new arrangement to him as a *fait accompli*. Once the transformation was already in place, he would have to agree it was for the best. After all, he didn't spend every moment in the mercantile. He had to go home and sleep sometime.

And when he went home to sleep, she would still be in the store.

6

"Shall I lock the door behind you?" Melanie smiled sweetly at Caleb as he hung up his storekeeper's apron on its hook near the back door.

Caleb's eyes narrowed, and Melanie caught her breath. Had she given him some reason to feel suspicious? His gaze darted from the *Closed* sign at the locked front door to the freshly swept floor and back to Melanie.

"I often stay on awhile after closing the store to go over the bookkeeping. Since I got sidetracked yesterday, I thought I'd spend the evening catching up on the accounts. But now . . ." He ran his fingers through his sandy hair as if frustrated by yet one more complication her presence brought with it.

Caleb pursed his lips and let out a long breath. "I guess now that you're here, it wouldn't be appropriate for me to be alone with you after hours. I'll have to make time to take care of the bookkeeping during the day."

Melanie kept her smile intact but said nothing, hoping her innocent demeanor concealed her eagerness to see him gone so she could get started on her project.

"Yes." Caleb nodded slowly. "Go ahead and lock up. That'll be fine." He swept one more look around the store, as if reluctant to leave, then put his hand on Levi's shoulder. "It's been a long day, son. How would you like to eat at the café tonight instead of me fixing supper?"

When the little boy yipped with pleasure, Caleb gave a tired grin and ruffled his son's hair. "Let's go home and get washed up, then." He gave Levi a second glance and added, "While you're at it, you'd better change your shirt and slick that hair down a little. It's standing up all over."

Melanie followed them to the door and made sure it was locked before she let her smile broaden into a grin. *Alone at last!* Turning, she planted her hands on her hips and looked around the store, trying to decide where she should begin.

A yawn caught her by surprise, and a wave of weariness swept over her. Caleb was right. It had been a long day, trying to adjust to her new situation and learn as much as she could about the people of Cedar Ridge, the mercantile—and the man who ran it.

Caleb was undoubtedly attractive, with his strong, honest face and direct gaze. And after seeing him in action all day, she knew for a fact that he was a hard worker who cared about the store and its customers. Then she remembered the note she'd found that morning and drew her brows together. Try as she might, she couldn't reconcile what she had seen of Caleb's character with the underhanded nature required to write such a malicious message. But then again, she barely knew the man.

Pivoting on her heel, she headed into the small kitchen. A cup of tea would be just the thing to revitalize her before she started reorganizing their merchandise. As she filled the kettle, another yawn stretched her mouth wide.

Melanie shook herself and blinked her eyes rapidly. Despite her eagerness to carry out her plan for the evening, even tea would not be enough to banish the exhaustion that dragged at her. Setting the kettle down on the sideboard, she started up the stairs to her room. She would lie down for a few minutes, long enough to give her weary body a brief rest and clear her mind for the task ahead. After all—she grinned again—she had all evening.

She stretched out on the coverlet and closed her eyes. Just a few minutes to relax, to let her mind drift. . . .

Something was smothering her, closing her nostrils, tightening her throat. Melanie sat bolt upright, trying to push the obstruction away. It took her a few seconds to wake up enough to recognize the acrid stench of smoke. She blinked, trying to get her bearings, then realized where she was—in her new room above the mercantile. And smoke meant there was a fire.

That's right, a fire in the alley. The men were putting it out.

No, that had been the day before. This was something different.

Fully awake now, she shoved herself off the bed and ran to the door. She yanked it open long enough to see smoke filling the stairwell, then slammed it shut again.

There was no other way to get to the ground floor, no way of escape. She was trapped upstairs.

Panic choked her even more than the smoke that stung her nostrils as she raced across the room to the window overlooking the alley. Flinging it open, she stuck her head out. She took two gulps of the clear outside air, then screamed at the top of her lungs. "Help! Fire!"

She heard a shout and poked her head out farther. Craning

her neck, she saw Caleb and Levi running her way from the direction of the café. "Help!" she cried again, waving her arms to attract their attention.

Caleb skidded to a halt below her window. "What's wrong?"

"Help me! There's a fire down below, and I can't get downstairs for the smoke."

His face paled, and he ordered Levi back with a wave of his arm. "Let me see what's going on. I'll try to find a way to get to you."

Melanie gripped the windowsill with both hands and cast a fearful glance back over her shoulder as smoke continued to seep under her door. "Be careful!"

Caleb nodded and leaped onto the back porch, where he was lost from view. Melanie could hear him fumble with the lock, then heard the door crash back on its hinges as he entered. She sent up a quick prayer for his safety while she strained her ears for any sound of impending rescue.

Moments later, footsteps pounded up the stairs. Caleb burst through her door, then slammed it shut behind him. He leaned back against it, gasping for air.

Melanie rushed to him and clutched his arm. "How are we to get down? Should I start knotting my sheets together?"

A brief smile curved his lips before he answered. "No need for that. The fire is out." He held up his other hand, and Melanie saw the teakettle dangling from his fingers.

An icy hand clutched at her heart, and her hand flew to her throat. "You mean I started it? I know I was sleepy, but I'm sure I left the kettle on the sideboard."

Caleb's smile returned. "You did . . . leave the kettle on the sideboard, I mean. The fire was in the office. I used the water in the kettle to put it out."

Relief turned Melanie's knees to jelly. Then she frowned. "How could you put out a fire that created so much smoke with a kettleful of water?"

Caleb's smile dimmed, and his face took on a grim expression. "I'll show you once we've thrown the doors and windows open to air the place out."

Ten minutes later, Caleb led her to the office and pointed to a sodden mass of rags in a metal bucket near the far wall. "It was more smoke than flame."

Melanie stared, then shook her head. "I don't understand. How did this get here?"

The floorboard creaked behind her, and she turned to see Levi gaping at the blackened remains. She whirled back around to face Caleb. "Or do I even need to ask?"

Caleb's brow furrowed, then his eyes widened when he caught her meaning.

"I was here when you put out that fire in the alley, remember? And we both know who started that."

Levi's head wagged from side to side. "It wasn't me. I didn't start the fire—not this one."

Melanie choked back a sob. How many times had she heard young Clarence proclaim his innocence just as convincingly? "How do you expect me to believe that? I locked the door behind you both when you left. No one could have gotten inside." She felt Caleb's hand on her arm and turned to meet his eyes.

"I know it looks bad, but Levi couldn't have done it. He and I were together when we went home and all through dinner at the café. This fire was started after we left."

Melanie lifted her chin and faced him squarely, but she saw only truth in his steady expression. She drew in a shuddering

73

breath. "But I locked the door. How could anyone have gotten inside?"

"They didn't have to." Caleb nodded across the room at the half-raised window. "All it took was prying the window open enough to lower the bucket inside and toss a match on top of those oily rags."

Melanie's lower lip trembled. "Why would anyone do that?"

Caleb avoided her gaze as he bent to lift the bucket. "A prank, maybe. Who knows? Nothing makes sense right now."

Melanie watched him carry the bucket and its reeking contents outside, feeling the sting of his words. Though he hadn't come right out and said so, she knew he'd been referring to her unexpected arrival. All the more reason to implement her ideas for bringing customers into the mercantile, thereby making herself indispensable. But not tonight—she'd had enough.

As soon as she gave the store a good scrubbing and made sure all the windows were locked, she went upstairs again.

7

Caleb pushed open the back door of the mercantile and listened. Surprised when he didn't hear any bustle of activity, he nudged the door open farther and eased his way inside. In the days following the fire, his would-be business partner seemed to have lost her initial panic and set her focus on making herself more at home in the mercantile. But today no bright greeting or lively humming met his ears—none of the relentless flurry he had come to associate with Melanie Ross's cheerful but inexorable takeover of his store.

Levi edged past him, tiptoeing as if he, too, was unnerved by the unaccustomed quiet. "Where's Miss Ross, Papa?"

Caleb shushed him and kept his own voice low. "I don't know, son." *Let's just be grateful for small favors.*

He shut the door softly, then took off his jacket and hung it on the nearby peg. "Keep your voice down. Maybe she's still asleep."

He wouldn't be surprised if she had overslept, considering her level of activity over the past few days. Every morning since she'd moved into the rooms above the mercantile, he had arrived to find some new change in place—a section of merchandise completely rearranged, new displays set up on small tables scattered about the store. It reminded him of the story he'd heard as a boy about the shoemaker and the elves, where the cobbler came downstairs every morning to make some happy discovery. But the discoveries he'd been making of late weren't pleasant ones—they were downright irritating. And they hadn't been orchestrated by friendly elves. These annoying alterations were the work of that human cyclone of activity, Melanie Ross.

After checking to make sure Levi had taken up residence in his fort, Caleb went to get his apron. His toe caught on some protruding object, and he had to grab at a nearby shelf to keep from falling. He looked around for the cause of his stumble and scowled when he realized he had tripped over one of Melanie's displays. He had warned her those little tables were apt to cause some unsuspecting customer to take a spill, but she hadn't paid him any mind. She insisted the display tables made their goods more visible and would draw more interest, and thus help increase their sales.

It was a disaster in the making—Caleb knew it. A double disaster, since she refused to use the tables to showcase their less expensive items. No, that would be too simple. Melanie Ross's idea of salesmanship was to bring out the more costly items that hadn't been selling well.

And she knew they hadn't been selling because—in addition to cleaning, setting up a new inventory list, and devising endless ideas for "improvement"—she had been going over the store's records after hours. Just the thought of it all was enough to make Caleb tired.

He had no idea when the woman managed to get any sleep. She was some sort of dynamo, one that never seemed to run out of energy. He had seen a light burning in the store every night when he looked out the window of his house before going to bed. And every morning he and Levi arrived to find her busily sweeping the back stoop. Until this morning, that is.

Apparently even dynamos ran out of steam eventually. And here was the perfect opportunity to undo some of the upheaval she had created. Caleb grinned and rubbed his hands, ready to make good use of the gift of time he'd been given. Where to begin?

His eyes lit on the case holding the mercantile's stock of pistols, now partially obscured by a collection of doilies and antimacassars she had arranged on the glass top. He scooped up the crocheted goods and started back toward the shelf where he kept the decorative oil lamps.

A piercing shriek split the morning quiet, and the doilies slipped from his fingers, raining down onto the floor. Another shriek sounded, followed by the clattering of feet as Levi plummeted down the stairs and dove into his fort.

Caleb forgot all about the doilies. He dashed toward the stairs, shooting a quick glance under the counter, where Levi curled into a little ball as though trying to make himself invisible. "What's going on, son?"

"I'll tell you what's going on."

Caleb looked up to see Melanie at the top of the stairs. She descended halfway to the ground floor with an ominous tread. Caleb's eyes widened when he realized she wasn't even dressed yet. With one hand she clutched a light, flowered wrapper around her trim waist. Her bare toes peeped out from under the hem. Her hair, which he'd only seen pulled back in a low coil, hung over one shoulder in a heavy braid.

He stared, unable to tear his gaze away. It took him a moment to realize she was still speaking.

"Are you listening to me, Mr. Nelson?" Her toes tapped a steady beat on the wooden step.

Caleb moved his focus from her slim figure to her face and flinched when he met her outraged expression. "I'm sorry. What were you saying?"

Her nostrils flared, and her expression grew even more indignant. "As I have been trying to tell you, I was awakened by a noise, and when I opened my eyes, what should I find but your son peering down at me. In my *bedroom*, Mr. Nelson!"

Caleb cast an uneasy glance toward the counter.

"I had just opened my mouth to ask him what he was doing there, when he shoved *this* into my face." She pulled her other hand from the folds of the wrapper and held up a wriggling green object.

Caleb gaped at the sight of Levi's pet frog. He sucked in his breath. No wonder she'd screeched.

"Levi," he began in a stern tone.

Only a slight scuttling noise gave any hint of the boy's presence.

Caleb raised his voice. "Levi, come out here now."

Levi emerged from his hiding place and shuffled over to stand beside Caleb, his gaze fastened on the floorboards. "I only wanted to show her Freddie."

"What have I told you about—"

Melanie cut in. "I am not finished. Can you imagine the shock I felt? And when I cried out, he dropped the creature on my—" A dark red flush suffused her face and neck. "On my bosom." She raised her hand to pat the area beneath her throat, then realized Freddie was still in her grasp. She grimaced and held the amphibian out at arm's length.

"Be careful. You might drop him." Levi hurried over to rescue Freddie from her grasp. He cradled the frog to his skinny chest and glared at his accuser. "I couldn't help it. You scared him, and he jumped out of my hand. I tried to get him back, but . . ."

Levi's voice trailed off as Melanie raised her eyebrows and narrowed her eyes.

It didn't take much imagination for Caleb to picture the scene: Freddie leaping from Levi's hand onto Melanie Ross's . . . chest . . . and Levi diving to retrieve him. He squeezed his eyes shut. That would explain the second shriek and Levi's precipitous retreat.

Melanie cleared her throat like a schoolmistress calling a daydreaming student back to attention. "I realize I overslept this morning, Mr. Nelson. But that is no excuse to have my privacy invaded in this manner. I am quite aware that my presence here is unwelcome, but surely even here in the West a lady has a right to expect—" Her voice cracked and her chin began to tremble. Without another word, she whirled and ran back upstairs. A moment later, Caleb heard the sound of her door closing, followed by the decisive click of a lock.

He bent over, scooped Levi up in his arms, and set the young miscreant on the counter, putting him at eye level. "Let me explain something to you. Gentlemen do not enter a lady's bedroom. Ever. Is that clear?"

Levi opened his mouth as if to argue, then studied Caleb's expression and seemed to change his mind. "Yes, Papa."

"When Miss Ross comes downstairs again, you will apologize to her. Like a gentleman. Do you understand?"

The boy's shoulders sagged, but he nodded. "Yes, Papa."

Twenty minutes later, Melanie descended the staircase for the second time that morning. The difference in her appearance couldn't have been more striking. This time, her hair was drawn back into its usual loose coil, with not a strand out of place. Instead of the flowered wrapper, her slender figure was now encased in a pale blue dress. Her face, however, was still set in the same taut lines.

"Good morning, Mr. Nelson."

Caleb nodded.

"Good morning, Levi."

"Good morning, Miss Ross." Levi spoke in a subdued tone. He started to edge away toward his fort, but Caleb cleared his throat and gave his son a meaningful look.

Levi's face assumed a stoic expression, and he stood at attention, like one of his tin soldiers preparing to face a firing squad. "Miss Ross, I'm sorry for scaring you like that. I just wanted to show you Freddie. He really is a nice frog. You'll like him once you get to know him better."

Melanie folded her hands in front of her waist and looked at him with a steady gaze. "If and when I decide to make Freddie's acquaintance, it will be at a time of my own choosing. Is that clear?"

Levi gulped. "Yes'm."

Caleb braced himself for another round of arguments in Freddie's defense, but Levi merely retreated to his hideout. Keeping a wary eye on Melanie, Caleb went back to the task of restoring the mercantile to its previous state.

She disappeared into the back and returned carrying a

rectangular rosewood box adorned with a delicate tracery of inlaid wood. "I found this music box on a shelf in the storeroom. Where would you like me to put it?"

Caleb gritted his teeth. "Right back on the shelf where you found it."

"Why? This is part of our inventory, isn't it? It's a beautiful item, but you can hardly expect to sell it if it isn't on display."

"I don't intend to sell it." When Melanie arched her eyebrows in a silent question, he continued, "Uncle Alvin always kept it there in the back. I asked him about it once, but all he said was that it had a certain sentimental value to him. Therefore, it holds a sentimental value for me, as well. Which means it stays on its shelf in the storeroom, and not out here."

She opened her mouth as if to argue, but then to Caleb's surprise, she turned and flounced into the storeroom without further protest. When she returned, she hesitated near the foot of the stairs, obviously wanting to comment on the changes he was making. Instead, she pulled a feather duster from under the counter and went to work on the shelves holding bottles of patent remedies.

Caleb watched her while he went through the motions of folding and restacking a pile of men's shirts. As he worked, his thoughts strayed back to the way she'd looked earlier, standing before him barefoot in her wrapper. The sight had affected him more deeply than he'd been aware of at the time, bringing back memories of comfortable family times spent around the fireplace with Levi and Corinna. Back in the days when everything seemed right with his world.

Melanie readjusted a bottle that wasn't quite lined up with the rest, then bent to dust the bottom shelf. Caleb took in the smooth lines of her skirt. Despite her assumptions that he had no concern for his female customers, he had been studying the most recent issues of *Godey's Lady's Book* in an effort to educate himself on the current fashions. Unlike Ophelia Pike, the majority of the women in Cedar Ridge shunned the recent resurgence of the bustle, opting for practicality over style. Melanie Ross appeared to be of the same mind, since a bustle obviously was not part of her attire.

Caleb's eyes widened, and he whipped his head around, concentrating all his attention on folding shirts instead of letting his eyes rove where they shouldn't. What was he thinking? He had no business noticing whether she wore a bustle or not. For all her irritating qualities, Melanie was obviously a lady.

A lady, to be sure, and an irritating one at that. One who didn't hesitate to stand her ground when she believed she was right, which seemed to be most of the time. One whose gray eyes flashed like a stormy sky when she grew angry. But that pretty well summed up what he had learned about her to date. And those were mostly superficial things. What of the person that lay underneath?

Without thinking, he blurted out, "What were you doing before you came out west?"

Melanie straightened and flicked the feather duster over a row of bottles. "I was a governess."

A governess? Then surely Levi wouldn't have been the first high-spirited child she had come across.

As if reading his thoughts, she tucked the feather duster under one arm and tilted her chin. "I am not unfamiliar with the antics of headstrong children. In my last position, the young boy in my charge was every bit as—" She broke off and shot a glance toward the counter, then cleared her throat and continued. "I apologize if my behavior this morning seemed a bit overdone, but I was taken utterly by surprise. You have to admit, being roused from sleep to find a frog dangling just inches from one's face would be enough to unnerve almost anybody."

Caleb grimaced, but he had to agree she made a good point. "You're right. Under the circumstances, I believe you handled yourself rather well." A sudden inspiration struck. "You've been working hard ever since you got here. I think you ought to take a little time off."

She looked at him as if weighing the possible meanings behind his offer. The doubt faded and her face brightened. "That is an excellent idea. I've been longing for a chance to see more of the town, and some fresh air will do me good."

Her quick agreement took Caleb off guard. Could it be the hard work was beginning to take its toll, and she was losing interest in becoming a storekeeper? He tried not to let his sudden spurt of optimism show.

"Yes," she continued with a decisive nod. "If we're going to make a success of this joint endeavor, it's imperative that I learn more about the people we serve. I'll just get my shawl and be on my way."

Caleb watched her go upstairs, his brief hope fading as quickly as it had been born. That didn't sound like the statement of a person who was ready to give up.

8

Melanie smoothed her skirts, looped the strings of her reticule over her left arm, and stepped out into a perfect spring day. Cottony clouds floated in a brilliant blue sky. Even the light breeze that caressed her cheeks seemed to celebrate the joy of spring, carrying the hint of apple blossoms mingled with the scents of the high desert. The fresh, clean tang did wonders to dispel the heavy weight that had settled on her shoulders ever since she'd first stepped through the doors of the mercantile.

She stood on the boardwalk and drew in a lungful of the invigorating western air. Other than sweeping off the stoop behind the store and the boardwalk out front, she had barely set foot outside since her arrival. Caleb was right. She had been spending too much time indoors. If she intended to make Cedar Ridge her new home, she needed to become more a part of it. And if she hoped to improve business at the mercantile, she had to get acquainted with the people in the area. Knowing their customers would be a key to making the store a success.

Which way to go? She scanned the length of Lincoln Street. From the limited time she'd spent outdoors, she had already seen the businesses directly opposite the mercantile and the saloon to the left.

To the right, then. She set off briskly, taking note of each building she passed. Next door to the mercantile was the freight office, Rafe Sutton, proprietor. Melanie sniffed as she walked past. The sight of the building brought back the memory of her arduous trip over the rutted trail from Fort Verde to Cedar Ridge, perched beside a scraggly-bearded driver who seemed compelled to launch a stream of tobacco juice at every bush they passed. Their journey was an event she—and her aching backside—would long remember.

A little farther down the street she came to a dressmaker's shop, a neat little establishment with a sign in the window reading *By appointment only*. That was more like it. Melanie cupped her hand around her eyes and peered through the window. A smile lit her face as she took in the array of fabric and notions. She had already seen copies of *Godey's Lady's Book* in the mercantile. She would study them carefully for clues as to what the dressmaker might need, as well as the ladies in the community who didn't avail themselves of the seamstress's services.

As she passed the bakery, she grinned and dug in her reticule for a pencil and scrap of paper. She'd better start making notes. Ideas were coming fast and furious, and she'd never be able to remember them all. She licked the tip of the pencil and began to write.

A small clapboard building was next, set back a little way from the boardwalk. Above the door hung a wooden placard bearing the words *Jonas Mills, M.D.*

Melanie's brow furrowed. Doctors needed medicine, of course, along with some very specialized equipment. Apart from the patent medicines she'd seen on the shelves, did they carry anything of that sort in the mercantile? She made a note to ask Caleb.

The doors of the plaster building that housed the bank stood wide open to the fresh air. Behind the teller's window stood Mr. Henderson, the young man she had seen on the day of her arrival. Melanie tapped her pencil against the paper. What kinds of things could they keep in stock for babies and children? That opened up a whole new array of items to explore. She scribbled a quick note and walked on by.

She reached the end of Lincoln Street and stepped off the boardwalk onto the hard-packed tan dirt, so different than the black, loamy soil she had been accustomed to in Ohio. She stood for a moment gazing to her right, then to her left. It appeared that Lincoln Street comprised the full extent of Cedar Ridge's business district. Little more lay beyond, save for a few scattered houses. And in the distance . . . *Oh, my!*

Beyond the edge of town lay a vast landscape dotted with the sprawling cedars that must have given the town its name. Farther out, a line of trees bearing darker foliage meandered off in an undulating line. And behind those trees hung a backdrop of tawny hills. Some of the pale brown slopes were adorned with more cedars, while others, streaked with pinkish layers, rose up in sheer cliffs surmounted by a ridge of barren rocks. The effect was absolutely breathtaking.

Melanie pressed one hand against her throat and stared in wonder. *Is this the place where I'm going to live out the rest of my days?* The scene before her couldn't have been more different from the one she'd grown up with. There were no tree-lined streets, no lush green lawns with carefully tended shrubs. This was raw. Rugged. Wild.

And yet a sense of rightness washed over her, a feeling of coming home.

She swept her gaze over the landscape, letting its beauty fill her senses, before circling around to the other side of the street. She strolled past a good-sized home made of bricks the same color as the sandy soil, its neat yard surrounded by a white picket fence. The door opened, and a familiar-looking figure wandered down the front walk.

Melanie smiled, recognizing Mrs. Fetterman. The plump woman didn't seem to notice Melanie until she'd nearly walked into her.

Mrs. Fetterman squeaked an apology and squinted up at Melanie, recognition dawning on her face. "Ah, the nice young lady from the mercantile!" A smile wreathed her weathered cheeks. "What a pleasure to see you again."

Melanie returned her smile. "I'm glad you're pleased, because you'll be seeing a lot more of me. Right now, I'm just taking some time to learn my way around town."

Mrs. Fetterman beamed with pleasure. "I was on my way to the mercantile, but I'm not in any rush. Would you like to come in and try some of my scones? I just took them out of the oven."

Melanie wavered, remembering the mix-up with the horse tonic. "Thank you, but perhaps another time."

Mrs. Fetterman patted her arm. "Not to worry. Since you're planning to stay, we'll have plenty of chances to visit."

Melanie watched the woman move along the boardwalk toward the opposite end of town. Did any of their catalogs offer spectacles that might be stronger than the ones Mrs. Fetterman was wearing? It might be worthwhile to find out.

She waited a moment before starting on toward the unattractive wooden building ahead. Its unpainted boards lent the structure a dreary air, and the walls didn't seem to be quite at right angles with the roof. Melanie noted the sign hanging over the boardwalk and quivered like a hound on the scent when she saw the name: *O'Shea's Emporium*. What a perfect opportunity to get to know their competition!

Tucking her pencil and paper back into her reticule, she pushed open the door and entered the store. No bell jingled a welcome as she stepped into the dimly lit interior and peered around. Her first impression was that it seemed much smaller than the mercantile, making it feel almost cramped in comparison. A quick perusal told her the store carried only basic items—certainly nothing to compare with Ross-Nelson's selection of goods. She moved along a set of rough shelves, noting several brands of coffee, bags of beans, and a scattering of canned goods.

The emporium's general appearance wasn't as clean as the mercantile's, either. She ran her finger along a shelf surreptitiously and wrinkled her nose when she inspected her fingertip. Dusty. Just as she'd expected.

The scrawny man who slouched behind the counter paring his fingernails with a pocketknife matched the unkempt look of the store. He rubbed his thumb across one fingernail and sent an indifferent glance in Melanie's direction. "If you see something you want, let me know."

Melanie murmured a noncommittal response and moved back toward the exit, holding her skirt close to her in an effort to keep it clean. There was no point in staying any longer—she had seen everything she needed to. She emerged back out on Lincoln Street with a sigh of relief. She had no need to worry about their competition. From what she'd seen during her brief foray, it was a miracle the other store stayed in business.

She went on her way with a lighter step. The sign on the next building proclaimed it to be the Verde Valley Land Company. And the building just beyond . . . Melanie couldn't hold back her grin when she saw that it was the marshal's office. She chuckled, remembering Caleb's reaction when she threatened to take up her case with the lawman. Despite her brave words to the contrary, she had little confidence in claiming any legal right to the store, but she wasn't about to let Caleb know that.

The door swung open as she passed. Melanie caught her breath and turned, expecting to meet the marshal face-to-face. Instead, Will Blake, the rancher she'd met on the day of her arrival, stepped out. A broad grin spread across his face when he saw her.

"Morning, Miss Ross. This beautiful day just got even prettier."

Melanie felt the blood rush to her cheeks. "Good morning, Mr. Blake. I'm surprised to see you in town again so soon. I had the impression you spent most of your time in the company of your cows."

The corners of his lips quirked up. "Cattle tend to take care of themselves. They don't need me nursemaiding them every second." He fell into step beside her as though they were longtime friends. "I had some business with the marshal. I rounded up a few strays with brands I didn't recognize, and I needed to let him know so he can put the word out and locate the rightful owners. But I also had other business that brought me to town today, and I need to thank you."

Melanie laughed. "I don't know what you have to thank me for, but whatever it is, you're welcome."

His smile deepened. "You saved me making a stop at the mercantile to ask Caleb where I might find you."

She drew back and looked up at the rancher, puzzled. "You were looking for me?"

A deep laugh rumbled from his chest. "You haven't been out of my thoughts since I met you last week. It isn't often we see a fresh face around Cedar Ridge, and it's even more special when that face is as pretty as yours."

Once again, Melanie felt the warmth of blood rushing to her face. When was the last time a man had complimented her like that? After spending the past few days feeling like little more than a nuisance, Will's words of admiration made her feel as if she were floating along with those bright clouds overhead.

"I know things are taken more slowly back east," he said, "but I'd like to get to know you better, if you're agreeable." Seeming to take her stunned silence for consent, he went on. "Where might I find you if I wanted to come calling?"

Melanie's heart raced, and she waved her hand to fan her flushed cheeks. "Why . . . I'm afraid you'll still have to come to the mercantile." His look of surprise brought forth a genuine laugh that suddenly put her at ease. "George Ross was my cousin," she explained. "I came out to work in the mercantile."

A frown creased Will Blake's forehead. "But your cousin is . . ."

"Yes, I know." She took a deep breath and forged ahead.

"He left all his belongings to me—which includes his share of the store." She waited for Will's reaction, hoping the story sounded convincing. If people around Cedar Ridge began to accept her as part of the town, it might help persuade Caleb she ought to stay.

"Well, what do you know?" Will shook his head and grinned. "I always liked George, but he never spoke much about his family. I knew he had a cousin, but I never expected it to be anyone as intriguing as you."

Melanie fluttered her hand again and let her breath out in a sigh of relief. Will had accepted her explanation without question. If only Caleb would credit it as readily!

Will pushed his Stetson farther back on his head. "That sun is getting a mite warm. How would you like to continue our conversation someplace where it's a little shadier. . . . Unless you were heading straight back to the store."

The hope in his eyes made Melanie want to giggle. A chat with someone as genial as Will Blake sounded like the perfect way to set her day aright. "Actually, I'm taking a little break and enjoying a few minutes to myself. I realized I've been spending all my time in the mercantile, and I haven't gotten to see much of the town."

Will glanced up at the sun as though checking its position in the sky. "It's a little early to have lunch. Why don't you let me escort you over to the bakery and treat you to some of the finest doughnuts in the territory?"

Melanie's sunny mood grew even brighter. "Thank you. I'd like that." She tucked her hand into the crook of his arm and smiled up at him. "I would like that very much."

Caleb carried an open crate of canned peaches from the back room and plunked it down on the floor next to the wooden stepladder. Tucking one can under his arm, he picked up another one in each hand and climbed the ladder to add them to the neat stack on the top shelf. Ophelia Pike had once informed him she didn't care for peaches, so she wouldn't have any objections to him putting them there.

"Can I help, Papa?"

Caleb looked down into the eager face of his young son, whose wide brown eyes held an earnest expression. Maybe he was trying to make up for the incident with the frog. Caleb glanced at Levi's hands. "Where's Freddie?"

The little boy pointed toward the counter. "I put him away like you told me to. He's in a box in my fort."

"In that case, why don't you hand me those cans one at a time so I don't have to keep going up and down this ladder? That would be a big help." He smiled at the way his son's chest puffed out. Maybe that was all the boy needed—a little more responsibility.

The bell jingled as he set the last can in place. Putting one hand on the shelf to maintain his balance, he turned to see Benton Woodbridge step inside. Caleb never called him by his given name, though. From their first meeting, he had picked up on the locals' habit of calling him the Professor. As far as Caleb knew, the man had never been a teacher of any kind, but his air of culture and his store of knowledge had earned him the nickname.

The Professor walked across the store, dressed as always in neat black trousers and matching coat, a dark gray vest over his gleaming white shirt, and a jeweled stickpin in his cravat. Caleb smothered a grin. Definitely not typical western garb. Caleb still didn't know why the Professor had chosen to live in Cedar Ridge, but having learned early on that prying into someone else's background wasn't tolerated in the West, he'd never tried to find out. Whatever the reason Woodbridge had for being there, Caleb was glad to have him around, and he was gratified that the Professor counted him as a friend.

He descended the ladder, picked up the empty crate, and set it on the end of the counter. "What can I do for you today?"

The Professor brushed an imaginary bit of lint from his sleeve. "I'm in need of a pound of sugar, if you please . . . and a bit of conversation."

Caleb grinned. "It'll be a pleasure to oblige you . . . on both counts."

The door burst open, and a wild-eyed woman stormed inside the mercantile. Caleb recognized her as Ava Morgan, one of the town matrons who swarmed around Ophelia Pike like flies drawn to honey.

She skidded to a halt as the door swung closed behind her and peered around the store's interior with a frantic expression.

Concerned, Caleb stepped forward. "May I help you?"

Mrs. Morgan pinched her lips together and looked askance at him and the Professor. "I wish to speak to Miss Ross."

"I'm afraid she isn't in at the moment. Is there some way I can assist you?"

His customer wavered, then reached into her reticule and produced a dark brown bottle. Holding it aloft, she advanced on Caleb. "I purchased this tonic from Miss Ross three days ago."

Caleb nodded, eyeing her warily.

"It's supposed to calm the nerves and help the digestion. It says so right here on the label." She waved the bottle in front of his nose.

Caleb resisted the urge to back away. If this tonic was guaranteed to soothe the nerves, it obviously hadn't lived up to its promise. He gave her his most reassuring smile. "The effects may not be immediate. Sometimes it takes a little while to work."

"Oh, it worked, all right." The irate woman shook the bottle, sloshing the liquid inside.

Caleb tilted his head and spread his hands wide. "I'm afraid I don't understand."

"It started working right after I swallowed the second spoonful. It's worse than castor oil. I couldn't get ten steps away from—" A crimson wave suffused Mrs. Morgan's cheeks. "I honestly thought I was going to die. I would have come in yesterday, but I could hardly hold myself erect."

Caleb took the bottle from her hand and frowned. The label was for Mrs. Bickham's Nerve Tonic. But Mrs. Bickham's remedy came in a green glass bottle. That dark brown bottle looked more like . . . *Oh, no.* He moved to the shelves that held the vet supplies.

"Mr. Nelson, I am not finished." His red-faced customer trailed behind him.

Without answering, Caleb pulled a bottle of Peterson's Drenching Solution off the shelf and weighed it in his hand. Sure enough, it was the same shape and color as the one Mrs. Morgan had returned.

"Mr. Nelson, are you listening to me? I demand that you take this dangerous substance off the shelves at once. It's a menace to the public."

"I'm dreadfully sorry." Caleb interrupted the diatribe and held out both bottles. "The labels must have gotten switched somehow. What you took was actually a solution to be given to bloating cattle."

"Oh!" Mrs. Morgan pulled a lace-edged handkerchief from her sleeve and pressed it to her lips. A small convulsion rippled across her shoulders.

"I'll be happy to refund your money," he said. "Or I can exchange this for a bottle of the real Mrs. Bickham's remedy, if you'd prefer."

Mrs. Morgan's shoulders shook again. She returned the handkerchief to her sleeve and drew herself erect. "I'll take the refund. I have no intention of giving you the opportunity to poison me a second time."

Apologizing profusely, Caleb withdrew a handful of coins from the register and counted the refund amount into the woman's outstretched hand. Giving him a curt nod, she pivoted and marched out the door.

The Professor moved closer and peered at the mislabeled bottle. "How do you suppose such a mistake could have taken place?"

Caleb returned the drenching solution to its place on the shelf, then held the offending bottle up to the light. "It was no mistake. Look at this." He traced his finger along the edge of the label, where a faint residue showed on the brown surface. "The original label has been removed. You can see a bit of the torn edge remaining. The Mrs. Bickham's label was pasted over the same spot."

The Professor gave him a questioning look. "You're saying it was done deliberately?"

Caleb nodded grimly. "It would appear so." He strode out

the back door and poured the contents of the bottle into the dust of the alley. *Who could have done such a thing?*

Levi?

He rejected the notion as soon as it entered his mind. Replacing the label like that was beyond a six-year-old's ability. Besides, that kind of subterfuge didn't fit Levi's character. Caleb couldn't deny that his young son created more than his share of mischief, but the boy wasn't truly malicious. He stepped back inside the mercantile and tossed the empty bottle into the wastebin.

Wiping his hands on his storekeeper's apron, he turned back to the Professor. "Sorry for the interruption. Let's get back to your order." He measured the sugar into a small cloth bag and set it on the counter next to the crate. "Shall I put it on your tab?"

"If you would, please." The Professor glanced toward the stepladder. "A couple of cans of those peaches it appears you just put up there would do nicely, too."

Caleb climbed the ladder again, retrieved the peaches, and then rejoined his friend, leaning back against the counter.

"I was rather hoping to meet that new partner of yours I've been hearing about." The Professor's dark eyes twinkled when he spoke. Caleb couldn't tell whether that was due to amusement or anticipation.

"She stepped out for a while." Caleb raked his fingers through his hair. "And thank goodness for that. This has been the longest week of my life."

The Professor's eyes widened. "How so?"

Caleb sighed, glad for the chance to confide his woes. "I'm beginning to wonder whether or not this venture is going to work out for me. It was hard enough to make the decision to pull up stakes back in Missouri and move to Arizona to come help my uncle and make a new start. Then there was the challenge of settling in and learning the business. And then to have Uncle Alvin up and die just as I was starting to get the hang of things . . ."

The Professor nodded. "I can only imagine how difficult that must have been, but I believe you've handled the transition admirably. From everything I've seen, you have an innate business sense that will stand you in good stead in making this store a success."

"I hope so. If I don't succeed, it won't be for lack of trying—that's for sure."

"I can attest to that," the Professor agreed. "Everyone in Cedar Ridge has seen how hard you've worked."

Caleb rolled his eyes. "Not nearly hard enough, according to some people."

The Professor's eyebrows shot up. "Oh?"

Gratified by the other man's interest, Caleb gave vent to the frustration that had built up since the moment Melanie Ross entered his store. "It's this niece of George's. My 'new partner,' as you called her. She sashayed in here assuming she owned his share of the business. I don't think she has a valid claim, but I'm honestly not sure what will happen if it comes to a legal battle."

He groaned and smacked his palm on the counter. "We butt heads every time I turn around. She has a raft of ideas for 'improving' the store." He spread his arms wide, taking in the displays of merchandise. "What needs changing? Keeping things the way they've always been worked fine for Uncle Alvin, so it's good enough for me, but I can't convince her to leave well enough alone."

The professor's somber look reflected Caleb's mood. "What kind of woman is she? What would happen if you just explained all this to her?"

Caleb blew out a huff of air. "You think I haven't tried? All she does is stiffen her neck and keep on doing whatever she wants. You wouldn't believe some of the crazy ideas she's come up with—rearranging the store every time my back is turned, reorganizing the merchandise in a way that makes no sense to me, but one she insists will be better for business. It seems her family owned a store back in Ohio, but that doesn't mean *she* knows the first thing about running a business. But just try to convince her of that! She wants to have her finger in everything."

"Where is she now?" The professor looked around as if expecting to see Melanie pop up from behind the flour barrel.

"I sent her out to explore the town. She'd hardly been out of the store since she got here, so it seemed like a good excuse to get her outside. Truth to tell, though, I'm the one who needs the break." He glanced over at the mantel clock. "It's been nice, but I can't expect it to last much longer. She'll probably stroll back in any minute."

Caleb looked at the Professor, whose features had taken on a faraway expression. "What is it?"

The dapper man pursed his lips. "I was just thinking about your uncle and wondering how he would have handled this."

Caleb raised his hands and let them fall back at his sides. "I honestly don't know. No, that isn't true. Uncle Alvin was a God-fearing man. He probably would have welcomed her as George's rightful heir with open arms."

The Professor nodded. "I suspect you're right. Alvin was

one of the fairest men I've ever known. I expect he would have done just that."

"But he didn't have a son to raise." Resentment rose up, choking Caleb until he had to force the words out. "Levi needs stability, and it's been hard enough for me to provide that for him without having some pig-headed woman keeping everything in an uproar."

"So what are you going to do?"

"I don't have any idea. I'm at my wit's end trying to figure out how to make this work and still keep my sanity intact."

The Professor gave a dry chuckle. "It sounds as if you need some time to yourself, time to be able to think clearly so you can sort things out."

Caleb snorted. "How am I supposed to get that? It's bad enough having her shuffle things around every night. I don't dare leave her here alone during the day. There's no telling what she'd do. I can't seem to make her understand that this is a business, not a lark. She simply has no idea the amount of work that's involved in managing the store on a day-to-day basis."

The Professor tilted his head and smiled. "Maybe that's exactly what she needs to learn." His smile broadened at Caleb's blank look. "Think about it. If she really wants to have a managing role, she ought to know more about the kind of responsibility that entails. It might be enough to persuade her this isn't really something she wants to do."

He tapped his cheek with one finger. "On the other hand, it might do exactly the opposite. There's really no way to know until you try. Either way, it would give her a better look at what she's getting into . . . and you would have the few hours' respite you so obviously need."

His smile faded, and he looked at Caleb with a serious expression. "George and Alvin operated this store as partners, but you've been running it singlehandedly ever since Alvin passed away. Maybe it wouldn't be a bad idea to have someone who can help carry part of the load."

Caleb stared at the odd little man, wondering if his friend had a point. He had spent every waking moment since Melanie arrived trying to undo every change she made so he could keep a tight rein on the mercantile. Was it possible that he'd been doing them both a disservice?

The more he thought about the Professor's suggestion, the more the idea grew on him. Maybe loosening his hold was the best way to regain it in the long run. Could it really be that easy to persuade her to leave? He suspected that might not be exactly what the Professor had in mind, but as a strategic move, it just might work.

Or it might make her feel she had gained even more of a toehold.

But he needed some time away from the store and Miss Ross—needed it desperately. And he could take Levi along, make it a special outing for the two of them, something they hadn't enjoyed for months. Maybe it was worth the risk. After all, how much damage could she do in one day?

He clasped the Professor's shoulder. "I think you may have hit on something. I believe I'll give your idea a try."

The Professor sketched a bow, then gathered up his purchases. "I'm happy to have been of service. And on that pleasant note, I will be on my way. I look forward to hearing the results of your little experiment. They should prove quite interesting."

The bell jingled as the door closed. Caleb returned to

the storeroom for another crate and finished restocking the shelves with Levi's help. He had just put the stepladder away when Melanie breezed inside with a spring in her step he hadn't noticed before.

When he smiled at her, the surprise on her face took him aback. Hadn't she ever seen him smile before? Well, maybe not, come to think of it. Not often, at least. But he had plenty of reason to smile now. He'd accomplished a lot in her absence. And thanks to the Professor, he now had some hope of getting his life back on track. He dusted his hands on his apron and smiled at her again. "How was your walk?"

"Marvelous." Her face lit up. "I was able to get a better sense of the businesses in town and their needs. I have a whole new list of ideas I'd like to implement."

The news produced a queasy feeling in Caleb's stomach, but he refused to let it upset him. He stepped closer to her and squinted. Were those crumbs and traces of powdered sugar on her chin? He reached out to brush them off with his thumb. "It looks like you discovered the bakery, as well."

Her blush made him grin. She looked just like Levi caught with his hand in the cookie jar. Encouraged at seeing her caught off guard like that, he forged ahead. "How would you like to tend the store tomorrow?"

Melanie's mouth dropped open. "On my own?" She couldn't have looked more shocked if he'd suggested she climb onto the store's roof, sprout wings, and fly.

Caleb suspected he might be taking much more pleasure in her discomfiture than befitted a gentleman. Maybe she wasn't always as self-assured as she tried to appear. "Why not?" he answered with a casual wave of his hand. "If you're going to be part owner, you ought to have a taste of what it's like to be in charge. I thought I'd take Levi down to the creek in the morning and do some fishing."

Levi popped out from his cubbyhole under the counter, his eyes wide as saucers. "Fishing? Really? Just you and me?"

The innocent question brought a lump to Caleb's throat. He and Levi spent their days together in the store, but that wasn't the same as just the two of them spending time focused on something his son enjoyed. The unmistakable excitement in the boy's voice at the prospect of having his father all to himself spoke volumes about how hungry he was for Caleb's attention.

Melanie seemed just as quick to recognize Levi's need. She smiled over his head at Caleb and nodded. "That sounds like a fine plan to me."

Caleb felt a twinge of misgivings about his scheme. He'd expected more trepidation on her part instead of this calm display of confidence. But maybe this was all for the better. Let her start off with an overabundance of assurance. All the easier for a few setbacks to burst her bubble and force her to accept that Cedar Ridge wasn't the place for her.

"Make sure you have everything ready before it's time to open," he cautioned. "It's a lot more taxing than you might expect, trying to manage everything on your own."

"I'll do that," she promised. Her eyes sparkled, not seeming daunted in the least.

"On the other hand, it might be very slow tomorrow morning. It's hard to know what to expect sometimes. I hope you won't be too disappointed if there isn't much to do."

"Oh, I won't be." She was practically glowing now, like a child awaiting Christmas morning. "If that turns out to be the case, it will give me an opportunity to put some of my ideas into practice right away."

Caleb felt his heart drop like a stone.

She turned toward the stairs. "Let me put my shawl away and freshen up a bit. Then I'll be ready to buckle down and get back to work."

Caleb watched her hurry up the stairs, wondering if he had somehow miscalculated. She didn't seem at all put off by the idea of carrying the full weight of responsibility for the store on her shoulders.

Maybe his stroke of genius hadn't been so brilliant after all.

9

Caleb leaned back against the trunk of a towering syca-more and watched the milky-blue waters of Walnut Creek ripple at his feet. He tipped his head back and looked up through the tree's soaring branches, where a light breeze rustled the glossy leaves. The sun's rays filtered through the lacing of branches, dappling the blanket he'd spread out for the two of them to rest on. The first true peace he'd felt in months washed over him in a wave of contentment.

Turning his attention back to the creek, he called to Levi. "Keep away from the edge, son. If the fish see you, they'll hunker back in the rocks and won't take your bait." He saw no need to mention that stepping back would also lessen the chances of Levi falling in. The spring rains up north had melted the snow on the mountaintops, sending an excess of water downstream. The creek flowed at a rapid pace, rising high along the banks and eddying in a pool right below the tree where he and Levi had taken up their positions.

Caleb's cane pole leaned against the mottled bark of the

sycamore's trunk. He'd had success enough to make him happy. Three good-sized trout were tied on the stringer anchored to a fallen log a short way downstream—more than enough for their supper. For the rest of their time there, he planned to relax and enjoy their day together, and give his determined son a chance to hook the "whopper" he was sure lurked in the swirling pool.

"Do you think Freddie will like his new home?" Levi asked.

"I think he'll be very happy here. It was time to let him go free, and you made a good choice, turning him loose by this pool. He'll have lots of bugs and flies to eat, and maybe he'll find some frog friends to play with." And there wouldn't be any more incidents between Freddie and Melanie Ross or any of their women customers.

At the reminder of Melanie, a ripple of unease intruded into his peaceful reverie. Would he recognize his store when he got back to town? How many customers had she managed to alienate in his absence? He sat up and rubbed his hand across his face, trying to shake off his sudden gloom.

"Why art thou cast down, O my soul?" The verse from the Psalms came to his mind like a healing balm. *"And why art thou disquieted within me? hope thou in God."*

The words of the psalmist brought renewed solace to his soul. The ancient composer knew exactly where to find his hope.

Then again, the psalmist didn't have Melanie Ross to contend with.

Enough! Caleb slapped his palms against his knees. His purpose in taking Levi fishing was to have some time to think and pray about his situation. If he let worries eat away at him, his time away from the store would be wasted.

He leaned back again and watched as Levi focused his

attention on the wooden bobber that floated on top of the water, following its progress as the current carried it in a circuit the length of his fishing line around the edge of the pool. "Keep an eye on your line," Caleb called. "You don't want it getting snagged on those cattails."

Rousing himself, Caleb gathered up the remains of their picnic lunch and tossed the crumbs a dozen feet away, much to the delight of the sharp-eyed scrub jay keeping watch from one of the sycamore's limbs.

Getting to his feet, he shook out the blanket, dislodging the last of the crumbs, then spread it out again. He had to give the Professor credit for a clever idea. If Melanie's shift in the store turned out to be anything less than total disaster, he would have to take advantage of more times like this for as long as she stayed in Cedar Ridge.

"Should I check the hook again?"

Caleb raised his hand to cover his smile. "You've already checked it three times in the past ten minutes. You have to give the fish a chance to see it. Just keep your eye on the bobber."

"I haven't even had one little nibble with this worm. Maybe it fell off. Don't you think I ought to pull it up and make sure? Maybe there's nothing there for the fish to see."

Caleb stretched out on the blanket, propping himself up on one elbow. "Give it time, son. If you're going to be a good fisherman, you need to learn to be patient."

Levi shot him an impish look. "I guess Miss Ross wouldn't be a very good fisherman, then, would she."

Caleb gave his head a quick shake. After six years, he still hadn't gotten used to his son's abrupt changes of subject. "What do you mean?"

"She wasn't very patient with you this morning."

Caleb winced at the memory. "No. No, she wasn't." His mind drifted back to his words of instruction just before they left that morning. He'd only wanted to impress upon her the fact that tending the store involved more than prettying up their displays. Being a successful storekeeper meant being aware of a number of different things, all at the same time.

"You have to know your customers. Most of the people around here are easy enough to deal with, but a few need special treatment. There's the mayor's wife, for instance." Caleb gave her a quick description of Ophelia Pike, omitting any mention of protruding bustles or a resemblance to the letter *S*. "Remember, she and her husband buy a lot from us, and we want to keep it that way. If she asks for anything we don't have in stock, tell her we'll order it, and make sure you follow through on that right away."

Melanie's nod was a bit impatient. "Of course. It's the same treatment I would expect for myself as a customer. That's exactly the kind of service we ought to be giving."

"Then there's Andy Jenkins. I've noticed several small items missing a time or two after he's been in the store. I haven't caught him at it yet, but if he comes in, don't let your attention get diverted. You can't take your eyes off that one for a minute."

Melanie's brow crinkled. "And if he's in the store when someone else asks about an order, and I need to check in the storeroom . . . ?"

It isn't as simple as you thought, is it. "You'll have to figure that out for yourself. That's what running a store is all about. It isn't a lark, it's a business. Now if some stranger comes in who looks like they may try to give you trouble, I keep a pistol in the drawer next to the cash box."

That was when she'd told him not to borrow trouble and practically thrown him out of his own store.

A whoop from Levi broke into his thoughts. "Look, Papa! The bobber's gone!"

Caleb sat straight upright. Sure enough, Levi's cane pole bent in an arc, its quivering tip nearly touching the water's surface. He sprang to his feet and ran to the bank. "Hold your pole up high. Don't let him get away."

"I'm trying, but he's too big. Help me!"

Caleb grabbed the pole with one hand above and the other below Levi's and held it in a firm grip. "Okay, let's pull him in. Come on now, you can do it."

The veins stood out in Levi's neck as he heaved back, pulling for all he was worth. After a moment, the pole went slack as the water broke and the fish cleared the surface in a mighty leap. Caleb took advantage of the opportunity, keeping the pole high in the air and swinging it over to the bank. He held tight and kept the line taut, while Levi ran over to inspect his prize.

The look on the boy's face was one of pure delight. "It's the biggest fish I've ever seen! I did good—didn't I, Papa?"

Caleb laughed aloud at his son's exultant expression. "You sure did. That must be the granddaddy of all the trout in this stream. I'm going to have to set up a separate stringer just for him."

He busied himself pulling out the hook. Then taking the fish from Levi's grasp, he took a length of heavy cord from his pocket and threaded it through the fish's mouth and back out through the gills. Then he carried it over to the bank and knelt to tie the cord to the half-submerged log.

"Why did Mama have to die?"

The question took Caleb so off guard that he nearly lost his grip on the line. He made a quick grab to hold it fast before the trout took advantage of his lapse and swam away. With his free hand, he looped the line around the branch holding the other three fish and knotted it tight.

Straightening, he wiped his hands on his pant legs and turned to face Levi. "To be honest, son, I really don't know." And that was the absolute truth. Hadn't he bombarded his heavenly Father with that same question for countless nights after Corinna's death?

Levi broke a dry cattail from its stalk and wandered over to the blanket. He plopped down on it, sitting cross-legged. Avoiding eye contact with his father, he picked at a patch of dried mud on the knee of his overalls. "Do you think she would have liked me?"

Caleb felt like he'd taken a fist to the chest. "Of course. She loved you, son. You were the joy of her life."

Levi nodded, seeming to accept the assurance without question. He ran his thumb along the dry cattail, peeling off clumps of the tiny seeds. "What about Uncle Alvin? Why did he die?"

Caleb drew a long breath. Those were weighty questions for a boy Levi's age. He'd never expected their little outing to take such a philosophical turn. He picked his words carefully, trying to decide how much a six-year-old ought to know. "Well, he got sick, son."

Levi bobbed his head. "But he was getting better. I thought he was going to get well."

"We all did." Caleb felt a renewed sense of grief, remembering how quickly Alvin had taken a turn for the worse. "But sometimes things don't work out the way we expect them to."

Levi nodded again, appearing to ponder the concept. "Uncle Alvin liked me."

Caleb smiled. Kneeling beside his son, he reached out and ruffled the boy's hair. "Yes, he did. He liked you very much."

Levi tossed the bits of cattail aside and started digging in the dirt with the stick. "What about Miss Ross?"

Caleb felt a little like the bobber in the pool, being spun this way and that. What had made Levi connect Melanie to this line of questioning? He tried to keep his voice light. "Well, when we left the store, she was alive and well. I assume she'll be in the same condition when we get back."

Levi looked up and crinkled his nose. "I mean, how long is she going to stay here?"

Caleb shifted uneasily. "I don't know for sure. It kind of depends on how things go."

Levi stretched out on the blanket and stared at the puffy clouds overhead. "One of the cowboys asked her to marry him again."

Caleb stared at him. "Really?" He couldn't say the news surprised him, although he'd never expected his son to be the one to tell him. The shortage of women in the West made any new female arrival fair game for men who longed for a home and family, so the idea of one of them offering marriage on such short acquaintance wasn't unheard of. But in the brief time she'd been in Cedar Ridge, Melanie had already racked up an impressive number of proposals. "Which one?"

Levi lifted one shoulder. "I was in my fort, so I couldn't see him. I just heard what he said." The boy's eyelids fluttered and seemed to grow heavy. His mouth stretched wide in a yawn. "Are you going to ask her to marry you?"

Caleb bit back a yelp. "Me? Whatever gave you that idea?"

"I just wondered. I heard some ladies in the store talking about it."

Caleb gritted his teeth. Bad enough for him to be the topic of the local gossips' speculation, but he hated the thought of Levi overhearing it. "Sometimes people just like to hear themselves talk. No, I have no intention of marrying Miss Ross."

"That's good," Levi murmured. "I don't think *she* likes me very much."

"Oh, I'm sure that's not—" Caleb stopped in midsentence, remembering the look on Melanie's face when she'd held up Freddie the frog. Her expression that morning hadn't been one of warmth and acceptance. He sought for some words of reassurance, then realized the boy's eyes were closed, and his gentle breathing confirmed that Levi had fallen asleep.

Caleb lay back and clasped his hands behind his head. *Thanks, Lord. I've had enough of fielding difficult questions for the moment.* He stared up through the leafy screen and watched the clouds drift across the sky. This was what he and Levi needed—time together without the distractions of the mercantile.

He would find a way to make it happen more often. If Melanie agreed, he could ask her to mind the store once in a while so he and Levi could get away on a regular basis. Assuming she didn't up and accept one of those proposals. If she got married, she'd move away to start a home of her own and lose all interest in running the mercantile.

Lose interest . . . Caleb sat straight up as an idea struck him. If Melanie got married, it would put an end to his problems. Why hadn't he thought of that before?

And what was she waiting for? She'd certainly had enough offers. He could see why suitors like Dooley and Rupert

Hatcher wouldn't appeal, but there were plenty of well-established men in the area, men who could provide a good home and a solid future. He considered the possibilities, his excitement growing by the moment.

It wasn't as if he was only thinking of himself. A good marriage would provide her with security and a comfortable future. All she needed was for the right man to ask. Apparently, she hadn't met him yet.

A smile tugged at Caleb's lips as an idea blossomed, then burst into full, glorious bloom. Maybe he could hurry up the process, or at least help it along. He knew most of the men in the area, from Cedar Ridge and Fort Verde all the way over to Prescott and Fort Whipple. Surely she could find someone suitable out of so many possibilities. All he had to do was spread the word that a comely young woman of good breeding had settled in the area, and they'd come running. In droves.

And that wouldn't hurt his business, either. He rubbed his hands together. It was a great plan, as brilliant as anything the Professor could conceive. It would be the perfect solution for both of them. He couldn't wait to put it into action.

10

Melanie reached for the pair of scissors on the fabric table and guided them carefully, cutting along the lines of the pattern in the blue gingham. Business had been slow so far, but the lack of customers didn't bother her. The lull had given her time to work on one of her pet projects. With any luck, she would have it finished before Caleb and Levi returned from their fishing expedition.

She grinned as she wrapped the loose end of gingham around the bolt, remembering Caleb's insistence on reviewing every detail of his daily routine before they left. His panic at the thought of leaving her in charge was almost palpable. She spread the two cut lengths of fabric on the table and smoothed them with her hands. What did he think she was going to do—burn the store down in his absence?

The thought brought a chuckle, which faded quickly when she realized that might be exactly what had been worrying him. It was painfully obvious that the only reason he'd taken the day off was because Levi needed time with him, not because he believed her capable of tending the mercantile on her own.

She folded several inches of the first length of fabric over along one long edge and began to sew it in place with small, neat stitches. She would show him just how capable she was. In addition to spending her days watching Caleb to learn how he ran the business and handled customers, she had been working equally hard after hours, dividing her time between studying the store's records and making the changes she felt sure would improve the mercantile.

She reached the end of the fabric and made a few tight stitches to anchor the thread before snipping off the end. Today, she had the luxury of having the store to herself during daylight hours, a perfect opportunity to prove what could be done with a little ingenuity and effort. She looked up when the bell sounded and a woman who could have stepped straight out of the pages of *Godey's Lady's Book* swept into the store.

Melanie blinked. The modish attire would have fit right in with the Deavers and their circle of friends, but it looked oddly out of place in Cedar Ridge.

The woman turned in a slow circle, as though looking for someone—for Caleb, Melanie realized. At the sight of her imperious mien and stylish dress, the pieces came together. The woman fit Caleb's description of Ophelia Pike to a tee. As the woman turned sideways, Melanie noted the jutting bustle and pressed her lips together to keep from laughing out loud. She had heard Levi mention the *S*-shaped lady, but she hadn't realized that lady and the mayor's wife were one and the same.

Smoothing her apron, Melanie put on a bright smile. "Good afternoon. It's Mrs. Pike, isn't it? May I help you?"

Mrs. Pike stopped short and stared. Melanie kept smiling, enduring the woman's inspection and feeling painfully certain she had been found wanting. Mrs. Pike cast another look around the store. "Where is Mr. Nelson?"

Melanie struggled to maintain her composure, feeling as though her smile had frozen permanently in place. "He took the day off to go fishing with his son."

Mrs. Pike's eyes widened, and she drew herself up like a pouter pigeon. "What can he be thinking of, lollygagging outdoors on a day the store is supposed to be open for business? I came in here intending to place a sizable order . . . if he's able to fulfill it." She sniffed. "And rewarding that scalawag of a son of his with a day at the creek? What that child needs is a firm hand applied to the seat of his britches. That's the way to keep him in line."

She swept the store with another icy glare and huffed her displeasure. "How does he expect to keep my patronage if he's not here when I need him? I may just go down the street to Mr. O'Shea's and give him my business instead."

Melanie came around the fabric table and approached Mrs. Pike with her most helpful expression. "You won't need to do that. The store is most definitely open for business, and I will be happy to place an order for you."

A surge of excitement rippled through her. What a coup it would be if Mrs. Pike placed a sizable order. She could just picture Caleb's expression when he came in to find that she'd not only managed to keep from incinerating the mercantile, but had been responsible for making a significant sale.

Mrs. Pike peered down her nose, obviously unimpressed by Melanie's assurances. "Who might you be, and why would Mr. Nelson leave you in charge?"

Melanie held herself primly erect. "My name is Melanie Ross, and I am part owner of the Ross-Nelson Mercantile." She placed a slight emphasis on the first part of the store's name, in case Mrs. Pike missed the connection.

"Is that so?" The other woman's nostrils flared slightly, and she hesitated, seeming at a loss for words—a situation Melanie suspected didn't happen often. She glanced from Melanie toward the door, as if debating whether or not to leave.

Melanie held her ground and refrained from groveling. She didn't believe the woman's threat about patronizing Mr. O'Shea for one moment. Having seen the emporium with her own eyes, she knew for a fact they wouldn't provide the kind of goods or service the mayor's wife undoubtedly expected.

Mrs. Pike's shoulders sagged a fraction. "Very well, then. I'll give you a chance. I would like to order a new set of china, and I want it to be something special, not the heavy crockery you keep in stock here. Have you any patterns you can show me?"

It was all Melanie could do to contain her elation. "Let me show you the catalogs, and we can go over them together. I'm sure we'll be able to find just the right pattern to suit your needs."

They spent the next hour poring over the pages of one catalog after another, debating the relative merits of various china patterns. In the end, Mrs. Pike rapped the table with her knuckles. "I've made up my mind. I'll take the Wedgwood Columbia."

Melanie nodded her enthusiastic approval. "I think that's a perfect choice." She pulled out a sheet of paper and dipped her pen in the inkwell. "How many place settings would you like?"

Mrs. Pike pursed her lips as she considered. The bell jingled, and Melanie looked up to see Earl Slocum saunter inside. She smiled and gave him a little wave. "I'll be with you as soon as I've finished here."

The wizened man grinned. "No rush. I've got all day."

Melanie turned back to Mrs. Pike.

"I'll take eight. No, wait. Make it ten. In for a penny, in for a pound. Isn't that right?"

Melanie offered a demure smile in return, when what she really wanted to do was let out a loud whoop. She wrote down the necessary information and blotted the completed order before putting it in an envelope. A slight flutter of doubt stirred. Should she ask for payment now, or wait until the order arrived? Caleb's instructions hadn't covered that eventuality. "Would you like me to put that on your tab?" She held her breath and waited for the answer.

"No, I intend to pay you today and have it settled. There isn't any point in giving my husband a chance to change his mind." Mrs. Pike chuckled at her little joke as she counted out the payment, then watched while Melanie addressed the envelope and affixed a stamp to it. "You'll be sure that order goes out right away?"

Melanie carried the envelope over to the bag of outgoing mail and dropped it inside. "There. It will go out when the next mail delivery arrives. Is there anything else I can do for you today?"

"No, I've taken up enough of your time." Mrs. Pike gathered up her reticule and rose to her feet. "I must say it has been very pleasant dealing with another woman on matters of the home. You made some excellent suggestions."

Melanie felt her cheeks grow warm at the compliment.

"Thank you, Mrs. Pike. I hope to see you again soon." She walked the other woman to the door, then joined Earl Slocum, who was studying a pair of work boots. "I can help you now, Mr. Slocum."

Slocum hung the boots back on the wall. "To be honest, ma'am, I'm not looking for anything in particular. If you don't mind, I'll just putter around a bit."

Melanie smiled at the grizzled man. "I don't mind at all." Relieved to have a moment to catch her breath, she straightened the catalogs, stacking them neatly. As she did so, a scrap of paper fluttered to the floor.

Even before she stooped to pick it up, she had a sick feeling in her stomach. Her queasiness was justified when she turned the paper over in her hand and saw the words written in an angry scrawl that had become all too familiar.

Get out of Cedar Ridge while you still can.

Melanie swallowed back the bile that rose to her throat when she read the brief message. Tearing the note into tiny shreds, she tossed the fragments into the dustbin. As she returned to the fabric table, a sudden thought struck her. Going back to the table where she'd stacked the catalogs, she selected one and flipped it open to one of the pages she and Mrs. Pike had studied. Fetching a fresh piece of paper, she dipped the pen in the inkwell and wrote out another order. She read over it once more, making sure she had copied all the information accurately, then addressed a second envelope, sealed her order inside, and dropped it in the mailbag.

Buoyed by a heady sense of accomplishment, she strolled

over to check on her customer. "Are you sure there isn't anything I can help you with?"

Slocum shook his head. "I really don't need a thing. I come in every so often when I want to kill a little time." His lips parted in a snaggletoothed grin. "I have to admit the scenery in here is a whole lot better than it used to be."

Melanie laughed. "Thank you for the compliment. Since you're looking for a way to fill your time, would you mind helping me with something?"

Earl Slocum's chest swelled. "Why sure, ma'am. Anything you need."

Melanie pulled two curtain rods from a barrel holding odds and ends of household goods and led him over to the fabric table, where she gathered up a length of the blue gingham material and began threading one rod through the long pocket she had made.

Slocum eyed her as she worked. "Curtains?"

Melanie nodded. She pulled the last of the gingham over the end of the rod, then picked up the other rod and did the same with the second length of fabric.

Earl Slocum whistled through his few remaining teeth. "That ought to pretty the place up even more."

"That's my plan. Would you mind carrying that stepladder over to the window for me and holding it while I put these rods up?"

He complied with alacrity, positioning the stepladder with care and offering his hand to steady Melanie as she stepped onto the bottom rung. When she moved up to the next rung, she heard a cracking sound and felt the wood beneath her foot give way.

With a yelp of surprise, she grabbed Slocum's arm and

jumped down. The curtain rod dropped to the floor with a clatter.

Earl Slocum's expression was one of pure amazement. "Are you all right, Miss Ross?"

"Something's wrong with that stepladder." When he didn't respond, Melanie gave a nervous laugh, wondering if she sounded as foolish as she felt. "It seemed as if it was going to splinter right under me."

Slocum knelt down and examined the offending step. "Well, what do you know? Looky here." He pointed to a faint crack across the top of the second rung. "You're right. It looks like it's ready to split apart."

"How odd." Melanie leaned over and drew her eyebrows together. "Caleb and I both used it yesterday, and nothing seemed to be wrong then."

"Well, it's sure a problem now." Slocum glanced around the store, his gaze lighting on the display of hardware. "If you don't mind me taking one of those bed slats you have for sale and borrowing a couple of tools, I can have this fixed in a jiffy."

Melanie hurried to fetch the saw, hammer, and nails he asked for. When she returned, she saw him staring at the bottom of the broken rung with his forehead screwed up in a puzzled frown. "What's wrong?" she asked.

"See that?" He ran his finger along a groove in the wood. "It looks like someone's sawed it partway through. But that doesn't make a lick of sense."

Melanie peered at the spot he indicated. Sure enough, she saw what appeared to be a freshly sawn cut in the middle of the wooden rung. She stared. "You're right. That doesn't make any sense at all."

She watched while he removed the damaged rung and made the necessary repairs, all the while wondering why anyone would do such a thing. The damage had to be intentional—and it was obviously aimed at causing trouble for her and Caleb, since they were the only ones who used the stepladder.

But who would want to cause them harm?

Her thoughts were interrupted when Slocum set the newly mended ladder on the floor and stepped on the second rung to test it.

"Good as new." He grinned. "Ready to try again?"

Melanie pushed the unanswerable questions to the back of her mind and took his outstretched hand. To her relief, the stepladder held this time. "Thank you. That's much better." She gave him a smile. "Now would you mind handing me the curtains?"

Her helper scooped the curtains up from the floor and held one end of the rod while she placed the other in the bracket she'd nailed above the window earlier that day. Then he moved the stepladder to the other end of the window and repeated the process.

"Thank you." Melanie climbed down and stood back to admire her work. "Yes, I think those will do nicely." The new curtains still needed hemming, but she wanted be sure to have them up so she could see Caleb's expression when he walked through the door. She gathered up the second curtain, then moved to the other window and waited while Slocum set the ladder in place and helped her up.

He waited until she got her balance, then handed the curtain to her. "Did the mayor ever change his mind about having fireworks at Founders Day?"

"Not that I know of." Remembering something she'd over-heard Caleb saying to Will Blake, she added, "From what I understand, he feels it's not the best use of the town's resources." She fit the curtain rod into place on the bracket and darted a quick glance out the window in the hope she might spot Will's lanky form striding down the street. He always had a smile for her, and his good-natured attitude had more than once proven balm to her soul when Caleb seemed more bent on turning her out than allowing her to stay in the store.

"That gingham sure is pretty," Slocum said, interrupting her thoughts. "Reminds me of the time I saw that Indian brave wrap a bolt of red calico around him, climb on his horse, and ride away with it streaming out behind him."

Melanie froze with her hands resting on the curtain bracket. "Oh my! Where did that happen?"

"Right out in front of this store." The man's tone was as unconcerned as if he'd been discussing the weather. "Back in the early days of Cedar Ridge, there wasn't much more than the mercantile here, and only a handful of people."

Melanie felt her knees grow weak as she climbed down the ladder. "You mean it happened *here*? At this store? How long ago was this?"

"Let me see." Slocum squinted his eyes, moving his lips as he calculated. "Musta been ten years or more ago, but I never will forget that sight." He glanced at Melanie, seem-ing to recognize her distress for the first time. "But don't let that bother you none. There haven't been any depredations around these parts in . . . oh, three or four years now." He offered the information with a smile, in the manner of one bestowing a gift. "That kind of thing has settled down all over the territory. . . . Well, pretty much, anyway. No sign of 'em around here anymore, unless you count the ruins out on the other side of the creek."

If his words were meant to give her comfort, the attempt had failed. Melanie swallowed hard, scooted the ladder across the floor, and climbed up to put the other end in place.

The bell jingled, and Melanie swiveled around on her precarious perch as Caleb and Levi walked inside carrying their fishing poles.

Levi fairly radiated excitement as he struggled to lift up a stringer holding a sizable trout. "Look what we got! Papa caught three little fish"—he dismissed Caleb's string of fish with a flick of his head—"but I caught the big one!"

Melanie couldn't keep from smiling at his infectious joy. "Good for you. It sounds like you had a wonderful time." She turned to include his father in her statement.

Caleb stood stock-still, gaping at the front windows with bulging eyes. "What is going on here?" Setting his fishing pole next to the door, he stepped toward the nearest window, fingered the curtain Melanie had just put up, and turned to glare at her and her helper. "What on earth do you think you're doing?"

Earl Slocum shuffled and glanced at the door. "I reckon it's time for me to be moseyin' on." He helped Melanie step down, then touched his finger to his forehead. "I'll be seein' you again one of these days." He exited the store with far more energy than he had shown thus far, leaving Melanie face-to-face with Caleb.

She swallowed and forced herself to meet his outraged expression, refusing to be intimidated by his obvious pique. "Mr. Slocum has been very helpful this afternoon," she said in an airy tone. "I had a problem with the stepladder, and he repaired it for me."

When Caleb continued to glower without speaking, she added, "It was a very curious thing. One of the rungs was broken nearly all the way through. Mr. Slocum thought someone might have done it deliberately."

Caleb brushed her comment off as though shooing away a pesky fly. "Earl Slocum is a good man, but he has a tendency to embellish. Don't try to distract me by changing the subject."

He retrieved his fishing pole and stringer and handed them to Levi, then spoke in an even tone. "Take these fish home and put them in the kitchen, son. We'll have them for supper tonight." After the little boy scampered off, Caleb turned back to Melanie, his brows knotted together in a fierce scowl. "I asked you a question. What is all this?"

Melanie drew herself up, bracing for battle. "They are known as curtains. Surely you've heard the term before."

Caleb's eyes narrowed down to slits. "I am quite aware of what they're called, Miss Ross, but what are they doing hanging in my store?"

"Don't you think they're attractive?" Melanie chose to ignore the issue of ownership. One battle at a time was enough. "They aren't quite finished. I'll have to hem them this evening after the store closes, but I wanted you to be able to picture the full effect when you got home."

His only response was a low grating noise that sounded like teeth grinding together. Melanie swallowed. This was not quite the response she had hoped for.

"And what's the idea of putting all that stuff in the window?"

Melanie turned to follow his pointing finger and stepped

across to pull the curtain back, revealing the display she had arranged so carefully. "You mean the table holding the oil lamp, the reticule, and the lace fan?"

Caleb jerked his head in a brusque nod. "And that bonnet, hanging off to the side all by itself."

Melanie favored him with a bright smile. "When women look in store windows, they like to see items they can use. Displaying them in a group like that helps them picture new ways to use them, which in turn boosts sales. I've seen it done back east, and believe me, it's quite effective."

Caleb waved his arm toward the window. "But that table and the few things on it are all you can see from the outside. You can't look in beyond the curtains."

Melanie dropped her hand and let the gingham panel fall back into place. "That's the point. Draw their interest with the window display, and they'll clamor to come inside and see what else we have." She looked at him hopefully, but his forbidding expression told her he wasn't convinced. Before he could start ranting again, she decided to share her news of the day's success.

She strolled toward the counter with an air of nonchalance. "You'll be pleased to know that things went quite well in your absence. Mrs. Pike came in a little while ago."

Caleb grew still and gave her a wary look. "Was she able to find everything she wanted?"

Melanie beamed. He couldn't have set this up better for her if she'd written his lines out for him. "She was interested in purchasing a new set of fine china. We didn't have that in stock, of course, but she placed an order before she left. She even paid for it in advance."

Caleb drew in a deep breath and some of his earlier tension

125

seemed to melt away. "That's good. She's a valuable customer, and her opinion carries a lot of weight in this town."

Basking in his unexpected approval, Melanie added, "I went ahead and placed another order after she left."

Caleb's countenance brightened even more. "Oh? Who was this one for?"

"For us." Melanie couldn't keep the satisfaction from showing in her voice. "If Ophelia Pike is interested in china, we can be sure the other ladies in the community will follow suit. So I ordered another set."

"You *what*?" Caleb's roar shook the rafters. "You ordered an entire set of china? Without anyone actually interested in purchasing it?"

Melanie gulped and managed a small nod. "I thought it would be helpful to have a set on display."

Caleb's face turned beet red. "You mean you didn't think at all. Don't you realize putting money into something like that is merely speculative? It'll be tied up until someone decides to buy that china . . . if anyone ever does." He raked both hands through his hair, leaving it standing straight on end. "We are trying to make a profit here, in case you hadn't noticed. This is not the same as stocking up on items like flour and sugar, things we know people will want."

Melanie tried to recapture the enthusiasm she'd felt earlier when she made the impulsive decision. "But as an investment—"

"It isn't an investment if a future sale isn't a certainty. That's gambling, not good business. We can't afford to speculate on frivolous items like that."

The back door swung open, and Levi scampered inside. He drew up short when he saw his father's dark scowl.

Caleb shuffled through some loose papers on the counter, then turned on Melanie. "Where is that order?" he demanded. "I want you to tear it up right now. And don't ever do anything like that again without consulting me first."

Melanie planted her fists on her hips and raised her chin. "It's too late to do that now. The order is already in the mailbag."

"Then we'll just take it out again." Caleb rounded the counter and strode over to the bag. Thrusting his arm inside, he began rummaging through the envelopes there.

Melanie folded her arms across her chest. "I wouldn't do that if I were you."

Caleb only glared at her and continued rooting in the mailbag.

"You do realize, don't you, that once an envelope is placed inside that bag, it officially comes under the protection of the United States Postal Service? And that tampering with the mail is a criminal offense?"

Caleb's arm froze and he stared at Melanie. Except for the convulsive movement of his jaw muscles, he looked as if he'd been turned to stone.

Soft steps scuffed across the floorboards, and Levi came to stand beside Melanie, gazing at his father in awe. "You mean Papa's going to jail?"

Caleb withdrew his arm from the mailbag and clenched his hands together to keep them from reaching out and throttling the infuriating woman. "No, son, I am not going to jail. Miss Ross is making a little joke." He glared daggers at Melanie, daring her to contradict him.

Instead of responding, she merely smiled as if enjoying

her small triumph. Then she strolled across to a back shelf, picked up an antimacassar, and disappeared behind one of the blue gingham curtains. Adding it to her window display, no doubt.

Caleb struggled to control his ragged breathing, hardly able to believe the audacity of the woman, even though he could see the evidence right before his eyes. Blue gingham curtains. In *his* store.

What did she think she was doing? It was one thing to barge in, claiming George Ross's share of the store as her inheritance, but this . . . He squeezed his fists until his fingers ached. This was out-and-out subversion.

His gray-eyed nemesis reemerged from behind the curtain and started to carry the bolt of the remaining blue fabric to its shelf. Caleb closed the distance between them in three long strides and planted himself in her way. "What other havoc did you manage to wreak while I was gone?" He fixed her with a fierce gaze intended to make her wither like a delicate flower under a blazing sun.

Instead of wilting, the obstinate female faced him squarely and held her ground. "We had a scattering of customers here and there, but not a lot. I made a few sales, but none of them amounted to much . . . except for Mrs. Pike's order." The sweet smile she bestowed on him made Caleb's blood simmer. Was she laughing at him?

Levi trotted over to join them. "Did any more cowboys ask you to marry them while we were gone?"

Melanie's gaze flickered to one side before she gave a tiny nod.

Caleb's interest quickened. "Oh? How many?"

The simple question achieved what his blustering hadn't. She seemed to shrink before his eyes.

"One." The word came out in the barest whisper.

One? The proposals were slowing down. It was time to put his plan into motion. He just had to encourage the right man to ask her.

With her eyes cast down toward the floor, Melanie skirted around him to replace the bolt of fabric. Then she picked up a matching tortoiseshell comb and brush and headed toward the front of the store.

"Oh, no you don't." Caleb reached out and caught hold of the brush as she tried to scoot past him, intending to pull it from her hands, but she only tightened her grip. "What were you planning to do with this?"

Melanie set her jaw and looked up at him with a mulish expression. "I am putting the finishing touches on my window display."

Caleb felt a wave of heat rise up his neck. "No. Enough is enough. I really must insist—"

She wrapped the fingers of her other hand around the brush handle and tugged on it. "Did I happen to mention that Marshal Hooper was one of the customers who came in earlier? I was so pleased to finally have the chance to meet him. Such a kind and gracious man. We had a lovely chat."

Caleb snapped his mouth shut to hold back the angry words threatening to spill out. Her features were bland enough, but he hadn't missed the quick tilt at the corners of her lips, gone as quickly as it had appeared. Even in that fleeting instance, he had recognized the expression for what it was: the assurance of victory. As long as she could wield the marshal's name as a weapon, she had Caleb right where she wanted him, and he knew it.

And she knew he knew it.

All the more reason to put his plan into action without delay.

"I'm telling you, fellows, she came out west planning to stay. She isn't some frail little flower who's afraid to get her hands dirty, or someone who'll go running back east the moment a problem arises."

Caleb leaned back against the counter and surveyed the group of men circled in front of him and hanging on his every word. It almost seemed like divine intervention in favor of his plan when a contingent of soldiers from Fort Verde sauntered into the store only moments after Melanie left on some errand. He'd been quick to take advantage of the situation and had been holding forth on the winning attributes of the charming Miss Ross for the past ten minutes.

A short, wiry man near the front of the group regarded Caleb thoughtfully. "I've seen her, and I'll admit she's a looker. But can she cook?"

A murmur of assent ran around the group, and Caleb fought to maintain his glee. They were interested, all right. Like dry tinder waiting for a spark. All they needed was a little encouragement. Surely at some point, one of the men in the surrounding area would catch Melanie's notice and win her favor. His task was to provide her the widest field possible to choose from.

A barrel-chested officer scuffed his boot and slanted a skeptical look at Caleb. "If she's as great a catch as you're making her out to be, why are you so anxious to see her married off to someone else?"

The unexpected question made Caleb sputter. Before he

could frame a satisfactory answer, he heard a loud "Hsst!" from the man nearest the front window.

"She's comin' back!" he whispered. "She's almost here!"

Caleb pushed himself away from the counter and leveled a stern gaze at the group of potential suitors. "Act natural, men. Women have sensitive feelings, and we don't want to let on that we've been talking about her."

He picked up the feather duster and began swiping at the nearest shelf while the men spread throughout the store. Several of them slipped out the back door, apparently not ready to begin a matrimonial pursuit just yet. Just as Melanie entered the front door, one of them turned and gave Caleb a broad wink.

Caleb smothered a chuckle as he continued to dust. He had set the wheels in motion. All he had to do now was stand back and let nature take its course.

11

Melanie leaned over the basin, dipped her hands into the water, and splashed it on her face. Immediately, a series of goosebumps prickled up her arms and rippled across her shoulder blades. She hurried over to the bed, where she had laid out her dress, and pulled it over her head, fastening the buttons with chilled fingers.

Throwing a light shawl over her shoulders, she walked to the window, where she pushed the curtain to one side and leaned her arms on the sill, taking in the invigorating sight of the rolling hills and jagged cliffs silhouetted against the sunrise. And what a sunrise! Shades of scarlet, gold, pink, and orange blazed across the sky in a breathtaking array. Had she ever seen such brilliant hues back east?

"Thank you for this beautiful day." The words escaped her lips on a sigh of pure delight. Ever since her walk around town, she felt an increasing sense of assurance that she'd made the right choice. She belonged in Cedar Ridge. Though the town lacked many of the advantages of city life, its untamed quality brought with it a sense of connecting with the world around her in a way she had never experienced before. Like a storm-tossed wayfarer sailing into port, she felt she had found her home at last.

Melanie breathed deep of the crisp morning air. She had to agree with the words of the poet Browning—God indeed sat enthroned in His heaven, and all was right with her world.

Turning from the window, she retrieved her buttonhook from the top of the dresser and sat on the edge of her bed to fasten her shoes, reflecting on how quickly life could change. Only a short time ago, she assumed she would spend the rest of her days caring for other people's children. Now she was establishing her place as a merchant in a growing community. And all through an incident that seemed at first like an utter disaster.

She smiled. How like the Lord to create beauty from the ashes of her despair and turn her heartache into rejoicing! Young Clarence Deaver's accusations, intended to bring about her downfall, had instead opened the doorway to the opportunity of a lifetime, something like the way God had turned calamity into victory for Joseph in the Bible.

True, her presence in Cedar Ridge hadn't caused any rejoicing on Caleb Nelson's part, but he would come around in time. If God could help Joseph find favor in Pharaoh's eyes, He could do the same for her where this stubborn man was concerned.

She crossed the room to the dresser and arranged her hair, smiling at her reflection in the mirror while she undid her night braid and picked up her hairbrush. Smiling came more easily to her these days. Once relieved of her position as the

Deavers' governess it seemed as though a heavy burden had been lifted off her shoulders.

No more being caught in that lonely middle ground between gentry and servants, interacting with both worlds but a part of neither. She was a businesswoman, a merchant, on an equal footing with anyone in town. All she had to be concerned with now was building her own future. No more having to deal with overindulged children like Clarence Deaver Jr.

Her smile dimmed, remembering the boy's perfidy and the way the poisonous lies had slipped so easily off his tongue without one whit of concern as to how those untruths would affect her . . . or anyone else. She drew the brush through her hair in long, smooth strokes. Whose life was he making miserable now? She pushed away the twinge of guilt that arose at the realization that by now someone else would have stepped into her place as the one the boy would use as his scapegoat.

That burden of guilt wasn't hers to carry. With all her heart, she wished she could have made more of a difference in young Clarence's life, but the damage had been done before she'd ever appeared on the scene. The years of excessive pampering that instilled an inflated sense of self-importance in the boy weren't so easily overcome.

She jabbed a hairpin in with unnecessary vigor and winced when it grazed her scalp. If she ever had children of her own, she would see to it that they grew up to be civil, decent people who understood the value of honor and integrity. But that wasn't likely to happen anytime soon.

Her hands stilled for a moment. She already had another child in her life. And he was likely to be a part of her life for the foreseeable future. She pushed the last hairpin in and checked her appearance in the mirror once more before making her way downstairs.

Levi could be an adorable child . . . when he wanted to be. She smiled, remembering the look on his face when he held up his "whopper" of a trout. At the same time, she was painfully aware that another side of his personality existed—the part that set the fire in the alley on her first day in Cedar Ridge.

She shuddered at the memory of him dropping his pet frog on her chest, then diving after it—and at the recollection of bolting after him in her nightdress and wrapper. Admittedly, she hadn't been at her best that morning, either. She must have looked like some wild-eyed banshee following in his wake.

She went into the kitchen and put a kettle of water on to heat for her morning cup of tea. His father should have been keeping a closer watch on him, she told herself for the dozenth time. But although she wasn't Levi's governess, the two of them were destined to have an ongoing relationship for a number of years. Maybe she could exert a positive influence on the boy. It could be a perfect way to use the skills she had acquired as a governess.

As she measured out the loose tea leaves, her mood brightened. What God had done for Joseph also blessed those around him. Maybe part of the reason He had guided her to this situation was to have her help mold Levi's behavior. She poured the boiling water over the tea leaves, determined to begin right away. She could talk to Levi, get to know him better.

The more she thought about it, the more her excitement grew. If she could draw the boy out, it would help her learn which facet of Levi's personality reflected his true nature. And once she had that information, she would be better equipped to know how to proceed. With a little influence of the right sort, he could grow into a delightful young man, one other people would enjoy having around.

Leaving her tea to steep, she donned her apron and went into the storeroom for the broom. As she walked past the shelf where the ornate music box stood, she paused for a moment to trail her finger along the delicate tracery of multicolored wood. Such a shame that Caleb insisted on keeping it hidden away. Someday she would try again to persuade him to let her play it. Maybe hearing its music pour forth would encourage him to set it out on display, where it could be enjoyed—and possibly purchased—by their customers.

She carried the broom to the rear door of the mercantile, ready to begin her workday by sweeping the back stoop. She enjoyed the early morning chore, which gave her a chance to have a few quiet moments outdoors before the day's busyness set in.

She pulled open the back door, turning her face up to greet the morning sun. Her foot struck an object as she stepped out, and she caught hold of the doorframe to keep from falling. She looked down to see what she had tripped over and frowned. Why would anyone leave a bundle of clothes in back of the mercantile?

On second glance, she realized the clothes were still occupied. A man dressed in a canvas duster lay crumpled at her feet. Neat black trousers extended past the hem of the duster, ending in a pair of feet encased in highly polished black shoes.

Her mind whirled as she tried to make sense of what she

was seeing. Why was someone lying on the back stoop? Maybe he was a traveler who had spent too much time in the nearby saloon and only managed to stagger to the stoop before passing out to sleep off the results of his bender. That notion was dispelled the moment she noticed the pool of blood that had accumulated beneath the man's head.

Melanie swayed and clutched at the doorframe with both hands. The broom clattered to the boards below, and a scream tore from her throat.

The piercing scream stopped Caleb in his tracks. It was a woman's voice—Melanie's. And this was no startled shriek, like the one she'd let out when she met Freddie. This scream held a note of fear, of danger.

"Wait here." He tossed the curt order to Levi as he sprinted toward the store's back entrance, a thousand thoughts whirling through his mind. Had Melanie fallen or injured herself somehow? Had someone broken in and was even now trying to rob the store?

Late spring was the time for rattlesnakes to be awakening from their winter's hibernation. Maybe she'd discovered one when she came out to sweep the back stoop. The possibility made him put on a burst of speed, wishing fervently that his view of the stoop wasn't blocked by the wing of the building that jutted out into the alley.

He rounded the corner at a dead run, skidding to a halt when he saw Melanie on the stoop with both hands pressed over her mouth, her wide eyes staring down at the motionless body of a man at her feet.

Caleb's eyes bulged at the sight. He tore his focus away

from the man's body and looked back up at Melanie. "Who is he?"

She shook her head and lowered her hands, like one in a daze. Caleb noticed her fingers were trembling. "I don't know," she said. "I came out to sweep and found him . . . like that."

Caleb stepped forward. "Is he dead?"

Her head dipped in a tiny nod. "I'm pretty sure he is. Look." She pointed with a shaking finger, and Caleb saw the puddle of blood.

His bewilderment grew. "Did he fall?" He cast a glance upward toward the store's roof. "Did something drop on him?" Try as he might, he couldn't fathom what might have happened. His eyes took in the scene before him, but his mind refused to make sense of it. The whole situation seemed absurd—dead men didn't just show up on a person's doorstep.

He knelt beside the stranger, ready to turn him over so he could get a better look at his face. Even before he took hold of the shoulders, he felt sure Melanie was right. That gray pallor didn't belong to the living. His instinct was confirmed when he rolled the body stiffly to one side and got a glimpse of the back of the man's head.

Caleb retched and swallowed hard to keep his breakfast from coming back up. That dent in the man's skull hadn't been made by any mere fall. He pulled his hands away, and the body rolled back into place of its own accord.

Feet pounded along the alley, and Micah Rawlins, owner of the livery stable, dashed up, panting. "What's going on?" he asked. "I was feeding the horses and I heard someone scream."

Caleb got to his feet, still staring at the body of the stranger.

Micah followed his gaze, and Caleb heard his sudden intake of breath.

Rawlins pursed his lips and let out a low whistle. "You want me to go fetch Doc?"

Caleb shook his head. "He's beyond any help a doctor can give him."

Micah snorted. "Probably just as well. I spent a little time in the Silver Moon last night, and Doc came in while I was there. He was already pretty well in his cups and didn't look like he planned on slowing down anytime soon."

Caleb's gaze returned to the massive wound on the back of the stranger's head, and he swallowed again. "If you want to go get someone, better make it the marshal."

Melanie stood pressed against the back wall of the mercantile, watching Marshal Hooper finish his examination of the dead man. The initial shock of discovery had begun to wear off, and her mind was beginning to function more clearly again.

The burly lawman pushed himself to his feet with a grunt and motioned for Caleb to cover the body with a tarp fetched from the store. Keeping his eyes fixed on the corpse, he asked, "Do you know who he is?"

Caleb shook his head. "I have no idea. There were no identifying papers in his pockets."

Melanie didn't miss the quick glance his comment earned from the lawman.

"You went through his pockets?"

A dull flush colored Caleb's face. "I checked them while I was waiting for you. I thought I might find a wallet or some other identification."

139

The marshal grunted. "As stiff as he is, it looks to me like he's been dead awhile. This must have happened sometime during the night."

He turned to face Caleb, fixing him with a keen stare as he said, "You're sure you don't know him?"

"I've never seen him before." Caleb tucked his hands into his pockets. "It seems that he intended to come to the store, but why? And why the back door?"

The marshal flicked a quick glance at Melanie, and she felt heat rise up her neck to stain her cheeks. Pushing away from the wall, she faced the marshal directly. "I assure you, I've never seen this man, either. I have no idea why he was lurking around here at night."

Marshal Hooper held her gaze for a long moment, then gave a brief nod as if satisfied. When he turned away, Melanie felt an unaccountable sense of relief. She turned her attention back to the dead man.

Death wasn't completely unfamiliar to her. She had handled the funeral arrangements for both of her grandparents, but she had never been associated with a violent death before. She supposed that in cases like this, the lawman in charge had to look at everyone in proximity to the death with some degree of suspicion, but she'd never imagined how uncomfortable that would be for the parties involved.

Much as she wanted to look away, her eyes kept returning to the spot where the poor man's body lay. Thankfully, the tarp now covered the wound on his head. It didn't cover the pool of blood, though. It would have to be scrubbed away soon, before it left an indelible stain. The thought of that job falling to her made her stomach roil, and she pressed her hand against her waist to quell the sick feeling.

Her beautiful morning had turned into a nightmare. Had that man really been murdered? Right on her doorstep?

Her bedroom window on the second floor overlooked the back stoop. Why hadn't she heard anything?

And what if she had? Her mind continued its relentless questioning. Could she have done anything to prevent the murder, or would the attacker have turned on her, as well, leaving two bodies for Caleb and Levi to discover when they came to the store?

Her body began to tremble, and her knees threatened to give way. A long, shuddering sigh escaped her lips, and she leaned back against the wall for support.

Caleb looked at her, his face a mask of concern. He turned to the marshal. "Is there any reason the body can't be moved now?"

The marshal shook his head. "No, I think I've seen all I need to."

Caleb stepped over to Melanie and spoke in a low tone. "Why don't you let the undertaker know he's needed? You should be able to find him at the barbershop."

Melanie nodded and pulled herself erect. Still unsteady on her feet, she tottered around the corner of the mercantile toward Lincoln Street, appreciating Caleb's consideration in providing her with a way to make a graceful exit

Her steps quickened as she left the scene of death behind her. By the time she reached the town's main street, she was nearly running. Looking to make sure the way was clear, she crossed the road quickly, relieved when she saw two men standing in front of the barbershop. She hurried over to them, focusing her attention on the one dressed all in black.

"Could you come with me, please? Your services are needed at the mercantile."

The one she addressed tilted his head, and a flicker of interest lit his eyes. "Dear lady, I would be happy to assist you, but what kind of service would you like me to provide?"

Melanie resisted the urge to shake the man by his starched collar and tried to keep her voice level. "A man has died at the mercantile. Could you please come?"

A smile flitted across his face. "I'm afraid you've made a mistake. Mr. Bingham here is the one you're looking for."

Melanie looked his companion up and down. In shirtsleeves and a bow tie, the man's round cheeks and cheery expression seemed far removed from what she had expected. She stared for a long moment. "You're the undertaker?"

A merry smile lit his face. "Yes, ma'am. And the barber." He cupped one hand around his mouth and added, "And a decent substitute for a dentist, if you happen to need a tooth pulled when Doc has been bending his elbow a bit too often down at the Silver Moon." He doffed his bowler hat and bowed. "Andrew Bingham, at your service."

His face took on a solemn expression better suited to his second profession. "You say someone has died at the mercantile?" The somber look changed to one of alarm. "You wouldn't be speaking of Caleb Nelson, would you?"

"No, I don't know who it is. He's a stranger to us both. Someone seems to have . . . killed him . . . during the night." Her voice choked, and she pressed her hand to her throat.

Both men gaped at her. Andrew Bingham nodded and started for the barbershop. "Let me get my jacket, and I'll be right over." He stopped in the doorway and turned back to

Melanie. "You don't need to accompany me if you'd rather stay away."

Melanie nodded her thanks, suddenly feeling at loose ends. She had done all she could for Caleb and the marshal, and the poor stranger was beyond any human aid. There was nothing left for her to do, except go back to the mercantile to pick up her morning routine where it had been interrupted and get ready to open the store for business.

But she didn't particularly want to go back at the moment. And she wasn't sure she had the stamina to do so, even if she did. Her legs began to tremble again, and she swayed.

The black-clad man beside her cupped her elbow with his hand and steered her along the boardwalk. "Would you care to sit on this bench?" He indicated one of a pair of benches in front of the barbershop.

Melanie let him escort her to the seat without protest. His offer hadn't come a moment too soon. She didn't think her legs could hold her up one minute longer. "Thank you very much."

"You're quite welcome." Her dapper escort waited until she sank onto the bench and seated himself at the other end. When he tilted his angular face toward hers, she could see that his eyes were so dark they appeared as black as his clothing. He assumed a kindly expression and regarded her with a look of keen interest. "We haven't been introduced yet. My name is Benton Woodbridge, but people around here call me the Professor."

Melanie accepted the hand he extended. "I'm pleased to meet you. I'm Melanie Ross."

The Professor smiled. "I thought as much. I have heard of your arrival, of course. It doesn't take much time for news to make its way around Cedar Ridge. I'm delighted to make your acquaintance. Your coming has added a spot of beauty to our little community."

Melanie drew a long breath, feeling the first glimmer of normalcy she'd experienced since walking onto the back stoop and discovering the murdered man.

The Professor went on without waiting for a response, seeming content to carry on the conversation alone. Melanie was more than willing to let him, relishing the calming effect created by his soothing stream of words.

After a while he paused, then said, "It's my understanding that you are a relative of George Ross."

Melanie nodded, relieved to find the energy to speak again. "He was my cousin. A much older cousin," she added with a smile, "but he was the only family I had left."

The Professor's lips curved in a gentle smile. "I met George the day he and Alvin Nelson rode into Cedar Ridge and bought the mercantile. I always enjoyed visiting with him. He was a fine man, a decent man—as was Alvin." He kept his eyes focused on her as he spoke, as if watching to make sure she wasn't about to succumb to an attack of the vapors. "I was very sorry when they passed on. They have been sorely missed. I'm glad Caleb was here to take over and keep things going in the store, carrying on their legacy, you might say. He's a good man."

Melanie blinked at the change of subject, and then she nodded. "Yes." She thought again of the concern she'd seen in Caleb's eyes when she'd sagged against the wall, and the opportunity he'd given her to escape the grisly scene. "Yes, he is."

At the reminder of the stranger's demise, she shot to her

feet and pressed her fingers to her lips. "What are we going to do? About a funeral, I mean?"

When the Professor only tilted his head and looked at her with a puzzled expression, she explained, "We don't know anything about him—his name or where he came from. How are we supposed to send word to his family? Who is responsible for making arrangements?"

The Professor stood beside her with half-closed eyes and pursed his lips, as though calculating something in his head. Finally he nodded, seeming pleased. "The timing is good, if anything like that can be said about such a tragic situation. Today is Monday, and the circuit rider is due to arrive this weekend." Seeing the blank look Melanie gave him, he went on. "Pastor Dunstan has the responsibility for preaching to a number of communities in this part of the territory. He rides from one town to the next—making a circuit, you see—and stops in Cedar Ridge once a month or so."

"Oh." Melanie pondered this new concept. "But surely we can't wait that long before we bury this man."

The Professor made a clucking sound with his tongue and reached out to pat her hand. "I know this must seem strange to you. Andrew will see to the burial—probably tomorrow. Pastor Dunstan won't be able to officiate, of course, but I'm sure he'll be willing to say a few words at the graveside after the service on Sunday."

Melanie looked around as she let the Professor's words sink in. "Where will the service be held? I've walked all around town, and I haven't seen a church."

A dry chuckle rose from the Professor's throat. "When the circuit preacher comes to town, we hold services in the mercantile." He chuckled again at her look of surprise. "It's something George and Alvin instituted when they came to Cedar Ridge. It is a common practice in western towns, as odd as it may seem to someone fresh from the East."

Melanie caught her breath. "And the only services for that poor man will be held out at the cemetery?"

The Professor nodded. "That, too, is common out west, especially when the person in question doesn't have any family in the area."

Melanie latched onto the Professor's assurance as the only bright spot of news she'd heard that morning. Bad enough to think of the stranger being murdered right under her window. She couldn't have borne seeing his body laid out inside the mercantile.

12

The next Sunday, Melanie fidgeted on the rough wooden bench, more intent on relieving her discomfort than on listening to the low hum of conversation filling the mercantile. All her life, she had heard people talk about feeling as crowded as sardines packed in a tin. Now she understood exactly what that meant. She couldn't move more than a fraction of an inch without bumping Mrs. Fetterman on her right or Levi on her left.

Mrs. Fetterman's sturdy figure blocked Melanie's view farther along the bench on that side, but she could see Caleb's solemn face on the other side of Levi, and Dan Crawford, the saddlemaker, sitting beyond him. Up front, she spotted Mrs. Pike and her husband, the mayor. The Professor sat in the row just ahead, along with Andrew Bingham, Micah Rawlins, and Rafe Sutton, the scraggly-bearded freighter.

She looked in vain to find Will Blake, then remembered him mentioning he had to take care of some business over at the county seat. The ride to Prescott and back would take the better part of three days, so she couldn't expect to see him back yet. A soft sigh escaped her lips. Will's presence would have been a comfort on this sad day.

Across the aisle, she saw the scrawny figure of Thomas O'Shea, owner of the emporium. He turned at that moment and their eyes locked. O'Shea drew his brows together in a fierce scowl, then swiveled around to face the front again.

Melanie caught her breath at the show of animosity and dropped her gaze to the floor. When she recovered her composure, she went back to scanning the benches, careful to avoid the area where O'Shea sat, his back rigid.

She met the glances of several of the area's single men, some of whom had already offered proposals of marriage. She let her gaze slide away from theirs, grateful that none of them seemed to be focused on continuing their amorous pursuits now that the mercantile had been transformed into a church. It was not a day to have to worry about fending off would-be suitors.

The rest of the benches were filled by an array of people whose names she didn't know. Who would have thought there could still be so many people in the area she hadn't met yet, and that they all could fit into the mercantile at the same time? The transformation from store to sanctuary had been remarkable. Three men had walked in the door at closing time the previous evening, ready to help Caleb set up. It was clear they had done this before, needing no direction in pushing all the stacks of merchandise—including the tables holding her new displays—back against the walls, leaving the center area open. From the wagon one of them backed up in front of the store, they produced a number of crude benches and set them up in rows.

They worked steadily, leaving little for Melanie to do, other than hover over her displays like a mother hen protecting her chicks. After a while, she found herself standing off to one side, reduced to the role of onlooker, feeling out of place, as though she didn't belong. Not unwanted—the way those horrid anonymous notes made her feel—but unnecessary. And that was almost as difficult to bear.

She shifted as much as she could in the confined space. The benches had not been made for comfort. Her backside already felt numb, and the service hadn't even started. As if in tune with her thoughts, Levi squirmed beside her. Melanie quieted him with a finger to her lips, although she understood exactly how he felt.

The murmurs died down as Pastor James Dunstan rose from his seat on the first row and stepped to the front. Melanie had met him when he'd ridden into town the night before. A lanky man with features weathered from riding back and forth across the harsh Arizona terrain, he seemed like one who would be more at home behind a plow than a pulpit. His voice was surprisingly gentle, in contrast to his rugged appearance, although it was strong enough to carry throughout the building.

"Friends, I know disturbing events have occurred here since we last worshiped together. Circumstances like this can shake the foundations of our faith and show us what we truly believe. In the book of Matthew, our Lord says that we must build our foundation on the rock, so that our house will be able to withstand whatever storms may come."

While he spoke, Melanie scanned the crowd as well as she could from her cramped position, wondering if all these people typically turned out for one of the circuit rider's services, or if a greater number than usual had come that morning to draw comfort after the killing.

Beside her, Levi stirred again. Melanie quelled him with a pointed look, then glanced over at Caleb, wondering why he wasn't dealing with the distraction his son was creating. His eyes were fixed on a point at the front of the store, but he looked as though his thoughts were miles away from the service and the preacher's words.

What could he be thinking about? Melanie wondered if his thoughts, like hers, had strayed to the puzzle of the murdered stranger. Only the day before the marshal had told them the man's identity was still a mystery. The only clue that had turned up so far was a horse left at the livery stable on the night of the murder. Micah Rawlins had been in the Silver Moon Saloon at the time, so he hadn't seen the man and didn't know his name or anything about him.

Chiding herself for letting her attention stray, Melanie turned her focus back to Pastor Dunstan.

"He is our Rock," the preacher was saying. "And He is big enough for us to trust with everything—our hopes, our labors, and our fears. Please bow your heads with me while we pray."

After the final amen, the pastor raised his head and looked out over the crowded room. "I hope you'll all proceed now to the cemetery and join me in laying our unknown brother to rest."

The congregation rose and started to file out. Beside Melanie, Mrs. Fetterman dabbed at her eyes with a lace-edged handkerchief. "That poor soul. Imagine dying all alone, far from home and unknown, buried in a grave that won't even bear a name."

Unable to speak past the sudden lump in her throat, Melanie

could only nod and walk beside Mrs. Fetterman. Outside, it looked as though the whole congregation had taken the preacher's urging to heart and joined him in following the route Melanie had taken on her walk through town. Once they reached the south end of Lincoln Street, the crowd turned left, circling the scattered buildings that lay beyond, and followed the rough, rock-bordered path that led from town to the top of a low cedar-studded hill.

At the edge of the path, Levi leaped from one rock to another. Melanie frowned and looked around for Caleb, finally spotting him some distance ahead, deep in conversation with Dan Crawford. Reaching out, Melanie caught Levi's hand and held it fast. After a tentative tug, which got him nowhere, the boy settled down and walked along beside her.

They joined the rest of the group in forming a circle around the rim of the hill, surrounding the open area where headstones and simple crosses marked the final resting places of a dozen or more departed souls.

On the other side of the circle, Melanie watched Caleb glance around and saw a furrow appear between his brows. When he spotted Levi standing next to her, he gave her a brief, relieved smile and remained where he was.

Pastor Dunstan opened his well-worn Bible and lifted his head toward the heavens, as if speaking to one whose presence was evident. "Father, while this man is a stranger to us, he is known to you. You have watched his life on this earth unfold in its entirety. We are gathered together today in your name to acknowledge that every life is precious, and we commend his spirit to your keeping."

Lowering his gaze, he smiled at those gathered before him.

"Moses wrote a psalm that speaks of the brevity of life. On an occasion like this, it seems especially appropriate."

Looking down, he began to read: "'Lord, thou hast been our dwelling place in all generations. Before the mountains were brought forth, or ever thou hadst formed the earth and the world, even from everlasting to everlasting, thou art God.'"

Melanie closed her eyes, the better to focus on the words penned so long ago.

"'The days of our years are threescore years and ten; and if by reason of strength they be fourscore years . . .'"

Melanie's throat tightened. The stranger's life hadn't lasted anywhere near threescore and ten years. How old had he been? Probably little more than fifty. Old enough to have a wife, maybe even a family of grown children somewhere. But not nearly old enough to say he'd experienced the joy of growing old with his wife beside him. A silence followed, and she opened her eyes again.

Pastor Dunstan closed his Bible. "God knows the number of our days, and He tells us to be prepared for the time they will end and we step into His presence. This man"—he gestured toward the mound of fresh-turned earth at his feet— "didn't expect his life to end so abruptly . . . and in a place where he was alone and unknown."

He scanned the assembled group as if he were looking into each face there and reading each one's heart. "None of us know when we will face that day of judgment. Let me urge you in the strongest terms to make sure you are ready for that day, whenever it may come." He paused, then added, "Thank you for joining me here. This concludes the service."

Levi slipped his hand free and scampered over to his father, who smiled and gave Melanie a nod of thanks. The crowd began to disperse, with people breaking into small groups and talking among themselves. Melanie looked around, wishing she had someone to share the moment with.

"You thought you were pretty clever, didn't you, Miss Ross?"

Melanie whirled upon hearing the voice at her elbow and came face-to-face with Thomas O'Shea.

His eyes glittered with undisguised malice. "Coming into my store like that, never saying a word about who you were or what you were doing there."

"Why, I . . ." Melanie sputtered. She looked around, hoping to see a friendly face coming to her rescue, but no one seemed to be paying the least bit of attention to her.

O'Shea waved a bony finger under her nose. "Sneaking and prying around like that! If that's the way you want it, fine. Two can play that game."

With that, he turned and stalked away, leaving Melanie standing wide-eyed and short of breath. Apparently, her ploy to scout out the other store in town hadn't been so clever, after all. Berating herself for her ill-conceived plan, she started back toward the path leading to town.

A sudden thought halted her in her tracks, and she turned to stare at O'Shea's retreating back. The owner of the emporium knew who she was—had known it all along—and was clearly angry at what he perceived as an attempt to spy on him.

"Two can play that game." What had he meant by that? Was O'Shea the one who had sawn the ladder rung nearly in two, knowing it would only be a matter of time before either she or Caleb stepped on it and might be injured?

153

Melanie shook her head. She would have noticed Thomas O'Shea if he came into the mercantile, and she'd never seen him there.

But he might have sent an emissary sneaking around to do the deed for him. Melanie's chest tightened, and she forced herself to breathe. Was that the way it had happened? There was no way to know for certain, but she promised herself she would be more watchful from now on. Once again she turned her steps toward town.

A stone marker several yards away caught her eye, and she moved closer, bending to trace the name with her fingertips: *George Martin Ross.* Tears stung her eyes, and she dashed them away. So this was Cousin George's final resting place, the spot where his body would lie until the resurrection. Next to his grave, she spotted another marker, this one belonging to Alvin Nelson. The tears came again, along with a watery smile this time. Cousin George wasn't resting alone. He had his treasured friend beside him, his partner throughout his life's adventures.

And who did she have?

The thought caught her up short, but then she smiled, remembering the preacher's words. She had the Lord. He was her foundation, and that was enough. Setting aside the temptation to be drawn into self-pity, she began to make her way back down the hill alone. As she walked, snatches of conversation drifted her way.

"Such a sad thing, coming here, only to be killed."

"Who do you think he was?"

"Nobody knows, not even the marshal."

"Well then, who do you think did it?"

"I'm thinking it must have been someone he was traveling

with. Maybe they got into an argument and his friend bashed him over the head."

Melanie quickened her pace. She'd had enough of thinking about the stranger's untimely demise for one day. Or any number of days.

But her mind refused to focus on anything else, fretting over the scrap of conversation she'd just overheard like a terrier gnawing on a bone. Could there be something to the idle speculation? Was the killer another stranger just passing through Cedar Ridge . . . or could he be someone local?

Her steps lagged, and she turned to look back at the scattered group with a fresh awareness, wondering if the murderer could be standing right before her eyes, a familiar face in the place she was beginning to think of as home.

13

W hat about this one, dear?" Mrs. Fetterman plucked a tall, slender box with gold lettering off the shelf and held it out to Melanie.

Melanie scanned the box and shook her head. "This is Scott's Nerv-O-Sol. The label says it's a speedy and reliable remedy for headache and neuralgia."

Mrs. Fetterman sighed and went back to browsing the shelves.

Melanie pressed her fingers against her right temple. Shaking her head had been a mistake. It had been throbbing all afternoon, and the quick movement only made it worse.

Glancing at the front window, she took note of the sun's position. After their initial clash over the curtains, she and Caleb had reached a compromise. The curtains could remain in place—as long as they were tied back during the day to allow passersby to view the store's interior. Melanie had dug her heels in at first, but it proved to be one issue on which Caleb steadfastly refused to budge. Now she grudgingly admitted his plan was an improvement, allowing sunlight to stream inside the store—and show off their wares to better advantage—while maintaining the pleasing appearance she'd been striving for. Not that she would ever admit that to him.

Judging from the length of the shadows outside, she had another two hours to go before she could set the *Closed* sign in the window.

She turned her attention back to the selection of patent remedies—now set well away from the veterinary supplies—and perused the shelves. "Look at this one." She selected a brown bottle with a black label. "Dr. White's Dandelion Alterative, the great liver corrector, blood purifier, and tonic."

Another nostrum caught her eye. "H. H. Warner & Co. Safe Cure, beneficial for the liver and kidneys. Either of these might be helpful. What do you think?" She handed both bottles over for Mrs. Fetterman's inspection, although she doubted whether the other woman could see more than the largest print at the top of the labels. While the older woman turned the bottles this way and that, Melanie closed her eyes and massaged her temple again.

Mrs. Fetterman clucked like a setting hen. "Are you feeling all right, dearie? You look like you might need one of these tonics yourself."

"I have a bit of a headache—that's all." Melanie summoned a weary smile. "I've been meaning to talk to you about something."

Mrs. Fetterman cocked her head like a curious sparrow.

"Would you like to look through the catalogs with me some day and see if we can find a better pair of spectacles for you? I don't mind reading labels to you at all, but I hate

157

to think of you missing out on all the other things you would be able to see."

"What a lovely idea!" Mrs. Fetterman clapped her hands. "Do you really think a change of spectacles might improve my vision?"

A man dressed in a bowler hat and a herringbone suit walked toward them, and Melanie shied like a frightened colt, relaxing only when he passed them without a second glance and continued on to the counter where Caleb stood tending their other customers.

Mrs. Fetterman's forehead puckered. "Are you sure it's just a headache? You seem a bit on edge."

"I thought he was going to propose."

The crease between Mrs. Fetterman's brows deepened. Melanie tried to brush off the other woman's concern with a laugh. "I know that must sound vain, but it keeps on happening, over and over again. You were here the first time. Remember?"

"How could I forget?" Mrs. Fetterman's face lost its frown, and her pale blue eyes danced. "The way Dooley Hatcher leaped over that crate of washboards was a sight to behold." She cocked her head and peered up at Melanie. "And you say that hasn't been the only time?"

"Far from it!" Melanie wailed. "It's been going on since I arrived."

Mrs. Fetterman waved her hand. "That isn't unusual when a good-looking woman like you moves into the area. With such a shortage of eligible ladies, a few proposals are to be expected."

Melanie shook her head. "I might be able to understand a few, but this has been happening almost nonstop. . . . In fact, it seems to have gotten worse, especially over the past week or so. Miners, cowboys, even some soldiers from Fort Verde—all men I've never seen before! It's like watching bees swarm out of a hive. I can't imagine what I might have done to encourage this."

Tears pricked, and she blinked them away. The onslaught of proposals had proven to be an immense distraction—so much so that she hadn't been able to rearrange the merchandise or set up the new display she'd planned for the front window.

Oddly enough, Caleb didn't seem upset by the steady stream of suitors. She cast a baleful glance toward the other end of the store, where he stood talking to Will Blake. After he'd chased off the Hatcher brothers and practically threw Slim Applegate out the door, she would have expected the current influx of would-be beaus to make him erupt like Mount Vesuvius. Instead, he seemed to take it all remarkably in stride.

Melanie winced as a stabbing pain shot through her temples. She had found another of the hateful anonymous notes that morning, which only added to her worries. She'd decided to ignore them as an ugly nuisance, and the fire in the office as a malicious prank. But after discovering a murdered corpse on her doorstep, she had to wonder if the earlier incidents were merely cruel jokes or if they added up to a true and personal danger.

Between that worry, the ongoing stream of proposals, and her headache, she was always so exhausted by the time evening came that she hadn't even found the time to sort through Cousin George's things. All she could manage was to retreat upstairs with a plate of cheese and crackers and a cup of chamomile tea. *Ayer's American Almanac* touted the tea as particularly beneficial when it came to soothing headaches, but the cup she'd prepared earlier that day didn't seem to be helping. The pounding throb had settled in as her constant companion.

"This looks interesting." Mrs. Fetterman held a squat blue bottle three inches from her nose and squinted at the label.

"Excuse me, are you Miss Ross?"

Melanie turned to find a stocky man standing close behind her—entirely too close. Something about his intent expression sent warning bells clanging in her mind, which served to intensify the hammering in her temples. She moved back a step. "Yes?"

He pulled off his straw hat and held it before him in both hands. "I don't have a lot of time, so I'll get right down to business. My name is Nehemiah Curtis, and I've been farming a quarter section a ways south of town. It has fairly promising prospects, and there's a good, solid house. I don't drink, I don't gamble, and I don't spend my evenings at the saloon." He reached up and stroked his chin with one hand. "I may not be much to look at, but I'm steady, and I'd make you a good husband. How about—"

"No."

Nehemiah Curtis's eyes widened, then narrowed, and the corners of his mouth curved downward. "What do you mean, no?"

"I mean I have no intention of marrying you." Melanie fought down the urge to scream out her frustration and struggled to maintain an even tone. "Thank you for your offer, and I wish you the best in your search for a wife, but I'm afraid you will have to look elsewhere."

Curtis's face turned the color of the red bandanna tied around his neck. Jamming his hat back onto his head, he turned on his heel and strode away, leaving Melanie staring after him. He stomped to the far end of the store and jabbed a pudgy finger in Caleb's face. "I thought she was supposed to be anxious to wed."

Caleb's head whipped around. "Excuse me?"

Even at that distance, Melanie didn't miss the furtive glance he shot in her direction.

"You heard me," Curtis said. "I thought she was eager to get a husband. Ripe for the plucking—that's the word that's been going around."

Caleb's face paled, and he patted his hands in the air, as though trying to shush the angry man. "Why don't you come out back where we can talk without disturbing anyone?"

"I'm done talking. I didn't come in here to be made a fool of. Good day to you, sir." He turned and walked out the door, slamming it with such force that Melanie feared for the window glass.

The store grew quiet, reminding Melanie of the calm before a storm. So quiet she could hear the mantel clock ticking away on its shelf at the far end of the mercantile.

Thrusting the bottles into Mrs. Fetterman's hands, she stalked down the length of the store with a measured tread, only vaguely aware of customers scuttling toward the door to make a hasty exit. She kept her eyes focused straight ahead, her attention locked on the turncoat . . . the snake . . . the *weasel* standing in front of the counter.

Melanie pointed her finger at Caleb's face in the same way Nehemiah Curtis had done only moments before. "What did he mean, 'that's the word that's been going around'?" She stepped forward and jabbed the finger into his chest. "Are you behind all this?"

161

Caleb stood with his mouth half open, darting glances from Melanie to the rear door and back to Melanie again, as if gauging whether he could get past her to make his escape.

"Anxious? Eager?" Melanie's voice rose higher with every syllable. "'*Ripe for the plucking*'?" She heard a soft snicker off to one side and whirled on Will Blake. "Were you in on this, too? All the times you've stopped here to visit, all the times you've sought me out." She jerked her thumb toward Caleb. "Did he put you up to that?"

The amused expression on Will's face dissolved, to be replaced by a look of alarm as she advanced on him, step by threatening step. He raised his hands, palms out, in a gesture of surrender. "Hold on a minute. I'm no party to this . . . whatever it might be." He added the last phrase with a guilty look at Caleb.

Turning back to Melanie, Will captured her gaze and held it. "Think back. If you'll remember, the first time I expressed interest in you was on the day we met—the very day you came to town. That was done all on my own, with no coaxing needed. I don't need anyone's help to know you're the most attractive woman in these parts." One corner of his lips quirked up, and he tipped his hat. "And now, if you'll excuse me, I believe I'll be on my way and leave the two of you to sort things out." He wasted no time in putting his words into action.

The moment the door swung shut behind him, Melanie rounded on Caleb again. "How could you? Of all the despicable, underhanded schemes!" Her voice cracked, and she swallowed back the tears that threatened, despising her show of weakness. "If you think you can get rid of me by marrying me off to some farmer . . . or soldier . . . or the undertaker, of all people . . . you've got another think coming."

Caleb gulped. Then he swept his arm toward the window as if taking in the town and the landscape beyond. "Look out there. This is a land of promise, but it can be a lonely one. Most of the men around here are hungry for married life and a family, and you're a fresh new face. And not a bad looking one, at that."

"So you felt compelled to sic them all on me?" Melanie heard a scuffling sound behind the counter, and Levi emerged from his fort. He scooted across the floor to take up a stand slightly behind his father and stared at her with a look of awe.

Melanie was aware of his presence, but it didn't dampen her anger one whit. She fixed a scorching glare on the object of her wrath. "Do you think I'm desperate?"

"No, not at all." Caleb's soothing tone was belied by the way he inched toward the back door, with Levi keeping pace. "You're quite pleasing to the eyes. Certainly pretty enough to attract a man without any help from me."

Levi nodded vigorously. "That's right. I heard Papa say that to Mr. Crawford. He told him it was a good thing, too. He didn't even have to pay those men to come and ask you to marry them."

Melanie's eyes bulged, and she glowered at Caleb through a red haze. "So you really did it. You encouraged all those men to . . . to . . ." Finding herself bereft of further speech, she grabbed for the broom that stood propped against the counter and brandished it like a weapon.

Caleb backpedaled a few more steps. "Get ahold of yourself, Miss Ross. You're letting your emotions get the better of you."

"My emotions?" Melanie tightened her hold on the broom handle and raised it over her shoulder, bringing it down on the counter with a mighty *whack*. "I'd say there's plenty of call for emotion when I find out I'm being treated like a piece of merchandise . . . and unwanted merchandise, at that." She lifted the broom again and advanced another step.

Caleb opened his mouth, then seemed to think better of it. He grabbed Levi by the shoulder. "Son, sometimes retreat is the better part of valor. Let's get out of here."

The two of them backed to the door, and Caleb reached around to turn the knob, never taking his eyes off Melanie. "Once you've had a chance to calm down a little, perhaps we can discuss this a little more rationally." He looked like he wanted to say more, but he appeared to change his mind when she raised the broom again. Without another word, he drew Levi out onto the back stoop and shut the door behind them.

Melanie stood staring at the closed door and felt her knees begin to tremble. Had she just chased Caleb out of his own place of business? She looked down at the broom in her hand and shook her head. Maybe she really was as crazy as she must have looked to him and Levi.

She leaned the broom back against the counter and tottered over to the front door. Snapping the lock in place, she reached for the *Closed* sign. It was still a little early for the store to close, but she didn't care. Not today. Not after discovering the callous scheme Caleb Nelson had hatched. She started toward the kitchen to brew herself a pot of chamomile tea. With any luck, she could fall into a dreamless sleep. She had already lived through one nightmare . . . and in broad daylight.

"Are you all right, dearie?"

Melanie started and whirled around to see Mrs. Fetterman still standing where Melanie had left her before beginning her onslaught on Caleb. She pressed her lips together to stifle a moan. Another witness to her humiliating outburst. The tears she had managed to hold back now flowed in earnest.

Mrs. Fetterman pattered across the floor and pressed a handkerchief into Melanie's hand. "There, now. You needn't fret like that. Every once in a while, a man needs something to wake him up, and today was one of those times for Caleb. You'll see, it'll all blow over and be forgotten in no time."

"Forgotten?" Melanie choked back a sob. "How could anyone forget what happened after seeing the way I made a total idiot of myself? He already despises me. This is just going to make it worse."

To Melanie's astonishment, Mrs. Fetterman only chuckled. "Stuff and nonsense. Right now, you feel like you've been caught up in a whirlwind, but these things have a way of working themselves out. You'll see." She held up the bottle of Dr. White's Dandelion Alterative. "I think I'll take this with me, if you don't mind putting it on my tab."

"I'd be glad to." Melanie showed the older woman to the door, unlocked it, and relocked it behind her, then slumped against it. She squeezed her eyes shut, wishing she could erase the incidents of the past half hour from her memory. It was bad enough to be the target for the attentions of every available man in the area, but to find out Caleb had orchestrated it all in the hope of driving her off was simply unbearable.

Melanie strode across to the shelves of patent remedies and picked up a bottle of Scott's Nerv-O-Sol. Maybe she needed a dose of the tonic even more than chamomile tea.

14

Caleb ushered Levi up onto the back stoop of the mercantile, both surprised and relieved when he didn't encounter Melanie outside sweeping as usual. He hadn't been sure what to expect after the way she'd chased him off the day before. Had she calmed down yet, or was she ready to pick up again where she left off?

He looked down, frowning when he saw the thin layer of dust on the boards. Sweeping the stoop was always her first chore of the morning, but apparently she hadn't gotten around to it yet.

And what did that mean? Was she planning to give him the silent treatment? Was she upstairs packing, ready to give up and go home?

Or was she lurking just behind that closed door, armed with the broom . . . or an even more substantial weapon this time?

Motioning Levi to stand back, he gripped the knob gently, intending to open the door as quietly as he could. He looked down in surprise when the knob refused to turn. He tightened his grip and wiggled the knob back and forth.

Locked. His brow furrowed. What did that mean? Melanie had always unlocked the door by the time he and Levi arrived.

Levi stepped closer. "Is Miss Ross still mad at you, Papa?"

Caleb gritted his teeth and fished in his vest pocket for his key. He had been gentleman enough to leave yesterday when Melanie had run him off the premises like a whipped dog. The woman had obviously been overwrought, unable to deal with things in a rational manner. Thinking back to what Nehemiah Curtis had said, though—plus the fact that she had tumbled onto the scheme Caleb had been promoting— he had to admit there might have been some justification for her behavior.

He unlocked the door and shoved it open, ready for a confrontation, but Melanie wasn't there to meet him, only an empty silence.

And as far as he could see, she hadn't even come downstairs that morning. Everything looked just as it had when he'd scurried out the day before. Maybe his theory was right and she was making preparations to leave. His brief sense of elation was cut short when another thought struck him. Not that long ago, a murder had occurred on their back steps. Had some harm befallen Melanie during the night?

He put his hand on Levi's shoulder. "Stay here, right by the door." Taking a few steps inside, he scanned the mercantile, but there was no sign of her. Not sure whether to feel relieved or concerned, he raised his voice. "Melanie, are you here?"

Again there was no answer, only the quiet. With his heart in his throat, Caleb bounded toward the stairs, calling her name again. Just as he cleared the top step, the door to her bedroom opened and Melanie emerged, tightening her wrapper around her waist.

"Are you all right?" Caleb looked her up and down. There didn't seem to be anything wrong with her, apart from the dark circles under her eyes and a tightness at the corners of her mouth. "I thought . . . I was afraid . . ." He took a quick step back, suddenly aware of her proximity and the fact that she was still in her nightclothes.

Melanie didn't seem to notice. She lifted one hand and touched the tips of her fingers to her forehead. "Would you mind if I stayed upstairs this morning? I'm not feeling quite like myself today."

"Of course." Caleb moved down one step. "I'm sorry you're not feeling well. Is there anything I can bring you?"

She shook her head, then winced. "No, thank you," she said in a faint voice. "I believe I'll just go lie down for a while." Without waiting for a reply, she turned and disappeared into her bedroom.

Caleb trotted back down the stairs, where Levi waited for him with an anxious expression. "Did she try to hit you again?"

"Not at all. She simply isn't feeling well. It looks like it's just the two of us manning the store this morning." He grinned and tousled the boy's hair. "Why don't you grab the extra broom and help me by sweeping off the back stoop while I take care of the boardwalk out front. We'll need to hurry if we're going to open on time."

The morning sped by with a steady stream of customers, most of whom inquired about Melanie's whereabouts. With every conversation, Caleb became increasingly aware how much of a fixture she had already become in the mercantile. All the more reason he needed to break her connection with the store before it became too strong.

At midmorning, Rafe Sutton walked through the door and strode up to the counter. "My wagon's out back in the alley. I've got a delivery for you. Where do you want me to put it?"

Caleb frowned. "Are you sure it's for me? I wasn't expecting any orders."

Rafe moved the ever-present wad of chewing tobacco from his right cheek to his left. "It's for that pretty partner of yours. Her name is lettered on top of the crate, right above where it says *Ross-Nelson Mercantile: Fragile*."

"Fragile?" Caleb stared at the freighter. Ophelia Pike's china had arrived several days before. *What could this be?*

A memory stirred, and he felt the muscles in his neck tense. It must be the china Melanie had ordered to put on display. His lips thinned, but he tried not to let his anger show. It wasn't Rafe's fault, after all. He jerked his head toward the doorway behind the counter. "Put it in the storeroom, if you would."

Rafe nodded and moved toward the back door. He paused with his hand on the latch, looked around the store, and turned back to Caleb. "Seems funny not to see Miss Ross around today. That smile of hers sure brightens up the place."

Caleb managed a weak smile in return.

Looking at the line of customers awaiting his attention, he had to admit Rafe wasn't the only one who missed Melanie's presence. In many ways, she had proven to be more a help than a hindrance. Under different circumstances, he might even have enjoyed her company.

By lunchtime, he still hadn't heard a peep from upstairs, not even a creak of the floorboards to indicate she had moved around at all. Had he missed hearing her while he'd been occupied with customers, or was she still abed? And if that was the case, did she merely have a headache, or was she truly ill?

Even though he didn't appreciate most of her contributions when it came to running the store, there was no question that she was a hard worker. Maybe she had pushed herself to the point of utter exhaustion. After all, she said she wasn't feeling like herself.

Caleb grunted. She certainly hadn't acted like herself when she came after him with that broom yesterday. The shadow of concern that had been hovering over him since he'd discovered her uncharacteristic absence that morning deepened. If it turned out that she was sick due to exhaustion, how much of that was his fault? His addlebrained scheme to inundate her with proposals would only have added to the strain she already carried.

He rubbed the tight muscles at the back of his neck. If the truth be told, he owed her an apology. Maybe a thoughtful gesture extended as an olive branch would show his goodwill and help to make amends. Going into the kitchen, he put the water on to brew a pot of tea. While he waited, he took out the ham sandwich he'd brought for his own lunch and arranged it on a tray, then carried the peace offering upstairs. He stopped at the top step, surprised to find Melanie kneeling beside an open trunk under the window, pressing an armful of fabric to her face.

"Oh, you're up."

Melanie turned around at the sound of his voice. When she lowered her hands, Caleb saw she was holding a man's woolen coat.

She followed his gaze and gave an embarrassed laugh. "It belonged to my cousin George. I was just remembering the way he always smelled of pipe tobacco and licorice. There's still a trace of it on his coat." She folded the garment and set it aside atop a stack of clothing already piled next to the trunk.

Caleb glanced down at the tray in his hands. "I thought you might be hungry."

A soft smile brightened her face. "How thoughtful. Would you mind setting it over there?" She indicated a small table nearby. "I'll be ready to take a break in a moment. I haven't had a chance to go through George's things, and I suddenly felt the need to reconnect with him a bit, so I thought I'd make the most of this opportunity. I hope you don't mind."

Caleb set the tray down and turned back to her. "No, I don't mind at all. I understand what it's like to lose someone you love."

"Your uncle Alvin?"

Caleb cleared his throat and made himself answer truthfully. "Yes . . . him too."

A frown appeared between her brows, replaced by a look of awareness. "Your wife?"

Caleb nodded. He walked back to the head of the stairs and sat down on the top step. "Her name was Corinna, and we'd been married for four years. Levi was three at the time, and we were so excited about the new baby that was due."

He swallowed past a sudden obstruction in his throat. Other than Uncle Alvin, he hadn't spoken to anyone about Corinna since he'd arrived in Arizona. "But there were complications. The baby—our little girl—only lived a few minutes, and Corinna died within the hour."

He glanced at Melanie, surprised and oddly touched when he saw tears brimming in her eyes.

"I'm so sorry," she said. "That must have been terribly difficult for you."

"It was." Caleb took a deep breath. "If it wasn't for the Lord and Levi, I don't think I could have kept on going. My mother took care of him while I worked the farm, but then she died about a year ago, and things got even harder. When Uncle Alvin wrote and asked me to come out here and help him, it seemed like an answer to prayer. I sold our farm in Missouri, and Levi and I headed west."

Melanie looked down at her hands, clasped in her lap. "That's why this store is so important to you."

"It's our future," he said simply. He planted his hands on his knees and pushed himself to his feet. "And I guess I'd better get back to tending it."

Melanie looked up at him. "Do you need me to come down and help with anything? I can finish sorting through the things in this trunk another time."

Caleb smiled his thanks. "That's all right. Take your time. I can manage for a while." He decided not to mention how much he could have used her help during his busy morning. They had reached a truce of sorts. There was no point in stirring up more animosity. Leaving Melanie to her rummaging, he went back downstairs and set up Levi's lunch, then fixed some cheese and crackers for himself. He was just clearing away the remains of their meal when the bell jingled, and the door swung open to admit Marshal Hooper.

"Good afternoon." Dusting the cracker crumbs off his hands, Caleb stepped forward to greet the lawman. "What can I help you with today?"

The marshal closed the door behind him and stepped farther inside the store. "I'm not looking to buy anything today, Caleb. I'm here on official business." He leaned against the counter and hooked his thumb under his gun belt. "I'm trying to learn more about that fellow who got his head bashed in on your porch."

Caleb flinched at the reminder of the grisly discovery. He shook his head and rested both arms on the counter. "I don't know that I can help you. As I told you then, I never saw him before."

"You can't think of any reason he would have been outside your store in the dead of night?"

"Not a single one. There isn't any explanation I can think of. It's as much of a puzzle to me as it is to you."

The marshal nodded thoughtfully, as if filing Caleb's words away in his mind for future reference. "From the quality of his clothes, it's evident that he was probably a man of good standing. Wherever he came from, I expect there's at least someone back there who's wondering where he is."

Caleb tapped his fingers on the counter. "I've been thinking the same thing."

"The only connection I can find at all is that someone left a horse in the livery stable the night before the body was discovered. But Micah was over in the saloon at the time, so he didn't see who left the horse, and there was nothing to indicate what the man's name was or where he came from or why he was in Cedar Ridge. Nobody in town seems to know anything about him . . . but he was found here on your stoop."

The marshal leaned over the counter and peered into Caleb's face. "I can't help but feel that there's some kind of tie-in here, but I don't know what it is. It just doesn't make any sense."

Caleb straightened and leaned away from the intensity of the lawman's gaze. "This is the West, after all. It isn't always a safe place to be."

"True, but this isn't just some drunken brawl ending in a shootout. This is outright murder. A murder that happened right under my nose, which is something I take personally. It might have been done by someone passing through—that seems to be the prevailing theory around town—but it might just as well be someone who lives here. And if the murderer is still around, I intend to see justice done."

"I couldn't agree more." Melanie appeared at the bottom of the stairs, carrying a sheet of paper in one hand.

Caleb turned, surprised to see her looking much more refreshed than when he'd left her a few minutes previously.

She walked over to join them at the counter. "Whoever that poor man was, the people who cared about him deserve to be notified."

The marshal squinted at her. "Did he look familiar to you? He had to have some reason for coming to your store."

Melanie shook her head. "I can't imagine what that might be . . . especially in the middle of the night. Perhaps he didn't intend to come here at all. Maybe he was being pursued by whomever it was who killed him, and he was simply trying to hide."

Marshal Hooper regarded her thoughtfully. "Maybe. What-ever the case, it happened in my town, and I'm going to keep on digging until I find the answers I'm looking for."

Melanie nodded solemnly, then she brightened. "Look what I found." She held the paper out to Caleb. "It's Cousin George's will."

Caleb's jaw sagged. Feeling as if he'd just been kicked in the gut, he reached out to take the document, a single sheet of paper with the words *Last Will and Testament* across the top. He scanned the writing below, letting his eyes skim past several mentions of debts to be settled from his estate down to the only words that mattered.

I leave all my worldly possessions, including my share in the Ross-Nelson Mercantile, to my cousin, Melanie Esther Ross.

With a sense of disbelief, Caleb went over the will a second time, giving it a more thorough scrutiny. He recognized the handwriting as George's, having already seen it on paperwork pertaining to the store. And if the writing belonged to George Ross, that meant the will was truly his—which meant . . .

He looked up and into Melanie's eyes. "I guess this makes it official."

Her face fairly glowed, and she bounced up and down on her toes, looking as if she wanted to break into a joyous dance. "That's right. We're partners. You can't run me off now."

The marshal raised his eyebrows and looked at Caleb.

Caleb squirmed under the man's sharp scrutiny and tried to keep from looking as if he'd just had his legs kicked out from under him. Melanie was right. There was no way he could ease her out of the store now. George's will made it clear—she had as much right to be there as he did.

15

Melanie hummed while she bent over the wooden crate lid she had sanded smooth that morning and wielded her paintbrush with care as she put the finishing touches on a new sign. She took her time cleaning her brush and putting the paint jar away in the back room. Returning to her newly painted sign, she touched the bright crimson letters with her fingertips to make sure they were dry before carrying the placard to the window and angling it so it would be visible from the street.

Caleb looked up from the back shelves, where he stood atop the stepladder, restocking cans of vegetables. "What are you doing?"

"Putting up a sign."

"I can see that." Caleb climbed down from the stepladder and walked over to the window. "What's it for?"

Melanie favored him with a placid smile. "I'm going to run a special on those chamber pots."

"You're *what*?" Caleb's look of horror would have been comical if not for the scowl that accompanied it.

Melanie clasped her hands in front of her. "We haven't sold a one of these in the time I've been here. It's far better to move the existing inventory so we can make room for new stock, even if we have to sell it at a discount. Don't you agree?"

He didn't. Melanie could tell by the way his chin jutted out. She continued to smile sweetly, all the while bracing herself for the argument she knew would ensue. Instead, Caleb returned to the stepladder and went back to restocking, setting the cans of peas on the shelf with more force than necessary.

Melanie checked the position of her sign again, singing softly under her breath. Finding Cousin George's will had made things infinitely easier for her . . . if not for Caleb. With her position finally established, she no longer had to prove herself. The discovery of the will made her a bona fide partner, and the two of them would have to learn to get along . . . whether Caleb liked it or not.

Which he didn't. He had, however, accepted defeat. Although the glowering looks he sent her way made his feelings plain enough. *Too bad*. Melanie chuckled under her breath.

She looked up every time someone passed by the window, half expecting Will Blake to stop by. Her lips curved at the memory of the visits he'd made to the store over the past few days, sometimes making some small purchase as an excuse, other times merely to stop and pass the time with her. Obviously her tirade last week hadn't been enough to deter his interest. And she was glad of that. The better she got to know Will, the more she valued his friendship.

Shooting a quick glance at her unwilling partner, she ducked into the storeroom and headed straight for the intricately inlaid music box. She found her way blocked by a large crate she hadn't seen before.

Melanie bent over and peered at the label. Her pulse quickened when she saw her name and the word *Fragile* stenciled on the top. It must be the set of china she'd ordered. Reaching for a small crowbar, she pried the crate lid open and worked her hand down through the excelsior until her fingers encountered a smooth, curved object.

She pushed the excelsior away, lifted her find from its nest of wood shavings, and held the teacup up to the light. A smile curved her lips. The china's Blush pattern was even more beautiful than she had imagined.

And Caleb hadn't said a word about its arrival.

Fine. Melanie's smile broadened as she straightened and brushed off her skirt with her free hand. She wouldn't say anything to him about her discovery. She would take her time to plan the perfect display, then set it out and surprise him.

She bent to return the cup to the crate, but then thought better of it and dug through the excelsior again until she located a delicate saucer. Wiping both cup and saucer free of dust, she set them on a shelf in plain view. Caleb couldn't help but see them next time he came into the storeroom.

Melanie chuckled as she leaned across the crate and reached for the music box. Her fingers traced the scrolled pattern of inlaid wood on the top. Even if they didn't offer it for sale, such a beautiful piece deserved to be out on display, not hidden away where no one could appreciate it. Lifting it with care, she carried it into the mercantile and set it in a place she had already cleared on a shelf that held crockery and other breakable items.

She stepped back to admire the effect and felt something roll under her foot. Looking down, she saw she had stepped on one of Levi's tin soldiers. Scooping up the toy, she bent to peer under the counter and beckoned to Levi. "You mustn't line your men up on the floor like that. One of the customers might trip over them. Why don't you set them up on one of the shelves, where they'll be out of the way?"

Levi pushed his lower lip out but complied with her request, and was soon intent on arranging his troops on one of the shelves under the fabric table.

Melanie smiled. In addition to feeling more like a part of the store, she was beginning to feel more confident about using the skills learned during her time as a governess in dealing with Levi. The boy just needed more attention than he had been getting.

Caleb wasn't an uncaring father, she mused while she ran the feather duster across a display of bar soap. The poor man was just overwhelmed. She could only imagine the pressure he'd been under, trying to keep a business afloat and to corral his rambunctious son, all at the same time.

Here was another way she could add to their partnership. By helping with Levi, she could ease the strain Caleb had been under. She had already implemented several changes in that area, making it a practice to check on Levi's whereabouts at frequent intervals instead of assuming that silence meant he was staying in his fort and out of trouble. Experience had taught her that silence was not always golden. Knowing where he was and what he was doing at all times had proven remarkably effective in keeping the boy in line.

The bell tinkled, and a man dressed in dusty miner's garb stepped inside, holding the door open to admit the mayor's wife, as well.

Levi scooted across to Melanie and tugged at her skirt. "It's the S lady," he whispered.

Melanie shooed him back to play with his soldiers, smothering a smile at the boy's fascination with Ophelia Pike's exaggerated curves.

Mrs. Pike eyed Levi playing quietly and gave Melanie an approving nod.

"Good morning, Mrs. Pike. May I help you?" Melanie asked.

"Thank you," the other woman replied, "but I think I'd like to browse awhile."

The miner wandered to the other end of the store and began sorting through a selection of pick handles. A moment later, Caleb joined him, and the two were soon deep in discussion.

Melanie picked up the feather duster and continued cleaning the displays.

"Miss Ross, I need your advice." Mrs. Pike's voice carried clearly from near the shelves where bolts of fabric were stored.

Melanie set the feather duster aside and turned toward the fabric table to check on Levi. He wasn't there.

She shot a frantic glance around the rest of the store, but the boy was nowhere to be seen. But he'd been busy lining up his soldiers only a moment before. Where could he have gone in such a short time?

Mrs. Pike unrolled a length of calico and held it up. "I'm trying to decide if this would be suitable for a morning dress." She raised the cloth for Melanie to see. She turned slightly as she did so, revealing Levi standing directly behind her.

Melanie gasped, and her throat went dry. She now had a clear view of Levi, his little face screwed up in a mask of concentration. The tip of his tongue protruded from one corner of his mouth as he focused on setting up a skirmish line of soldiers ever so neatly . . . on the shelf created by Ophelia Pike's bustle.

Melanie watched in fascinated horror, wondering what she should do. She discarded her first impulse to leap across the intervening space and snatch the soldiers up in her hand. But the mayor's wife was certain to discover the battalion on her backside any moment, and Melanie cringed at the thought of her reaction.

Caleb left the miner looking through a stack of canvas-duck work trousers and strolled her way, unaware of the little drama playing out before him.

Melanie waved, trying to send him a silent signal without catching Mrs. Pike's attention.

The lady in question reached for a different bolt of fabric. "Or perhaps this shade of blue would suit my complexion better. What do you think?"

"That would be lovely, too, Mrs. Pike."

Melanie recognized the exact moment Caleb realized what was going on from the terrified expression on his face. He shot a questioning look at Melanie, who could only shrug a response and gesture at him. He was closer, and Levi was his son. It was up to him to do something to save the situation.

Inching up behind the unsuspecting Mrs. Pike, Caleb stretched out one hand and picked up a soldier between his thumb and forefinger, removing it from its perch with infinite care.

Levi opened his mouth to voice a protest, but Caleb quelled him with a warning look.

"Or perhaps this would be better?" Mrs. Pike swung around to face Melanie. Her movement also brought her face-to-face with Caleb, who stood with his hand hovering over the spot where her derriere had been a moment before.

Mrs. Pike's mouth formed an O, and her eyes grew round. "I *beg* your pardon!"

Caleb stood as though he'd been turned to stone, his hand still reaching into open air. "I . . . I was just . . ."

Mrs. Pike backed away from him a step. As she did so, Melanie saw the soldiers teeter, then slide off the bustle and down the back of the voluminous skirts to hit the floor with a muffled clatter. Melanie held her breath, but Mrs. Pike was so caught up in her indignation she didn't notice.

She held Caleb in place with an icy stare. "May I ask what you think you are doing?"

Caleb continued to stammer. "I thought I saw . . . something . . . on the back of your . . . um . . ." His voice trailed off, and his face turned dark red.

"Well, I never! A gentleman doesn't accost a lady like that, regardless of what he thinks he may have seen." Holding her head high, Mrs. Pike pushed the bolt of fabric into his hands and swept out of the store.

Levi ran to Melanie and buried his face in her skirt. Melanie couldn't blame him. From the look on his father's face, she could only imagine the dire consequences he was planning for the boy for putting him in that predicament.

Caleb looked over his shoulder at the miner, who didn't seem to be paying them the least bit of attention. When he turned back around, he crossed the floor to where Levi cowered next to Melanie and spoke in a fierce whisper. "What do you think you were doing?"

Levi flinched. "I was just lining up my soldiers."

Caleb ran his finger around the edge of his collar. "But why on . . . ? Why there?"

Levi pointed at Melanie. "She told me to."

Melanie gasped and stared at Levi in shock. "What? I did no such thing!"

The little boy bobbed his head up and down. "You did. You told me to set them up on a shelf."

Caleb shifted his smoldering glare to Melanie. At that moment, she wished she had someone to hide behind. Judging by Caleb's expression, Levi wasn't the only one in hot water.

Melanie watched Levi scamper ahead of her along the boardwalk, reveling in the freedom of being outside, in the open air. *As he should be*, she thought. Children needed to be outdoors instead of spending their days cooped up inside. Perhaps she should suggest to Caleb that he take his son out for some time together every day. If he felt uneasy about leaving her to her own devices in the store while he was gone, she could offer to take the boy herself.

Today, though, she had simply taken Levi by the hand and left. Outdoors was the best place for both of them to be at the moment, on the far side of Lincoln Street, away from Caleb's steely glare.

Not that he didn't have some justification for his anger, she thought, remembering Ophelia Pike's face when she saw his hand hovering near her backside.

Melanie glanced over her shoulder and saw Caleb watching them from the doorway. She let out a sigh of relief when a pair of customers arrived and Caleb went back inside to help them.

She continued strolling south on Lincoln, nodding to the people she passed. Every day, it seemed, she met more of the citizens of Cedar Ridge and felt a little more like a part of the community, and a welcome one at that—where everyone but Caleb was concerned.

Levi picked up a stick that had been lying in the street and straddled it as if it were a horse. Melanie smiled at the little boy's active imagination. He was full of energy and mischief, to be sure, but his mischief was of a different sort than Clarence Deaver's. Levi wasn't hurtful or intentionally malicious. He was just a spirited young child who needed a firm, consistent hand to bring him into line.

A cowboy from one of the nearby ranches rode by, tipping his hat to Melanie as he passed, presumably on his way to the livery stable, or perhaps the Silver Moon. She heard a brisk clatter of hooves on the street behind her. Looking over her right shoulder, she saw Marshal Hooper on his buckskin gelding. She raised her hand to wave a greeting but lowered it when she saw his stern, unsmiling expression. She'd already dealt with one man in a sour mood that afternoon. She had no desire to strike up a conversation with another.

The marshal pulled his horse to a stop in front of his office. Then he dismounted and started to loop the reins around the hitching rail. Levi chose that moment to gallop past, firing an imaginary six-shooter as he went by.

The buckskin set his feet and jerked back, nearly upsetting the marshal, who let out a string of words unsuitable for the ears of ladies and children.

Levi watched the lawman struggle to get his horse under control, listening in wonder at his display of language.

Marshal Hooper retied the gelding, then strode over to Levi and stood towering over the boy. "What's the matter with you?" he roared. "Don't you know better than to run up on a man while he's tying his horse?"

Melanie took a tentative step forward, wondering if she ought to intervene.

Levi craned his neck to look up at the marshal. Then without a word, he drew back his right leg and kicked the lawman squarely on the shin.

The marshal let out a howl, snatched Levi up by the back of his belt, and marched toward the mercantile, bellowing for Caleb.

Melanie flew into action, charging into the street to cut him off. She took up a stance squarely in front of the marshal and planted her feet. "Put that child down!"

Marshal Hooper stared at her, open-mouthed. He lowered his arm a few inches, but Levi's feet still flailed well above ground level. Out of the corner of her eye, Melanie could see people stopping along the boardwalk to gape at the scene she was making, but she was too angry to care.

She spoke again in her most severe tone. "You heard me. Put the boy down at once. You're scaring him."

The marshal eyed her steadily, then swept his gaze along the boardwalk, taking in the gathering crowd. Slowly, he set Levi on his feet.

As if to prove her right, Levi dashed over to Melanie and wrapped both arms around her waist. Clinging tight, he raised his face to hers. "Save me, Mama!"

Melanie put her arm around his shoulders and held him tight, ignoring his slip of the tongue. "Don't worry, Levi. I intend to."

Marshal Hooper's face turned a dull red, and his eyes shifted from one side of the street to the other. "I wasn't planning to do the boy any harm, ma'am. But it isn't the first time he's done a tomfool thing like that." He pointed at Levi, who had once again buried his face in the folds of Melanie's skirt. "He doesn't need to be mollycoddled. The boy has to take responsibility for his actions. What he needs is a good talking to, maybe even a trip to the woodshed."

Melanie didn't take her eyes off the lawman, but she heard the scattered murmurs of assent clearly enough. Over the buzz from the rest of the crowd, Ophelia Pike's voice rose clearly: "That's what I've been saying all along."

Melanie tightened her arm around Levi's shoulders. "He has a father who can see to that. I'll be sure to let him know."

She glanced down at the little boy, who was still cowering against her, and her throat thickened. How could she ever have thought he was like Clarence Deaver? Levi wasn't a self-centered, manipulative, spoiled brat. He was just a scared little boy who needed attention, and she had the skills to provide that, to help steer him away from the path Clarence's life had taken.

She reached down and tilted up Levi's chin so he had to look into her face. "Young man, you need to apologize to the marshal for kicking him. That is not acceptable behavior."

Levi looked at her in mute appeal, but she stood firm. She could tell the moment he recognized he'd lost when his shoulders slumped and he looked down at his feet. "I'm sorry," he mumbled.

"And . . . ?" Melanie prodded.

Levi heaved a sigh that seemed to come all the way from his toes. "And it won't happen again."

Melanie looked back over her shoulder at the mercantile and saw Caleb come to the door, apparently drawn by the commotion. She watched his mouth drop open when he spotted his son and his business partner as the center of attention.

She patted Levi on the head and gave him a tiny push. "Run on back to the store now. Your father is looking for you."

She turned to the marshal again. "If there is nothing further . . . ?" When he didn't answer, she gave him a polite nod and followed Levi, trying to look as though she saw nothing out of the ordinary about having an altercation with the local law in the middle of the street.

When she reached the door of the mercantile, she hesitated, then decided to walk a bit farther. There was no telling what Caleb's reaction would be to her public squabble with Marshal Hooper. If he planned to take her to task for that, she didn't feel ready to face him just yet.

Turning left, she headed toward the bakery. Maybe one of their powdered sugar doughnuts would help settle her nerves. As she stepped down into the street at the corner of Pine Street, her heel caught on the edge of the boardwalk, and she pitched forward onto the dirt with her hands splayed out to break her fall. Sand and small pebbles tore at her palms as she slid across the ground.

Melanie heard the sound of boots thudding along the wooden walk. "Miss Ross? Are you all right?"

A moment later, Dooley Hatcher knelt beside her, concern etched in his face.

"I'm fine." She grimaced as she tried to push herself upright.

"You sure? Here, let me help you." Dooley offered his arm with a gentlemanly flourish. She put her hand in the crook of his arm and winced when her palm touched his sleeve.

Dooley led her to a bench just outside the dressmaker's shop. "What's wrong with your hand? Better let me take a look."

Melanie extended her arm. While Dooley wasn't someone she would ever encourage as a suitor, she found his solicitude touching.

He knelt in front of her and cradled her hand in his, turning it so he could examine her palm. He pursed his lips and let out a low whistle. "You'd better get that cleaned up and put some iodine on it. It could have been worse, but it's going to be sore for a few—"

"Hey!"

Dooley's head jerked up, and his face paled. Melanie spun around to see Caleb barreling toward them, eating up the distance on the boardwalk with angry strides.

"Leave her alone!" Caleb bellowed.

Dooley sputtered. "But I was just—"

"No, it's off, I told you! No more proposals."

"But, Caleb, I wasn't—"

"Not another word. Just get yourself out of here, and leave Miss Ross alone."

Dooley put his hand on the bench and levered himself to his feet. As he shuffled away, Melanie heard him mutter, "And people say *I'm* crazy."

With his chest still heaving, Caleb turned to Melanie and opened his mouth, then closed it again. Then he turned on his heel and marched back to the mercantile.

Melanie stared at his retreating back, trying to comprehend what had just happened. She heard a quiet *tsk* and whirled around to find Mrs. Fetterman standing behind her.

The older woman's faded blue eyes twinkled. "It's amazing how many ways a man in love can find to make a fool of himself."

Melanie's eyes widened. "What?"

Mrs. Fetterman gave a gentle laugh. "Why, the man's besotted. I've seen the way he looks at you."

Melanie knew all too well the way Caleb usually looked at her. She'd caught the same expression on his face the other day when he stomped on a spider he'd discovered near the back shelves. She shook her head. "I'm afraid you're mistaken."

Mrs. Fetterman chuckled again. "I've been wrong about many things in my lifetime, dearie, but this isn't one of them. You'll find that out in due time—trust me." Giving Melanie a conspiratorial wink, she turned and walked away in the direction of her boardinghouse.

Her words echoed in Melanie's mind. *"I've seen the way he looks at you."* Mrs. Fetterman's simple comment triggered a surge of emotions the woman could never have anticipated. Caleb Nelson might be set in his ways to the point of mulishness, but he was also a man of honor and integrity— the kind of man Melanie could allow herself to be drawn to . . . if there was any hope he might be attracted to her as well.

"I've seen the way he looks at you." A flutter of hope stirred within her, soft as the beat of a butterfly's wings. Was there any possibility Mrs. Fetterman could be right? After all, the woman had experienced more of life than Melanie had. And having been married herself, she knew more of the ways of men.

On the other hand, Mrs. Fetterman had also remarked on the striking resemblance between Melanie and Cousin George. The flutter of hope shriveled and died, like a moth flying too close to a flame.

Caleb Nelson attracted to her? It wasn't possible. Unless . . .

She thought back over his altercation with Dooley. Obviously, he had mistaken Dooley's kneeling posture for yet another proposal of marriage.

A warm glow swept through her. Just then, Caleb had looked more like an avenging angel than an ardent suitor, but that wasn't the reason for her sudden contentment. Mistaken or not, he had come to her defense for the very first time.

And she found she rather liked it.

16

That night Melanie drifted off to sleep listening to a light rain falling on the roof, certain that its gentle patter would lull her into a restful slumber.

But in the middle of the night something jolted her awake and brought her sitting bolt upright. Had she heard a noise? She listened, hands clasped to her chest in an effort to control her ragged breathing. Long moments passed, and she'd almost convinced herself she'd imagined the whole thing when she heard it again—a faint scraping sound coming from downstairs.

She clutched the sheet up under her chin, straining to identify the sound. Surely it was only a mouse or some other small intruder. But she couldn't shake the feeling that she'd heard the distinctive click of the back door latch—that someone had come inside and was moving about down in the mercantile.

Perhaps Caleb had had trouble sleeping, too, and came back to retrieve his ledgers to work on at home. In that case, the stealthy sounds made perfect sense. He would assume she was fast asleep and be careful not to bother her.

But what if it wasn't Caleb? She needed to be sure.

Melanie slipped out of bed, pulled on her wrapper, and padded barefoot to the stairs. She inched her way down step by step, peering through the gloom. The stair creaked underfoot and she froze, barely able to breathe.

A dim glow of light flickered from inside the office, and her shoulders sagged with relief. Her assumption that Caleb had come back for his ledgers had been correct after all. She called his name softly, not wanting to startle him.

No sooner had the word escaped her lips than the light went out. In the stillness, a floorboard creaked near the back door, and she heard the click of the latch again.

Melanie waited, but no other sound disturbed the stillness of night. She headed back upstairs, calling herself a silly goose for being so frightened . . . and for the emptiness she felt when Caleb hadn't responded. She had barely whispered his name, after all. He must not have heard her. It was the only thing that made sense.

When she climbed back into bed, she pulled the covers up over her shoulders in a protective cocoon. The rain had stopped, but a steady *drip-drip* from the eaves continued. The gentle sound should have helped her relax, but her thoughts were a jumble. When sleep returned at last, it was interrupted throughout the night by worrisome dreams and fits of wakefulness.

Early the next morning, when she finally accepted that more sleep would be impossible, Melanie groaned, kicked the sheets aside, and sat up on the edge of the bed, rubbing her eyes. A new day was at hand, whether she'd gotten the sleep she needed or not. A faint glimmer of light filtered in through the bedroom curtain, but it was not yet enough for her to read by, so she lit her bedside lamp, then reached for her Bible and pulled it onto her lap.

"'I will lift up mine eyes unto the hills, from whence cometh my help. My help cometh from the Lord, which made heaven and earth.'"

Melanie continued on, reading the rest of the psalm. When finished, she closed the book and ran her fingers over the worn leather cover, drawing comfort from the verses. She set the Bible back on her bedside table and crossed over to the window. A rosy pearl hue tinged the sky. In a few minutes the rising sun would offer a spectacular view of the hills surrounding Cedar Ridge.

Why not be part of that scene, instead of observing from the window? She grinned as the thought took root in her mind. She could enjoy a brisk walk in the crisp morning air and still have plenty of time for her morning routine when she got back.

Donning her blue paisley dress and pinning her chestnut hair into its customary coil, she grabbed a light shawl and made her way downstairs. Halfway between the bottom step and the counter, she felt something crunch under her foot.

Melanie pulled up short. What had she stepped on? She peered at the wooden planks in the dim light and rubbed her foot back and forth across the spot. The action produced a grating sound, as if coarse sand had been sprinkled across the floorboards.

Frowning, she walked behind the counter, where they kept a lantern hanging on the wall. She lifted it from its hook and fumbled for a match. A moment later, the wick glowed bright, and she held the lantern high while she retraced her steps.

Her breath caught when she saw shards of china scattered

across the floor. Dropping to her knees, she picked up one of the larger fragments. Her throat tightened when she recognized the delicate pink pattern of the teacup she had set out on the storeroom shelf to taunt Caleb.

Tears sprang to her eyes at the loss of the lovely piece. She studied the remnants again. There were a few large chunks, but most of the teacup had been ground into a fine powder, as if crushed under an angry bootheel.

A burning sensation rose in her throat, and she swallowed hard. Who could have done such a thing, and why hadn't she noticed the mess when she was locking up the evening before?

She retrieved the broom and dustpan from the storeroom and swept up the remains of the china. While she worked, a thought struck her. Did this have something to do with the noises she'd heard during the night?

If that was the case, Caleb must have done it. But the cup had been in the storeroom. How had it ended up out here? And why had the china been ground to a powder? If Caleb was responsible, the destruction of the cup had to be an accident. Crushing something in anger didn't fit what she knew of his character.

Besides—her mouth twisted in a wry grin—Caleb had been upset enough at the thought of spending money on the china with no guarantee it would sell. He would never squander such an investment by destroying it.

Melanie brushed one hand across her eyes. A night of tossing and turning was hardly conducive to clear thinking. She would take up the matter of the broken china with Caleb when she returned from her walk. Dumping the remains of the smashed cup into the wastebin, she returned the broom and dustpan to their places and stepped outside to meet the dawn.

The tangy, fresh-washed smell Mrs. Fetterman had identified as cedars, creosote bush, and cliff rose filled her senses
and chased her weariness away. Drawing new energy from
the invigorating air, Melanie stepped out briskly, heading
toward the south end of town.

Though her brief walk with Levi the day before hadn't
ended well, her foray outdoors had helped shake the cooped-
up feeling that had beset her after spending the majority of her
time inside the store. She felt ready to stretch her legs again
and explore a bit. She strolled past the café and the bakery,
past Doc Mills's office and the bank. When she reached the
assay office at the end of Lincoln Street, she decided to keep
going.

The sun crested the horizon, sending a shower of golden
light across the landscape. Melanie shielded her eyes and
pivoted in a slow circle. To the east, a faint trail led out of
the valley where Cedar Ridge nestled and meandered upward
toward the neighboring hills with their pink-streaked sides
and chalky cliffs. Nearer at hand, crystalline drops of dew
coated the grass and bushes like a silver mist, lending the
scene an ethereal beauty that took her breath away.

The rolling slopes held her attention. She had heard stories
from several customers about the Indian ruins in those hills,
dwellings of a people who had come and gone before.

She set out along the trail in a pensive mood, thinking
about those early inhabitants. Among them, there had been
women . . . like herself. Had some of them walked the same
path her feet trod now, wondering what life had in store for
them? What hopes and dreams filled their thoughts?

Melanie stopped and scanned the breadth of the valley.
What did anyone now living know about the people who

lived there centuries before? No one was left to recall their names or remember any of them as individuals. A sudden loneliness swept over her. Who would know anything about her a hundred years from now? Would anyone then remember her name?

She shivered and drew her shawl closer around her, not sure whether to attribute her sudden chill to the cool morning air or the fresh awareness of the transitory nature of life. Her thoughts turned again to the stranger who lay buried in the cemetery. His life had ended only a short time ago, yet even the people he died amongst didn't know his name.

Sorrow smote her anew. For the thousandth time she wondered why she hadn't heard anything when he'd been attacked. Could she have done anything to stop the murder? Not by brute force, perhaps, but a loud cry for help would have brought Caleb and the other townsmen on the run. If nothing else, she might have at least identified the killer and helped bring him to justice.

Melanie glanced at the hills again. She had been walking for a good twenty minutes, yet she seemed no closer to the cliffs than when she'd set out. It was time to turn back and leave further explorations for another day. Responsibilities awaited her at the mercantile.

She retraced her steps toward town, lost in somber reflection. The moment she arrived in Cedar Ridge, she'd felt a sense of coming home. Now it seemed that her newly discovered Eden harbored its own serpent. She lifted her gaze again, looking up to the hills. "Lord, why does there have to be such heartache in the midst of all this beauty you've created?"

And the heartache wasn't limited to the mystery of the murdered stranger. There was her relationship with Caleb, for instance. If only he would cooperate a bit, life in the store could be so much more pleasant. Granted, the two of them hadn't butted heads in a major way since Cousin George's will came to light. To all appearances, Caleb had reached a grudging acceptance of her presence at the mercantile, but she knew full well that he still didn't appreciate her suggestions for change.

She started when a roadrunner dashed across her path. A surprised laugh gurgled from her throat at the sight of his comical gait. His perky crest and oversized beak gave him a clownish appearance, and she could almost imagine him smiling at her. His whole demeanor seemed so simple, so carefree. What would it take for her to feel that happy?

Her steps dragged, and a longing filled her heart. *A home*, she thought. That's what it would take. A place to belong, to be loved.

She had a home waiting for her in heaven. The Bible teachings learned at her grandmother's knee assured her of that. Her grandparents were there, along with the mother who died while she was barely a toddler and the father she had never known. And, of course, Cousin George. They would all be waiting to greet her when she arrived at the pearly gates one day, and what a grand reunion they would have!

Still, it would be so good to have someone to love her while she lived out her days on earth. Someone to talk to, to share times both happy and sad, to hold her in a gentle embrace.

But it couldn't be just anyone. If human company was all she sought, she could have taken her pick from any of the men who had proposed to her already. What she longed for was true companionship—a meeting of hearts and minds, a union of souls—and she didn't intend to settle for anything less. In the meantime, she had the Lord. And that would be enough.

She frowned when she passed Dan Crawford's saddle shop, surprised to see the *Open* sign already hanging in the mercantile's front window. Had she spent more time on her walk than she thought? Hastening across the street, she ran up the steps to the boardwalk and hurried into the store.

The Professor was standing near the coffee grinder, chatting with Caleb, who was turning the crank with an easy rhythm.

Melanie stumbled to a stop. "Am I late?"

A puzzled scowl shadowed Caleb's face. "Where have you been? I thought you were still upstairs. We were trying not to disturb you."

Melanie gestured toward the door. "It's such a beautiful morning. I decided to go out for a walk and enjoy the sunrise."

Caleb's frown deepened. "Please tell me you didn't go outside alone while it was still dark." When she didn't answer, his voice sharpened. "While a killer may be on the loose? Are you out of your mind?"

Melanie bristled at his incredulous tone. "I was perfectly safe. There was nobody else around."

Caleb rolled his eyes. "That is exactly my point."

The brusque reminder caught her up short, but she didn't want to give him the satisfaction of knowing that. Ignoring Caleb, she turned toward the Professor, who offered her an apologetic smile.

"It's my fault that the store is open earlier than usual. When I realized I was out of coffee, I decided to drive into town and have breakfast at the café. Caleb saw my buggy and waved me over. When I told him what I was doing, he took pity on me and offered to grind some Arbuckle's for me."

Melanie smiled back at him. "I'm sure Caleb could commiserate with you. He's like a grouchy bear if he doesn't have his coffee." She shot a look at Caleb, who continued turning the crank without comment.

She decided to change the subject, wanting to throw off the sense of unease brought on by Caleb's mention of murder. Trying to keep any hint of accusation out of her voice, she asked, "What happened to that cup last night?"

Caleb looked up from the coffee grinder with a puzzled frown. "What do you mean?"

When he continued to stare at her as if she were speaking in a foreign tongue, Melanie planted her fists on her hips and glared at him. "You know very well what I mean—the china teacup that broke when you came back last night."

Caleb shook his head slowly. "What are you talking about?"

Melanie felt her irritation rise. "Don't deny it. I heard you. I came downstairs and called your name. You must have been going out just then, because all I heard was the click of the door latch."

His face softened, and a slight smile curved his lips. "I was never here last night. You must have been dreaming."

Melanie let out a huff. "It wasn't a dream, and it wasn't my imagination." She strode over to the wastebin. Picking it up, she carried it to where Caleb stood and held it up so he could see the broken shards inside. "I certainly didn't imagine this."

Caleb's mouth dropped open, and he stared at the remnants of the shattered cup a long moment before he lifted the wastebin from her hands and set it on the floor. When he straightened, deep lines creased his forehead. "How could that have happened?" he muttered.

Melanie bristled. "That's what I'd like to know."

He leaned toward her and cupped her shoulders in a light grip. "I'm sorry the cup got broken, but I can assure you I had nothing to do with it."

Melanie stared into his eyes, mere inches from her own, and saw only truth reflected there. The warmth of his gaze and his touch on her shoulders nearly made her knees buckle. She glanced down to break the spell, and Caleb stepped away.

When she looked up again, she saw the Professor step over to the shelf where the music box stood and run his finger across the top. Lifting the lid with tender care, he stared at the inner workings with a look of admiration. "An exquisite piece," he said. "What wonderful craftsmanship."

Melanie shook herself and tried to pull her thoughts together. "Thank you. I thought it was wrong to keep it hidden away in the back. I'm glad someone appreciates it."

The Professor lowered the lid and turned to face her. "It's obvious you have an eye for beauty. I have quite a collection of interesting items at my home. Would you be interested in dining with me one evening? I'm sure you would enjoy seeing them."

Melanie's lips parted. She didn't know the Professor well, but he hadn't struck her as the type of man who would invite a woman to visit his home unchaperoned.

As if reading her thoughts, the Professor smiled and inclined his head. "The invitation is meant for Caleb, as well. And Levi, too, of course."

Caleb looked up from sacking the ground coffee. He looked at Melanie with a question in his eyes, then he smiled and nodded. "If Miss Ross is agreeable, we'd all be happy to enjoy your hospitality."

Melanie felt her spirits lift, buoyed more by Caleb's smile than the prospect of dinner at the Professor's house. "Thank you. We'd love to."

The bell jingled, and Marshal Hooper strode through the door.

The Professor reached for the sack of coffee. "I'd better be leaving now. Would you put this coffee on my tab, Caleb? I'll plan on seeing you at my house the day after tomorrow, if that works for you."

Melanie watched him leave, then turned back to see the marshal saunter over to where Caleb was wiping down the coffee grinder with a clean rag.

"Good day to you," Caleb said. "You're out and about early this morning."

Hooper nodded toward the Professor's departing figure. "I'm not the only one."

Melanie drifted over to join them.

The marshal tilted his hat back on his head and eyed Caleb. "Does the name Lucas Weber mean anything to you?"

Caleb set his rag down and squinted at the abrupt question. "No, I can't say it does."

"What about you, Miss Ross?" The marshal turned to Melanie. "Have you ever heard that name?"

Melanie edged closer to Caleb. "No, I don't believe so." She exchanged a quick look with him. "Why?"

The marshal studied them both as he spoke. "That's the name of the man you found on your doorstep."

Melanie caught her breath. At last they knew his name. She felt the sting of tears and tried to swallow past the lump that swelled in her throat. She raised her hand to dash the moisture from her eyes but caught the marshal's stony stare and linked her hands in front of her waist instead.

The lawman cleared his throat. "You remember that letter I received yesterday?"

Melanie nodded, recalling the envelope addressed to the marshal that had arrived in the previous day's mail delivery.

"It was from Lydia Weber, Lucas's wife. She said he was missing. She hasn't heard anything from him since he set off on a trip to Cedar Ridge, and she wanted to know if I'd seen him or knew anything about his whereabouts." He pulled a small photograph from his vest pocket and held it out. "She sent this tintype along so I'd know for sure if I'd run across him."

Caleb took the tintype from him. After a long glance, he handed it to Melanie. She held the picture up, studying every detail. *So that's what he looked like in life.* She remembered the slack features and the grayish skin and shuddered, wondering if she would ever be able to banish that image from her memory.

The bell over the door jingled. Doc Mills entered, squinting as he peered around the store. When he spotted the three of them, he ambled over and took up a stance next to Melanie.

She wrinkled her nose against the lingering odor of stale alcohol and cigar smoke that seemed to accompany the doctor wherever he went, and backed away a half step, hoping the move wouldn't be too obvious. Turning her head slightly to one side, she studied him out of the corner of her eye. Looking at his shaking hands, she wondered that any patients at all sought his help and sent up a quick prayer of thanks for her own good health. What a sad thing, to see the toll drink could take on a man!

Doc looked at Caleb, moving his head from side to side, as if trying to bring him into focus. "I've got a sizable order for you. The list is right here." He held up a sheet of paper half covered with writing.

"We'll be with you in a minute," Caleb said. "Just as soon as we're finished here."

"Marshal Hooper has learned who the dead man was," Melanie told him. "He was telling us about it just now." She held up the tintype.

Doc gave the photograph a cursory glance, then let out a puff of air that stirred his drooping mustache. He pocketed his list and turned away. "I can see you're busy. Why don't I come back when you have more time?" With a nod that included all of them, he shuffled toward the door and went out. Through the window, they could see him turning left on the boardwalk.

"Probably on his way to the Silver Moon for a little hair of the dog that bit him last night," the marshal muttered.

Melanie followed the doctor's unsteady progress along the walk, then turned back to the marshal with a sigh and handed him the photograph. "You're going to return this to Mrs. Weber, aren't you? It will be doubly precious to her now that her husband is gone."

Marshal Hooper shook his head. "She said she has another and told me to hang on to it. I'm hoping it will help me in my investigation." He tucked the tintype away again, then hooked his thumbs in his gun belt. "You're sure you don't recognize the name Weber?"

"No," Caleb repeated. "Why?"

Melanie drew her brows together. They had already told him the name was unfamiliar. Why did he keep harping on the question? From Caleb's expression, she suspected he wondered the same thing.

The marshal raised one hand and stroked his chin. "According to Mrs. Weber's letter, her husband came to Cedar Ridge to look into his brother's death."

His brother? Melanie looked up at Caleb, who appeared to be every bit as confused as she felt. Then comprehension lit his face.

"Weber? Wait a minute." He bowed his head as if deep in thought, then he nodded. "I remember now. I think a letter came to my uncle from an L. Weber—in Colorado—shortly after his death. I returned it, marked *Deceased*." His brows knit together. "You mean to tell me the man who sent that letter was the same man who was murdered?"

The marshal nodded without speaking.

Melanie stared from Caleb to the marshal. "I don't understand. Who was his brother?"

The lawman turned his attention back to her. "Charley Weber was one of George and Alvin's old prospecting buddies. He came into town last November, all fired up about a gold strike he'd heard about in South America, thinking he would talk them into pulling up stakes and joining him so the three of them could have one last adventure together." He patted the pocket where he'd put the tintype.

Caleb rubbed his forehead. "That's the first I've heard of it." He looked at Melanie. "Do you know anything about this Charley?"

She shook her head. "I don't ever remember Cousin George

mentioning him, but he didn't really mention anyone other than Alvin—in his letters or when he visited us." She looked back at the marshal. "So what happened to Charley? Obviously they didn't all go off together."

Marshal Hooper shook his head. "Nope. Both George and Alvin told him their roving days were over. They'd had their fill of panning for gold in icy streams and sleeping on the cold, hard ground. They said they'd found their last home right here, and they intended to stay in Cedar Ridge for the rest of their lives. Which they did."

He rolled his shoulders. "Of course, no one knew then how little time any of them had left. Charley got sick and died before he ever got a chance to head off to that new strike. And he was quickly followed by George and then Alvin. All three of them are buried out there in the cemetery. And now I'm wondering about the real reason Charley showed up in Cedar Ridge."

Caleb frowned. "What do you mean?"

Marshal Hooper rested one hand on his holster. "Lucas Weber's wife—his widow, I should say—said her husband got a letter from your uncle Alvin, saying he had some misgivings relating to Charley's death. Lucas wrote back to Alvin for more information, but his letter was returned." He eyed Caleb, who swallowed and nodded.

"My uncle was already gone by then," Caleb said. His brow furrowed. "But that was nearly three months ago. Why did Charley's brother wait until now to come out here himself?"

"Lydia Weber wrote that she'd been ill for several weeks. He didn't want to leave her until he was certain she'd recover."

"And now he's left her forever." Melanie's breath came out in a soft sigh. "How very sad."

The marshal folded his arms, and his probing gaze returned. "Sad, yes. But I also find it a little odd that we now have one murder and one suspicious death occurring in Cedar Ridge in a few months' time—especially since they both have a connection with this store."

17

I had no idea your house was filled with so many wonders, Professor." Caleb waved his arm, taking in the large room where they all sat sipping coffee after a congenial meal. "It's almost like a museum."

"Thank you." The Professor's angular face grew pink with pleasure. "Learning about the past and the people who inhabited it is one of my greatest joys in life."

Melanie could well believe that. She stared around at the glass cases that lined the whitewashed walls of the rambling adobe building the Professor called home.

The Professor got up and beckoned to Levi. "Do you know what this is?" He knelt beside a porous oblong stone the size of a breadbox and rubbed his hand along its concave surface.

Levi walked over to inspect the stone and shook his head.

"It's called a *metate*. It was used to grind corn and other grains into meal."

Levi's brow wrinkled. "How does it work?"

"Like this." The Professor picked up a smaller stone the size of a brick and hefted it in his hand. Kneeling beside Levi, he reached into a small stone jar and drew out a handful of dried corn, which he sprinkled across the metate's surface. "Put your hands here," he directed.

Levi knelt in front of the Professor and gripped the smaller stone in both hands.

"Good. Now push it back and forth over the corn."

Levi complied, grunting with the effort to roll the stone grinder across the dried kernels. A few minutes later, a grin wreathed his face. "Look! I did it!"

"So you did." The Professor chuckled and ruffled the boy's hair.

"That's fascinating," Melanie said. "I've never seen one of those before." She took another sip of coffee and walked over to get a closer look at some of the other items on display. "What a marvelous collection you have! How long has it taken you to accumulate it all?"

The Professor joined her, and Caleb followed. "I've picked it up one piece at a time over the past twenty years or so." He surveyed the room with a loving eye. "Some would see the life I've chosen as a lonely existence, but it suits me well."

He tilted his head to one side and looked at Caleb. "Local gossip has it that the marshal now knows the identity of the murder victim. Is that true?"

Caleb blinked at the abrupt change of subject, then he gave a sour laugh. "For once, the rumor mill got it right. The man's name was Lucas Weber. It seems he came out here to check on the circumstances surrounding his brother's death. Apparently my uncle had some suspicions and wrote to Mr. Weber about them.

"I didn't know his brother, Charley—hadn't even heard about him dying out here until the marshal filled us in. All that happened before I came to Cedar Ridge."

He looked over and saw Levi arranging a series of arrowheads in a neat row according to size. "Leave those alone, son. They don't belong to you."

The Professor waved away his concern. "What he's doing won't hurt them a bit." He watched Levi for a moment, then added, "I believe you can expect great things from that boy. He has an orderly mind."

Melanie wondered if the Professor saw in Levi a reflection of himself as a child.

The Professor smiled at his guests. "I can't tell you how much I've enjoyed this evening. It is a rare pleasure for me to be able to share my collection with people who can appreciate them."

He ran his fingers along the top of a display case, then turned back to Caleb and Melanie. "I remember Charley Weber."

Melanie stared at him. "You do?"

The Professor nodded. "He was an old mining associate of George and Alvin's."

"That's what the marshal told us," Caleb said. "Funny, but I never heard Uncle Alvin mention him. I'm surprised he didn't say anything about a friend of his dying while visiting, especially if there was any question as to what caused his death."

The Professor tilted his head. "I don't find it odd at all. That fits perfectly with Alvin's character. He wasn't a man to stir up gossip or indulge in idle speculation."

"True." Caleb glanced down at the floor, then turned his

209

gaze back to the Professor. "Do you remember anything about the way Charley died?"

The Professor took a moment to straighten his jacket cuff before answering. "As I recall, he had been here a couple of weeks when he became ill. He seemed to be recuperating nicely, but then he took a turn for the worse and died quite suddenly . . . in his sleep, I believe. His death took everyone by surprise." He narrowed his eyes and stroked his chin. "Or maybe not everyone."

Melanie started. "What do you mean?"

"Don't you see? If Alvin's suspicions were well founded, and Charley Weber was murdered, there was at least one person who expected it." The Professor spoke in a matter-of-fact tone that sent gooseflesh chasing up her arms.

She leaned forward. "But people get sick and die unexpectedly all the time. You said Mr. Weber passed away peacefully in his sleep. He wasn't stabbed or shot or—" she gulped—"hit over the head."

A smile touched the Professor's thin lips. "True, but not every murder involves something so violent . . . or so obvious. Poison, for instance, has been used for centuries."

A long silence followed his statement. Melanie found her voice first. "So you think someone poisoned Charley Weber?"

The Professor shrugged. "Who can be sure? It's certainly one possibility. Anyone who was around him during the time of his illness could have added some substance to his food or drink that would have had the desired effect."

Caleb drew himself up. "If you'll remember, he was staying with my uncle and his partner at the time. I hope you aren't suggesting either of them had anything to do with this?"

The Professor held up his hands. "Not at all. I knew both

George and Alvin well, and I cannot conceive of such a thing. But"—he raised one forefinger—"with him staying in the rooms above the mercantile and so many people passing through on a daily basis, it opens up a wealth of opportunities."

"What did you make of all that?" Melanie asked while Caleb guided the wagon along the road on their way back to town. Silvery moonlight glinted on Levi's hair as he drooped against her side. She circled her left arm around his shoulders.

"He really does seem like some sort of a professor, doesn't he." Caleb chuckled. "Throwing out all those theories and challenging you to come up with a logical solution."

Levi slumped farther down in the wagon seat, coming to rest with his head in Melanie's lap. By the light of the moon, she could tell his eyes were closed, and he appeared to be fast asleep. She smiled and stroked the boy's silky hair with her fingertips.

The wagon jolted as one of the front wheels bounced over a rock in the road. Melanie gripped the edge of the seat with one hand and held Levi steady with the other. The sudden lurch threw Caleb's shoulder hard against hers.

He righted himself and brought the wagon under control, then gave her an apologetic smile. "I'm sorry," he said. Their eyes met and held, and the smile faded from his face.

"Don't apologize. I'm all right." Melanie's voice came out in a breathy whisper. Lowering her head, she readjusted her position as best she could without waking the sleeping child, still able to feel the pressure of Caleb's shoulder against her own. She watched his hands, strong and sure on the reins, then risked a quick glance at his face.

Seeing his eyes focused on the road ahead, she let her gaze linger over his profile, silhouetted in the moonlight. It was a strong face, one she could imagine looking at for the rest of her life.

The thought left her breathless, then she pulled herself together. What was she doing, building up castles in the air?

18

Melanie finished arranging a single place setting of Blush by Blair china on a table in the front window and stepped back to judge the effect. *Beautiful.* The lace tablecloth she had used as a table covering set off the dinner-ware with its rose design and blue highlights to perfection.

Leaning forward, she adjusted the cup and saucer slightly. A shadow fell across the table, and Melanie looked up to see Will Blake watching her through the window. When she smiled, he tipped his hat and came into the store.

Caleb looked up from sorting mail behind the counter when the bell jingled. "Morning, Will." He took a second look and his eyes widened. "Look at you, all spiffed up this morning. What's the occasion?"

Melanie took one last look at her china display and strolled over to join the men at the counter. Will did look different this morning. Now that he had removed his Stetson, she could see that his hair, usually tousled with dark curls tumbling over his forehead, was neatly parted and slicked down, and his strong jaw showed evidence of a recent shave. Instead of his usual work clothes, he was dressed in a crisp white shirt with a string tie at the collar and neatly creased dark trousers. She looked up again at his face with interest, awaiting his reply.

Caleb set the mailbag under the counter and grinned. "The preacher's not in town, so we aren't holding a church service. Nobody has died this week that I know of, so you can't be going to a funeral."

Will grinned back, showing no offense at Caleb's bantering tone. "I'm glad you like the way I look, but you aren't the one I'm trying to impress." He cleared his throat and turned toward Melanie. "I asked the café to pack a basket of food, and I picked it up a few minutes ago. Would you like to join me for a picnic?"

Melanie felt her lips form an O. Out of the corner of her eye, she saw Caleb's mouth drop open. "Why, I . . . I don't know."

She glanced at Caleb, whose mouth was now closed, his lips drawn tight in a thin line, wearing a look similar to the one he'd worn when he'd interrupted Dooley's "proposal."

Melanie looked back at Will. "I have some things I really ought to be doing around the store."

"I'm sure those will keep. Things are usually pretty slow in the middle of the week." Will smiled at Caleb. "Right?"

Caleb grunted. Will apparently took the sound for an assent and nodded at Melanie. "I thought we could take a ride in my rig, and I'd show you a bit of the countryside. Maybe we could go across the creek and eat near the ruins." Crinkles formed at the corners of his eyes when he smiled.

The smile warmed Melanie like sunlight on a spring day, and she felt her interest quicken. The prospect of spending some time outdoors and seeing the ruins she had heard about sounded much more appealing than staying indoors all day. And as Will observed, business was slow at the moment. They'd only had one customer all morning.

She looked at Caleb again. "Would it be all right with you?"

Caleb grunted again, adding a curt nod this time.

Melanie beamed at Will. "Thank you, that sounds like a lovely plan. Just give me a few minutes to run upstairs and change into a different dress."

Will's smile broadened. "You look just fine the way you are. There's a bit of a breeze, though, so you might want to take something to throw over your shoulders in case it cools off later."

Caleb stiffened. "How long are you planning to be gone?"

Will chuckled. "It's a beautiful day. Why rush?"

Melanie laughed, caught up in his lighthearted mood. "All right, let me get a wrap." She hurried to the back room, where she kept a light shawl on a hook. When she turned to go back into the mercantile, she nearly collided with Caleb.

She yelped and took a quick step back, startled by the intensity of his gaze. "What is it?"

His brows formed a straight line above his eyes. "I just don't want you getting the idea that you can go running off anytime you want."

Melanie stared up at him. "But you said it would be all right if I left for a while."

Caleb went on as if she hadn't said a word. "As I told you the other morning, it's the height of folly for you to be off on your own, with a killer on the loose."

"But I won't be on my own. Will is escorting me."

The muscles in Caleb's jaw worked. "And Will is one of the few people I'd let you go off with like this."

Melanie arched her eyebrows. "*Let* me?" She flung the shawl over her shoulders and pushed past him.

Will settled his Stetson back on his head when she reappeared and grinned at Caleb. "We'll see you later." He crooked his elbow at Melanie.

When she accepted his proffered arm, she saw a look pass between the two men but couldn't tell what it meant. She followed Will's lead out to the street, where a gleaming buggy awaited them. She looked up at him in surprise. "We're going in this?"

There was that smile again. "Only the best for a special lady." He helped her up into the buggy, and Melanie arranged her skirt on the tufted leather seats.

Will circled around behind the buggy and swung up beside her, then picked up the reins and set the flashy bay mare in motion with a click of his tongue. People stopped along the boardwalk and stared as they drove by. Melanie returned their nods, feeling a bit self-conscious as she proceeded down the street sitting at the side of a man who thought she was special.

Before long the buildings were behind them, and the buggy rolled across open country. Melanie felt her spirits rise with every turn of the wheels, reveling in the fresh-scented breeze that brushed her face and the sights and smells of nature, all seeming to promise them a glorious afternoon.

She watched the way Will guided the bay mare with strong, sure hands, the economy of motion in his gestures showing his proficiency. She relaxed and leaned back against the padded buggy seat. "Thank you for inviting me. I love working in the store, but I have to admit I enjoy spending time outdoors as much or more."

She sighed and let the buggy's gentle motion ease away

the tension of her odd encounter with Caleb. Looking out over the vast landscape, she said, "How long have you been ranching here?"

Will tugged on the right rein to guide the bay in a gentle curve that brought them alongside a sparkling creek. "I came out from Texas five years ago with a herd of five hundred breeding stock."

Melanie raised her eyebrows. "So many?"

Will smiled. "That's considered a pretty small number in ranching circles. Right now, I'm running around ten thousand head. That's about all I can handle at the moment."

Melanie shook her head. "I can't imagine how you manage to keep up with it all."

The clear whistling calls from a bevy of quail met her ears, and she smiled when she spied their heads bobbing as they scratched beneath the underbrush. The mother quail darted from the undergrowth at the base of a cedar tree, heading toward a low creosote bush with quick, determined strides. The plume on her head bobbed in rhythm with her movements. Six babies, identical to their mother except for size, scurried along behind her.

Melanie laughed, then looked around. "So where are these ruins I've heard about?"

Will pointed off to the left. "Over there. You'll see them in a minute." He turned the buggy in that direction as he spoke, heading straight toward the creek.

Melanie gave a loud gasp, and Will chuckled. "Don't worry. The water's shallow here. We can ford it easily enough."

She watched as they splashed through the flowing water, relieved when she saw it didn't even come up to the level of the wheel hubs. A hundred yards beyond, they reached the base of the cliffs. Will pulled the mare to a halt under a huge sycamore tree at the edge of a large meadow. "Here we are. This is also where we'll have the Founders Day celebration. Plenty of room for races and games out here on this meadow."

He hopped down and circled the buggy. Melanie put her hands on his shoulders and let him help her step down. She scanned the area, looking for piles of broken rocks and rubble from forgotten, tumbledown dwellings. "I still don't see the ruins."

Will grinned. "Well, let's start off with these caves at the base of the hill." He pointed to several round openings along the cliff wall. "Those were used for storage for shocks of corn and other food supplies. But the actual 'houses' are up here." He led her close to the cliff wall and pointed overhead.

Melanie raised her eyes and caught her breath. Fifty feet above them, narrow clay structures resembling a giant swallow's nest clung to the sides of the sheer rock. The mud walls matched the coloring of the cliffs, providing perfect camouflage. No wonder she hadn't noticed them before. Slots in the walls, which apparently served as windows, looked like dark eyes peering down at them.

Melanie stared upward, utterly fascinated. So these were the ruins of the ancient people she had heard about. She shook her head. "What are they like inside? How could the people who lived here even get up to them?" When Will didn't answer, she turned to find he had returned to the buggy and was busy arranging their picnic on a blanket he had already spread on the ground.

She repeated her questions after she'd seated herself on the blanket and filled her plate with fried chicken and two buttery rolls. "And why would anyone want to live on the side of a sheer wall like that?"

Will took a moment to swallow a bite of chicken. "For protection, mainly. Enemies couldn't get at them from above or behind. The only access is from below. And that ties in with your other question about getting up there. They used ladders to climb up to the ledges. They could pull those up if trouble came along. Then there wasn't any way for an attacker to reach them."

Melanie bit into a juicy drumstick, unable to take her eyes off the remarkable sight. "I'm trying to imagine what it would have been like to live that way. What did they do about their children? How could they keep them from tumbling over the edge?"

Will shrugged. "I have no idea. I'm sure they probably lost a number of people that way." Seeing her startled expression, he added, "It's a hard life out here. For them and for us. Nature has a way of keeping all of us on our toes. I'm sure they did what they could to protect their youngsters, though. Just like your parents must have watched over you."

She sighed and crumbled one of the rolls between her fingers. "I'm sure they would have . . . if they'd been able to."

When Will looked at her questioningly, she set the roll aside and moistened her lips. "I was raised by my grandparents. My mother died of typhoid when I was only a year old. I never even knew my father. He was a part of the 79th Ohio Infantry. He left home before I was born, and he fell at the Battle of Peachtree Creek."

Will reached out and covered her hand with his. "That must have been hard, not knowing your parents." He gave her fingers a squeeze and slid his hand away. "I guess life can be difficult, no matter where you live. I know it's different out here than what you're accustomed to, but that doesn't mean it's bad. It's a good life if you learn how to work within nature's boundaries instead of trying to fight against them."

Melanie pondered Will's comment in silence while she ate the rest of her meal. His attitude toward the value of life seemed altogether too indifferent to her, but maybe he was right and that was just the way things were done out west. If she planned to make her home in Cedar Ridge, it appeared that she would have to make some adjustments to her thinking.

They polished off the apple pie—with Will eating two slices. Licking the last crumb from his fingers, he glanced up, and a shadow crossed his face.

"What's wrong?"

"See those dark gray clouds blowing in over the ridge? There's a storm coming. We'd better pack up and head back." He suited his actions to his words as he spoke. "We may not get a heavy rain here, but if there's a downpour upstream, it'll raise the water in the creek until it becomes a torrent, and we'll be caught on this side of the creek."

A glimmer of humor lit his eyes. "Not that I wouldn't like to spend more time with you, but it wouldn't do your reputation any good if we didn't get home until sometime tomorrow."

Melanie felt a blush tinge her cheeks at his teasing. She helped him load the basket and the blanket into the buggy, then climbed aboard.

Will shook the reins, sending the bay mare into a brisk trot. Melanie held fast to the buggy seat as the rig rocked along at a far more rapid pace than when they'd traveled out.

"I really wanted to tell you more about myself," Will said. "I know I like what I see in you, but I wanted to give you a chance to get to know me better. After all, you see Caleb every day."

Melanie twisted around on the seat to get a better look at him. "What is that supposed to mean?"

Will flashed a glance at her, his easy grin fading into a more serious expression. "When two men are interested in the same woman, and one of them has the inside track, the other one needs to take advantage of every opportunity he can find."

Melanie threw back her head and laughed. "You're talking about Caleb? You saw what happened the other day. He's been trying to marry me off to anyone who would have me. He'll do anything to get rid of me so he can have the store back."

A low chuckle rumbled from Will's chest. "And that is my advantage. Caleb is attracted to you, but he hasn't admitted it to himself yet. I want to get my bid in before he wakes up."

They reached the edge of town only moments before the first drops of rain began to fall. Will pulled the buggy up in front of the mercantile, then helped Melanie down and escorted her to the front door. "It doesn't seem very gentlemanly of me to leave in such a rush, but I need to hurry back to my ranch." He turned his face up to scan the sky again. "It may be only a sprinkle now, but from the looks of things, it'll be coming down in buckets before I get home."

He rested his hands lightly on Melanie's shoulders. "Thank you for spending the day with me. I hope we can do this again sometime soon."

Melanie watched him drive away before she entered the store, where Caleb was hunched over a stack of papers spread out on the counter. At the sound of the bell, he looked up long enough to see that it was her, then bent his head down again.

Melanie took off her shawl and shook off the raindrops. "I take it you weren't overwhelmed with customers in my absence?"

Caleb grimaced and ran one hand through his hair. "This is the quietest day we've had since I came here. There have been plenty of people out and about on the street, but none of them have stopped in." He gave Melanie a sharp look as she walked past him toward the back room. "Did you have a nice time?"

"Very nice, thank you," she called back over her shoulder as she replaced her shawl on its hook. She returned to the mercantile and smiled at him. "I had heard about the ruins, but they're very different than what I'd expected."

A shadow at the window caught Melanie's attention, and she looked over to see two women peering inside, studying the display of china. She waited until they looked up, then she smiled and waved. The women only frowned, nudged one another, and hurried off down the boardwalk.

Mystified, she turned to Caleb, who merely shrugged. "See what I mean? It's been like that all day."

19

Melanie stood in the open doorway of the mercantile, looking out onto Lincoln Street. At the far end of the road, she could see a hum of activity as the other businesses in town began to shut down for the day. A handful of customers walked out of O'Shea's Emporium.

A moment later, Mr. O'Shea himself came out to carry some merchandise back inside, ready to close up shop for the evening. Signs boasting rock-bottom prices on staple items festooned his windows, and Melanie had watched a steady stream of shoppers going in and out of the emporium.

She made a face. More customers were leaving O'Shea's establishment than she and Caleb had seen at the mercantile all day. Business had picked up a little over the day she'd gone on her picnic with Will, but it hadn't approached the level they would normally expect for a Friday.

Without shifting her position, she looked over her shoulder at Caleb, who stood flicking a feather duster over already spotless shelves. "Do you want me to go ahead and put the *Closed* sign out?"

"No, we'll stay open until the usual time. You never know, someone might come in at the last minute. We can't afford to lose any business."

Certainly not after the bleak showing we had today. Melanie rubbed her hands along her arms, then marched out to the boardwalk to pick up a keg holding an assortment of brooms. She carried it inside and set it down with a thump.

She went back for a crate filled with scrub brushes and had just reached the doorway when she heard the echo of bootheels on the boardwalk and saw Dooley Hatcher approaching. She smiled and propped the door open for him with her hip. "Hello, Dooley. We were just about to close, but we'll be happy to stay open for you."

To her astonishment, he ducked his head like a turtle pulling into its shell and hurried past without speaking.

Melanie stared in disbelief. What had gotten into him? She stepped inside and let the door swing shut behind her. Was it because of Caleb's moratorium on proposals, or their altercation the other day? No, that couldn't be it. Dooley and his brother had both been in the store since then, seeming to hold no grudge. Today, though, Dooley had acted as if he didn't even know her—the same way nearly everyone else in town had been acting.

She looked at Caleb, seeing by his expression that he'd noticed what had happened. Melanie spread her hands. "Might we have done something to offend the entire town?"

Caleb shrugged. "You'd think so from the way people are acting, but for the life of me, I can't think what it could be."

She didn't know, either, but it must have been something awful for them to be shunned by one of the area's most eccentric characters.

She busied herself drawing the curtains behind the window displays while the mantel clock ticked off the final minutes until closing time. The moment the minute hand reached the twelve, she set the *Closed* sign in the window and locked the door.

Levi crawled out of his fort. "I'm hungry, Papa."

Caleb laid the feather duster on the counter. "Me too. Let's go home and I'll fix some supper."

"Would you like to stay and eat with me?" The words popped out of Melanie's mouth before she realized she was going to say them.

Levi's face brightened. "Could we, Papa? Whatever she's cooking smells really good. That's what's making me hungry."

Caleb sniffed the air appreciatively, then grinned at his son. "It does indeed, but we don't want to be a bother." He raised one eyebrow and looked at Melanie. "Are you sure you have enough to feed all three of us?"

"There's plenty," she assured them. More than enough, she told herself. With time hanging heavy on her hands that afternoon, she had kept herself occupied by puttering in the kitchen, slicing and dicing enough carrots, potatoes, onions, and beef to make enough stew to feed half a dozen hungry people.

"I've made far too much for me to eat by myself. You'd be doing me a favor. I could even whip up some biscuits, if you'd like."

A broad smile stretched Caleb's lips at the mention of biscuits. He winked at Levi. "Say no more. If a couple of hungry men are what you need, we'd be glad to help you out."

While the biscuits baked, Melanie pulled three bowls from the cupboard in the small kitchen and ladled a hearty portion of the rich stew into each one. Where would they all sit? She had been in the habit of carrying her food up to her room and eating at the chair by the window, but that wouldn't be an option tonight. No matter—they would manage somehow. Perhaps they could improvise stools and eat perched at the counter.

She closed her eyes and inhaled the mingled aromas of beef stew, biscuits, and brewing coffee. She hoped Caleb and Levi were as hungry as they claimed. Even if their appetites lagged, the savory smells coming from the kitchen ought to help stir them up.

She opened the oven door and pulled out a pan of flaky golden biscuits. It would be a simple meal but a pleasant one, a way to boost their spirits after such a discouraging day.

Melanie pulled off her apron and hung it on the nail by the kitchen door, then smoothed her hair back with both hands and patted it into place, hoping she looked presentable for their impromptu dinner party.

She loaded the bowls of stew and mugs of steaming coffee onto a tray and carried it out into the store. When she reached the doorway, she stopped short, and a delighted smile spread across her face. While she had been busy in the kitchen, Caleb and Levi had moved several of her display tables out of the way to clear a cozy space between the potbellied stove and the fabric shelves. A makeshift table—which on closer inspection proved to be a door borrowed from their stock of building supplies and balanced atop two small barrels—was draped with a tablecloth that bore a suspicious resemblance to a canvas ground cloth.

Two chairs that usually sat out on the boardwalk in front

of the mercantile flanked the table, along with the stepladder, which she assumed would serve as Levi's seat for the evening. Caleb and Levi stood on the far side of the table. Caleb's hand rested on Levi's shoulder, and both of them wore identical expressions of boyish pride. Caleb had even started a fire in the potbellied stove. Melanie could hear the firewood sputter and crackle as it burned, sending tendrils of warmth out into the room.

"What a transformation! It's almost like having a proper dining room." She set the bowls and mugs on the table and went back to the kitchen for the biscuits. When she returned, Caleb helped her into her seat with a flourish. Melanie noticed Levi eyeing the coffee and frowned. "Oh dear. Let me go get you a glass of water."

Caleb pushed his chair back. "Wait, I have an idea." He went over to one of the shelves and came back with a bottle of ginger ale. Levi's eyes glowed as he watched his father open the bottle and set it in front of him. Caleb smiled at the boy's excitement. "Enjoy it, son. It's a special treat for a special occasion."

They bowed their heads while Caleb asked the blessing on their meal. The moment the prayer ended, Levi scooped up a spoonful of stew and popped it into his mouth. "Mmm . . . this is good!"

Caleb tilted his head. "Are you sure?"

Melanie blinked. He'd seemed eager enough to sample her cooking earlier. Had something put him off? She watched him take a taste and saw his eyes widen in feigned surprise.

"Mmm . . . you're right!" He grinned at Levi and gave Melanie a conspiratorial wink. The flush that crept up her neck at his smile warmed her more than the woodstove.

They ate their meal with few words, and Melanie was glad she didn't feel pressured to keep a conversation going. The silence was a comfortable one, giving her a feeling of companionship she'd long gone without.

Levi started yawning over his second bowl of stew and asked if he could be excused. He wandered over to the basket where he kept his soldiers and started setting up a battle between two troops of them. Before long, he lay stretched out on the floor beside his toys. Moments later, he was sound asleep.

Caleb scooted his chair back and stretched his arms wide. "I guess I'd better go put a blanket over him. . . ." He glanced over at Melanie. "Unless you'd rather I just take him home now."

"No, please stay. I'm enjoying the visit."

Caleb lifted Levi so Melanie could spread a blanket on the floor, then he laid the boy back down again and wrapped the other side of the blanket over his sleeping son. The way the little boy's eyelashes fanned across his cheeks and the sounds of his steady breathing tugged at Melanie's heart.

She and Caleb settled back in their chairs and listened to the fire crackle. With Caleb looking as comfortable and relaxed as she'd ever seen him, leaning back with his feet stretched out toward the potbellied stove, and Levi asleep near their feet, the scene took on a homey atmosphere . . . almost as if they were a family.

The thought caught her up short. Maybe she was getting *too* comfortable. She straightened in her chair, determined to corral her wayward thoughts and bring them back to safer topics.

She took a sip of her coffee, then set the cup down on the improvised table. "I've been meaning to discuss something with you, and after today's dearth of customers, this seems like a good time to do it. I've been thinking of some new ways we could advertise—"

Caleb raised his hand, cutting her off. "Let's not spoil the evening." He turned his head slightly and gave her a wry grin, adding, "We can always get back to arguing tomorrow. For now, let's relax and— Wait a minute. I know just the thing."

He rose and went over to one of the shelves and returned with the music box in his hands. After moving their bowls aside to clear a space in the middle of the table, he wound the key and set the box down with care. Then he lifted the lid and slid the lever inside to the right. The mechanism whirred, then the cylinder began to rotate and a tinkling melody filled the air.

Melanie's heart quickened when she recognized the tune. "'Liebestraum.' That was one of my grandmother's favorite pieces. She used to play it on her piano when I was a little girl." She leaned her head against the back of the chair and let the music sweep her away, back to a time when she felt safe . . . protected . . . loved.

Closing her eyes, she could envision the way she used to bob and pirouette to the music while her grandmother's fingers moved nimbly across the ivory keys. When she opened her eyes again, she saw a glimmer of amusement in Caleb's eyes and realized she had been swaying in her chair, as though dancing again in her grandparents' parlor.

Her cheeks flamed when she thought how foolish she must have appeared. But Caleb didn't seem put off in the least. Instead, he stretched out his hand and bowed. "Would you care to dance?"

"Here? Now?" She studied his face. Was he making fun of

her? His smile was still in place, but it was a kind, inviting smile, not a mocking one. Wordlessly, she let him help her to her feet and placed her left hand on his shoulder.

His steps were light and sure as he waltzed her around the small open area of their "dining room." The touch of his fingers on hers and the warmth of his hand at her waist sent a tingle from her neck to her toes. She stared into his eyes, wondering if he felt it, as well.

Their feet glided across the floor in unison with the music, slowing as the mechanism wound down and coming to a rest as the last notes faded away. She could feel Caleb's pulse under her fingertips, matching the beat of her own heart. They stood together in the silence—not moving, not speaking, just staring into each other's eyes.

Caleb licked his lips and tilted his head down. "Melanie?" His voice sounded husky in the stillness.

"Yes?"

He caught his breath, and she heard him swallow.

"I think it's time for Levi and me to go home."

20

Melanie looked out the front window and sighed. Another slow morning, and this one a Saturday, usually their busiest day of the week. With all her routine chores out of the way, the lack of activity left her with unaccustomed time on her hands. Time enough to notice the way Caleb's hair curled near the edge of his collar as he bent over the ledger he'd been working on all morning. Time to wonder what it would feel like to weave her fingers through those soft, sand-colored waves.

The object of her daydreaming looked up at that moment and met her eyes, and she averted her gaze. Neither of them had spoken about their waltz to the tune from the music box the night before, and she couldn't decide whether that made her feel relieved or sorry. She had lain awake long after blowing out her lamp, reliving the warmth of Caleb's hand on her waist and the feeling of security his arms gave her as he swung her around the floor. It had felt as if they fit together perfectly. And the name of the piece they danced to couldn't have been more suited to the magic of that moment: "Liebestraum"—"Dream of Love." Her breath whispered out on a fluttering sigh.

What about Caleb? That was the question that plagued her through much of the night. Had he felt the same way, or did he now consider his impulsive invitation to dance a mistake?

The bell jingled—finally—just before noon. Melanie looked up with a smile of welcome when she saw Marshal Hooper, but her smile quickly faded at the sight of his grim expression.

The lawman walked over to the table where Caleb was working. "I'm afraid I'm going to have to impose on you."

Caleb got to his feet and raised his eyebrows in a silent question.

"I've been talking to people around town, trying to get any information I can about Charley and Lucas Weber—who might have talked to them, who might know anything about what happened to either one of them."

The marshal glanced toward the window. "Folks are starting to get scared, and there's been a lot of talk." He looked back at Caleb. "You've probably heard plenty of it already from your customers."

Caleb grimaced. "We haven't exactly been overwhelmed with customers lately, so I'm afraid we're in the dark."

"Rumors are flying, and I've seen what that can lead to. There's no telling what a group of people will do once they get spooked, and I don't want a lynch mob on my hands." The lawman hooked one thumb behind his gun belt. "I figure it's best to get things out in the open in front of everyone all at once, so I want to hold a town meeting. I'd like to use your store."

"Of course. When do you want to hold it?"

"Tonight. Right after closing, if that's all right with you."

Melanie saw the look of surprise that flashed across Caleb's face, but he nodded his agreement. "That won't be a problem. I'll be glad to do it."

"Thanks. I thought I could count on you. I need to go out now and spread the word. I'll send a couple men over this afternoon to help you set things up."

Melanie exchanged a look with Caleb after the marshal left the store. "A lynch mob?" Involuntarily, her hand reached up to press against her throat.

Caleb's smile didn't quite reach his eyes. "I'm hoping that was an exaggeration, but if wild stories are circulating around town, a town meeting would be a good way to help calm everyone's nerves. When people get upset, they can stir up a lot of gossip and do crazy things. This way, he'll not only be able to let the whole town know what's going on, but also make sure the word that's spreading around is based on truth rather than rumor."

Melanie nodded. "It makes sense when you put it like that." She caught her breath. "Caleb . . . he said people have been talking. If everyone knows now that the two men were brothers and assume their deaths have some connection with the store, maybe that's why they've been staying away."

Caleb looked pensive, then nodded. "You may have something there. That could explain a lot."

"But it doesn't make any sense. That would mean . . ." Melanie caught her breath. "They can't think we had anything to do with it, can they?"

Caleb chuckled. "I don't see how they could. Charley Weber died before I arrived in Cedar Ridge, and I've been here longer than you. Neither one of us had even heard of him before the marshal told us about him." He paused a moment, and his smile faded. "On the other hand, there's no accounting for the wild ideas people can come up with when they need answers and can't find any. Let's pray the marshal's meeting puts all this to rest."

Melanie pondered Caleb's words while she straightened a stack of canned goods. The more she thought about it, the more certain she felt that her theory about their sudden lack of customers had merit. And if that was the case, having the meeting in the mercantile could serve a dual purpose—to disseminate information and to help people feel comfortable about coming back in the store again.

By the time people began filtering into the store that evening, the general air of tension, the nervous glances, the murmurs that fell silent whenever she or Caleb walked by, made Melanie feel more certain than ever that her assumption was correct.

The sight of so many people packed onto the benches reminded her of the church service before Lucas Weber's funeral. But this time, instead of Pastor Dunstan, it was the marshal who got up to speak.

The murmurs died down as he took his place in the front of the assembly and stared around, looking into each face. "Folks, we all wanted to believe that Lucas Weber was killed by someone who was just passing through Cedar Ridge—maybe even someone Weber had been traveling with—who killed him here and kept on going. To be honest, I hoped that was the case myself."

His face grew stern. "But that was before I received a letter from his widow, letting me know not only who he was, but why he'd come here. He was Charley Weber's brother, and he was here to look into Charley's death. And it appears he may have had good reason for thinking there was something suspicious about the way his brother died. Now it seems we've had not one, but two murders here in Cedar Ridge, and they're connected in some way."

A buzz of conversation swept over the crowd.

On the far side of the room, Thomas O'Shea got to his feet. "This store is how they're connected. Charley was staying here, and his brother was killed on the back steps." He planted his hands on his hips and scanned the faces in the crowd. "Seems like all it takes to be murdered around here is to come to the mercantile. If you ask me, we're all taking a risk just being here."

A ripple of murmurs met his statement. O'Shea's skinny chest puffed up, and he opened his mouth to speak again.

The marshal shut him down with a glare. "You're out of order, O'Shea. I'm the one running this meeting." He cleared his throat and began to speak again. "Since those deaths occurred several months apart, I have to assume the person—or persons—responsible is still around."

From her vantage point at the rear of the building, Melanie could see the others looking around, eyeing their fellow townspeople with a dawning of suspicion.

The marshal continued. "I'm doing everything I can to find out who's responsible for these deaths, but until that is known, you all need to be aware that this person is dangerous. You need to be careful.

"And if anyone has information about either of these men,

or knows something that could shed light on what happened to them, I want you to come see me without delay. No matter how trivial or meaningless it may seem to you, it might be just the thing I need to put all the pieces together and solve this case." The lawman nodded. "Thank you for coming. That's all I have to say."

Wendell Trask, whose land office stood next door to O'Shea's Emporium, waved his hand. "Why are you only talking about the Weber brothers? Those aren't the only deaths we've had around here lately."

Melanie stiffened as a fresh wave of whispers swept through the room.

Marshall Hooper scowled and pointed to the speaker. "What are you talking about, Wendell?"

The land promoter stood and thrust out his chest. "I'm talking about George Ross and Alvin Nelson, two of our own who lived right here in Cedar Ridge . . . and they sure as shootin' had a connection with this store."

A connection with the store. Caleb tossed from side to side in his bed, unable to stem the echo of the words that had been running through his mind ever since he heard them at the meeting.

Could there be any truth to the notion that the mercantile had some link to the recent deaths? On the surface, the idea sounded like the ravings of a madman. But Marshal Hooper hadn't dismissed it out of hand, as Caleb expected. And judging by the reactions of the townspeople, they hadn't discounted it, either. It looked as if Melanie had been right about the reason for their business slacking off.

But it didn't make any sense. Caleb laced his fingers behind his head, trying to sort through his churning thoughts. He had heard stories of the Wild West throughout his growing-up years—tales of Indian raids and range wars. But the great migration of people moving into the West in recent years had brought civilization along with it. Such things belonged to the past.

Or so he'd thought. If he had believed for one moment that kind of danger still existed out here, or that it could strike so close to home, he never would have considered moving to Cedar Ridge with Levi.

But whether he wanted to believe it or not, people had been murdered. Strangers, though—people totally unfamiliar to him . . . until Wendell Trask brought up the possibility that George and Alvin's deaths might not have been due to natural causes.

Tossing the sheet back, he rolled out of bed and began pacing the dark bedroom, careful not to wake Levi, slumbering away in his little cot. Caleb had been with Alvin during his illness, was sitting at his bedside when he died. He hadn't noticed anything questionable then, but could he have missed something? Could someone have murdered his kindly uncle? Or Melanie's cousin? Bile rose into his throat at the thought. But now that the possibility had been raised, it had to be faced.

Assuming it might be true, then why? Caleb knew the mercantile better than anyone else in town, having spent practically every waking moment there for the past four months. He knew for a fact there was nothing about the store that would drive anyone to murder. The idea was simply ludicrous. And yet, people around town seemed willing to accept it as the truth.

Caleb scrubbed his palms across his cheeks. It seemed absurd to think that anything related to the store could be worth killing for. But absurd or not, somebody thought there was.

And Melanie was over there. Alone.

More restless than ever, Caleb went out into the parlor and looked out the window toward the mercantile. He could see no shadows lurking in the darkness, but a glow of light spilled out into the alley from the second floor. It looked as if Melanie couldn't sleep, either.

Worry knotted Caleb's stomach. Was she all right? She had a gift for puzzling things out. Had she put two and two together and reached the same conclusions he had? If so, she must be frightened out of her wits.

And maybe not without reason. If Trask's wild assertion was true, if there truly was some connection between the store and the murders . . . how safe was Melanie?

The question gnawed at him. His feelings had undergone a drastic change from their early days together, when he'd wanted to send her packing. Now he hoped the fear raised by the killings didn't prompt her to pack up and leave on her own.

Her presence made the store a better place, and he had to admit some of her crazy ideas had paid off. She seemed to have a knack for enticing people into the mercantile and persuading them to stretch their purchases beyond what they had intended.

He stared at the glow of light, remembering the feeling of holding her in his arms last night when they'd danced. The smoothness of her skin and the soft touch of her breath upon his cheek. He hadn't felt that kind of connection with another person since Corinna died, and he wasn't certain he

238

was ready to feel it again. He shoved his fingers through his hair. Was this new connection between them a blessing from above or a danger he should run away from?

Maybe flight was the best option. Not physically leaving Cedar Ridge, but distancing himself emotionally, being content to have her as a partner in business, nothing more. But he didn't want to run away. The realization struck him like a heavy weight.

And he didn't want her to make a run for it, either.

If that was the case, he would have to find some way to make the store secure and give her peace of mind about staying there on her own. New locks, certainly. Maybe bars to drop across both of the building's doors. He would see to that first thing in the morning.

In the meantime, though, he felt a responsibility to make sure she had locked the doors and was safe for the night.

He stepped back into the bedroom and pulled on his clothes. After checking to be sure that Levi was fast asleep on his little cot, Caleb slipped out the door into the alley that ran between his house and the store. He locked the door behind him, something he never did when just stepping out for a short time. But tonight was different.

He crossed the alley with quick, sure strides, but his steps dragged when he neared the back stoop of the mercantile. Now that he'd come that far, what should he do next? The key to the back door rested in his pocket, but if he opened the door and called upstairs, he ran the risk of scaring her to death—or of finding out she had already armed herself with something more substantial than a broom.

Stepping down off the stoop, he looked around for inspiration and saw the pebbles scattered across the surface of the alley, illuminated by the moonlight. Bending down, he scooped up a handful of the small rocks and flung one at Melanie's window.

Nothing happened. He raised his arm, ready to throw again, when he saw the curtain move.

Melanie's face peered out cautiously through the slit between the curtain panels. He waved to catch her attention. The moment she spotted him, she pushed the curtain to one side so she could raise the window and lean out over the sill. "Caleb? What's wrong?"

"Nothing." He kept his voice low. "I just wanted to let you know I'm coming inside." He trotted up the back steps and let himself in with his key, then locked the door behind him.

Melanie stood at the foot of the stairs, holding the oil lamp in her hand. She peered up at him, her face anxious in the lamplight. "What's the matter? Has something happened?"

Taking the lamp from her, he set it on the counter, where its soft glow bathed them in a circle of golden light. Caleb took in the sight of her, at the bare toes peeping out from under the hem of her wrapper and the trusting expression on her face. His breath left his lungs.

Melanie stepped toward him and laid her hand on his arm. "Caleb?"

The heat from her fingertips seemed to sear right through the fabric of his shirtsleeve. He tried to swallow, his throat suddenly dry. Maybe coming to the mercantile hadn't been such a good idea after all.

He took a deep breath and cleared his throat. "I saw the light in your window. I just wanted to make sure you were all right."

A tender smile lit Melanie's face in a way that threatened

to undo him. "That's kind of you, but I'm fine, really. I just couldn't sleep."

"I thought you might be worried about what Wendell Trask said at the meeting. I wanted you to know I'll be watching out for you. Remember, I'm just a moment away. If there's any problem, all you need to do is shout, and I'll be here."

A sheen of tears filmed her eyes. "Thank you," she whispered. "I appreciate that."

Caleb leaned toward her like a moth drawn to a flame. More than anything at that moment, he wanted to take her in his arms and shield her from all harm. But if he stayed any longer, they both might face danger of a different kind.

Summoning up all his resolve, he pulled away and edged toward the back door. "Tomorrow I'm going to do everything I can to make the store more secure. To begin with, I'll put new locks and drop bars on both doors. I don't ever want you to have to be afraid."

"That would be a comfort." Melanie padded toward him in her bare feet. "Can I fix something for you before you leave? Some chamomile tea, perhaps, to help you sleep?" She half turned toward the kitchen, and the neck of her wrapper slipped a few inches to one side. Caleb's gaze fastened on the creamy smoothness where her neck and shoulder met.

As much as he wanted to stay, Caleb recognized that accepting her offer would mean treading on dangerous ground—ground that threatened to crumble beneath him at any moment. It took all the willpower he possessed to shake his head. "No, thanks. I'd better leave."

He turned quickly to the door and fumbled to open it in the darkness. Stepping out onto the back stoop, he pulled the door shut behind him and drew in a breath of cool night air.

241

He inserted the key into the keyhole and twisted the lock. Then he stood for a moment, resting his forehead against the smooth wood.

The floorboards squeaked, and he heard Melanie's soft voice through the door. "Thank you for checking on me. Sleep well, and I'll see you in the morning."

Caleb pulled in a ragged breath and turned his steps toward home. Sleep was going to be a long time coming.

21

"Three lanterns." Melanie checked the count against the list in her hand, clicked her tongue, and penciled a quick note.

Caleb emerged from the back room, carrying a bag of flour over one shoulder. He shot a curious glance in her direction. "What are you doing?"

"Did you realize we have three of these big barn lanterns on this wall?" She tapped the list with her pencil for emphasis.

Caleb set the bag down next to the flour barrel. A cloud of fine white dust puffed up around him. He brushed off his sleeve and shrugged. "Nothing surprising about that. We've had those ever since I came here."

"Exactly. I've been going over our inventory and comparing it to the orders Cousin George and your uncle made over the past couple of years." She pointed to the lanterns. "We still have those three left, out of the five they originally ordered well over a year ago."

Caleb ripped the stitching along the top of the flour bag

243

and upended it into the barrel. "That's a good thing, isn't it? We have them on hand in case anyone wants to buy one."

Melanie tapped the toe of her shoe against the floor. "You're missing my point. They have just been collecting dust. Nobody is interested in them. They're taking up space we ought to be filling with merchandise people are more willing to buy."

Caleb shook the last of the flour into the barrel and folded the empty bag over his arm. He gave Melanie a wary look. "Such as?"

Finally the opening she had been waiting for. "I'm glad you asked. I've started a list of items I think will prove to be quite popular." She pointed to a sheet of paper on the counter.

Caleb walked over and picked up the page, already half filled with writing. His eyes grew round. "This is only the beginning of your list?"

She nodded. "We need to bring in more profit, and I believe introducing a wider variety of goods will be a good way to do it."

Caleb scanned the list again and ran his free hand through his hair, leaving a streak of flour across his forehead. Melanie braced herself, waiting for the inevitable objection. Instead he returned to the back room, still carrying the flour bag.

Melanie smiled, pleased at this indication that he was beginning to accept the idea of having her as a full partner. She went back to her inventory, checking it against the items on the next shelf. Even though Caleb obviously had his doubts, she felt sure her idea was a good one. Business had improved somewhat during the week since the town meeting, but it still hadn't returned to their usual level of sales. Thank goodness for loyal customers like Mrs. Fetterman, the Professor, Micah

Rawlins, and Andrew Bingham, who refused to be swayed by idle speculation. Broadening the store's inventory while keeping their staple items in stock should go a long way toward helping to bring back the rest of their customers, and maybe draw in some new ones.

And, she reminded herself, the circuit rider was due to arrive the next day. Seeing the store crowded for another worship service would surely help the townspeople overcome their newfound reluctance to set foot across the mercantile's threshold.

She hummed as she worked, feeling more rested than she had in days. Since Caleb changed the locks and put drop bars on both the doors a week ago, she had been sleeping much better. A smile curved her lips at the memory of his late-night visit. She couldn't have been more astonished when the pebble had rattled against her window and she'd discovered him standing outside, concerned for her well-being. It had been a long time since someone had watched out for her like that.

The bell over the front door jingled, and her spirits soared when Lena Andrews stepped inside. Melanie hadn't seen the town's dressmaker in the store in over a week. She gave the woman her brightest smile. "Good afternoon, Mrs. Andrews. What can I get for you today?"

Instead of answering, the woman fidgeted near the front door, darting anxious glances around the store's interior. "I need a bolt of muslin, please. And three yards of that blue calico." She edged a few steps farther inside, while Melanie set her checklist on the counter and pulled the bolts of fabric from the shelf.

Melanie watched from under her lashes as she unrolled the bolt of calico on the fabric table and prepared to measure out the requested yardage. What was wrong with the woman? She looked positively agitated.

Melanie offered another smile while she spread the calico out and smoothed it with her hand. "We're having beautiful weather," she said in a soothing tone. "Don't you love the smell of fruit trees in blossom?"

Mrs. Andrews ducked her head in a quick nod. She inched her way over to the table and watched Melanie cut the fabric. She flicked another glance around the store, then took a deep breath and leaned across the table. At that moment, Caleb walked in from the storeroom. Melanie grinned when she saw he still had a streak of white powder on his hair and forehead.

"Have you seen that ball of cotton twine?" he asked. "I thought it was on the shelf next to the wrapping paper, but I can't find it."

"Check under the counter," Melanie told him. "I used it to tie up a parcel for Mrs. Fetterman."

He retrieved the twine and nodded his thanks, then smiled at their customer. "Good to see you, Mrs. Andrews."

Instead of answering, the dressmaker shrank away and shifted her position to face the opposite direction.

Melanie folded the calico and pushed it across the table along with the bolt of muslin, staring at her customer with growing concern. "Is something the matter?"

Mrs. Andrews picked up the bolt of muslin and the cut length of calico and held them close against her chest. Then she leaned forward and pointed toward the door where Caleb had disappeared. "You seem like a nice young woman, so I thought I ought to warn you."

Melanie caught her breath in a quick gasp. "Warn me? About what?"

Mrs. Andrews looked over her shoulder. "Not what . . . *who*." She jabbed her finger toward the storeroom again. "There's something funny about this store and all the goings-on here. Those two brothers being killed was bad enough, but now it looks like someone may have done in George and Alvin, as well. Who's the one who stood to gain from that, I ask you? Who inherited this store? You'd best be on your guard—you could be next." She spun around and scuttled out of the store before Melanie could say a word.

Melanie was still staring at the door when Caleb returned carrying a parcel wrapped in brown paper and tied up with twine. She looked at him, wondering what on earth Lena Andrews could have been talking about.

The bell rang again, announcing the arrival of Micah Rawlins. He gave Melanie a genial nod, then crossed over to stand next to Caleb. "Have you heard about the town meeting?"

Caleb set the parcel down. "Another one? When?"

"This evening."

"No, Marshal Hooper hasn't said a word to me about it." Caleb folded his arms. "I'm glad you let me know. I still have time to get things moved around and set up in here."

Micah shuffled his feet and looked away. "It isn't going to be here, Caleb. They're having it down at O'Shea's."

Caleb's mouth fell open. "That doesn't make any sense. We have twice the room."

"Well, you know how people talk. I guess some of them aren't comfortable coming here, considering . . . well, you know." Micah edged toward the door. "Well, I'd best be on my way. I hate being the bearer of bad tidings, but I wanted to be sure you knew what was going on."

When the door swung shut behind him, Melanie walked

247

over to join Caleb. "Considering what? What was that all about?"

Caleb's mouth set in a grim line. "I don't know, but we're going to be at that meeting tonight, and we'll find out."

By the time they closed up shop for the day and walked down Lincoln Street to O'Shea's Emporium at the far end of town, the meeting was already underway, with Marshal Hooper trying to stanch the flow of questions being thrown his way.

There were nearly as many people inside the emporium as had been in the mercantile the night of the first town meeting, and those who found a place to sit were perched on crates, barrels, kegs—any available surface. The rest fit in wherever they could, standing shoulder to shoulder. Caleb held the door for Melanie, and they managed to squeeze inside. Micah Rawlins waved from a spot against the back wall and moved over as much as he could to make room for them. Glad that Mrs. Fetterman had volunteered to keep Levi at her home during the meeting, Melanie took her place beside Caleb. She turned her attention to the front of the room.

The marshal's face deepened to a dangerous shade of red. "I called this meeting to try to set some things straight, not to be harangued by a passel of tomfool questions. Now, simmer down, all of you. The sooner you let me speak, the sooner you can all be on your way and go home to your supper."

The rumble of dissent died down, ending altogether once the lawman sent a stern look from one side of the room to the other. "Rumors have been flying left and right over the past week, and I'm here to tell you that it has to stop. From what I've heard, some of you think that because there haven't been any arrests yet, it means I haven't been doing my job, and maybe I should be replaced."

Melanie's eyes widened.

Mayor Pike stood up from his seat at the front of the room and took a stance near the marshal. He turned to face the crowd and tucked his thumbs beneath the lapels of his jacket, as if getting ready to make a political speech.

"Fellow citizens," he began, "I want to assure you that I have complete trust in Marshal Hooper, and I am certain he is doing everything in his power to bring the perpetrator to justice. As you know, the safety of Cedar Ridge and its people has always been the highest priority of my—"

"Thank you, Mayor." Marshal Hooper stepped forward. "I appreciate the vote of confidence, especially in light of what I'm going to say next."

The mayor's face turned a dusky red. Returning to his seat beside his wife, he dropped back into his chair with a loud *harrumph*.

The marshal went on as though there hadn't been an interruption. "I've heard talk that some of you want to form a vigilance committee and take care of the situation yourselves. The last I heard, Arizona Territory was still a part of these United States. That means everyone—man or woman—is innocent until proven guilty in a court of law. Let me tell you right now, if any of you decide to go off half-cocked and take the law into your own hands, you'll be the ones who'll find yourselves arrested and facing charges."

An angry buzz broke out, as if someone had stirred up a hive of bees.

Wendell Trask stood and raised his voice to be heard above

the rest. "Then you'd better get the job done faster, Marshal. We just want to protect our families."

"I understand that, Wendell. But what you need to understand is that bringing criminals to justice is my job. And I'll get it done a whole lot faster if I don't have to deal with a bunch of interference from hotheads like you."

Rance Yeary, the saloonkeeper at the Silver Moon, stood up and thrust out his chin. "What exactly are you doing to keep this town safe? People are getting afraid to go out after dark anymore, and I'm losing customers because of it."

Melanie grimaced. She knew exactly how he felt.

Wendell Trask pushed his way forward through the crowd. "Some of us have been talking, Marshal. Things like murder don't happen without a reason. It seems to me that one of the questions you ought to be asking is why anyone would want to kill these men. Who stands to benefit by getting them out of the way?"

Marshal Hooper nodded. "Fair enough. All right, since we're all together, let me just ask all of you right now: Who stood to gain by Charley Weber's death? Is there anybody here who can shed some light on that?"

A man Melanie didn't recognize spoke up from the far side of the emporium. "Not many of us here were acquainted with him—at least, not before he came here. The only people he knew before he showed up in Cedar Ridge were George and Alvin."

Melanie sucked in her breath and shot a quick glance at Caleb, who looked just as shocked as she felt. Had her cousin and Caleb's uncle just gone from being thought of as possible murder victims to suspected killers? The idea was outrageous.

She waved her arm to catch the marshal's attention. "Just a minute!"

The man went on without paying her the least bit of attention. "And why stop with Charley? This may have started with him, but what about his brother? Who benefited by having him out of the way?"

Wendell Trask snorted. "Use your head. That's the only thing that makes sense. Whoever did Charley in didn't want anyone discovering what he'd done."

Micah raised his voice, "But that doesn't make a lick of sense—not if you're trying to say that George or Alvin had something to do with the first murder. They were both long gone by the time Weber's brother showed up."

Rance Yeary spoke up. "Forget the Webers for a minute. Let's ask the same question about George and Alvin. Is anyone better off having them out of the way? Who stood to benefit after they were gone?"

Every head in the emporium turned in unison. Every pair of eyes stared straight at Caleb and Melanie.

"Hold on!" Caleb stood rigid, his face as red as the mayor's had been only moments before. "That's crazy talk. Miss Ross and I are God-fearing people. What you're suggesting, that we had anything to do with the deaths of our relatives, is absolutely—"

"But who else stood to gain?" Rance Yeary jabbed his finger straight at Caleb. "You two are the only ones."

A stunned silence followed this pronouncement.

Then everyone seemed to speak at once.

"That's enough." Marshal Hooper's voice cut across the hubbub like the lash of a whip. "What we need is facts, not rumors and speculation. If nobody has any constructive information that will add to my investigation, it's time for you all to go on your way. Just remember what I said—you're paying me to do this job, so stay out of my way and let me handle it." He turned his head from one side of the room to the other, leveling a stern look at every person there. "And if anyone has ideas of forming a vigilance committee, know this: You will answer to the law for any illegal actions."

Melanie slumped back against the wall and watched the people mill around. Some collected in small, chattering groups, while others left the store. Those who departed scooted past Melanie and Caleb without speaking, or even looking at them.

She looked up at Caleb, struggling to find her voice. "What just happened?"

Micah shook his head sorrowfully. "Sorry about that, you two. I knew there were some whispers going around, but I had no idea anyone would take it this far, trumpeting a lot of nonsense out in public like that." He gripped Caleb's shoulder. "You know what it's like once people start talking. Trying to put a stop to it is like trying to rein in a runaway horse."

From the look on his face, Melanie suspected Caleb couldn't decide whether he wanted to crawl in a hole or start swinging his fists. He shook his head. "This isn't just idle talk, Micah. They're talking vigilantism. That's mob action, and there's no talking your way out once something like that takes hold."

Micah looked Caleb squarely in the face. "I don't think it will come to that. I'm fairly sure it will all settle down before too long. Besides, no one who knows either one of you would believe you could be involved in anything like this."

Marshal Hooper made his way through the crowd and stood before their little group, one hand resting on his holster.

He gestured back at the muttering crowd. "I never intended for things to take that kind of turn. I want you to know I'll do all I can to keep things under control."

Melanie put her hands on her hips and glared at him. "It seems to me the best way to do that is to find out who is responsible."

"I'm working on that, believe me." The marshal lifted his hat, then settled it back on his head. "I have to admit I've had more experience with rustlers and bar fights than anything like this."

His expression hardened, and he leveled a steely look at them both. "However crazy some of this talk may sound, I have to take it all under consideration. And while I may be slow at puzzling things out, I'm an expert tracker. So until this is settled, don't either one of you plan on leaving town." He turned on his heel and strode out the door.

Melanie clung to Caleb's arm, feeling as if she'd just had the breath knocked out of her.

He covered her hand with his. "Are you all right?"

After someone just implied we both are suspected of murdering our relatives? Of course I'm not all right. Aloud, she said, "I think I'm ready to go back to the store."

Caleb nodded. He turned to Micah. "We'll see you later. I appreciate you standing by us."

As they turned to leave, Melanie heard a woman's voice whisper, "But they seem so nice. You don't really think they had anything to do with this, do you?"

Ophelia Pike's voice rang out clearly. "Appearances aren't always what they seem."

Melanie turned to see the mayor's wife facing a small group of women, with her back to Melanie and Caleb.

"Just the other night," Mrs. Pike went on, "my husband was coming home late, and he saw something quite disturbing. Caleb Nelson was standing out in the alley behind the mercantile, throwing gravel up at her window."

Her announcement brought a round of scandalized giggles.

The woman who'd spoken first frowned. "That doesn't mean he's guilty of anything but being interested in her."

Caleb stopped to talk to Rafe Sutton. Melanie pulled away and moved closer to the group so she could hear better.

Mrs. Pike sniffed. "Don't be naïve, Nettie. They may have arrived here separately, but who's to say they didn't know each other before coming to Cedar Ridge? Maybe Rance Yeary has a point. What if they planned all this in advance?"

A gasp ran around the circle.

Mrs. Pike wasn't finished yet. "But that isn't the whole story. After he threw the gravel at her window, she came down to let him in . . . wearing only her nightclothes."

"No!" The other woman pressed a hand to her lips.

Mrs. Pike went on, a note of triumph in her voice. "Does that sound like the innocent actions of near strangers to you?"

"You mean they're in it together?" Lena Andrews bristled with indignation. "Well, I never! And to think I tried to do her a service by warning her about him!"

A gray-haired woman waved her hand for attention. "I don't see the sense in that. Why would anyone go to those lengths for a mercantile? It isn't like it's going to make either of them rich."

"And that isn't all." Mrs. Pike went on as though the other woman hadn't spoken. "How many of you were out on the street the other day when she flew to the Nelson boy's defense after he attacked the marshal?"

Two of the ladies raised their hands. The others leaned forward, with their lips parted.

"Did you hear what the boy said when he ran to her?" Mrs. Pike paused for effect. "He called her Mama." She let that bombshell sink in before she added, "Ladies, I believe it is possible that she is the boy's mother."

Melanie felt her face flame. Despite Micah's assurance to the contrary, it was obviously all too easy for people to believe the worst about them. She bit her lips to hold back a groan. The situation wasn't just a bad one—it was worse than they'd feared.

She couldn't let such a contemptible lie go unchallenged. Straightening her shoulders, she stepped forward, ready to defend her and Caleb's honor. At the same instant, Ophelia Pike turned around and spotted Melanie.

The mayor's wife drew herself up and sniffed. "Come, ladies. Let's be going."

At the sight of the icy stares from the women in the group, Melanie's courage faded and her brave words died in her throat. She had a sudden impulse to ask Rafe to hitch his wagon up right then and take her back to Fort Verde, where she could catch the stage and leave Cedar Ridge forever. But with the marshal's warning ringing in her ears, even that option had been cut off.

With a low cry, she turned and fled back to the safety of the mercantile.

22

"I f you measure out your preaching by so many minutes per person, I guess we're going to hear one short sermon today—eh, Preacher?" Andrew Bingham nudged Pastor Dunstan with his elbow, chortling at his own joke.

The circuit rider smiled at him. "I seem to recall that our Lord shared some of His most precious truths at times when He was alone with the twelve. I don't believe the size of the group matters to Him as much as the hearts of the listeners."

He grinned at Andrew's crestfallen expression, then turned to the rest of the little group. "Let's begin."

Melanie slid into the middle of one of the benches she and Levi had helped Caleb set up the night before. Even though she had questioned whether they needed to set up as many seats as usual after the spiteful words she'd overheard at the town meeting, finding her doubts confirmed had been a sore disappointment.

She made a quick count while Levi settled in his seat between her and Caleb. Idalou Fetterman was there, bless her, along with the Professor, Andrew, and Micah. Adding the three of them, that made a total of seven, not counting Pastor Dunstan—a far cry from the first service she'd attended there.

Levi snuggled close to her. "Where is everybody?" he whispered.

The pastor's opening prayer gave her an excuse to shush the boy and avoid giving an answer. How was she supposed to respond to his question when she didn't fully understand the reasons herself?

After singing two verses of "Onward, Christian Soldiers"—a feeble attempt that sounded nothing like a valiant army ready to march to victory—they settled back in their seats and Pastor Dunstan opened his Bible.

The bell over the door jingled softly. Melanie looked to the side and saw Will Blake slip inside. He closed the door softly and eased around to take a seat on Melanie's right.

A light blush tinged her cheeks. With so many empty benches, there was no need for him to choose the one the three of them already occupied. She didn't miss the dark look Caleb sent his way.

The pastor cleared his throat. "Today, we're going to take a look at the fourth chapter of Second Corinthians, beginning with verse eight: 'We are troubled on every side, yet not distressed; we are perplexed, but not in despair; persecuted, but not forsaken; cast down, but not destroyed. . . .'"

Troubled. Perplexed. Persecuted. The words summed up Melanie's feelings perfectly. Her hopes—and Caleb's—for making a new start in Cedar Ridge were being shot down at every turn, with the town she had come to love and planned to make her home turning against them both.

She truly did feel they were being threatened from all sides, not knowing where the next attack might come from. She blinked back tears and listened as Pastor Dunstan went on.

"When circumstances turn against us, it's easy to feel afraid . . . alone . . . forsaken. But as Paul reminded Timothy, God has not given us a spirit of fear."

Melanie sniffed quietly. Easy enough for the pastor to say. He didn't have the threat of vigilantes dangling over his head. And he was free to ride away once the service ended. He hadn't been warned to stay in town, with the promise of being tracked down like a common criminal if he dared to leave. Her thoughts continued along those gloomy lines until she realized with a start that the rest of the congregation were bowing their heads for the closing prayer. With a pang of guilt, Melanie ducked her head, offering a quick prayer for forgiveness and hoping no one had noticed her lapse.

After the service, Caleb picked up the small wicker basket that served as their collection plate and carried it to the preacher. "Based on the passage you chose this morning, I got the feeling you've heard what's been going on around here lately."

Pastor Dunstan nodded. "I tend to pick up most of the local news."

Caleb nodded at the basket. "I'm afraid it's pretty slim pickings this morning. I hate to suggest it, but you might want to consider finding someplace else to meet until all this has been resolved. None of this is your fault, but it's certainly affecting the offering."

The pastor put his hand on Caleb's shoulder. "God is in control, and He has never let me down yet." He looked away for a moment and cleared his throat. "I don't want to appear to have been listening to idle gossip, but I would like to leave you with another verse to ponder."

As he spoke, he darted a glance in Melanie's direction. "First Thessalonians, chapter five, verse twenty-two."

He squeezed Caleb's shoulder and looked at him earnestly. "Remember, a good name is rather to be chosen than great riches." With that cryptic remark, he gathered up his Bible and headed toward the livery stable, ready to ride on to the next stop on his circuit.

Melanie looked around for her Bible. "What was that verse?"

Caleb had already picked up his own and was leafing through the pages. "First Thessalonians, chapter five." He stopped at a page and ran his finger down the column. "Here it is." A moment later, his face tightened.

Melanie moved next to him and peered over his shoulder. "What does it say?"

The muscles in Caleb's jaw flexed. "'Abstain from all appearance of evil.'"

Melanie's heart sank, and her gaze locked onto Caleb's, wondering if she looked as mortified as he did. She knew one thing for sure. Pastor Dunstan hadn't just picked up a few stray tidbits concerning the happenings around Cedar Ridge.

He'd gotten an earful.

"I got the impression the minister's message struck rather close to home for the two of you yesterday." The Professor set three cans of peaches on the counter and gave both Melanie and Caleb a look of sympathy.

Melanie watched Caleb tear a sheet of brown paper from the roller above the counter and wrap it around the cans to make a neat parcel. "It certainly captured the essence of what we've been living through lately," he said.

The Professor nodded. "It's difficult when people talk about you behind your back."

Melanie studied the man in his fastidious black suit and ascot while she wrote up the order and added it to the Professor's running tab. She couldn't help wondering if his wistful tone spoke of his own familiarity with feeling excluded as well as hers and Caleb's.

She slid the parcel across the counter and smiled. "Will you be at the Founders Day picnic tomorrow?"

"What?" The Professor blinked, as if pulling his thoughts back from a place far away. "Oh, certainly. Are the two of you looking forward to the festivities?"

Caleb leaned against the counter and gave his friend a rueful smile. "I can't say we're exactly looking forward to them, not when the whole town seems to look on us as some kind of outcasts. But we're not going to let that stop us."

He looked to Melanie for confirmation, and she gave him a nod. They had talked about their situation during the slow morning hours at the store. As tempting as it would be to avoid the gathering, where they were bound to be on the receiving end of more stares and comments, it would be far worse to let it appear they were hiding out. Such actions would be taken as an admission of guilt.

"We're determined to go, no matter what," Caleb said. "We know we've done nothing wrong, and we can't let rumors convict us unjustly."

"Bravo!" The Professor's approving smile included them

both. "That is precisely the way to deal with nonsense like this. George and Alvin would be proud of the two of you."

Caleb's expression turned somber, and he drummed his fingers on the countertop. "I've been wanting to talk to you about something. When we were out at your place the other day, you mentioned something about poison."

Melanie sucked in her breath. What had prompted that abrupt change of topic?

"I've been thinking about Charley Weber's death," Caleb went on. "No one suspected it was murder at the time. From what you've told us, he became ill but seemed to be recuperating nicely. Then he took a sudden turn for the worse and died in his sleep. Is that right?"

"Yes, that's the way I remember it."

Caleb took a deep breath. "If Charley was poisoned, do you have any idea what might have been used? When I think of poison, I think of things like arsenic and strychnine that produce rather obvious symptoms. No one would mistake that for a natural death.

"But now I've started wondering whether there's some kind of poison that could kill a person without the cause being apparent."

The corners of the Professor's thin lips curved upward, giving him the appearance of a teacher beaming his approval upon a prize pupil. "You are quite right. Not every poison produces effects that are quite so dramatic or so easily identified. I happened to have a good book on the subject at home, if you'd care to look at it."

Melanie lifted her hand. "I don't think that will be—"

Caleb cut her off. "I'd appreciate that. It might be helpful."

The Professor's eyes gleamed. "Very well. I'll go get it and bring it back to you." With a pleasant nod, he picked up his parcel and went on his way.

Before the bell stopped jingling, Melanie turned to Caleb, her hands on her hips. "Poison?"

Caleb shrugged. "I didn't want to bring it up before, but it's a possibility I've been turning over in my mind. I thought as long as the Professor was here, I might as well ask him about it. How else can you explain a death that everyone around here, including Doc, accepted as natural?"

Melanie sagged against the counter. "Shouldn't you just tell Marshal Hooper about it? Remember what he said about letting him be the one to handle this?"

Caleb stepped over to her and cupped her shoulders in his hands. "Don't you see? The marshal told us himself he isn't any good with puzzles. He's going around asking questions, but he isn't getting any answers. And people are getting edgier by the minute. You heard them at the meeting the other night. They were talking about getting a vigilance committee together. I may not have been out here very long, but I've been here long enough to know that situations like this can turn deadly in a hurry."

Melanie felt the blood drain from her face as the meaning of his words sank in. "You mean, deadly for *us*?" His grim expression was all the answer she needed.

Caleb wrapped his arms around her and pulled her against his chest. Melanie clung to him, treasuring the feeling of being safe, protected.

She took a shaky breath and drew back, squaring her shoulders. "All right, what do we need to do? Where do we start?"

Caleb squeezed her shoulders. "I'm going to read the Professor's book and see if I get any insights from it. In the meantime, we need to watch the people around us—really look at them. Somebody around here is carrying around a heavy load of guilt. He's bound to do something that will give himself away."

"And just how are we supposed to do that?" Melanie asked. "Watch people, I mean. Business has fallen off to a trickle. It isn't like we have a parade of customers coming through our doors these days."

Caleb's eyes took on a gleam that reminded her of the Professor. "You're forgetting—tomorrow will be a perfect opportunity to see them all together in one place. Everyone in town will be at the Founders Day picnic."

23

The late afternoon sun slanted across the valley, high-lighting the pinkish striations on the hills overlooking the Founders Day celebration. Clumps of Indian paintbrush and lupine dotted the meadow where the potato sack race was in full swing.

Melanie stood beside Caleb under the spreading branches of a sycamore tree watching Micah Rawlins and Andrew Bingham bound along ahead of the rest of the pack, matching each other hop for hop. The race looked like it would end in a tie until Andrew surged ahead in a burst of speed and tumbled across the finish line first. Flopping to the ground, he scrambled his way out of the sack and jumped back onto his feet, ready to offer good-natured condolences to Micah for coming in second.

Melanie joined in the general applause, trying to hide her restlessness. As promising as Caleb's plan to study the crowd for signs of guilt had sounded, it had borne no fruit. They had scanned faces throughout the opening remarks by Mayor Pike, the picnic that followed, and three heats of horse racing, where the local cowboys pitted their mounts against each other.

A baseball game had taken up much of the afternoon. Levi tired of watching before the first inning was over, and begged to be allowed to play with some of the local ranchers' children. Pleased that he had children his own age to play with, Melanie encouraged Caleb to let him go, and the youngsters had spent several hours exploring the creek and darting in and out of the old storage caves in a game of hide-and-seek.

So now, with the festivities nearly ended and the sun hovering low in the western sky, Melanie felt the day had been a waste as far as their attempt at sleuthing was concerned. Other than enjoying the beautiful late spring weather and keeping Levi out of mischief, they hadn't accomplished much.

She nudged Caleb with her elbow. "Have you seen anything you think will help us?"

Caleb answered without taking his focus off the crowd. "I hate to admit it, but I haven't. I was so sure that if we kept our eyes open we'd be able to spot some clue that would point to the guilty party, but I haven't seen a single thing worthy of note." He let out a dry laugh. "Unless you count all the icy looks sent our way."

Melanie nodded wearily. She had seen them, too, and that was part of the reason she and Caleb had taken shelter under the sycamore instead of joining the rest of the onlookers.

"Here you are!"

Melanie swung around to find Mrs. Fetterman bustling up behind them, holding a plate in her hands.

"I noticed you didn't get any of my raspberry torte when you filled your plates, so I saved the last piece for you." She held the plate up under Melanie's nose. "I was going to save two pieces, but Wendell Trask beat me to it, so you'll have to share."

Melanie stared round-eyed at the slice of pastry, then sent a pleading look at Caleb. To her dismay, he only grinned.

"After you," he said.

Traitor. Unable to think of an excuse that wouldn't hurt the dear woman's feelings, she picked the cake up gingerly and took a tiny bite. Her eyes flared wide when the tangy flavor of sun-ripened raspberries exploded inside her mouth.

"Why . . . that's scrumptious!" While Mrs. Fetterman beamed, she took another bite and closed her eyes in sheer pleasure. "I do believe that's the most delicious thing I've ever tasted."

Mrs. Fetterman chuckled. "I'm so pleased you think so. Now, be sure to share the rest." With a merry wink, she walked away, leaving them alone again.

Melanie glared up at Caleb. "Did you know she could cook like that?"

Caleb burst out laughing. "It seems to me I told you she was a fine cook the day you arrived. You were the one who got worried about her mixing some of her patent remedies in with her food." He eyed the rest of the slice in her hand. "You did hear her tell you to share that, didn't you?"

Melanie pinched off a small morsel and handed it to him, then popped the rest into her mouth. "That's all you deserve."

Caleb raised his eyebrow when he took the tiny piece but didn't offer a protest.

Melanie laughed and asked, "What's supposed to happen

next? It'll be getting dark soon. Is there anything we need to stay for?"

"I think all we have left is a closing speech by Mayor Pike." Caleb gestured toward the edge of the meadow, where a handful of people were walking toward the bunting-draped dais.

Melanie made a face. "Do you want to stay and hear him speak?"

Caleb shook his head, looking as tired as Melanie felt. "I've heard about as much from the Pikes over the last few days as I want to." He glanced toward the setting sun. "We might as well head home."

"No, not yet!" Levi had run up just in time to hear Melanie's question and his father's answer. He stared up at them, hopping from one foot to the other and wringing his hands.

Caleb and Melanie stared down at the boy. "You want to stay and hear the mayor's speech?" Caleb asked in an incredulous tone.

Levi bobbed his head up and down. "We have to stay, Papa. We *have* to!"

Caleb looked at Melanie. "What do you say?"

She gave a little laugh and shrugged. "I guess it won't matter if we wait a little longer."

They moved over to the clearing where the crowd now gathered, spreading blankets on the ground in anticipation of the mayor's speech. They took up a position a few yards behind the group, at the edge of the light cast by lanterns strung between the trees.

Mayor Pike climbed up onto the speaker's platform and struck a pose, gripping the lapels of his jacket with both hands. He seemed to puff up as he stared out at his attentive audience.

"I hope you've all had a wonderful time today as we've commemorated the founding of our fair community. Though Cedar Ridge may be young compared to the cities of the East, let me assure you, it's going places. We have some of the best climate in the territory right here, and the possibilities are endless."

Scattered cries of "Hear! Hear!" met his pronouncement.

The mayor's chest puffed up even more. "I predict that with the increase in ranching and farming, and the new businesses moving in, our size will double in just a few short years."

Beside Melanie, Caleb stirred and whispered, "Where's Levi? I thought he was right here."

"So did I." Melanie swept her gaze over the lantern-lit area between them and the people sitting on their blankets. "I don't see him anywhere."

Mayor Pike went on, his voice building in a crescendo. "The folks in our territory's capital, Prescott, are taking notice of us. Make no mistake about it, my friends, Cedar Ridge is fast becoming a rising star in—"

As if on cue, a ball of flame with a stream of sparks trailing off behind it arced over the assembly. Melanie and Caleb watched as the small fireball reached its apex directly above the speaker's platform and broke apart, sending a shower of sparkling embers down over Mayor Pike and the crowd.

Shrieks rose as people leaped up off their blankets. Several of those nearest the platform, including Mayor Pike, beat the sparks from their clothes and stamped out the live embers before they could set the weeds and grass ablaze.

"Where did that come from?" Caleb demanded.

In the dimness behind them, a match flared, catching Melanie's attention. She pointed at the trees that lined the creek as another bundle of flame lofted skyward.

She clutched at Caleb's arm. "What can that be?"

"I'm not sure, but I have my suspicions." With a determined stride, he set off toward the creek bank with Melanie right behind him.

As they neared the water's edge, they heard spurts of muffled laughter. Caleb stopped and put his hand on Melanie's arm. "Shh. Let me get my bearings."

Another spate of giggles burst out, followed by the sound of a match striking. Melanie focused on a spot a few yards in front of them, where the sudden glow illuminated the excited faces of Levi and one of the boys he'd been playing with earlier.

The other boy, taller and stouter, clung to the tip of an alder sapling, bending it toward the ground. "Hurry up," he grunted. "I can't hold it down much longer."

Levi crouched beside his playmate. The tip of his tongue protruded from one corner of his mouth as he held the match under a small clump of something—Melanie couldn't determine what it was—wedged into the alder's top branches. "Hold on. It doesn't want to light."

"What's going on?" Caleb's voice boomed through the darkness.

Levi yelped and jumped back, dropping the match to the ground.

The other boy squealed and let go of the sapling.

The tree snapped upright, sending the small bundle flying in a wobbly arc overhead, then falling back to earth some distance from the young perpetrators.

Caleb strode over to the smoldering object. Melanie

glanced to make sure the fallen match had gone out on its own, then she spoke in her sternest governess voice: "Come here this instant—both of you."

Levi and his companion slunk out of the undergrowth and joined Melanie at Caleb's side. He knelt on the ground beside the smoking projectile, then glared up at the boys.

"Cattails?" He stood and kicked at the bundle. It dissolved in a spray of embers, which he stomped out with his boot.

The bigger boy stared down at the dirt and scuffed his toes. "Yes, sir."

Even in the dim light, Melanie could see Levi's chin quiver. "That was our fireworks. You spoiled it."

Melanie caught her breath. "Fireworks?"

Levi nodded. "People kept wishing we could have fireworks, but Papa said the mayor wouldn't spend the money to buy any. We were just trying to make Founders Day special."

Caleb grunted. "You made it a night to remember, all right. Come on. You two have an apology to make." He stooped to pick up a handful of the cattails the boys had piled on the ground, then led the way back to the speaker's platform.

The cries of alarm had subsided by the time he marched the boys back to the scene of Mayor Pike's interrupted speech. Most were still within the warm circle of light created by the lanterns, but they were on their feet shaking out their blankets, preparing to load their wagons and go home.

The mayor and his wife stood in the center of a circle of friends, accepting their commiserations for the way the day had ended. The people around them parted like the Red Sea as Caleb and Melanie escorted the boys to stand in front of the Pikes.

Mayor Pike stared down at the youngsters, then looked back up at Caleb. "What's all this?"

Caleb nudged Levi. "Go on."

Levi fixed his eyes on the middle button on Mayor Pike's coat, avoiding eye contact. "We're sorry."

The mayor's brows drew together.

Levi's shoulders slumped. "We didn't mean to mess up your speech with our fireworks."

Mayor Pike drew back. "Fireworks?"

"Cattails," Caleb explained. He held up the charred remains of the boys' pyrotechnic efforts.

Muffled laughter rippled through the crowd.

The mayor's face darkened. "What were you boys thinking? You could have injured people, or started a fire."

A weather-beaten rancher stepped through the crowd and looked down at Levi's companion. "Is this true, son? You had a part in this?"

The other boy's lower lip protruded. "Yes, sir."

Ophelia Pike wagged her finger toward the man's face. "If that were my son, I would—"

"That's all right, ma'am. I'll take care of this." The rancher turned, leading the boy away.

Mrs. Pike turned her wrath on Caleb. "I'm sure your son was at the bottom of this. It's just the kind of thing I would expect of him."

Caleb pressed his lips in a straight line. "We'll be leaving, too. Good evening, Mrs. Pike."

Melanie followed him as he strode from the lanterns' glow and steered Levi toward their wagon. She concentrated on picking her way along in the moonlight without tripping over a rock.

Caleb slowed and pointed. "Isn't that Doc up ahead of us?"

Melanie looked in the direction he indicated and nodded when she recognized the heavyset figure. "Yes, I believe it is."

"Come on." Caleb trotted off to catch up with the doctor, leaving Melanie to trail along behind with Levi.

"Doc Mills!" Caleb called. The older man looked over his shoulder and stopped to wait.

"I've been hoping for a chance to talk to you," Caleb said. "Do you have a minute?"

Doc watched Melanie and Levi as they came up to join them, and he shrugged. "I suppose so. What do you need?"

Melanie wrinkled her nose at the whiff of stale liquor that drifted to her when he spoke.

"I wanted to ask you something, but first I'll need to ask you to keep it to yourself."

Doc nodded. "I'm a medical man. I'm good at keeping a confidence."

"It's all this talk about Charley Weber's death maybe being due to murder, and not natural causes."

The moon rose over the hills to the east, illuminating Doc's solemn expression. "Go on."

"It seemed odd to me that something like that could have happened, since no one—including you—apparently saw anything suspicious about his death at the time."

Doc drew himself up, and his mouth tightened. "I know I have something of a reputation for imbibing a bit freely, but I can assure you—"

Caleb waved his hand. "No, I didn't mean to imply any negligence on your part. But on top of suspicions about what happened to Charley, now there's talk going around about the way my uncle Alvin died."

272

"And my cousin," Melanie added.

Doc gave her a brief glance before turning back to Caleb. "You were here when Alvin passed away. You saw how it happened."

"Yes, but I've been doing a little studying." Caleb pulled a book from his inside jacket pocket.

Melanie's eyes widened when she recognized the reference on poisons the Professor had loaned them the day before.

Caleb thumbed through the pages, then spread the book open and handed it to Doc. "Ipecac. It says right here that it causes extreme gastric upset. That sounds a lot like what happened with my uncle. You remember how we all thought he was getting better, and then he couldn't keep anything down at all."

Doc murmured a response, his eyes still fastened on the book.

Melanie moved forward a step. "Neither Caleb nor I were here when my cousin George died. What happened to him? I always assumed it was something to do with his heart, but could someone have done something to harm him?"

Doc lowered his head as if deep in thought, then he looked straight at Melanie. "George Ross died of heart failure. His symptoms were perfectly consistent with that diagnosis, and I have no reason to attribute his death to anything else. The other two, however . . ."

He turned to Caleb. "I didn't have any reason to look for something other than death by natural causes at the time, in either of those cases." He held up the Professor's book. "But now that you've drawn this to my attention, I have to admit it's a possibility."

He closed the book and turned it so he could study the

cover, his brows dipping low on his forehead. "Where did you get this?"

"The Professor loaned it to me," Caleb said.

A shadow flickered across the doctor's face, barely discernible in the moonlight. "The Professor? That's interesting. I knew he was a man of varied interests, but I wasn't aware he was a student of poisons." He handed the book back to Caleb without further comment.

"We need to take this information to the marshal." Melanie's voice shook when she spoke. "If it's a real possibility that Charley Weber and Caleb's uncle were poisoned, he needs to know."

Doc Mills tilted his head and looked at her from beneath his brows. "Are you sure you want to do that?" Seeing her shocked expression, he went on. "It might confirm the possibility that those two deaths were murder, and it might give him an idea of how it was done. But it still doesn't tell him who did it. With all the accusations flying around town, it would be easy for people to jump to assumptions and decide to take things into their own hands." He pointed to the book in Caleb's hands. "I believe you need to think very carefully about whether or not to make your theory known."

He turned away and ambled toward his buggy. Caleb, Melanie, and Levi walked back to their wagon in silence, with Doc's news—and his admonition—ringing in their ears. They settled a sleepy Levi on some blankets in the back of the wagon, and then Caleb clucked at the horse and they set off for home.

Melanie checked to see if Levi was asleep, then she scooted closer to Caleb on the wagon seat, drawing comfort from his nearness. She lowered her voice to a soft whisper. "So Alvin's and Charley's deaths really might have been murder?"

CAROL COX

"It appears so." In the moonlight, Caleb's face looked as if it had been chiseled from marble.

"Do you think Doc has any idea who might have done it?"

"I'm not sure. If he does, I don't think he's going to tell us. We'll have to find that answer ourselves."

"Us? How?"

"Whoever the murderer was, and whatever he used, he had to get his hands on that poison somewhere. What's the mostly likely place for him to get it from?"

Melanie pursed her lips. "I suppose he would have had to order it from somewhere." Her eyes widened, and her lips parted. "From our store. It could have come from the mercantile."

Caleb nodded. "It would have been the easiest thing to do. Starting tomorrow, we need to check through all our records."

275

24

"Can we go fishing, Papa? It's gonna be a beautiful day."
Caleb checked the lock on his front door and pocketed the key. "Not today, son. But if you're a very good boy, we'll plan on going fishing again someday soon." He glanced skyward. Levi was right about the weather—the morning was beautiful, but with the way the clouds were building up in the north, he suspected it wouldn't stay that way for long. Besides, he and Melanie needed to start checking their records to find out who might have purchased or ordered the substance used to poison Charley Weber and Uncle Alvin.

Levi scuffed a rock out of his way as they walked along the alley. "I guess after last night, you don't want me to make anymore fireworks, right?"

Caleb ruffled the boy's hair. "Right. No more fireworks, no more matches."

"Can I still play with my soldiers?"

"Sure, that's fine." Caleb slanted a look at his son. "As long as you don't—"

"I know. As long as I don't line them up on Mrs. Pike's——"

"That's right," Caleb cut in. "You've got the idea."

Levi picked up a pebble and flung it down the alley. "Can Miss Ross come with us? When we go fishing, I mean."

"I don't know about that," Caleb said. "We'd have to close the store." Even as he spoke, a picture formed in his mind: The three of them on the grassy bank overlooking Walnut Creek. Levi with his fishing pole in the water, or chasing grasshoppers and butterflies up and down the bank, and Melanie leaning back against the smooth bark of a sycamore trunk, the breeze stirring her hair, and the sun dappling her cheeks through the glossy green leaves.

His mood lifted. Maybe Levi had a point. Why not close the store up so they could all go together? It would only be for an afternoon—or maybe even a day. Once the marshal captured the murderer, there would be reason to take some time off to celebrate. He would have to pose the idea to Melanie and see what she thought of it..

Absorbed in his thoughts, he walked along the alley toward the store's rear entrance, with Levi skipping ahead of him. When Levi reached the back stoop, he turned and called to Caleb. "She's not here—and the porch isn't swept."

"What?" Caleb quickened his steps, his thoughts racing. Surely no harm could have befallen her, not with those new locks he had installed. Not with drop bars on both doors to keep intruders out. He reminded himself to breathe. The last time he had flown into a panic about her not being outside, it turned out she had been upstairs because she wasn't feeling well. Maybe she had another headache.

But what if she hadn't opened the door because she had fallen or hurt herself? The new worry gnawed at him as he hurried toward the stoop. If she was upstairs, sick or incapacitated, how could he get to her? He had the key to the lock, but the bars Melanie dropped across the doors each night would be just as effective at keeping him out as they were at barring trespassers.

He trotted up the steps, trying not to let his concern show so as not to frighten Levi. A bit of his worry ebbed away when the doorknob turned under his hand. He pushed the door open. Relief washed over him at the sight of Melanie standing before him, a sheet of paper in her hand. His relief faded when he saw the look on her face. "What's wrong?"

"This." She waved the paper at him. "It's the list I've been making, the one with my ideas for new items for the store. It was over on the table next to the catalogs when I came down a little while ago. But I know I left it right here on the counter before we left for the celebration yesterday afternoon."

Caleb shrugged. "We were in a hurry yesterday. Maybe you just thought you put it on the counter before we left. You might have set it down on the table and just forgot."

Melanie tapped the paper. "I could almost make myself believe that—but I didn't imagine this." She beckoned him into the office.

Caleb stopped short in the doorway. The small room looked as if one of Arizona's dust devils had swept through it, leaving chaos in its wake. Desk drawers stood open, and their record books, normally lined up neatly on a shelf near the window, now lay strewn across the desk and floor.

Melanie turned to face him. "We did not leave this room in this condition."

"You're saying someone came in while we were at the picnic? But we didn't notice any sign of a break-in when we returned. And there are only two keys to the new locks I put on. You have one, I have the other."

Melanie shook her head. "It didn't happen when we were at the picnic. I double-checked the locks on the doors and windows before I went to bed. Last night, this room was just the way we always leave it." She pointed toward the room's only window. "But this was open a crack when I came in here this morning."

Caleb stepped to the window and pushed it up a few inches.

Melanie moved beside him. "What are you looking at?"

"The lock. Do you see those scratches?" Before she could answer, he pivoted and went back outside. Melanie caught up with him while he was busy examining the lock from the alley side.

"See there?" He pointed out a series of gouges in the wooden frame around the lock.

Her forehead puckered. "I see them, but what do they mean?"

"Somebody slid a thin blade up between the two parts of the window frame and used it to work the lock open." He stepped back and frowned, trying to reason it all out. "The only reason someone would have needed to come in through the window"—realization hit him like a sledgehammer as he finished his statement—"is if they broke in during the night. With the bars in place on the doors, they couldn't get inside that way."

She nodded without saying a word, but Caleb could see the sheen of fear in her eyes, mirroring his own panic at the thought that someone had been inside the store in the darkest hours of the night while Melanie slept upstairs . . . alone and vulnerable.

A roll of thunder rumbled in the distance. Melanie watched the play of emotions on Caleb's face while they walked back into the mercantile.

When he spoke, his voice sounded taut and strained. "It's almost time to open. We'd better—"

A loud knock rattled the front door, and they both jumped. When Caleb went to open it, Will Blake rushed inside. "You've got trouble comin', Caleb. There's no time to lose."

Caleb stared. "What are you talking about?"

Will grabbed him by the arm and pulled him along toward the back of the store, where Melanie stood next to Levi, who had scrambled out of his fort at the sound of Will's voice. "You know all the wild talk that's been going on around town? I was just down the street waitin' for the bank to open, and there was a bunch talking out in front of O'Shea's. It sounded like they're forming a vigilance committee right now. You need to get Melanie and Levi out the back door and take them someplace safe. That crew may be here any minute."

The front door crashed open before he finished speaking. Melanie shrank back as a group of hard-faced men burst inside. She looked from face to face: Thomas O'Shea, Rance Yeary, Wendell Trask, and several others she didn't recognize. She pulled Levi against her and held him tight.

Caleb spoke sharply. "Levi, get upstairs now." Without taking his eyes off the intruders, he jerked his head in Melanie's direction. "You too."

Melanie pushed Levi toward the stairs but held her ground. She spoke just loud enough for Caleb to hear, trying to keep her voice from trembling. "This is my trouble, too. I'm not going to let you face it on your own."

Caleb didn't take time to argue. He stepped forward to put himself between her and the threat looming before them. "What are you *gentlemen* here for?"

His forceful stand seemed to take the group aback. They didn't answer but fanned out across the store like one of Levi's skirmish lines.

O'Shea, who seemed to fancy himself as the group's leader, looked at the others, then moved to the front.

"The boys and I been talkin', Nelson. We don't need your kind in this town."

Will moved over and stood shoulder to shoulder with Caleb. "These people have done nothing, O'Shea. Why don't you all just simmer down and go about your business before we have to call in the marshal?"

While the mob's attention was focused on Caleb and Will, Melanie cast a frantic glance around the store, looking for anything they could use as weapons to stand the vigilantes off. Pick handles. Pitchforks. What would work best?

O'Shea scoffed. "The marshal hasn't done anything but talk. But we've heard enough to believe these two aren't as innocent as you want to think they are. If the marshal isn't going to do his job, we're ready to take it upon ourselves and run these undesirables out of town."

Caleb hooked his thumbs in his belt and widened his stance. "What is wrong with you men? You're willing to jump at shadows and look at anyone as guilty without the slightest bit of proof."

O'Shea didn't back down. "You were at the meeting at my place the other night. You heard what Wendell asked—who's profiting from all these deaths? Follow the trail and the answer is clear enough." He stretched his arm toward Caleb and Melanie. "It's the two of you."

Caleb stared at the man without flinching. "If that's the line of thought you want to follow, let's take it one step further. What's the real reason *you're* so eager to get rid of the two of us? If you manage to run Miss Ross and me out of town and this mercantile goes under, who'll be the one to profit from that?"

A rumble of murmurs rippled through the rest of the group. Rance Yeary rocked back on his heels and eyed O'Shea thoughtfully. "He has a point there. You've had your mind set on running this store out of business ever since you moved here from Denver."

One of the men Melanie didn't know nodded slowly. "Yeah, you're always complaining about them having more customers than you do. If you cut out the competition, everybody in town would have to do business at the emporium."

Caleb's lips thinned. "Was setting those oily rags on fire in our office part of your plan to drive us out?"

O'Shea's mouth dropped open.

"And those hateful anonymous notes." The words came out before Melanie could stop them. "Are you the one responsible for them?"

Wendell Trask's eyes narrowed. "I remember Alvin talking about getting threatening notes. You mean it's still going on?" He took a step away from the storekeeper. "Maybe it's time to take a second look at all this. These two have only been here a few months, but the trouble started long before that. . . . Not too long after you came to town. What happened, did you decide if George and Alvin wouldn't turn tail and run, you'd step in and take care of things yourself?"

The blood drained from O'Shea's face, and he held up his hands. "Wait a minute, fellas. I don't know anything about that. I never left any notes or set any fire . . . and I sure never killed anyone." He shot a desperate look at Caleb. "You've got to believe me."

Rance Yeary moved toward him. "I don't know, boys. I think we may have found our killer. What do you say?"

The other vigilantes closed in behind the saloonkeeper and advanced on O'Shea.

Caleb brought his hand down on the counter. "Stop!" The group froze and stared at him.

"Do you see what you're doing?" Caleb shouted. "You're ready to convict O'Shea with no more proof than you had against Miss Ross or me. Now, get out of here, all of you, and leave it for the marshal to figure out who the real criminal is."

O'Shea didn't hesitate a moment. Shouldering his way through the knot of men, he bolted out the door. After a brief moment, the rest slunk after him.

Will turned to Caleb with a broad smile on his face. "Nice job, my friend. I don't know anyone who could have talked a group like that down better than you did."

Melanie rushed to Caleb and clung to his arm. "You were wonderful. I didn't know what they were going to do." She turned to Will. "Thank you for the warning and for standing with us. What on earth would make anyone behave like that?"

"Mostly, they're just scared." Will eyed the two of them for a moment, then rubbed the back of his neck. "Have you ever seen a bunch of cows get spooked? It doesn't take much—a gust of wind, or a tumbleweed skittering in front of them. Or maybe the tarp on the chuck wagon flapping. All of a sudden their ears go up, their eyes get big, and they all take off at the same time, each one tryin' to save itself and not caring what it runs over."

Caleb gave a rueful laugh. "That sounds a lot like what we've been seeing around town, all right."

Will grinned. "Cattle are some of the most brainless critters God ever put on this earth. The only thing dumber than cattle is sheep." His grin broadened as he headed toward the door. "And you know which one the Bible compares people to."

25

Thunder rumbled again in the distance, sounding like a portent of doom. Melanie shook off the melancholy fancy. They had problems enough to deal with without her conjuring up more. And the first issue at hand was getting the store ready to open. She closed the office door to shut out the sight of the havoc their intruder had left behind.

She paused with her hand on the knob. "Do you think Mr. O'Shea is the one who broke in last night?"

Caleb scoffed. "O'Shea? Not on your life. He's despicable—I'll grant you that—but I think he's more of a rabble-rouser, the kind of coward who wants to stir things up but has to have a group of cronies backing him up while he does it. I can't imagine him breaking in. It would take too much nerve for the likes of him."

The heaviness she'd felt since making her disturbing discoveries that morning settled in again like a dark cloud. "Then who?" She saw a shadow flit across Caleb's face. "What is it? What are you thinking?"

285

As Caleb opened his mouth to speak, a small voice called from the top of the stairs. "Papa, can I come down now?"

"Of course, son. Why don't you come play in your fort." He exchanged a glance with Melanie, and she knew their discussion would have to be postponed. She busied herself with the feather duster while Caleb got Levi settled and made sure he was happily occupied. A few minutes later, he approached and drew her to the far end of the store.

Melanie kept her voice low. "What were you getting ready to say?"

Caleb looked over his shoulder toward the counter, as if to assure himself that Levi couldn't overhear. "Did you notice the look on Doc's face last night when I told him that book came from the Professor?"

Melanie nodded slowly. "I did see something, but I didn't know what to make of it. Do you think he suspects the Professor?"

"I'm not sure, either, but I haven't been able to get it out of my head."

Melanie stared at him, unsettled by his somber expression. "What are you saying?"

"Think about it. Did you see all the weapons the Professor has in his collection? The man seems to have a fascination with instruments of death. And he was the one who brought up the possibility of Charley being killed by poison in the first place. It's almost like he steered us in that direction."

Melanie pondered the idea a moment, then shook her head. "I don't believe it. Why would he point you to that book if he was guilty?"

Caleb flung his hands upward. "I don't want to believe it any more than you do, but you have to admit he's an odd duck. Maybe he is trying to make himself appear innocent by giving us information—throw us off the scent."

Melanie tightened her grip on the feather duster. "But why would he break in here?"

Caleb shrugged. "I don't know. The obvious answer would be to get more poison. But if that's the case, why the mess in the office?"

Melanie measured her words with care, hating herself for even considering the possibility of the Professor's guilt. "I don't know . . . He may be odd, but he's also highly intelligent. He had to know that once the possibility of poison entered our thinking, we'd start looking at records of purchases and orders . . . and that at some point we'd begin to fit all the pieces together."

She flung the feather duster to the floor and clapped her hands to her cheeks. "What are we doing? We're just as bad as the rest of them, casting suspicion on someone—a friend, no less!—with nothing but the most circumstantial evidence to back it up. I know the Professor is a bit eccentric, but I simply can't believe he's capable of harming anyone." She lowered her hands and added, more to herself than to Caleb, "At least, I don't want to believe it."

"Neither do I." Caleb reached out and took both of her hands in his. "But we're dealing with murder here. I don't think we can completely discount the possibility. And I'm pretty sure Doc's mind is running along those same lines."

Melanie squeezed Caleb's hands, drawing strength from his touch. "In that case, we need to let the marshal know."

To her surprise, Caleb shook his head. "We can't do that, not yet anyway. As you just said, we don't have any solid evidence, only suspicion."

She pulled her hands away. "Then what are we supposed to do? You said it yourself—we're dealing with murder, and there are people in this town who think we're involved somehow. Are we supposed to just sit by and wait for a lynch mob to come back to our door? Or for whoever is behind these murders to come after us next?"

Caleb caught her shoulders and looked into her eyes. "First of all, we need to keep our wits about us so we can go on as we planned. We'll look through every record in the office if we need to—see if we can find something to point us in the right direction. Something solid enough to take to Marshal Hooper."

The bell jingled, and Andrew Bingham's cheery voice called out, "Hey, Caleb, I'm in need of some cakes of soap and shaving brushes. Can you help me out?"

"Sure thing. I'll be right with you." He bent close to Melanie's ear and murmured, "This may take a few minutes. You go ahead and get started. I'll join you as soon as I've taken care of Andrew."

Melanie nodded and hurried to the office, where she scooped up the scattered papers and piled them on the desk in an unorganized heap. No point in sorting them first; she could do that while she read through the stack. She sat down on the wooden chair and picked up the first sheet. After scanning it quickly, she set it aside, her frustration mounting. Their plan to look for evidence had sounded simple enough, but how was she supposed to recognize a clue when she didn't have a clear idea of what she was looking for?

She went on to the next sheet, and the next, seeing nothing that caught her attention.

She swiveled around in her chair and peered out through the office door. Caleb stood at the counter, chatting with Andrew Bingham as he bundled the barber's order into a neat parcel. She turned back to the desk, fuming. How long could it take to wrap up a few bars of soap and a shaving brush or two? She needed him searching, too, needed him to help her find the proof that would end their nightmare.

A soft scuffle of feet sounded behind her and she swung around, expecting to see Caleb. Instead, Levi staggered toward her, his skinny arms wrapped around a bulky object. Melanie gasped and leaped to her feet when she recognized the fragile music box.

Before she could reach him, Levi stumbled and thumped the music box down on the small table. He beamed up at her. "I brought you something to cheer you up, Miss Ross. Look, I winded it myself." He lifted the lid with a flourish and moved the lever to one side. Instead of launching into the lilting strains of "Liebestraum," two notes plunked into the air, and then the box fell silent.

"Oh no." Melanie jumped up and leaned over the box. Maybe he had wound the spring too tight. She gave the key a gentle twist with her fingers, relieved when it turned freely. She moved the lever from side to side, but to no avail. The cylinder refused to turn. Had the sudden drop onto the table damaged the box? Her heart sank.

"Levi Nelson, what have you done?"

His smile melted away, replaced by a look of alarm. Keeping his eyes focused on Melanie, he backed away toward the door leading out into the mercantile.

"Not so fast, young man." Melanie's authoritative tone stopped him in his tracks.

289

Caleb appeared in the doorway behind Levi. "What's going on?"

Levi twisted his head around and looked up at his father in mute appeal. "Miss Ross was looking sad. I was just trying to make her happy."

"By breaking an expensive piece like this?" Melanie sputtered.

Levi hung his head. "You said you liked that song. I thought maybe if you heard it you'd be happy again, like the night you danced with Papa."

Melanie felt her cheeks flame, and her gaze flew to meet Caleb's. She'd been so sure Levi had been asleep the night of their dinner party, but apparently he had heard the music and seen them dancing. What else had he seen? She remembered the way they'd stood after the music ended, staring into each other's eyes, and her face grew hotter.

Caleb bent down and addressed his son calmly. "You had no business touching that music box, son. You know better than to handle something like that without asking permission first."

The little boy's face crumpled, and tears spilled from his eyes to wind their way down his cheeks. "I was just . . . I just wanted . . ." Spinning around, he pushed past Caleb and darted out of the room. Melanie could hear his feet pounding across the wooden floor, followed by the sound of a door slamming shut.

Without a word, Caleb turned and strode after him. He returned a few moments later, alone, his face set in a stern line.

Melanie pressed her hands to her cheeks. "I am so sorry. I let my frayed nerves get the best of me, and I blew it all out of proportion. I never meant to upset him like that."

290

Caleb rubbed his forehead. "I know his heart was in the right place, and he only meant to help, but you're right—he had no business handling that box."

Melanie caught her breath. "Do you think you ought to go check on him?"

Caleb shook his head. "I'm sure he headed home. He just needs some time to himself so he can sort things out." He walked over and wrapped his arms around Melanie, rubbing his chin against her hair. "Don't be too hard on yourself. With everything that's going on right now, we're all on edge."

Melanie nestled against his shirt, feeling his heart beat beneath her cheek. "Are you sure he'll be all right over there by himself?"

Caleb gave her a quick squeeze, then released her. "I'll keep watch through the window. In the meantime, let's focus on looking for something that will give us the answers we need so we can bring an end to this."

An hour later, they were still at it, and Melanie felt ready to burst with frustration. "I can't believe it. We've gone through over a year's worth of records, and we have nothing to show for it."

"No," Caleb countered, "the problem is that we have too much." He held up the list they'd been making as they worked. "We sold stomach bitters containing ipecac to the Professor, and Merrell's Triturates to Will. Even some of Mrs. Fetterman's favorite remedies would be toxic if taken in a large enough dose. And the same could be said for most of our patent medicines. Half the people in town have come in to buy those at one time or another." He shook his head. "It isn't that we don't have any suspects—we have too many."

Melanie let out a bitter laugh. "Which means we're no

closer to the truth than when we started. The whole town can't be in on it. Maybe none of them are. How are we ever going to find what we're looking for?"

Caleb picked up the next sheet of paper. "We keep on sifting through this. That's all I know to do. Surely this will sort itself out if we just look hard enough."

"Go ahead," Melanie said. "I need a minute to clear my head." Looking for a distraction, she got up and moved over to the music box. If Levi hadn't damaged the internal workings irreparably, perhaps she could figure out what was wrong.

She closed the lid and turned the box over to examine the underside. Nothing seemed amiss, as far as she could see. Turning it back upright, she raised the lid again and peered down at the mechanism. Without taking her eyes off the cylinder, she moved the lever first to the right, then to the left.

The gears started whirring, and the cylinder jerked into motion, then stopped.

Wait a minute. Melanie repeated the maneuver, watching closely. Was something caught in one of the gears?

She looked over at Caleb, intending to show him and ask his advice, but he seemed intent on the records spread out on the desk before him. She turned her attention back to the music box. Did she dare attempt to meddle with the delicate instrument?

Lifting the box slightly to catch the light better, she tilted it from one side to the other. Yes, it was just as she'd thought. Something was wedged under the largest gear, next to the cylinder. She reached to try to pull it loose, but the space was too narrow to allow her fingers to touch it. Going out to the display of ladies' toiletries, she fetched a pair of tweezers and tried again. This time, she managed to catch hold of what appeared to be the corner of a piece of paper tucked under the mechanism. With infinite care, she pushed the corner from between the gear and cylinder and pulled the sheet of paper from beneath the mechanism.

Hardly daring to breathe, she set the paper on the table and pushed the lever again. The gears whirred, and an instant later the first notes of "Liebestraum" tinkled into the air.

Caleb swiveled around in his chair, a smile easing his harried frown. "You got it working again."

She nodded. "There was some paper jammed in the gears that was keeping the cylinder from turning."

He gave her a quizzical look. "That's odd. It was working fine the other night."

Their eyes met and held, and Melanie felt her throat go dry at the memory of their waltz together. She caught her breath and looked away. "Levi stumbled and set the box down on the table with quite a thud. That must have jammed a corner of the paper into the mechanism."

"Well, I'm glad it wasn't really broken." Leaving her to admire her success, Caleb turned back to his papers.

Melanie picked up the offending paper to toss it in the trash bin, then stopped and unfolded it, curious as to what it was and how it had found its way underneath the gears. A smaller piece slipped to the floor, and she bent to pick it up. The larger sheet, water stained and yellowed with age, was printed on both sides—a clipping from a Colorado newspaper, she realized as she scanned the partial masthead. She noted the date—August 1878. What on earth would an old news article be doing inside their music box?

Her eyes fastened on the headline, and she sucked in her breath. Straining to make out the faded words, she scanned the story that followed and then turned her attention to the smaller note. She was still staring at the papers when the last strains of the waltz died away.

Caleb turned around, the shadow back in his eyes. "I think I'm on to something. I listed all the purchases out again, by date this time. The Professor bought a supply of syrup of ipecac about the time Charley Weber came to town." His expression darkened even more. "It's enough to take to the marshal. Like it or not, it looks like we've found the killer."

Melanie shook her head and refolded the sheet she'd been reading. "You need to see this."

Caleb's brow furrowed. "What?"

"It's the paper I found in the music box. Actually, there are two of them. The larger one is from the front page of a newspaper. The other . . . is a note from your uncle."

"What? Let me see that." Caleb took the smaller paper from her hand and read aloud:

To whoever finds this note:

The newspaper story enclosed with this may be important. I found it folded up in Charley Weber's wallet while I was going through his things after he died. I had been feeling uneasy about my good friend's death. Something didn't sit right with me, although I couldn't put my finger on what that might be. I'm still not certain what it all means, but this news story may help explain it. After seeing it, I've begun to feel that Charley's invitation to George and me to go with him to South America was meant to cover up the real reason he came to Cedar Ridge, but I need to check into it further to make sure of my facts before I mention it to anyone else.

George Ross, my partner, knew of my suspicions, but he's gone now. I may be wrong, but if it turns out I am not, I want to leave some record behind in case anything happens to me before I get it all sorted out.

Alvin Nelson

Caleb looked up, a gentle smile softening his expression. "That sounds just like him. I can almost hear him saying those words. The man was fair to a fault. He never wanted to accuse anyone unjustly. So what did he hide? Is it going to tell us anything?"

"Maybe not everything, but it tells us a lot." Melanie handed him the yellowed clipping. "Look at this headline: 'Young Woman Dies at Local Man's Hand.' From what I can make out, the article tells about a girl who was killed in Pueblo, Colorado. Between these water stains and being faded with age, it's impossible to read the whole story, but one thing is clear enough." She pointed to one of the few legible lines.

Caleb took the paper in his hands and squinted at it, then his eyes flared wide. "Cecilia Weber?"

"There's more." Melanie leaned over his shoulder to read the rest of the sentence aloud. "'Daughter of well-known businessman Lucas Weber.'"

They stared at each other, then Caleb said, "Lucas Weber's daughter."

Melanie nodded. "Charley's niece."

Caleb held up the paper again. "What happened to her? Does it say?"

Melanie let out a bitter laugh. "I'm sure it does, but the rest of the story is nothing more than a blur, except for a couple of lines at the end." Caleb followed her pointing finger. "Right here, where it says the killer escaped, and the posse lost his trail. It looks like the killer got away."

Caleb stared at her. "Are you saying there's some connection between this article and Charley's death?"

"Your uncle apparently did. His note was folded inside the article."

26

Melanie felt her throat constrict. "That would explain why he never played the music box, never had it out on display."

Caleb raked his fingers through his hair. "It makes sense. He knew it would be easy enough for someone to break in and find these papers if he left them somewhere in the office, so he hid them in the music box for safekeeping."

Melanie drummed her fingers on the tabletop, trying to piece it all together. "But if Charley's death had something to do with this article . . ." Her lips parted as a thought struck her. "His niece had been killed. A loving uncle would never forget that. Do you think he found her murderer here in Cedar Ridge?"

"Could be . . . But if that was the case, why didn't he say anything?"

"He got sick. Maybe he planned to tell the marshal as soon as he recovered."

Caleb nodded thoughtfully. "That would make sense.

Charley was ill, but he seemed to be getting better. Then he took a sudden turn for the worse and . . . died." His face turned ashen. "Just the way it happened with Uncle Alvin."

He went to the back window and looked out.

Melanie struggled to keep her voice steady. "How much would your uncle have told Lucas Weber in his letter? Do you think he would have identified the man he suspected?"

"Not without solid proof." Caleb's voice held a note of certainty. "Remember, he didn't even give a name in that note he left behind. My uncle was a man who would stand unwaveringly for the truth, but he was equally fervent about not wanting to make accusations against anyone without having all the facts. He never said a word about his suspicions to me."

He paced the small office as he continued. "Let's assume he found the news story in Charley's things after he passed away. He may not have paid much attention at first to a story in an old newspaper—why would he, after all? But once he read that article, something must have raised a suspicion in his mind."

Melanie leaned forward, caught up in his excitement. "Would he have confronted the person he suspected?"

"I don't believe he would. Not right away, at least. One thing I've learned in my time in Cedar Ridge is that you don't ask men about their past. A lot of them have come out west to make a fresh start. Uncle Alvin would have known that, since he spent most of his life out here. He would have been more likely to extend grace than to point a finger."

He halted in midstride, and his voice took on a stern note. "But something must have made him feel his suspicions had merit. And once he made the connection between whoever the article was written about and Charley's untimely death . . . then it became something more than a man's actions in the distant past. A murder had happened here in Cedar Ridge, and Charley was his friend. He would have felt compelled to do something about it."

"And when he did . . ." Melanie felt a chill trickle up her spine. "That must have been when he decided to get in touch with Lucas."

Caleb hit his fist against his knee. "But why didn't he say anything to me? I could have helped him."

Melanie didn't have to wonder about the answer to that. "Because you're family. He cared about you and Levi. He wanted to see justice done, but he wanted to protect the two of you, as well. And he may have waited to take that step of writing to Lucas until he was taken ill himself."

"He must have," Caleb said. "It's the only way it all ties together—otherwise Lucas would have responded sooner."

Melanie nodded. "Lucas Weber wouldn't have known about your uncle's death."

"No, there was no reason for him to have heard about it. So when his letter was returned, that left him with a host of questions."

"And no way to learn the answers," Melanie said softly. "Unless he came out here to search for them on his own. And when he got here . . ." They stared at each other for a long moment.

Caleb spoke slowly, as if letting his words piece his thoughts together. "The man who murdered Lucas's daughter was apparently known in their town. If the man who killed Charley was the same person—"

"Lucas would have recognized him," Melanie finished

for him. She sucked in her breath, and her eyes flared wide. "Caleb, did you hear what Rance Yeary said?"

"About what?"

"When he was talking to Thomas O'Shea. He said O'Shea moved here from Denver." She gripped his arm. "Denver, Caleb! O'Shea is from Colorado."

Caleb's face grew taut. "That's right." He thrust the papers into Melanie's hands. "It's time to turn all this over to the marshal. He can take it from here. Hold on to these. The Professor's book is at my house. I'll go get it and bring Levi back with me. I won't feel safe having him out of my sight until this is all over."

In the distance, Melanie heard the faint rumble of thunder again. She closed her fingers around the papers and gave him a brisk nod. While Caleb hurried off on his errand, she locked the front door and put the *Closed* sign in the window.

No sooner had she finished than Caleb burst inside the back door, his face ashen. "Levi's gone."

Melanie stopped in her tracks. "What do you mean, gone?"

"I mean I can't find him anywhere." Caleb's voice was as taut as his features. "I looked all over the house, in the cupboards, even under his cot. He isn't there."

27

Melanie felt as if a giant hand had squeezed the air out of her lungs. "Where could he have gone?"

Concern shone in Caleb's eyes. "I don't know, but I need to find him. What about these papers?"

"Getting them to the marshal can wait," Melanie said. "Finding Levi is more important. Where shall we put them?"

Caleb looked around the office and picked up the music box. "They've been safe in here so far. I can't think of any-place better." Opening the box, he took the papers from Melanie and folded them together, then slipped them back underneath the mechanism. He started for the back door. "I'm not sure where to start looking."

Melanie followed close on his heels. "He might be playing in the alley."

"No, I already checked."

"Then let's look out front."

Melanie walked out into the middle of Lincoln Street, squinting her eyes against the dust blown up by the gusting wind. She scanned the street from one end to the other, but there was no sign of the little boy.

She thought about Levi riding his stick horse up and down the boardwalk the day he had his run-in with the marshal. "Let's check the livery stable. Maybe he went over there to visit the horses."

They ducked their heads against the blowing dust and hurried across the street.

Micah Rawlins looked up when they dashed inside the livery. "I don't usually see you both out of the store at the same time. What's the occasion?"

"We're looking for Levi," Caleb said. "Have you seen him?"

"As a matter of fact, I did." Micah set his pitchfork against a post. "He was headed out toward the south end of town . . . maybe an hour or so ago. He had a cane pole over his shoulder. Said he was going fishing."

"Fishing?" Caleb echoed. "On a day like this?"

Micah shrugged and grinned. "The wind wasn't whipping like this when I saw him. He told me he was going to try a spot he'd seen over by the ruins on Founders Day." His grin faded. "I figured it was just kid talk. That's a long way for a little tyke to be walking on his own. You don't really think he'd try it, do you?"

"The ruins . . ." Melanie looked up at Caleb with dawning anxiety. "But that's on the other side of the creek. He wouldn't try to cross by himself, would he?"

"He might," Micah said. "The water's plenty low enough for him to find places where he could get across. He'd get his feet wet, but he could still do it easy enough if he picked the right spot."

"And if he didn't . . ." Melanie felt a stirring of panic. "That's a long way for him to go on foot. Do you think he could make it that far?"

Caleb's grim expression made her panic rise even more. "I wouldn't put it past him. When he ran out of the store, he looked upset enough to tackle pretty much anything."

Melanie filled in the words he'd left unspoken: *And he was upset because of you.*

Micah stepped to the doorway and looked up at the sky. "See those black clouds massing up north? Looks like the rain is coming down pretty hard up there. That means the creek will be rising before long. If your boy is on the other side when that happens, he'll be cut off."

Caleb grabbed him by the arm. "Can you get a rig ready right away? I need to get out there and find him."

Micah started pulling a harness from its hook on the wall before Caleb finished speaking. "You bet. And as soon as I get the two of you on your way, I'll sound the alarm and start rounding up a search party."

Melanie clung to the wagon seat as it jounced along the trail. "This is my fault. I never should have scolded him so harshly. The music box is costly, but it's only a box. Levi is worth infinitely more than that."

"You had no way of knowing he'd take off like this." Caleb held tight to the reins and kept his eye on the road. "If it helps any, I'm blaming myself just as much. I was supposed to be keeping an eye on the house through the office window. How did I miss seeing him slip away?"

Melanie sat up as tall as she could on the swaying seat and

studied the trail ahead. "Can you see any tracks? How do we even know he came this far?"

"We don't." Caleb's tension was evident in his voice. "But what he told Micah is the only thing we have to go on. I have to follow up on it."

They reached the creek and splashed across the ford, the horse's hooves sending up plumes of water. Fear clutched at Melanie's throat. As Micah said, the water was still shallow enough in that spot, but would Levi have known to cross there?

"Look!" Caleb shouted.

She whirled around. "Where? Do you see him?"

Caleb hauled back on the reins and circled the horse back around to the edge of the creek bank. "Not Levi, but see those prints?"

Melanie followed his pointing finger. Small boot-shaped imprints stood out clearly in the mud at the water's edge. And they were coming up *out* of the water on that side of the creek. Relief swept over her. So Levi had gotten that far, at least. She stood up in the wagon—balancing against the thrust of the wind, feeling it pulling strands of her hair loose from its pins—and searched the area.

Beside her, Caleb cupped his hands around his mouth. "Levi! Where are you?"

Melanie shook her head. "The wind is blowing too hard. He won't be able to hear you."

"Then we'll just have to cover as much territory as we can. Keep a sharp lookout." Caleb shook the reins and set the horse into motion, heading across the meadow and toward the cliffs.

Melanie twisted from side to side, trying to see in every

direction at once. Movement to their rear caught her attention, and she tugged at Caleb's arm. "It's Micah, and he has someone with him."

He turned to look where she pointed. Two horses plunged across the creek, approaching them at a rapid clip. Behind them, a line of horses, wagons, and buggies stretched out along the trail from town. True to his word, Micah had brought a search party.

Micah reined his sorrel gelding to a halt beside the wagon. Will pulled up alongside him a second later.

"Micah caught me just as I was ready to ride back to the ranch," Will said. "Have you found any sign of him?"

Caleb nodded. "We saw some tracks on this side of the creek, so we know he came this far, but I don't know where to look next. He told Micah he was going fishing, but we didn't see him anywhere along the bank. He could be down in the trees, or up in one of the storage caves, or anywhere else around here. Where do we start?"

Will gestured toward the line of approaching wagons. "We have enough people to do a thorough search, and more are on their way." He hailed the new arrivals, waving them over to join the group, and raised his voice to be heard above the wind. "We don't have much time, men. It's already raining heavy up north, and the storm is on its way here. We have to find the boy quick—before a flash flood hits. Some of you head upstream, and some of you take the other direction. Better have at least one man on either side of the creek. We know he got this far, but he might have crossed back over at some point.

"The rest of you, fan out. We've got a big area to cover. Look in the underbrush, check the caves, anywhere you think a youngster might decide to go exploring . . . or hole up to get out of the wind. If you find him, fire off a couple of rounds to let the rest of us know."

As the searchers hurried off, Will turned to Caleb and Melanie and pointed toward the trail. "Looks like more people are arriving. I'll go meet them and get them organized." He dug his heels into his horse's sides and galloped off.

Caleb cast a glance around the open area and appeared to make up his mind. "He told Micah he was going fishing. Maybe that hole he spotted was down near where he and the rancher's boy were setting off their fireworks on Founders Day. Let's start there."

Melanie laid her hand on his arm when he lifted the reins. "I think Will is right, we need to cover as much ground as we can. He and the other children were playing hide-and-seek up around the caves. Why don't I look at them while you check the creek?"

Caleb held the horse steady while she climbed down from the wagon, then he drove off at a brisk trot.

Melanie sprinted off toward the nearest storage cave. She leaned into the opening and peered around the dim interior. "Levi? Are you here?"

No answer. Pulling her head back, she turned and ran to the second cave, farther along the cliffside. As she bent to look inside, her shawl snagged on the rocky wall, bringing her up short. She snatched it off with an impatient cry and tossed it on the ground. A quick check inside revealed only an empty darkness.

The third cave yielded no more results than the first two. Melanie looked at the next opening twenty yards away, unable to keep her thoughts from returning to the small tracks by the creek. If Levi had taken refuge in one of the storage caves, he might be lonely and afraid. But if he was down by the rushing waters of the creek, he could be in mortal danger.

Hiking up her skirt, she ran toward the stream. She could see Caleb off to her right, and a ragged line of volunteers moving along the bank. For a moment, she wavered, wondering if she had made a mistake in abandoning the caves to check the creek. She glanced to her left. The line of searchers hadn't gotten that far. She could move beyond them and check the part of the creek that lay farther downstream.

She pushed her way through the trees, hearing the voices of other searchers calling Levi's name farther up the bank. The dark, angry clouds building up overhead obscured the sun, making it seem more like dusk than midafternoon there in the shade of the trees and undergrowth.

Melanie ducked under an oak limb and made her way to the edge of the bank, struggling to keep her footing on the slippery mud while she kept a close lookout for any signs that would indicate Levi had come this way . . . or fallen into the creek.

She pressed forward, with the wind whipping her skirts and the bushes catching at her clothes. Rounding a bend in the creek, she spied a pool not far ahead on the other side of a fallen log. *Levi's fishing hole?* It looked fairly deep.

A pile of debris lay trapped along the underside of the log. Melanie clambered onto the rotting trunk, praying she wouldn't find Levi caught in the muddy water that swirled against a cut in the bank.

Her foot slipped on the water-soaked log, and she slid back a step. She tried again, bunching her skirts in one hand and using the other to grip a broken branch that protruded from the side of the trunk. Planting her foot atop the log again, she pushed herself up. She teetered for a moment, then regained her balance and looked for a spot farther along the log that would afford solid footing.

She moved slightly to one side and felt something press into the small of her back. She leaned forward, moving away from the obstruction. Before she could take another step, the pressure on her back increased, and a sudden thrust sent her tumbling.

With a shriek of terror, Melanie plummeted toward the roiling pool below.

Melanie heard the splash as she plunged into the pool. Then all sound was wiped away as the frigid water closed over her head. A moment later she bobbed up again, with her head above the surface. Opening her mouth wide, she sucked in a breath of air and tried to shout for help, but the weight of her waterlogged skirt pulled her down, dragging her under the surface again and cutting off her cry.

She kicked her legs, attempting to free them from the clinging fabric, and flailed her arms, trying to catch hold of something, anything, she could use to pull herself above the water.

Calm down, she admonished herself. She couldn't help herself if she couldn't think straight. She sank through the murky water and tried to focus her thoughts while her aching lungs screamed for air.

Her feet quickly touched bottom, and bending her knees slightly, Melanie pushed with all her might. The propulsion shot her back toward the surface.

The instant her face cleared the water, she let her breath

out, then caught a precious lungful of air while her hands scrabbled for a handhold. This time her fingers touched a small branch extending over the pool. She gripped the slender stick and held on for all she was worth, using it to pull herself over toward the bank.

Clinging to the branch with one hand, she stretched out her other arm and grabbed for the bank. But when she tried to pull herself up, the dirt crumbled away, leaving her with nothing but a handful of slick mud balled in her fist.

Melanie kicked as much as the entangling skirt would allow, desperate to keep her head above water. The cold had begun to sap her strength, and she knew if she went down again, she might not come up.

The branch slackened in her grasp, and Melanie saw that it was about to give way. Looking around, she saw a partially exposed tree root several feet away. Pushing herself toward it as far as she could, she gauged the distance, then breathed a prayer and lunged for it. Her fingers touched the root and she hurried to wrap both hands around it.

The water seemed to grow even colder, and numbness seeped into her fingers. She didn't know how long she could keep holding on. The murky water, stirred up by her struggle, splashed into her mouth, and she choked.

Melanie spluttered and coughed, knowing she wasn't going to be able to make it out on her own—she had to get someone's attention. "Help me!" she screamed. "Is anybody there?"

There was no answer. "Help me, Lord," she begged. Pressing close to the bank, she heaved against the root and raised herself as far above the water as she could. Drawing on her last remnant of strength, she called out again. "Somebody, please! I'm in the water and I need help!"

Footsteps crashed through the underbrush, and a voice shouted, "Where are you?"

Melanie wanted to weep with relief. Taking a deep breath, she managed to choke out, "Here! I'm down here."

A moment later, Caleb's face appeared above the edge of the bank, and she saw him take in the situation at a glance. Kneeling, he reached down and clasped one of her wrists in both his hands.

"Hang on," he told her. "This is going to get rough." Leaning back on his haunches, he began to heave. Melanie reached up with her other hand and caught hold of his arm as he dragged her up and over the bank to the solid ground beyond.

She lay facedown for a long moment, digging her fingers into the dirt, reassuring herself she had escaped her watery prison.

Caleb bent over her, his anxious face peering into hers. "Are you all right? Can you breathe?"

Marshal Hooper ran up, followed by Andrew Bingham and two other men. "We heard shouting. Did you find the boy?"

"No. Miss Ross took a tumble into the creek."

With Caleb's help, Melanie struggled to a sitting position, then moved over to a dry log, where she sat huddled over with her arms wrapped around herself.

Caleb knelt in front of her, catching her hands in his and gripping them tight. "What happened?"

Melanie felt a pang of guilt. He was already frantic about Levi going missing, and she was only adding to his troubles. A shiver shook her from head to toe.

He pressed his hands tighter around hers. "Where's your shawl?" Without waiting for an answer, he stood up and peeled off his coat.

22

"I took it off up there by the caves. I must have left it there when I came back to help look down here."

"Here, you need to stay warm." He wrapped the coat around her shoulders.

"Thank you," she said, nestling into its warmth. "I was so scared," she whispered. "I didn't think I was going to get out of there." She looked up and gave Andrew a shaky smile. "It looks like we cheated you out of some business."

The barber, sometimes undertaker, looked puzzled for a moment, and then his face cleared and he laughed. "Think nothing of it. I'm more than happy to wait a long time for that kind of business from you."

Marshal Hooper took up a stance directly in front of Melanie. "Tell me what happened," he said in a gruff tone that caught her by surprise.

When she hesitated, Caleb looked up at the lawman. "She'll be all right. She must have just slipped and fallen into the water."

Melanie shook her head and looked up into Caleb's eyes. "I didn't fall. Somebody pushed me."

28

What!" Caleb's hands tightened on her shoulders. Melanie spoke clearly, enunciating each word with care. "I didn't fall in—I was pushed. Micah said Levi had spotted a fishing hole over here, so I wanted to take a look at that pool. I was trying to make my way over that log"—she pointed to the fallen tree—"when I felt someone's hand on my back. The next thing I knew, whoever it was gave me a shove, and I fell in the water."

Caleb's face tightened. "You didn't see who it was?"

"No, it happened too fast. In fact, at first I thought I'd backed into a branch. It wasn't until I felt the push that I realized it had to have been a person."

Caleb faced the group of men, his expression grim. "Have any of you seen O'Shea out here?"

"Not me," Andrew said with a puzzled expression. "How about the rest of you?"

The others shook their heads.

Melanie gripped Caleb's arm. "You think . . . ? Of course!"

She scrambled to her feet and looked up at the marshal. "We found something you need to know about. Mr. O'Shea—"

The lawman cut her off with a wave of his hand. "Hang on a minute." He turned to the onlookers and said, "The rest of you need to get back to searching. We have to find that little boy before the storm breaks."

Realizing the marshal wanted to speak to her and Caleb in private, Melanie waited until the others were out of earshot. Then she blurted out, "We think Mr. O'Shea may be the one behind the murders."

When Marshal Hooper raised his eyebrows, Caleb picked up the tale. "We found a newspaper clipping about Lucas Weber's daughter being killed in Colorado."

"And Mr. O'Shea lived in Denver before coming here." Melanie leaned forward. "That's quite a coincidence, don't you think?"

"I'd have to agree with you," the marshal said, "if I hadn't just gotten another letter from Lydia Weber. She told me about her daughter's death." He drew an envelope from his jacket pocket. Reaching inside, he pulled out a photograph and handed it to Caleb. "And she enclosed a picture of the man responsible."

Caleb's jaw sagged. He stared at the paper, then looked back at the marshal. "Is this who I think it is?"

Melanie crowded close to him and peered at the image in his hand. Her eyes widened at the sight of the face that looked back at her. It was a younger face, and clean-shaven, but the features were unmistakable. She raised her head to meet the lawman's gaze. "Doc?"

Marshal Hooper nodded. "No doubt about it. He's changed his name, but it's him, all right. There's a lot more to the story, but we can go into that back at my office after we've found your boy. It doesn't prove he's the one behind all the deaths we've had around here, but there's a definite connection between him and the Webers."

Melanie stared in the direction the other men had taken. "Why didn't you want the others to know? They could be on the lookout for him."

The marshal snorted. "And if they found him, what then? You've seen for yourself how riled up this town has been. I intend to bring him to justice, but if word of this gets out before I get my hands on him, I'm likely to find him swingin' from a tree branch."

Two shots rang out in quick succession. Micah came running up, panting for breath. "They found him, Caleb. They found your boy!"

Caleb ran toward the sound of the shots, with Melanie right behind. When they reached the open meadow, they saw Will approaching with Levi in his arms. As soon as their paths met, Caleb reached for his son and held him close.

"I found him up in the farthest storage cave," Will said. "It seems the little fellow crawled in there to get out of the wind, and then he fell asleep. He never heard us yelling for him. I wouldn't have known he was in there, except for spotting his fishing pole leaning up against the cliff."

Melanie clapped one hand to her mouth. If only she'd gone a little farther, she might have been the one to find Levi and end Caleb's agony that much sooner.

Levi turned a tear-streaked face up to peer at Caleb. "I'm sorry, Papa. I shouldn't have run away like that."

Melanie choked back a sob. "I'm the one who needs to apologize, Levi. I should never have spoken to you that way."

To her amazement, Levi reached out for her with one hand. She stepped closer so he could wrap his arm around her neck. The move brought her up against Caleb, who wrapped his own arm around her waist, and the three of them stood for a long moment in a tight, healing embrace.

"Looks like she's made her choice."

Melanie lifted her head to see Will bending close to Caleb's ear. When Will saw her looking at him, he winked and moved away.

What did he mean by that? Brushing the question aside, she laid her head on Caleb's shoulder. She might not understand the meaning of Will's cryptic remark, but one thing she did know: This was her home, the place she belonged—right there in Caleb's arms.

Caleb kept his arm around Melanie as they walked back toward the wagon, accepting the congratulations and well-wishes from the searchers. Rain began to sprinkle down, with large drops that splatted against their clothing and faces.

Micah looked up at the clouds. "We didn't find him a minute too soon. It's going to start coming down hard pretty soon, folks. Better get on the other side of the creek and head back to town."

Melanie looked at Levi, snuggling against his father's shoulder, taking in his tousled hair and the streaks of dirt on his face from lying on the floor of the cave. She suspected she looked even more bedraggled after her plunge into the creek. Pulling Caleb's coat from her shoulders, she draped it around the little boy. "Here, we don't want you to catch cold."

Caleb tucked the coat tighter around Levi. "But what about you? You're the one who's soaking wet."

She touched her hand to her throat. "My shawl. It's still up by the caves."

Caleb started to hand Levi over. "I'll run up and get it for you."

She shook her head and smiled. "Stay here with Levi. He needs you. . . . You need each other. I'll be right back. It will only take me a couple minutes, and I'll meet you at the wagon."

Caleb nodded, cradling Levi against his chest.

Melanie hurried toward the caves along the cliff side, finding the shawl just where she remembered leaving it. Snatching it up, she started back to rejoin Caleb. She had taken only a few steps when an eerie sound stopped her in her tracks. She cupped one hand around her ear to block out the noise of the wind and listened, straining to hear it again.

There. It came to her a little louder this time. It sounded like a moan, a cry for help.

Melanie spun in a circle, looking around her. Who else could be out there? The band of searchers had already started home. Had one of them been injured and unintentionally left behind?

Another moan. She followed the sound to the cliff wall, where she discovered a low opening partially screened behind a clump of sagebrush. She made her way over to it and knelt to call inside. "Hello? Is anyone in there?" She heard no words in response, only a low groan.

Her concern mounting, Melanie tossed her shawl across the sagebrush and crawled into the opening, peering into the dim interior. "Where are you? Are you hurt?"

A hand closed around her upper arm and yanked her inside. Melanie flew forward, sprawling on the hard ground. Before she could push herself up, her shoulders were seized in a viselike grip.

Melanie screamed, twisting on the ground, straining with all her might to break away.

The punishing hands dragged her backward, then wrapped around her from behind, holding her in a smothering embrace. Melanie could feel her captor's chest pressing against her back and struggled in vain to turn enough to try to make out his face in the darkness.

"Who are you?" she gasped. "What do you want?"

Her assailant bent his head close to her ear, his breath warm against her cheek. Even before he spoke, the stench of stale alcohol told her who he was.

Caleb stood with Levi cradled in his arms, marveling at the sweet feeling of his son's arms twined about his neck. Though he'd wrestled with it throughout that long afternoon, he hadn't been able to escape the fear that he might never experience a hug from his son again. And he'd come near to losing Melanie, too. His throat thickened. Two near misses and two rescues, all in the same day. *I don't deserve that kind of blessing, Lord, but I thank you.*

Micah Rawlins laid a hand on his shoulder. "We'd better get moving."

Caleb nodded. "Just as soon as Melanie gets back." Joining his friend, he carried Levi to the wagon. Andrew and Will stood nearby, tightening the cinches on their horses' saddles. Caleb lifted Levi onto the wagon seat. He would get the boy settled in and be ready to leave the moment she returned.

He climbed up onto the seat beside his son, thinking back to the comment Will had made a few moments before and wondering if his friend had been right. Had Melanie made her choice? And if so, had she truly chosen him?

He checked Levi, making sure the coat was firmly tucked around him, and looked around for Melanie. Where was she? She'd said she would only need a couple of minutes to retrieve her shawl. Maybe she hadn't been able to find it, but even so, she was surely aware of their pressing need to get across the creek.

Andrew Bingham trotted up on his horse and called to Micah. "Is everyone accounted for? We don't want to go off and leave anybody stranded."

"I think so." Micah swung up onto his sorrel gelding. His brow knitted as he scanned the line of wagons heading homeward. "I don't remember seeing Doc leave, though." He reined the horse over to the other side of a group of cedars, and his frown deepened. "No, his buggy's still here."

"We'd better find him quick." Andrew kicked his horse and trotted downstream along the creek, calling Doc's name.

Caleb felt like he'd been kicked in the stomach. He stared at Micah. "Doc was here today? I never saw him." His thoughts jumped back to Melanie insisting she had been pushed into the creek.

Micah looked at him oddly. "Yeah, he was one of the last to arrive. Why?"

Caleb threw a frantic glance toward the meadow and the cliffs beyond. No sign of Melanie . . . or Doc. "Micah, would you stay here with Levi? I need to go find Melanie."

Micah dismounted without hesitation. "Sure, I'll stay with him. But hurry."

Will stepped down from his mount and came over to the wagon. "What's wrong?"

"Come on." Caleb grabbed his friend's arm. "I don't have time to explain now. I'll fill you in on the way."

"What do I want? I'm just going to finish what I started."

Melanie writhed and twisted, trying to escape the fingers that bit into her shoulders like steel pincers. She managed to free one arm enough to bring her hand up and rake her nails across Doc's face. When he let out a howl and slackened his hold, she scrambled to her feet and struck her head against the low ceiling. The impact dropped her to her knees, and she moaned.

Doc let out a harsh laugh. "That ought to take some of the starch out of you." Taking hold of her shoulders again, he dragged her across the rocky floor of the cave into the corner farthest away from the entrance, where the ceiling sloped down even more. He crouched down and sat, pulling her with him and holding her with her back tight up against his chest. "You have more fight in you than I expected after that dunking in the creek."

Melanie's head swam, and she tried to make sense of his words. "You pushed me?" *Of course.* She should have known. "But I didn't see you with the searchers."

"As intended. With everyone coming out from town, no one would question my joining the search party, but that wasn't the reason I came. I was hoping to find a chance to get either you or Caleb alone, and I did . . . but it didn't work out quite the way I'd planned."

Melanie squirmed against the arms that encircled her body. "Meaning I didn't die?"

He grunted. "If he hadn't come along to pull you out, it

would all be over now. They'd have been fishing your body out of the creek half a mile downstream."

Melanie gasped, and her stomach roiled at the thought of him standing on the bank, watching her drown.

"It would have been so much easier that way," Doc lamented. "After the boy was found, I was ready to head back to town with the others when I saw you coming out here alone, and I realized I'd been given a second opportunity. This time I won't leave anything to chance."

Doc laughed, his chin rubbing against the back of her neck. "This time I'm going to hold your head under the water and make sure I've finished the job. I was really hoping all the killing was over, but after Caleb showed me that book last night, I knew the two of you were going to figure out what happened with Charley and Alvin. A drowning will be perfect. There will be nothing to connect it to a poisoning, and no one will question something that's so obviously an accident."

Fear clutched at Melanie, threatening to choke her. She swallowed against the knot in her throat and screamed as loudly as she could. "Help! Somebody help me!" Her cry echoed off the walls of the cave.

Doc's rumbling laugh sent another puff of alcohol into the air. "No one can hear you out there, not with that wind. If there's anyone left to hear. They've probably all started back to town by now. That's what I've been waiting for."

Melanie shook her head violently. "Caleb wouldn't just leave. He'll come after me."

Doc chuckled. "But he won't find you . . . not until after it's too late."

A sob ripped from Melanie's throat. "Even if you do kill me, Caleb will know you're the one who did it. We already knew that you're the one behind the other murders. If you kill me, he'll come after you."

Doc's voice hardened. "He won't have time to do that. I'll get to him first . . . just as soon as I've finished with you."

"But it isn't just Caleb and me." Melanie's voice quavered so much she could barely form the words. "The marshal knows, too. He's the one who told us."

Doc's harsh laugh echoed off the cave walls. "Don't think you can lie your way out of this. You aren't the first lying woman I've dealt with."

29

Will shot an incredulous look at Caleb as they neared the caves. "You're telling me that Doc is the one behind killing Charley Weber and his brother?"

"That's right." Caleb didn't break his stride. "I have a suspicion he may have killed my uncle, too. And unless I miss my guess, he's the one who pushed Melanie into the creek today." He stopped when they reached the storage caves and looked around. "Where is she? She said she was coming straight here." Worry gnawed at him at the thought of Doc being in the area.

"Don't jump to conclusions," Will said, reading the cause of his anxiety correctly. "It doesn't necessarily mean Doc has done anything to Melanie. Maybe we just missed her."

"Where else would she be?" Caleb demanded. "She said she was coming up here to get her shawl." Cupping his mouth with his hands, he shouted for her. Will joined in, the two of them calling Melanie's name over and over again.

Only the wind answered.

CAROL COX

From somewhere outside the cave, Melanie heard faint voices calling her name. "Caleb!" she shrieked. With a strength borne of desperation, she jabbed her elbow into Doc's stomach and wrenched away, scrambling for the cave opening on her hands and knees.

She had only moved a few feet before Doc's hand closed around her right ankle and jerked back, yanking her leg out from under her. Melanie slammed flat onto the ground, face-down on the hard dirt floor. Before she could move, he grabbed her other foot and held it fast.

Melanie clutched at the ground for a handhold. Her fingers raked across the dirt, and she felt her skirts ride up to her knees as he dragged her all the way back to the farthest cave wall.

He released her for an instant, then he seized her by her waist and hauled her backward like a sack of potatoes, catching her up against his chest again. He wrapped one arm around her body, pinning her arms to her sides, and planted his other hand over her mouth.

She heard Caleb call her name again and tried to scream but could only produce a muffled wail. Her chest heaved and tears clogged her throat. Caleb was out there, looking for her . . . and she could do nothing to let him know where she was.

Doc's chest heaved and his voice grated in her ear. "Don't try that again."

Melanie heard Caleb call once more. His voice sounded farther away this time. Tears stung her eyes and flowed down her cheeks. He wasn't going to find her. She was going to die. And she would never have a chance to tell him how much she cared for him.

Sobs overtook her, shaking her whole body. Doc tightened

his arm around her chest and pressed his hand closer over her mouth, his fingers digging into her cheeks.

Melanie strained against the increasing pressure on her mouth and ribs, fighting to draw in a breath.

Doc moved his hand upward a bit, keeping his palm over her mouth while he pinched her nose shut between his thumb and forefinger.

Melanie's eyes flared wide and her lungs heaved, trying to draw in the slightest breath of air.

Doc clamped his hand down even tighter. "Calm down," he ordered. "This will be easier on you in the long run than drowning. It'll all be over in a minute. You won't feel a thing."

Caleb tried to fight down the despair that threatened to overwhelm him. "She can't have just disappeared, Will. She has to be here . . . somewhere." Worry clawed at him like a wild animal. What if Doc had found her before she got to the caves and dragged her off into the woods, or down by the creek?

Or maybe Will was right and they had just missed her somehow. Even now she might be down at the wagon, waiting . . . and worrying about him.

God, help me! Show me what to do. He turned to Will, trying to keep his voice even. "It looks like she isn't up here. We would have seen her by now. Why don't you go on back to the wagon and see if she returned without us seeing her. I can't keep the thought of Doc grabbing her out of my mind. I'll check down by the creek."

"Right." Will nodded and started to trot off, but he stopped after taking a few steps. "What's that?"

Caleb looked in the direction Will pointed. "It's Melanie's shawl. She never made it back this far." The realization hit him like a blow to the chest. "Forget the wagon—she won't be there. I need you to check the trees behind the creek while I look along the bank. We don't have any time to lose."

"You're right." Will flinched as a bolt of lightning streaked across the sky. "And that storm is nearly on us."

30

Melanie arched her back and writhed like a snake, jerking her head from side to side, desperate to free herself from Doc's oppressive hold. Her lungs cried out for air as she put every bit of strength she possessed into this last-ditch effort. She wouldn't get a second chance.

Doc cursed, wrestling her into submission. "Don't make this any harder on yourself," he panted.

She managed to open her mouth a fraction and felt the skin of Doc's hand against her teeth. Sending a quick prayer heavenward, she caught the flesh between her teeth and clamped down.

Doc yowled and yanked his hand away, long enough for her to suck in a lungful of the blessed air.

"Stupid woman!" Grabbing her by the hair, he yanked her head back hard, pressing it tight against his shoulder. He squeezed his hand over her mouth again, redoubling the pressure.

Melanie fought for her life, scrabbling against the cave

floor in a futile effort to gain enough purchase to get away. Her violent struggle pushed her back against Doc, knocking him off balance. She heard him grunt when he came up hard against the wall.

She curved her fingers into talons and tried to claw his arms, but she couldn't raise her hands high enough with her upper arms held captive. Her hands beat against the ground, feeling around for a handful of dust to fling into his face. Her fingers closed over a fist-sized rock.

What could she do with it? With Doc holding her from behind, she couldn't see to aim, but she could feel his chin digging into the top of her head. She gritted her teeth and lunged, trying to raise her arm enough to bring the rock around behind her and hit him in the face.

"It's no use," Doc panted. "You're as good as dead."

Despair washed over Melanie in a crushing wave. *He's right. I'm going to die—right here, right now*. Maybe it would be easier to accept the inevitable and just give in. Her painful struggle would be over that much sooner. The light filtering in through the cave's opening began to dim, and she felt her fingers loosen on the rock.

The next instant, a blinding flash of light burst through the opening, accompanied by an explosion of sound that reverberated through the cave.

Doc flinched, and his hands loosened their hold. Melanie gulped in air and tightened her grip on the rock. She swung her arm up with all her might, aiming at a spot just behind her head.

A solid *thunk* told her she'd connected with her target. Doc's arms grew limp and fell away. Melanie spun around, still clutching the rock, and raised her arm to strike again. At the shadowed sight of Doc's still form, she let the rock slip from her fingers and clawed her way to the exit.

Caleb picked himself up off the ground and stared around, dazed. "What was that?"

A few yards away, Will got to his feet and pointed to a spot a hundred feet up the hillside where a massive oak looked like it had exploded. "I've been around when lightning struck before, but that one was too close for comfort."

Caleb looked with awe at the riven tree, its trunk still smoldering. Limbs of all sizes lay strewn across the clearing where he and Will stood.

The rain started coming down in earnest, pelting them with stinging drops. Caleb stooped to pick up his hat. He had to find Melanie and get back to Levi so he could take them both to safety.

He looked at Will. "I think we need to start searching lower ground." The rancher nodded and set off at a brisk pace. Caleb started to follow, then turned back to get Melanie's shawl. He *would* find her. And when he did, she would need it.

As he reached for the shawl, the clump of sagebrush it lay on began to shake. A moment later, Melanie appeared behind it. Caleb stared open-mouthed, feeling like he'd just been witness to a conjuror at work.

A radiant light spread across her face when she saw him, and the next minute he was holding her in his arms. Rivulets of water streamed down her cheeks. Tears or raindrops, Caleb couldn't tell.

He wrapped his arms around her and pulled her close. She clung to him as though she never wanted to let him go, and Caleb had no intention of turning her loose. Bending his head, he lifted her chin and pressed his mouth to hers. The touch of her lips sent a surge of energy through him, every bit as electrifying as the lightning bolt.

When he pulled away, Melanie cupped her hands around his face and stared up at him with a look of wonder. Caleb looked at her, taking in every aspect of her appearance as she stood before him in her sodden dress, her hair in tangles, and water streaming from her skirts. She had never looked more beautiful to him.

"I thought I'd lost you," he whispered.

A shadow dimmed her happy look. "You nearly did." Without leaving the circle of his arms, she turned and pointed at the rough fissure behind the bush. "Doc is in there." Her voice faltered. "I think I killed him."

Will came up behind them in time to catch her remark. "Did I hear right? Doc's around here?"

Melanie nodded and pointed again. "Right over there, in that cave."

Fury darkened Caleb's vision. "He tried to hurt you?" He stepped away from Melanie and started toward the cave.

Will stopped him with a hand on his shoulder. "Let me take care of Doc. Melanie needs you right now."

Looking back, Caleb saw her tremble. He retrieved the shawl and spread it over her shoulders. "I'm not sure how much good it's going to do. It's almost as wet as you are."

She looked up at him with a trace of a smile on her face.

Will crawled from the cave, using his pistol to prod Doc along in front of him. Doc stood and stumbled, holding his hand against a bloody gash on his head.

Melanie shrank back against Caleb. "I thought he was dead."

Will's eyes held a glint of steel. "No, but when he faces the music for everything he's done, he may wish he was."

Rage of a sort he'd never known filled Caleb as he stared at the man who had murdered his uncle and tried to take the life of the woman he loved. More than anything at that moment, he wanted to exact justice on his own, make the murderer feel the kind of pain he had caused to so many. He wanted vengeance.

"Vengeance is mine; I will repay, saith the Lord." The Scripture he'd heard more than once from Uncle Alvin blazed in his mind.

All right, Lord. But I sure hope you hurry.

He tightened his hold around Melanie's shoulders. "Let's move. We still need to get across the creek and back to town."

31

Melanie wound her hair into a coil and pushed the hairpins into place. She leaned closer to the oak-framed dresser mirror and ran a fingertip along the puffiness under her eyes, still there after a good night's sleep.

Out of habit, she'd awoken as usual at first light, but remembering Caleb's insistence that she sleep in that morning, she'd pulled the covers over her head and sunk back into slumber. She hadn't stirred again until the sun was past its zenith.

At least she had been able to wake up. A shudder rippled through her at the thought of the time she'd spent with Doc in the cave, wondering if she would ever see another dawn. Bruises marred her arms where Doc's fingers had dug into her shoulders, and her body bore a multitude of scrapes and scratches from being dragged across the ground. It would be days before the marks on her cheeks from the pressure of Doc's hand faded. But those reminders of her ordeal would disappear in time. She had lived through it, and that was what mattered.

That, and whatever the future might hold for her and Caleb. She would never forget the sight of him standing before her when she made her desperate escape from the cave. And now he would be waiting downstairs.

She took her time descending the stairs, realizing afresh how sore her muscles were. When she reached the bottom step, she heard a voice call out, "There she is!"

Melanie looked up to see a crowd of people congregated in the mercantile, stretching from the counter over to the far wall . . . and all of them looking at her.

When Caleb stepped toward her, she whispered, "What's going on?"

He smiled. "It's been like this all day. As soon as the news about Doc got around, people started pouring in here, all of them asking about you. Some of them have been waiting for more than an hour to see you."

Andrew Bingham grinned. "We needed to see for ourselves you were all right. Caleb made us keep quiet so we wouldn't wake you up."

Someone cleared his throat loudly. The crowd parted to allow Mayor Pike and his wife to make their way through.

The mayor cleared his throat again. "Miss Ross, it appears this town owes you a debt of gratitude for bringing the truth to light and helping to bring a perfidious villain to justice."

Melanie nodded her thanks, not sure what to say.

Mrs. Pike fastened her gaze on the top of Melanie's head, not quite meeting her eyes. "I'd like your assistance with a number of items I plan to order. I'll be back in to discuss them when you've had a chance to recuperate."

Melanie watched with a faint smile as the mayor's wife swept out of the store beside her husband, knowing that was the closest thing to an apology she was ever likely to get from Ophelia Pike.

A buzz of conversation sprinkled with laughter swept over the crowd, giving the gathering a festive air. Melanie looked around, marveling at the number of visitors to the store. She nudged Caleb. "Have they just come to say hello, or are they buying anything?"

His delighted grin answered her even before he spoke. "If sales keep on going as well as they have today, we'll make up for the business we lost by the end of the month."

Melanie breathed a happy sigh. "So maybe we won't lose all our customers to O'Shea, after all."

Micah cleared his throat and nodded toward the door. "Speaking of O'Shea . . ."

The owner of the emporium made his way through the crowd and took a stance in front of Melanie and Caleb. He kept his eyes fixed on the floor. "Miss Ross. Caleb."

Melanie drew nearer to Caleb, who circled his right arm around her.

"Afternoon, O'Shea," he said.

The skinny man slapped his hat against his leg, and his Adam's apple bobbed up and down. "I just want to say— I'm sorry for what happened yesterday." He risked a glance up at them. "Having the tables turned on me that way, when everyone thought I was the one trying to scare you into leaving town, kinda woke me up. It brought me up short to realize I'd been so intent on getting all the business in town for myself, I didn't realize the kind of trouble I might be stirring up for the two of you."

He took a deep breath and cleared his throat. "If you can find it in your heart to forgive me, I'd like a chance to do better." He held out a tentative hand. "Do you think there's room enough for both of us in this town?"

Caleb gripped the other man's hand without hesitation. "I'm sure there is. I'm more than willing to get along, Thomas. I'd much rather have you as a friend than as an enemy."

A quick grin flitted across O'Shea's face, and he ducked his head in a brief nod. "Thanks, Caleb. It feels good to clear the air." He shuffled his feet and then added, "Well, I'd better get back to my store. Good day to you both." He turned and made his way to the door, pausing to give them a brief smile as he went out.

A series of customers lined up at the counter, and Caleb went to take care of them. Melanie turned to see Will and the Professor approaching.

The Professor sketched a little bow, his black suit and cravat as tidy as ever. "From what Will tells me, you showed a remarkable amount of wit and courage yesterday. I hope this dreadful experience hasn't soured you on the West. It would be an honor to have you remain in our midst."

"I don't have any plans to leave." Melanie smiled at the Professor, thinking of the town, the store, and the dear people she had gotten to know since coming to Cedar Ridge. And Caleb. God truly had taken her frightful situation with the Deavers and turned it around for her good. She couldn't imagine being happy anyplace else.

Will tilted his hat back on his head and smiled. "I'm glad to hear that."

The bell jingled, and Mrs. Fetterman pushed her way into the room. When she spotted Melanie, she waved and hurried over to enfold her in a tight hug. "Oh, my dear! What a horrible time you've been through."

She held up a plate and beamed. "Look, I brought you some of my raspberry torte to celebrate your rescue. Two pieces this time," she added with a grin.

Melanie felt her mouth water at the sight of the delectable pastry. Without a moment's thought, she picked up the nearest slice and finished it off in three quick bites. Mrs. Fetterman chuckled, and Melanie's cheeks flamed. "I didn't mean to gobble it up like that. I think you'd better take Caleb's slice to him before I completely lose control."

"Mrs. Fetterman!" Caleb hailed her from the counter. He reached underneath and held up a parcel. "This package arrived for you this morning."

The gray-haired woman clapped her hands and hurried over to the counter. She took off the paper in one swipe and crowed, "It's my new spectacles!" Taking off the old pair, she set the new ones in place, hooking the side pieces over her ears.

Melanie grinned at Caleb, enjoying the older woman's eagerness.

Mrs. Fetterman turned around and let her gaze travel over the store.

"Well," Melanie said, "what do you think?"

Mrs. Fetterman's voice held a note of awe. "I had no idea how much difference a new pair could make. When I think what I've been missing . . ." She grinned up at Melanie. "I guess now I'll be able to read labels for myself."

Melanie bent and gave the older woman a quick hug. "I'll still be here to help out anytime you need me."

Mrs. Fetterman nudged Melanie's arm and lowered her voice to a whisper. "I didn't miss everything, though. I was right, wasn't I."

Melanie tilted her head, puzzled.

Mrs. Fetterman's eyes twinkled. "About the way Caleb looks at you. It didn't take a new pair of specs to see that. He's doing it right now."

Melanie laughed and felt a blush color her cheeks. Her laughter faded when she saw Marshal Hooper winding his way through the crowd to stand before her.

Melanie's heart constricted. The sight of the lawman brought back the memory of the previous day's ordeal, flooding her with emotion. She wondered how long it would be before she was free of that nightmare.

The marshal took off his hat and nodded to her and Caleb, then glanced around the store. "I wanted a word with the two of you, but I didn't count on the whole town being here. Is there any place we can go to talk in private?"

When Caleb hesitated, Will stepped forward. "Go ahead. I'll keep an eye on things and call you if you're needed."

Caleb nodded his thanks, then led Melanie and the marshal back to the mercantile office.

The marshal turned his hat in his hands. "Now that the storm has passed, I'm getting ready to take Doc over to Prescott. He'll stay in the jail there until he stands trial for murder. He'll be charged with the deaths of Cecilia, Charley and Lucas Weber, and your uncle Alvin. Not to mention the attempted murder of Miss Ross."

"Will we have to testify at the trial?" Caleb asked. "I don't like the idea of putting Melanie through that."

Melanie's eyes widened. Once they'd made their way back to town—crossing Walnut Creek only moments before a wall of water came rushing down the streambed—Caleb and Will had delivered Doc Mills to the marshal, and Melanie felt like a chapter of her life had closed. The thought of having to relive it all again, in public and before a group of strangers, brought back all the dark emotions she wanted to forget.

The marshal shook his head. "I don't expect we'll need you there. The court might send someone over to take an affidavit, but this trial is going to be more a formality than anything. Doc gave me a full confession after you brought him in last night."

"So easily?" Surprise sharpened Melanie's voice. A forthright admission of his guilt seemed at odds with the man who had gone to such lengths to conceal his crimes.

"It was that letter from Mrs. Weber that did the trick. That, and the photograph. Once I showed those to him, he broke down and owned up to everything."

"What was in that letter?" The curiosity in Caleb's tone matched Melanie's own desire to know the rest of the story. "You said you'd fill us in on that later."

Marshal Hooper leaned back against the edge of the desk. "You already know about Cecilia Weber's death."

Melanie nodded. "But just that she was killed, not how or why it happened. The newspaper article was so blurred, we couldn't make out any of the details."

"It happened nearly seven years ago," the marshal said. "Miss Weber and Doc—who was going by another name at the time—were engaged to be married."

"Engaged!" Melanie felt the air whoosh out of her lungs.

"But she broke it off just before their wedding date. Turns out she found out about Doc's drinking, and it gave her second thoughts. Then she turned around and accepted another man's proposal, one of Doc's good friends."

Caleb grunted. "That would be hard for a man to take."

The lawman nodded. "Especially someone who'd been diving into the bottle. Outwardly, Doc seemed to take it with good grace, but inside, he was looking for a way to get even. He found his chance when they were all at a dinner party one evening, and he managed to catch her alone outside. When the other guests heard screaming, they rushed outdoors and saw Doc running away. They found Cecelia's body in the garden. Her neck had been snapped."

"How awful!" Melanie exchanged a look of horror with Caleb and put her hand to her throat. How easily the same thing could have happened to her!

Caleb cleared his throat. "From what little we could read of the article, it sounded like Doc got away."

"That's what Mrs. Weber's letter said. By the time they started after him, he had just enough of a head start to grab a horse and get out of town. He managed to lose the posse, and he's been on the run ever since."

Caleb ran his fingers through his hair. "What about Charley? Are you saying he just happened upon Doc while he was visiting my uncle here?"

The marshal shook his head. "Lydia Weber said she was going through her husband's papers and came across a letter written to him by his brother. He told Lucas he'd met a soldier on leave from Fort Verde who talked about a lush of a doctor, as he put it, in the neighboring town. Charley thought it was worth checking into and told his brother he might be on the trail of the snake who had killed his niece. He said a couple of old pards of his lived in Cedar Ridge, so no one would suspect the real reason for his visit. He promised to keep Lucas posted and let him know what he found out."

338

"But he didn't," Melanie said softly.

"He may not have had time," the marshal said. "Once he took sick, he needed medical attention, so Alvin and George called in the only doctor in town. Doc recognized the Weber name right off, of course. He didn't know Charley was on his trail, and he hoped he wouldn't be recognized after all those years, but he didn't want to take any chances."

Caleb picked up the story. "Then when Uncle Alvin had his suspicions about Charley's death, Doc decided to take care of him, too."

The marshal nodded. "He seemed to think that one more murder would keep him from being caught. Then Lucas rode into town. Doc was just coming home from another session at the Silver Moon, and he recognized him at once. Weber must have been heading to the back door to rouse your uncle when Doc caught up with him."

They were silent a moment, then Caleb spoke. "Did he happen to mention whether he'd been leaving threatening notes around the store?"

"Yes, he mentioned those. He said something about setting oily rags on fire in your office, too." The marshal let out a dry laugh. "As long as he was in a confessing mood, I guess he figured he'd make a clean breast of everything. Not that it will do him any good when it comes to his trial. Murder is murder."

"What about Cousin George?" Melanie asked, not sure if she wanted to hear the answer.

"I asked him about that," the marshal said. "Doc swears George's heart just gave out on him, nothing more than that." He settled his hat back on his head and turned toward the door. "Since he owned up to all the others, I don't see any reason to believe he's holding anything back. I'm sure he's telling the truth about that."

Melanie dropped the bar in place to secure the front door, then repeated the process with the back door and turned to make her way up the stairs. She had only spent a few hours dealing with customers and the well-wishers who continued to come in throughout the afternoon, but even that limited activity left her feeling utterly spent.

Up in her room, she pulled the pins from her hair and ran her fingers through the long chestnut strands, letting them fall loose across her shoulders.

Something rattled against the window, and Melanie spun around with her hand pressed to her throat. When the noise sounded again, she pushed the curtain aside and peered out. Caleb stood below her in the alley, a basket in his hand and Levi by his side.

Melanie pushed the window up and leaned her arms on the sill. "Is everything all right?"

"I was going to use my key, but you've barred the door. Would you mind coming down to let us in?"

A smile curved Melanie's lips. "What if someone already saw you flinging pebbles at my window? Are you trying to sully my reputation?"

"This is broad daylight, not the middle of the night. Besides"—he nodded at Levi—"I brought along a chaperone."

Melanie laughed. "Give me a minute. I need to put my hair back up."

"No, leave it just the way it is." The look he gave her sent a tingle from her scalp to her toes.

"All right," she said. "I'll be right down."

When she opened the door, Levi darted inside. "We brought dinner, Miss Ross."

Caleb grinned and held up the basket. "I figured you'd be too worn out to fix yourself anything substantial, so I got some food from the café. I hoped we could all eat together, and it would give us a chance to talk."

Melanie's exhaustion began to slip away. "How thoughtful of you. I was only planning to put together a plate of cheese and crackers."

Levi hopped from one foot to the other. "And Papa said I get to eat in my fort. I'm going to pretend I'm out on bivouac with my soldiers."

Caleb carried the basket into the office. "While he's playing, I'd like to discuss our partnership."

Melanie followed him, fighting the feeling of letdown at the prospect of talking business after a long, tiring day.

Caleb set the basket on the desk. "I don't want the food to get cold, so we won't take time to set up a table like we did before. Why don't you get some plates from the kitchen, and we'll just eat in here?"

She went to do as he asked, wondering what lay behind the desire to discuss their partnership. A queasy feeling settled in her stomach. Did he still want her out of the store? The kiss they'd shared the day before had seemed to be full of promise, but maybe she'd read it all wrong.

She carried the plates back to the office, where Caleb put a drumstick and a biscuit on Levi's before sending him off to play. While Levi scampered off, Melanie set food out for her and Caleb.

When she turned around, he stood in front of her, only

inches away. His nearness made her breath come quickly, and she stared into his face, trying to discern what was on his mind.

He glanced away for a moment before he began to speak. "When you first came here, I wasn't very gracious to you. In fact, I was quite rude, and I want to apologize for that."

He looked up again, meeting her eyes. "But the more I watched you, the more I saw the kind of person you are. I saw your kindness, the way you care about people like Mrs. Fetterman and the Professor, the way you've captured Levi's heart . . ."

His eyes darkened in a way that left her breathless. ". . . and mine."

Melanie felt like her own heart had stopped beating.

Without taking his eyes off her, Caleb leaned to one side and reached behind a stack of catalogs. The lilting strains of "Liebestraum" filled the office.

Melanie decided she'd been wrong. Her heart was beating, all right. She could feel it pounding in her chest at double speed.

Caleb straightened and moved even closer. He framed her face in his hands and traced her cheekbones with his thumbs.

Melanie's eyelids fluttered closed, and she stood lost in the moment, listening to the music, drinking in Caleb's nearness, thrilling to the wonder of his touch.

When he spoke again, his voice sounded husky. "When I said I wanted to talk to you about our partnership, I didn't mean the mercantile."

Her eyes flew open, and her breath caught at the intensity of his gaze. He bent his head down, and she felt his breath graze her cheek. "I don't want to spend another day of my life without you by my side."

A film of tears blurred her vision, and she blinked them away.

"I want us to go on together as partners in life." Lowering his hands, he grasped her fingers in his and sank down onto one knee. "Melanie, would you do me the honor—the very great honor—of becoming my wife?"

A joyous laugh escaped her lips while tears spilled over onto her cheeks. Finally, a proposal she wanted to hear! "There is nothing I'd like better in the world."

With a jubilant smile, Caleb got back to his feet and pulled her into his arms again. Melanie raised her face to meet his kiss, knowing in her heart she had found her home at last.

AUTHOR NOTE

Dear Reader:

It has been a joy to write another story set in the early days of Arizona's history. With such a rich variety of settings to draw from, I've loved being able to focus on a completely different area of my home state this time.

People often ask where the ideas in a book come from. In the case of *Trouble in Store*, I can trace the inspiration for several scenes back to my ninth summer, when my mother, grandmother, and I set off on a tour of northern Arizona. With its rolling hills and flowing creeks, it was quite a change from the cactus-studded desert where I'd grown up! I'll never forget my first view of Montezuma Castle, a pueblo built into the side of a limestone cliff by the Sinagua people many centuries ago. The sight of cliffside dwellings sparked my imagination as a child. Who were the people who lived there? What were they like? Those questions lay buried in my mind all through the years, and Melanie pondered them as well during the early part of her stay in Cedar Ridge.

When Melanie arrived in Arizona, she already felt like her life had been turned upside down. Becoming the proprietor of the mercantile she inherited from her cousin wasn't a turn she'd expected her life to take. Little did she know that God had even more surprises in store! I don't know about you, but I often feel like Melanie did when life throws me a curve. I'd like to have things planned out well in advance and know exactly where I'm going and how to get there . . . but more often than not, it doesn't work out that way.

What then? How are we supposed to react when the path we expected to follow turns out to be far different than the one God gives us? We can kick up a fuss, wail, and complain—something I'll confess I've done more than once. But if we want true peace, we'll find that in trusting the Lord and seeking His perfect will for our lives. No matter how wonderful I think my plans are, His are always so much better. And that's where our happy ending truly lies—in trusting Him to know what's best.

Thank you for taking the time to read *Trouble in Store*. May you find your own happy ending in following God's best for your life!

Carol
Philippians 4:4

Author of nearly 30 novels and novellas, **Carol Cox** has an abiding love for history and romance, especially when it's set in her native Southwest. As a third-generation Arizonan, she takes a keen interest in the Old West and hopes to make it live again in the hearts of her readers. A pastor's wife, Carol lives with her husband and daughter in northern Arizona, where the deer and the antelope really do play—within view of the family's front porch.

To learn more about Carol, please visit her at:
Her Web site: www.AuthorCarolCox.com
Her blog: www.AuthorCarolCox.com/journal
Facebook: www.facebook.com/carol.cox
Twitter: www.twitter.com/authorcarolcox

If you enjoyed *Trouble in Store*, you may also like...

When undercover Pinkerton agent Ellie Moore's assignment turns downright dangerous—for her safety *and* her heart—what's this damsel in disguise to do?

Love in Disguise by Carol Cox
authorcarolcox.com

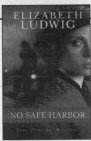

Desperate to locate her brother, Cara travels to America, where she is thrust into a web of danger. Her questions may bring her closer to her brother, but they also put her at the mercy of dangerous revolutionaries—including a man she's grown to love.

No Safe Harbor by Elizabeth Ludwig, EDGE OF FREEDOM #1
elizabethludwig.com

When Lily Young sets out to find her lost sister amidst the dangerous lumber camps of Harrison, Michigan, she will challenge everything boss-man Connell McCormick thought he knew about life—and love.

Unending Devotion by Jody Hedlund
jodyhedlund.com

◊ BETHANYHOUSE

Stay up-to-date on your favorite books and authors with our *free* e-newsletters. Sign up today at bethanyhouse.com.

Find us on Facebook. facebook.com/bethanyhousepublishers

Free exclusive resources for your book group! bethanyhouse.com/anopenbook

If you enjoyed *Trouble in Store*, you may also like...

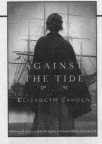